Deadly Reunion

DEADLY REUNION

RON HANDBERG

AUTHOR OF *CRY VENGEANCE*, *MALICE INTENDED*, AND *SAVAGE JUSTICE*

N S

NORTH STAR PRESS OF ST. CLOUD, INC.
St. Cloud, Minnesota

For our nine wonderful grandchildren,
who fill our lives and hearts with joy

Cover art: Jeffrey Holmes

Author photo: Jon Yeager

ISBN: 0-87839-362-5
ISBN-13: 978-0-87839-362-6

First Edition, September 1, 2010

Printed in the United States of America

Published by
North Star Press of St. Cloud, Inc.
P.O. Box 451
St. Cloud, Minnesota 56302

www.northstarpress.com

AUTHOR'S NOTE

In the late '60s, as a young reporter for WCCO Television in Minneapolis, I was assigned to cover the brutal, unsolved rape and murder of a suburban high school girl.

It was a relatively routine assignment, one that I had all but forgotten when—more than three decades later—I received a letter from one of the detectives I had interviewed at the time. Now retired, he had just finished one of my novels, Dead Silence, and wanted me to know that the murder I had covered so many years before has remained unsolved.

If I was interested, he said, he would be willing to talk to me about it and provide me with the full file of the investigation.

That conversation, and his voluminous, meticulous file, provided the springboard for this novel. And while this story, a work of fiction, bears little resemblance to the real-life story, his files provided a treasure-trove of information on police procedures in this kind of a case, which—I hope—adds to the authenticity of my story.

Sadly, the real murder of the real girl remains unsolved to this day.

Ron Handberg
Minneapolis, MN.

(July 22, 1992)

THERE WERE ONLY THREE OTHERS on the bus when it pulled up to the woman's corner. They sat behind her, slumped in their seats, staring out the windows into the darkened neighborhood street and dimly-lighted homes. Only she got off, saying a soft, "Goodnight," to the driver as she stepped down onto the curb, leaving the cool of the bus for the heat of the July night. A long day and evening at work were finally over, leaving her eager for the cool shower and chilled glass of wine that awaited her at home.

She was alone, save for the murmur of mosquitoes in the night air.

The circle of light from the corner streetlight faded quickly under the shadows of over-hanging trees and faded to near total darkness in the park across the way. But she felt no fear; the neighborhood was safe and familiar. She had walked this street on nights like this many times before, knew every crack in the sidewalk, every light in every curtained-window.

She had no reason to believe tonight would be any different.

Perhaps it was her exhaustion, or the sound of an ambulance siren in the distance, or the barking of a dog two streets over, that kept her from hearing the soft-soled footsteps behind her.

No one would ever know.

She heard his voice before she heard his steps.

"Surprise."

She spun around, but he was too fast. One hand was over her eyes, the other clamped over her mouth. Hands so strong. Gripping, holding her fast. Helpless. Voiceless.

Where did he come from? My, God, what's happening?

She struggled, arms and legs flailing, her scream trapped deep in her throat.

He dragged her over the curb, onto the street. Neck stretched, heels dug into the asphalt.

The park! He's taking me to the park. It can't be. Don't let it be!

Another curb. Grass now. One shoe off, somewhere on the street. The grass cool and damp through her stocking heel. Twisting in his grasp, she reached over and behind her, trying to get at his face. Wool, not skin. A stocking mask. She tore at it, heard him grunt. His grip tightened, squeezing her eyes and mouth. So strong. Pain. No breath. Bite at the hand. Leather, not skin. A glove. Another grunt. Another word. "Bitch."

She was on her back, the ground hard, biting into her body. Looking up as he straddled her, his hand no longer over her eyes, seeing nothing but his dark mask, the umbrella of trees hiding whatever light the night sky held. So heavy, crushing her, smelling of rancid sweat. Reaching for something. What? His other hand came off her mouth, but only for an instant—replaced by a swath of tape, sticky, foul-tasting. No chance to scream or take a breath.

Her mind tumbled. Frantically. Fearfully. Fight or submit? Life could not end like this. Not for her, not without a fight. No way. She heaved her body, arching her back, twisting, kicking. But he held her wrists with one hand, riding her like a hobby horse, ripping at her blouse. A guttural laugh through the mask.

Her body ached, her muscles cried out, calling for the help her voice could not summon.

Help that would not come.

Suddenly, her hands were free. Flailing at him, but too weak to harm. Something was in his hands. A belt. She grabbed for it. Heard him laugh again. Playing with her. Then a slap. Hard, stinging. The belt around her throat.

The night closed in. The umbrella of trees vanished.

Bob and Karen Steele loved to jog, especially in early morning, before the sun was high enough to cook them. Their daily route took them through the quiet streets of their St. Paul neighborhood, two miles in all, ending in Garden Park. From there, they would walk and cool down on the final two blocks to their home.

On this morning, their routine changed slightly, bringing them through the park instead of the streets around it. Bob was slightly ahead of Karen, as he usually was, and it was only because she stopped for a sip of water that she spotted the body, lying beneath and slightly hidden by the drooping boughs of a pine.

She moved closer, not believing what she saw. Then she shrieked. And threw up.

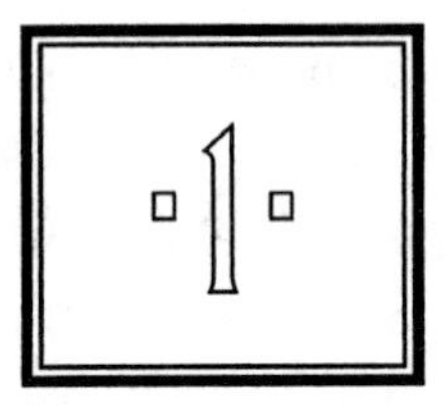

(Seventeen years, nineteen days later)

IT WAS THE LAST PLACE ANYONE who knew George Barclay would expect to find him. Including George himself. Yet there he was, standing awkwardly at the entrance of the hotel ballroom, a cloud of intertwined red, white and blue crepe paper floating above him. He was alone, clearly uncomfortable, and more conspicuous than he would have wished. On the hefty side of two-hundred fifty pounds, he was hard to miss.

At the moment, however, no one in the crowded room seemed to take notice, giving him the opportunity once again to tug at the fabric of his suit coat—trying without success to maneuver the middle button into the corresponding button hole. *Screw it*, he thought. He'd get the goddamned button moved.

"Excuse me," said a voice at his right shoulder. A woman's voice. "Have you picked up your name tag?"

"Ahhh, no, not yet," Barclay replied, glancing at her. "I just got here. Sort of getting the lay of the land."

She smiled. A nice smile. Freckles on her forehead and the tip of her nose. Reddish hair with the first streaks of gray. Cut short. Not much makeup. No effort to hide her age. He liked that. But he didn't have the vaguest notion of who she was. Nor, obviously, did she know him.

"Did you register?" she asked. Squinting at his face, struggling to remember.

"I think so. I sent in the money."

Just why remained the big question. Especially now, as he stood facing a roomful of people he didn't know, or at least didn't remember.

And the majority—from what he could see—looking in a hell of a lot better shape than he was.

"The registration desk's right over there," the woman said, pointing, still looking puzzled.

When he'd received the letter several months before, the reunion had seemed like an okay idea. Something different. A kick. What the hell? Twenty-five years. Where's the harm? But that was then. Now he wished he'd thrown the damn letter away.

As he turned toward the reception desk, the woman touched his arm and pointed to her own name tag, attached to a green silk dress that adhered nicely to her body. "I'm Rachel Armetage, Higgins back then, and I'm sorry but I can't seem to place you."

He grinned, although the smile was largely lost behind his well-trimmed black beard—which was also showing the first hints of gray. "I was George Barclay," he said. "Twenty-five years and a hundred pounds ago."

"Of course!" she exclaimed, standing back, examining him once again. "The beard confused me."

Right, he thought ruefully.

She studied him further. "Now I've got it," she said. "You were on the newspaper."

"And you have an amazing memory," he said, genuinely impressed. Then, as he was about to step away, it suddenly dawned. He snapped back. "Rachel Higgins. The cheerleader. Right? I remember you. Great legs."

She blushed slightly, but seemed pleased. "Talk about memory. Now go get that name tag."

Big tits, too, he recalled, but he didn't say that.

The banner over the reception desk read:

TWENTY FIVE AND STILL ALIVE!
Welcome Armstrong Class of '84, Home Again

Alive? Well, maybe. His doctor, who was also an old friend, would take issue with that. "You're a damned mess," he was fond of telling him. "If a heart attack or stress doesn't get you, a stroke sure as hell will."

At least he didn't smoke anymore.

ARMSTRONG HIGH WAS A BIG SUBURBAN Minneapolis school—bigger then than now—that had boasted a graduating class of more than six-hundred kids from a mixture of blue- and white-collar families. Strong academics were given lip service, but at Armstrong, sports were king. If you didn't play hockey, football, or basketball you were . . . well, George.

He played chess.

But Rachel was right, he also wrote for the high-school newspaper, *The Odyssey*. Aside from a couple of other kids on the newspaper staff, he'd had few real friends. No kick-ass buddies, as most other guys seemed to have. Especially the jocks, who liked to travel in packs. And certainly no girlfriends. Except for Jennifer, and it was hard to count her. She hardly knew he was alive.

Truth was, however, it was his curiosity about Jennifer Bartlow that had brought him to the reunion. But why now? He hadn't had the guts to check on her in all of these years. Not that he hadn't thought of her often enough. But she was almost certainly married by now, he guessed, with a flock of kids. Probably with a good job, too. She had that kind of talent.

Once he had his name tag, and after taking a deep breath, he walked back beneath the crepe paper and into the ballroom, pausing just inside the door to once again muster his courage. It was hard to tell, but it looked like a couple of hundred people were already there, with more arriving by the minute. He was surrounded—and isolated—by the squeals of delight and peals of laughter as old classmates greeted one another, many expressing apparent surprise at how little the others had changed in a quarter-century,

Yeah, right.

Feeling more of a stranger than ever, he scanned the crowd on the off-chance he might recognize someone—and when he didn't, he headed straight to the bar. He wished now that he'd kept his old yearbook; maybe then he'd remember somebody from the old pictures.

To be fair, part of his problem was that he had spent less than two years at Armstrong, having moved with his family in his junior year from a small town in South Dakota. So he'd not only found himself stuck in a new school but in a new culture, the prairie boy come to the big city.

"What'll it be, sir?" The bartender had finally found him.

"Amstel Light, if you've got it," Barclay said.

"No problem," he replied. "Need a glass?"

"Nah."

Beer in hand, Barclay wandered off to one side of the bar, certain he looked as uncomfortable as he felt. Most of those around him appeared to be with spouses or significant others. Holding hands. Clinging, talking to one another, if not others. Barclay was unmarried, always had been. While he was at peace with that most days, at times like this he wished there could be someone by his side.

He'd thought about trying to get a date for the night, but knew anyone he'd ask would be even more uncomfortable than he was, knowing no one and caring even less than he did.

He returned to the bar for another beer, then retreated to his solitary outpost.

Unlikely as it might sound, until he got the reunion letter, he'd not heard from or seen any member of his class since the day of graduation. True, he'd left home soon after to go out of state to college, and then on to a series of television news jobs in other parts of the country. Still, he'd returned to the Twin Cities ten years before as the news director of Channel Seven. And while he was seldom seen on camera, it was a visible position in the community.

As he surveyed the crowd, he was approached by a well-built big guy with long, reddish hair, and a flushed face, who'd obviously arrived at the party much earlier. He stopped not six inches away, swaying badly, as he looked closely at Barclay, then squinted at his name tag.

"Who the fuck are you?" he asked, his words slurred, his breath a sickening combination of beer and cigarettes.

Barclay tried to ignore him.

"Hey, don't you hear, chubby? I asked you a question. I don't 'member you. What the hell's your name?"

Barclay stood his ground, grinning. "George Clooney."

"What?"

"You asked. I told you. George Clooney. I grew a beard."

The man guffawed and stepped back, almost falling over. "You can't shit a shitter."

Barclay shrugged.

In a drunken blink, the man's smile turned to a snarl. "You're screwin' with me, man. Nobody does that."

"Take it easy, pal. I was kidding you. I don't want a problem."

He pushed a fist into Barclay's chest. "You are the problem, fatso."

As Barclay was about to grab his nose and twist, the same woman, Rachel, stepped between the two of them. "What's happening here?"

"Nothing," Barclay replied. "Just a quiet conversation."

The drunk shoved a middle finger in front of Barclay's face, then turned aside, muttering more expletives as he moved on to his next victim.

It was all over in less than a minute.

"I'm sorry about that," Rachel said. "There's one in every class."

"No harm done."

"C'mon," she said, "let's mix a little."

"I'm not much of a mixer," he said. "At things like this, I mean."

"When then?"

"When I know someone," he replied.

"You won't get to know anyone standing there like a stump," she persisted. "C'mon. There are a few people you should remember." Taking him by the hand, she led him like a lost child through the crowd, introducing him to others as she stopped to greet them. She seemed to know everyone. The Queen Bee of the reunion.

"You don't have time for this," he protested. "I can find my own way."

"Not so you'd notice," she replied over her shoulder.

So he tagged along, an empty beer bottle in his hand, feeling more than ever like a piece of overweight excess baggage. *Get a grip,* he told himself. *You manage a goddamned newsroom of scores of people, many of them with egos bigger than this ballroom, yet here you are, acting like you just walked in off the prairie. Again.*

Despite his discomfort, Barclay tried to put on his most pleasant face, doing his best to be charming, to make conversation as Rachel stopped to chat. But it was as if he'd stumbled into a wedding to which he'd not been invited, where the families of the bride and the groom each treated him as a guest of the other, politely but distantly.

All the while, though, his eyes moved across the crowd, hoping to catch a glimpse of the woman he had come to see, the girl he remembered as Jennifer Bartlow. But he quickly realized how hopeless it was; there were far too many people moving about, and he had no idea what she would look like today, this many years later.

At one point, Rachel paused and asked, "So what do you do, George?"

"I work at Channel Seven. I'm the news director there."

"Really? That's my favorite station."

"Glad to hear it," he said.

As they moved on, she introduced him to men he could only vaguely recall, with names like Stuart and Gerald, whose memory of him was no better than his of them.

I've got to get my ass out of here.

But before he could flee, there was a clinking of glasses, with someone at a microphone urging them to find their places. Dinner was about to be served.

Rachel pulled him along. "This way, George," she said. "I've saved a place next to me."

He held back. "To tell the truth, Rachel, I'm not sure I should stay. This isn't turning out quite like I hoped."

"Nonsense," she said. "The evening's young. Give it a chance."

What's with this lady? he wondered. *It's like she's adopted me. She sure as hell can't be attracted to me. No woman has been for a long time. Besides, she's got a ring on her finger.*

She led him to her table and quickly introduced him to the three couples sitting there. He graciously acknowledged the introductions but quickly forgot their names, which made little difference since they were all engaged in their own conversations anyway.

He leaned over to Rachel. "Aren't we missing someone?" he whispered to her. "Like your husband?"

"For him to hear, you'd have to speak up," she said, with a slight grin. "He's either in heaven or hell, depending on your viewpoint, but he's certainly not within earshot."

"You mean he's passed?" he asked.

"Yes, George, I mean he died. Two years ago. Of cancer. It was quite sudden. No one expected it, least of all me."

"I'm very sorry," he said, "that's horrible. But what about the ring?"

She held her left hand up, the diamond glistening next to a serious gold band. "Protection. Keeps away unwanted attention unless I decide it's wanted. Besides," she smiled, "who knows? I may need to pawn it someday."

A waiter made his way around the table, offering a choice of red or white wine. Barclay picked red, Rachel white. "So what about you?" she asked. "Are you married?"

"Single, straight, and happy to be both," he replied, for maybe the two-thousandth time in the past few years. "I live alone. Just me and an adopted cat. I bought a condo downtown, near the station. It's convenient, and I spend most of my time in the newsroom anyway."

"Doesn't seem like much of a life," she said. "All work and no play."

"About it," he admitted.

At that moment, her attention was grabbed by the woman sitting on her right, allowing Barclay to study the reunion program that had been left on each of their plates. He quickly scanned the document, seeing—among other things— the typical reunion statistics: who had come the farthest distance; who had been married the longest; and who had the most children and grandchildren. On and on. He recognized few of the names.

On the last page of the program, under the title IN MEMORY, was a list of seven names, classmates who had died in the past twenty-five years. *Seven out of six hundred isn't that bad*, he thought, as he went down the list. Then he stopped.

At the very bottom was the one name he did remember, the person he had most hoped to see at this reunion:

Jennifer Bartlow.

He tried to catch his breath. For an instant, her face with her flashing eyes was there. Mocking him. Beguiling him. Then she was gone.

Reaching for his glass of wine, he took a quick swig. No swirling it in the glass, no catching its aroma. Then another gulp. Rachel turned back to him. "George, are you okay?"

"Yeah," he said. "I just noticed something."

"What?"

He pointed to Jennifer's name. "Jennifer Bartlow. I didn't know she'd died," he said. "It came as a shock, that's all."

There was concern on Rachel's face. "You obviously knew her."

"Not well," he said. "I had a couple of classes with her. Probably didn't know I even existed."

"But what? You had a crush on her?"

"You could call it that, I guess. From a distance."

Rachel said, "You probably knew her better than I did. We traveled in much different circles."

By now, Barclay had collected himself. "Do you know how she died?"

She stared at him, puzzled. "Of course. Everyone does. Where were you?"

"When?"

"In 1992."

His mind went blank for a moment. Then, "In '92? In Rockford, Illinois. My second job in television."

"And no one ever told you?"

"What?"

Rachel's eyes fell. When she looked up, he could see the pain. "She was murdered, George. Raped and murdered. A block from her apartment."

He fell back into his chair. Stunned. Staring into space. Disbelieving.

"I'm sorry," she said with real sadness. "I thought everyone knew."

"No one ever told me," he whispered. "It never came up. Too old, maybe."

Death. Murder. No strangers to George Barclay. He'd covered more murders in the past twenty years than he could count. But in all of that time, in all of those cities, he had never known one of the victims. They were merely names on a script, read by a face on the television screen, as distant as the moon and the stars. Some were sadder, the murdered children especially, but still, they were someone else's kids. Someone else's heartbreak.

All of the faces around him seemed to blur. Only Rachel's stood out in stark relief. "Who did it?" he finally asked.

She shrugged. "No one's ever been caught. I would have heard. Her death was one of several around that time."

"What do you mean? Some kind of serial . . . ?"

The waiter was at his shoulder. "Did you order steak or chicken, sir?"

Barclay looked up. Then at Rachel. "Sorry," he said. "I don't think I can eat. I think I have to go." He pushed his chair back and got up. "Thanks for everything, Rachel. You've been great . . ."

She was on her feet as well. "I'm truly sorry, George. Can't you stay?"

"No, I don't think so. I wasn't really hungry, anyway."

She reached for his hand. "May I call you sometime?"

"Sure," he said, quickly fishing out one of his business cards. "Anytime." Then he was moving fast, stumbling, somehow navigating between the tables, finally making it through the ballroom door, under the crepe paper arch and past the big banner.

TWENTY FIVE AND STILL ALIVE
Welcome, Armstrong Class of '84, Home Again

2

The August heat was oppressive, with no hint of a breeze, as Barclay emerged from the air-conditioned hotel to walk the four blocks to his air-conditioned condo. The sweat was rolling down his back and under his arms before he hit the sidewalk, and he quickly shed the suit coat and loosened his tie. Not that it did much good.

It had been one of those sweltering days of a Minnesota summer when both the temperature and the humidity soared, prompting heat index warnings to be issued everywhere. In a state known to be an icebox in January, it could be like a furnace in August. Even the setting of the sun had brought little relief.

Extreme heat was one thing to a skinny guy, quite another to somebody like Barclay, who could work up a sweat in the dead of winter. He wasn't sure he could take much more of this, but he knew his own weatherman was predicting that more of the same stifling heat was on the way.

As he trudged along, he struggled with the shock of Jennifer's death, of her unspeakable rape and murder. He had gone to the reunion hoping for a glimpse of her, maybe a brief word in passing, a chance to reintroduce himself, to see if she had even the vaguest memory of him.

Now, it was not to be. It would never be.

By the time he reached his condo door, he was sopped, dripping sweat on the tile of the foyer. He flung his coat in the direction of a chair and had his shirt halfway off by the time he reached the refrigerator and pulled out an icy bottle of beer. Thankfully, the condo itself was like a refrigerator, Barclay having turned up the air before leaving for the reunion.

Sitting on the kitchen counter, eyeing him irritably, was Seuss, a Siamese cat he'd been forced to adopt when his longtime anchorman, Alex Collier, decided to leave the station for a job at CNN. Collier had made it plain: Barclay could take Seuss or watch him go to an uncertain future at the Humane Society shelter. "He's a giant pain in the ass," Collier had told him, "and I don't give a shit if he lives or dies. But I'd like to tell my kids he was adopted by a kindly old man."

After scouring the newsroom for other potential takers, Barclay reluctantly agreed to accept the cat—although he'd never owned a pet, even as a kid. And Seuss had taken some getting used to; he was not particularly friendly, and made no attempt to hide his displeasure over a late dinner or a dirty litter box, following Barclay around the condo, complaining noisily.

Seuss got his name because Collier's first cat was one of a litter born in an old hat left in a closet—and Collier's son had insisted that happenstance earned the cat that particular moniker.

Barclay quickly filled the cat's bowl and freshened his water, then returned to the living room with his beer.

His condo was on the twentieth floor of one of the high-rise buildings that now seemed to surround downtown Minneapolis, populated largely by aging empty nesters from the suburbs, or by singles like him, who worked downtown. The condo itself was nothing special: living room, small dining room, kitchen, two bedrooms, one of which he'd turned into an office, and one and one-half baths. And a balcony, which overlooked the downtown skyline in one direction and, on a clear day, the city's gorgeous chain of lakes in the other.

Since he spent relatively little time there and didn't entertain much, he'd shopped for only enough furniture and appliances to make it livable. But he did have four flat-screen TVs that dominated one wall, allowing him to monitor his own station and the competitors on the rare occasions he was at home and not in the newsroom.

The few paintings on the other walls and the occasional knickknacks on the shelves were courtesy of his mother, who'd gone shopping for him on one of her visits back to the Twin Cities from Florida. "Honestly, George," she'd said, "I swear you could live in a cave and be happy."

As long as it had air-conditioning.

His only personal memorabilia were a few broadcasting plaques in his bedroom-office, awards honoring him and the station for some of the investigative series they'd done over the years. And an old picture of Dan Rather shaking his hand at a news directors' convention.

Now, slouched on the sofa, he kicked off his shoes and stared at the blank TVs. Yet another Saturday night alone. He could have stayed at the reunion, and probably should have, but the prospect of listening to hours of small talk, of feigning interest in those around him, watching them laugh and trade happy memories while he could think only of a dead Jennifer Bartlow, was simply too much to bear.

The Twins were on television, but even that didn't peak his interest. Instead, he reached for the phone on the end table and hit the speed dial.

"Channel Seven News," said the answering voice.

"Wilson?"

Harry Wilson on the assignment desk. "George? That you?"

"Yeah."

"What's up?" Wilson asked.

"I need a favor," he replied.

"No problem, but I thought you were at some kind of reunion."

"I was. I left."

"Surprise."

"Don't get smart. What's going on?"

"Not much," Wilson said. "House fire in Maplewood. A drowning in Prior Lake. Some political bullshit. You know the routine. Trying to make chicken salad out of chicken shit."

Barclay chuckled. That was his line. "Have you got some time?"

"Sure."

"Check our archives. Find out what we've got on the murder of a woman by the name of Jennifer Bartlow. Killed in '92, I think. Maybe one of a string of murders."

There was hesitation on the other end of the line. Finally, "That's a long time ago."

"I know," Barclay said.

"A lot of stuff got lost when we moved to the new building, and when they switched over to the computers and all."

"Try, okay?"

"Sure. Shall I call you back?"

"I'll be here."

"You're the boss."

"Nice of you to remember."

Barclay picked up his empty beer bottle and retreated to the kitchen, finding Seuss stretched out on the kitchen table, giving himself a bath. Knowing full well he shouldn't be there, the cat glared defiantly at Barclay, daring him to do something about it. *Ungrateful bastard*, he thought. *This is what I get for saving your friggin' life.*

Reaching into the refrigerator for another beer, he suddenly remembered he hadn't eaten anything. But there wasn't much there: a couple of TV dinners, a leftover chicken breast, the soggy remnants of takeout salad, and a half-gallon of milk, probably sour by now. He'd been counting on that reunion dinner.

Hell with it, he thought, taking out the Hungry Man's beef TV dinner and sticking it into the microwave. Probably good for another half-inch around the waist.

He'd actually lost a lot of weight a few years before, shedding close to sixty pounds in a frenzy of exercise and dieting over a period of about six months. Partially because of his doctor's pleadings, and partially because he'd found a woman he cared enough about to try and improve his body image. Sweet, saucy Monica. But the romance and the diet ended at about the same time—and he was soon back to his old ways.

Once he'd swept Seuss off the table, and was about to dig into the dinner, the phone rang. Must be Wilson, he thought, although it would be an awfully quick call-back. Maybe his mother; she knew he was often home alone on Saturday nights. He picked up the kitchen extension.

"George?" A woman, with noise in the background. Not his mother.

"Yes."

"This is Rachel. From the reunion. Still at the reunion, actually."

Barclay wasn't sure what to say.

"I know this must seem odd, George, since we just met. But I got worried about you, leaving so suddenly. And I sort of feel responsible."

"What? Why in the world is that?"

"Because I was the one who told you about Jennifer. I could have done it in a different way . . ."

"Rachel, please . . ."

"No. Listen to me. I had no idea it would affect you like it did. I could have handled it better. I could have . . ."

Barclay got up and carried the phone into the living room. "You're being silly, Rachel. I'm a big boy. I can take bad news. I over-reacted, I'm not sure why. It was stupid to leave the party. And rude. Especially after you'd been kind enough to babysit me."

"The party's still going on," she said. "You could come back."

"And leave my TV dinner?" he laughed. "No way. Besides, it's almost past my bedtime."

He could hear her giggle. "Okay, then. How about lunch tomorrow? A Sunday brunch. You're downtown, right?"

"At the LaSalle Plaza, yes."

"Do you have plans?"

"No."

"Good. How about the Hilton? At eleven? I should be over any hangover by then."

He hesitated. What the hell was going on? "Okay," he said, then stood staring at the phone. This was either the nicest woman in the world, or someone with an agenda that was beyond his imagination. He'd just met her, for Christ's sake, and she clearly hadn't known who he was or what he did. So she couldn't be looking for any special favors. Maybe she knew more about Jennifer Bartlow than she'd let on.

What did she say? That she hadn't known Jennifer that well? That they'd traveled in different circles? He could believe that.

Jennifer was hardly the cheerleader type. In fact, he could never remember seeing her at any kind of game, let alone leading the cheers. Wasn't her style. Still, the two women must have crossed paths often enough in those high school years.

How was it possible that he'd missed learning of Jennifer's death all of these years? Simple. It was old news by the time he got back to the Twin Cities, and clearly nothing had happened since then to bring her name back into the headlines. Hers was just one of many unsolved murders, one of a long list of cold cases on the books, filling file cabinets or cop shop computers.

With a half-hour to go until news time, Barclay returned to the kitchen to finish his Hungry Man meal, now cold and looking even less appetizing than it had to begin with. He threw it into the garbage. Maybe the unintentional start of a new diet.

The news, when it came on, was just as Wilson had described it: routine. There probably was no worse time for a news department than a hot, humid weekend day in August. The dog days of summer. Aside from an occasional breaking story, the news seemed limited to summer parades and festivals and the conferences of no-name politicians trying to take advantage of stations' desperate need to fill their newscasts.

He was barely able to stay awake through the end of the newscast and was dozing off on the couch when the phone rang again.

"Yeah."

"Wilson here. What'd you think of the show?"

"Boring. And it's not a show. It's a newscast."

"Whatever."

Barclay sighed. Wilson was typical of a lot of the brash young people on his staff: Bright but not particularly well-read; confident, but bordering on smug; educated in the ways of television, but not necessarily well-schooled in the tenets of journalism. With time, and patience, Barclay hoped to change all of that—as he had for so many other kids who'd come through his newsroom. It's what kept his juices flowing.

"So what have you got?" he asked.

"Not much. A brief synopsis of the murder, but no tape. That's long gone, maybe lost in the move."

"So?"

"Jennifer Bartlow. Age twenty-six. Two years out of the University of Wisconsin in Madison. Raped and strangled on the night of July 22, 1992, a block from her apartment on Eustis Avenue in St. Paul. Attacked walking home from the bus. She worked in downtown St. Paul, at Ecolab. Her body was found in a park the next morning by some joggers."

"That's it?" Barclay asked.

"All we've got. I haven't had time to check newspaper archives."

"Don't bother. I'll do that."

"You knew this woman?" Wilson asked.

"Went to high school with her, but didn't know she'd died until tonight."

"Bummer."

"Nothing about any arrests?" Barclay asked.

"Not in our files. But like I say, it's pretty sketchy. We gotta' get a better system."

"I know," Barclay replied, although he doubted that he'd live long enough to see it.

There was a pause. "Anything else I can do?"

"No thanks. Go home. Get some sleep."

"You, too, boss."

Oh, yeah? Easy for him to say. For reasons he didn't fully understand, he slept fitfully these days, often tossing and turning late into the night. Despite Tylenol PM and a dozen other sleep remedies. And, tonight, he knew, might be another of those nights.

Once in bed, as he lay staring at the darkened ceiling, he tried to jar his memory, to take him back those twenty-five years—to piece together the picture of what once had been Jennifer Bartlow. But the passing years had left him with only a maddeningly vague image: tall, maybe five-eight, with a slim and straight body, narrow hips and small but luscious breasts, which she usually tried to hide, and a face that would turn heads in any room she entered. Dark skin, dark hair, and dark eyes that seemed to ignite when turned in your direction. And while she seldom smiled, at least in his direction, when she did, it made his knees weak.

The thought of this girl, once so alive, lying dead and discarded in some park, her glistening eyes lifeless, her wonderful body cold and violated, made him as angry—and as sad—as he'd ever felt. And, yet, he realized that if she were alive today, if she had been at that reunion, she'd probably have been as oblivious to him as others there.

But, as he turned over and began his struggle for sleep, he managed to maintain the hope that while she may not have recognized him, she might—just might—have remembered him.

Or maybe he was already dreaming.

RACHEL WAS WAITING IN THE LOBBY of the Hilton, sitting in one of the big overstuffed chairs near the reception desk. She gave a quick wave as he approached, showing no evidence of her feared hangover. If anything, she looked fresher and more attractive than she had the night before.

"Hey, George," she said, smiling warmly, rising to grasp his hand firmly.

"Hello, Rachel. Aren't you looking sharp. Very cool and comfortable."

And she was. In a light, sleeveless white summer dress with blue striping, showing off well-tanned arms and legs. The facial freckles he'd noticed the night before were even more evident—and charming—by day than they were by night.

"Well, thank you," she said, glancing down at herself. Then at him. "You're not that bad yourself."

Actually, he had made an effort to dress a little more carefully than usual: Pressed khakis and a loose, oversized and colorful Hawaiian-type shirt that somewhat disguised his ample paunch. He'd even fussed with his hair and beard, but a dry August wind had spoiled those efforts on his walk to the hotel. "I do what I can with what I've got," he said.

She laughed and took him by the arm, leading him toward the all-but-deserted restaurant. "Looks like we've got the place to ourselves," she said.

A waiter was by their side immediately, offering each a menu and asking if they'd care for anything to drink. Before Barclay could reply, Rachel said, "How about a mimosa? They're pretty harmless."

He would have preferred a beer, but knew it was too early and would appear gauche. "Sure," he said.

The waiter scooted off.

"So," Barclay asked, "how did the party turn out?"

"Great. I stayed to the bitter end. Got in a lot of visiting and dancing. But I was a good girl . . . drank coffee for the last two hours. I do wish you would have stayed."

"I'm not much of a dancer," he said. "I tend to crowd the dance floor."

She grinned and leaned across the table. "You know, you can be a very funny man. But a tad too tough on yourself, I think."

At that moment, the waiter appeared with their drinks and asked if they were ready to order. "Give us some time," Rachel said. "We're in no hurry and it doesn't look like you're too rushed."

"You got that right," he said, and disappeared.

As they talked, Barclay learned that her late husband had been older than she, a successful stockbroker at one of the local firms, who'd been a heavy smoker for most of his life and had died of lung cancer before he turned fifty. "He left me well enough off," she said, "but with half my life to live without him."

He didn't know what to say to that. "Children?" he asked.

"Two. A boy and a girl, Colleen and Joe, Jr., both away at college."

She went on to tell him that she'd sold the family home on Lake Minnetonka after the kids left, and had bought a loft condominium in the warehouse district—on the other side of downtown. "I had to sell a lot of stuff, but there's plenty of room for me—and enough for Joe and Colleen when they're back from school."

She said she'd worked occasionally during her marriage, but that her husband had wanted her at home for him and the children for most of those years. After his death, she said, she'd gone to school for interior design and had now started her own small decorating business.

"I'm not making much money yet, but I'm getting more clients every month—and enjoying every minute of it."

As she talked, he studied her more closely. For someone in her mid-forties, she was amazingly well-preserved. Could pass for late thirties, at least. Take away a couple of crows-feet around her eyes and her skin was wrinkle-free. She wore little makeup, aside from a touch of lip gloss, and what was there was skillfully applied.

So the question persisted: *Why's a woman like this sitting here with a guy like me?*

The waiter was back. Rachel gave the menu a quick glance and ordered a spinach quiche, with hash browns on the side. Barclay took a moment more, longing for steak and eggs but settling for a fruit plate.

"Are you sure?" she said. "I hope you're not doing that for me."

"For my doctor," he said, glancing around. "I know he's somewhere watching. He has spies everywhere."

She giggled again, as she had on the phone.

"Seriously," he said. "It didn't take me long last night to see that I was a lot larger than most of the people there. It's one thing to waddle around a newsroom, but something else at an affair like that. So I decided it was time to take off some weight. Maybe fifty pounds or so."

"You're kidding!"

"Oh, I can do it," he said, telling her of his previous massive weight loss, and how much better he'd felt. "It takes time, but as everyone knows, the secret is keeping the pounds off. I'm not too good at that."

Without realizing it, and without much prompting from her, he went on to tell her about his early life, his education, and the series of jobs he'd held before coming back to the Twin Cities. That his folks had retired to Florida a year after his return. "In part, I came back because of them, but now, in the winter, they're toasty warm in Naples while I freeze my buns in Minnesota."

It had been a long time since he'd felt as comfortable talking about himself to anyone, telling her more than she probably wanted to know. But she never seemed to lose interest.

By then their lunches had arrived, and they ate without much conversation, Barclay hoping that his growling stomach was not audible across the table. When they'd finished, he got around to asking the crucial question. "So, Rachel, as much as I've enjoyed this, and hoping not to offend you, I have to ask why you're doing it?"

She looked puzzled. "Doing what?"

He searched for the words. "Befriending me, I guess. Last night. Today. I'm nobody to you, yet you've gone out of your way to . . . I don't know . . . get to know me. That doesn't happen often to me, and it strikes me as a little strange."

Grinning, she said, "My, you're a suspicious one."

"No, just curious. I don't often attract the attention of attractive women."

"Well, I'm not out to jump your bones, if that's what you're thinking."

"Be serious."

"Okay. Since you ask. Last night, right off, you struck me as a shy, out-of-place guy. And cute, in your own way. Like a big, gentle bear. Maybe a little lonely." She paused. "I have scads of women friends, too many if you want to know the truth, but not many men friends—not since Joe died, and even then they were mostly his friends, not mine. And, now, those men I do know often want more than I'm willing to give, if you know what I mean."

He nodded. "I guess so."

She went on, "And I felt badly last night when you learned about Jennifer. You showed some emotion, some sensitivity. I don't see that in many men."

Before he could respond, she continued, "My mother was a widow, like me. And I remember how she loved to be invited to our parties. Not because she liked parties, but because she knew men would be there . . . and she loved to hear their voices. She spent so much time with other women, other widows, that hearing men talk and laugh gave her real pleasure, reminding her of my dad, I guess. Now I know how she felt."

That made sense to Barclay. The only real women friends he had these days were connected with work, and they were often younger, married or engaged. The result was that most of his friends were men, guys to go to a ball game or have a beer with. And even that was difficult since many of them also worked for him.

"So that's why I thought we might get together," she said. "You struck me as a funny, interesting man. And I think, I hope, I'm an interesting woman. I figured maybe we could become friends, spend some time together. Platonic time, George. That's my only motivation."

He studied her for a moment, still not entirely convinced. But before he could say anything, she added, "I'm also interested in your business. I'd like to know more about what you do and how it all works. My son, Joe, in fact, is taking broadcast journalism at the University of Missouri."

"Really? How's he doing?"

"Fine, so far."

"Good for him."

"And I also brought something for you," she said, reaching for her purse, pulling out what appeared to be a small piece of newsprint. "It's a clipping about Jennifer's death. I had it in some old high school files at home."

Yellowed and brittle, it was almost in pieces. From the *StarTribune*, dated July 23, 1992:

THIRD RAPE, MURDER VICTIM DISCOVERED IN ST. PAUL

Police have no leads.

St. Paul police discovered the apparent third victim of a serial killer who rapes his victims and leaves their bodies in secluded areas.

The body of 26-year-old Jennifer Bartlow of St. Paul was found in Garden Park, only a block from her apartment in the 300 block of Eustis Avenue in St. Paul. Police think the woman may have been attacked as she walked home from a bus stop two blocks away last night. Her body was discovered by joggers this morning.

Bartlow was an employee of Ecolab in downtown St. Paul, and police were told she had worked late Tuesday evening and had eaten downtown before boarding the bus for home.

The medical examiner is conducting an autopsy to determine the exact cause of death, but police have classified her death as a homicide.

Two other women were killed under similar circumstances in recent months, leading police to fear a serial rapist-murderer may be on the loose.

Twenty-two-year-old Sheila Hamsted was found raped and murdered in south Minneapolis in October, and the body of 23-year-old April

> Sullivan was found in suburban Brooklyn Center in February. Both women had been sexually-molested and strangled.
>
> No suspects have been arrested in any of the slayings, and a $50,000 reward has been offered for the arrest and conviction of the killer or killers.

Barclay read the story once, then again. Not much there that Wilson hadn't told him on the phone. But some.

"There were other articles that followed that one," Rachel said. "But I couldn't find them."

"That's okay," he said. "I appreciate this. May I keep it?"

"Of course."

They sat quietly for a moment, both lost in thought. "It was so long ago," she said, finally. "I wish I could remember more."

"Did anyone mention Jennifer at the reunion?"

"Not last night, but there was a big tribute to her at the tenth reunion. She was the first in our class to die. But now it's been so long . . . "

"You told me you didn't know her well," Barclay said.

"That's true."

"How well?"

He waited as she looked away, deliberating. Finally, she said, "We didn't mix, okay? She had her own small group of buddies, and they pretty much kept to themselves. You must have seen that."

"I didn't get that close," he said.

"None of us really did. Not that we didn't try. But she kind of stood alone, except for that small clique of hers."

"You didn't like her much."

"True. But there may have been a touch of jealousy involved, too."

"How so?"

"You must have seen that guys went gaga over her. And she led a lot of them on."

"Not me."

She laughed. "Then you were the exception. Unfortunately, she got the reputation as a real tease. A vamp, to put it nicely. So we left her alone."

He sat back, trying to reconcile his memory of Jennifer with Rachel's description. It didn't wash. But then again . . .

"I'm sorry to disappoint you," she said. "It's not fair to talk about the dead like that. But you asked."

"I know."

"So what do you plan to do?"

He sighed. "About this? I don't know. The cops have probably done everything they can . . . and, like you say, it happened a long time ago." He paused. "It just seems . . . that . . . to die like that is one thing, but to have it go unsolved, unpunished . . . well, that's something else."

"If there's anything I can do . . ."

"Thanks, but . . ."

"I do know some of Jennifer's friends that I mentioned. I could put you in touch with them, if you'd like."

"I might. Do you know if her parents are still living?"

"No, but I can check."

"Good."

The waiter was by their side, check in hand. Rachel insisted on paying. "After all, I invited you," she said. He argued, but it did no good.

As they got up to leave, he said, "You mentioned you'd like to know more about my business. The station's just across the street, and I'm going to stop in for a minute. You're welcome to come along and see the place."

"I'd like that," she replied.

4

THE TELEVISION STATION WAS A LOW, two-story building that stretched for most of a city block in the heart of downtown Minneapolis. Constructed of big chunks of Minnesota limestone with a copper dome, now turning green, it had a large window at one end of the building, allowing passersby to watch the news live on the air, and a giant-screen TV at the other end.

Once inside, Barclay led Rachel down a long hallway to the newsroom, the mahogany walls along the way covered with large, framed color portraits of the Channel Seven news personalities, and those of the network stars.

Barclay's picture was not among them.

Being Sunday, only a skeleton crew was operating the station, with virtually no one in sight. "It's usually a little more active than this," he said. "Especially around news time, when everybody's chasing their tails."

Along the way, they passed the big news studio with its remote-controlled cameras, which were once operated by actual human beings, and the technical operations center, where banks of equipment hummed and whirled, churning out the commercials that kept the station's cash registers ringing.

The newsroom itself was a large open area populated by shoulder-high cubicles, crowded together, housing the reporters and producers. Front and center in the room was the assignment desk, raised slightly above the floor, and behind that the dispatch room—where young college students monitored all of the police and fire radio frequencies, twenty-four-seven.

Barclay led Rachel through the maze, introducing her to the few people there. Harry Wilson was back on the assignment desk, a phone in each ear.

"Who's he talking to?" Rachel asked.

"Who knows? Trying to scare up some news, I'd guess. Not easy on a Sunday in August. Not with a couple of newscasts to fill."

At the far end of the newsroom was Barclay's small office, encased on two sides by wide windows—providing a vista of the newsroom. As they walked to it, Barclay said, "You might want to shut your eyes."

Inside, television monitors were stacked on one wall, and the desk, credenza and shelves, even the floor, were crammed with videotapes, discarded newspapers and old scripts. The carpet was worn bare, and the back of his office chair was obviously broken, leaning backwards at a precipitous angle.

"Not the tidiest place I've ever seen," she said. "How do you find anything?"

He laughed. "I don't."

As they turned to leave, Harry Wilson approached them. "George, you got a minute?"

"I guess so," he said, then quickly introduced Rachel.

"Nice to meet you," Wilson said, motioning Barclay to follow him.

"I'll only be a minute," Barclay told Rachel. "Grab a chair anywhere."

Walking away, Wilson said, "Nice looking babe. Where'd you find her?"

"Forget it. What's going on?"

"I just got a call from Pam Stewart at the *StarTribune*. She tried to reach Hawke. When she couldn't, she tried you at home. I didn't say you were here."

Nicholas Hawke was the vice-president and general manager of the station—Barclay's boss—and a man with whom he'd had his share of tangles over the years. By now, however, they'd managed to put aside their differences to coexist in their common interest.

"What did she want?" Barclay asked.

Wilson looked around, making sure he couldn't be overheard. "She works on the business page and says she just got a tip from somebody in New York. That the station's been sold."

"What? This station?"

"You got it. To an outfit called TriCom Communications. They own about a dozen other stations, she says, mostly in small and medium markets. She wants to know if we know anything . . . and if we have any comment."

Barclay sank into a chair. "Jesus. That has to be bullshit. I'd have heard something." His mind churned. Had there been any hints? Any signals he might have missed? Whispered conversations in the hallways? Unfamiliar suits wandering around? Not that he could recall, but then again, he wasn't privy to much of what happened on the second floor, what the technicians liked to call "management heaven."

By choice, he confined himself to the newsroom as much as possible, ignoring the intrigue and politics of upper management. As a result, he often was among the last to hear the rumors or be told of decisions by Hawke and others.

But something like this? Impossible.

"She's checking other sources," Wilson said, "and hopes to go with the story in tomorrow's paper."

"We're not saying anything," Barclay told him. "And where the hell is Hawke?" Then he remembered. He'd told him he'd be out of town for the weekend. New York? *Fuck me.*

"I told her I'd call her back," Wilson said. "What'll I tell her?"

"Tell her if it's news, it's news to us," Barclay replied with a sneer.

"Seriously?"

"Tell her she has to talk to Hawke. And that we don't know where he is. I'm not going to get my tit stuck in this particular wringer."

"You got it," Wilson said, starting to walk away.

Barclay grabbed his arm. "And don't tell anybody else about this. Not until we know what's going on."

Channel Seven, unlike many major market network affiliates in the country, was still locally owned by third-generation members of a family that had started out in the newspaper business but had turned to television years before when it became clear that broadcasting would be the cash cow of the future. Now large corporations could own multiple TV stations, making it ever more difficult for local owners to remain competitive and profitable. Especially in a recession, and with cable, satellites, the Internet, and other competitors taking an increasing share of audience and advertising revenue. Nonetheless, stations like Channel Seven still held substantial value for conglomerates like TriCom.

"Is anything wrong?"

Rachel was standing next to him. For how long he wasn't sure. "Sorry," he said. "No, nothing's wrong."

"You look a little pale. Bad news or something?"

He got up. "It could be. I'm just not sure."

"Well, I hope not," she said. "But I should be getting home. My kids check in with me every Sunday afternoon."

"I'll give you a ride."

"Not necessary. I parked in the hotel ramp."

He walked her to the back door. "I've enjoyed this," he said. "I'm glad you called."

"So am I." She reached over and gave his hand a quick squeeze. "You're a nice man, George Barclay. It'll be nice to have you as a friend."

She was halfway out the door when she turned back. "I'll call you with the names of Jennifer's friends. Okay?"

"Okay," he said. "And thanks."

Then, with a wave and a smile, she was gone.

Barclay was waiting outside Hawke's office on Monday morning, shuffling his feet and paging through that morning's edition of the *StarTribune*. He'd been through the paper several times, page by page, but had found no story on the pending sale of the station—in the business section or elsewhere.

The report must be bogus, he thought. *Another rumor*.

As he was about to get up and leave, Hawke's executive assistant, a woman named Maria Fallon, walked in, obviously caught off guard to find him there. "George? What a surprise." She rarely saw him in Hawke's office, unless he'd been summoned there. "What brings you up here?"

"Waiting for your boss," he said. "I mean, *our* boss."

"Is he expecting you?"

"I don't think so."

"Maybe I can help," she offered.

"Probably not."

She gave him a curious look as she sat down at her desk. "I'm not sure when he'll be in, George, and I know he has some out-of-town guests with him. Perhaps I can have him call you."

Out-of-town guests?

Barclay walked over to her. "Have you heard the rumors?" he asked.

Her face reddened slightly. "What rumors are those, George?"

She was lying. "C'mon, Maria. We're old friends. Remember? Why am I always the last one to know things around here?"

He'd known Maria since his first days on the job. An assistant in the sales department then, she had diligently worked her way up through the clerical ranks to her present position. Tall and quite proper, she had well-blushed cheeks and a flip-up hairdo that made her even more imposing. Known within the station as the power behind the throne, there was little that went on that was beyond her view.

But now, as she busied herself tidying up the top of her desk, she refused to look up. "I don't know what you're talking about."

He leaned over the desk, bending his head to try and catch her eyes. "The newsroom got a call yesterday, from the paper, saying the station's been sold. Pretty good story, if it's true. And our news department knows nothing about it."

"Nor do I, George," she said, finally facing him. "And even if I did, you know I couldn't say anything."

At that moment, there was movement behind him, and Barclay turned to find Hawke and three other men, all buttoned-up, standing in the office doorway. Corporate goons, he thought. Hawke appeared even more surprised than Maria to see him. "Hey, George," he said, leading his companions around him and toward his private office. "Don't know what you want, but it'll have to wait."

"I just need a minute," Barclay said. "It's important."

Hawke stopped, irritation in his voice. "I said it's going to have to wait."

The three suits smiled slightly and followed Hawke into his office.

Assholes, Barclay thought as he turned around and left.

ONCE INSIDE HIS OFFICE, one of Hawke's companions asked, "Who's the chubby guy?"

"George Barclay, the news director," Hawke replied.

"So that's him."

"I hope you're not paying him by the pound," another said with a laugh.

Hawke ignored the insult.

"You don't put him on the air, do you?" said the first.

"No, no."

"I hope not."

The third man spoke for the first time. "When we talked about him, and made our deal, I didn't know what he looked like. In most of our stations, we like our news directors to be . . . well, air-worthy. You know, capable of getting out on the street, reporting. Saves hiring another reporter."

"Yeah, well, that's not how it works here," Hawke said, somewhat defensively.

"Then things may have to change," said the first.

WHEN BARCLAY RETURNED to the newsroom, he was immediately confronted by Jeff Parkett, his assistant news director. "Have you seen the *StarTribune*'s website?" he asked.

His heart sank. "No," he said. "But I can guess what's there."

They walked over to Parkett's computer, already displaying one of the web pages. Barclay leaned over to read:

> The *StarTribune* has learned from reliable sources that WCKT-TV, Channel Seven in the Twin Cities, has been sold to TriCom Communications, a media conglomerate operating out of Charlotte, North Carolina. No purchase price was revealed, but the sources say the deal was finalized in weekend talks in New York—in the offices of the investment bank, Morgan Stanley.
>
> No official of WCKT-TV or TriCom would confirm the sale, or even that negotiations were underway, but the sources tell the *StarTribune* that secret talks have been held over the past several weeks. TriCom Communications owns fourteen television stations, forty-three radio properties, and twelve daily newspapers in markets across the country.
>
> The *StarTribune* made numerous efforts to contact management officials at WCKT-TV for comment or confirmation, but those calls were not returned.

As Barclay stared at the screen, Parkett asked, "Did you know about this?"

"Only rumors," he said as he picked up a phone and angrily punched in three numbers. "Maria? Tell Hawke to get on the Internet, and look at the *StarTribune* website. Maybe he'll talk to me then."

He slammed down the phone. "Screw it!" he shouted, kicking at an empty wastebasket. "Getting beat on our own story. What's going on around here?"

Those nearby moved away in the face of his rage. Barclay didn't get angry often, but when he did, the newsroom had learned to give him plenty of space. Only Parkett dared to remain nearby. "What do we do now?" he asked.

"Report the damn story, if I can ever get Hawke to talk to me."

Parkett persisted. "Forget the story. What about all of us?"

It was a question that was troubling him as well. "I don't know," he finally said. "But I wouldn't go making any big plans for a while."

MARIA KNOCKED ON THE DOOR of Hawke's office and opened it a crack. "Sorry to interrupt," she said, "but George says you should look at the *StarTribune* website. Right away. Says it's important."

Hawke hit some keys on his computer and waited a moment until the page appeared. The three suits gathered around him, reading what Barclay had read moments before.

"Looks like the cat's out of the bag," Hawke said. "Somebody leaked it."

"Don't look at us," one of the men replied.

"It's either one of your people, or me," Hawke said irritably. "And I know it wasn't me."

He called Maria into his office. "Tell George there'll be a news conference at two this afternoon, in the studio. Have the promotion department alert the other media." He paused. "One more thing. Set up an employee meeting immediately after the news conference."

Maria nodded and headed for the phone.

WORD OF THE SALE SPREAD QUICKLY, leaving the newsroom—the whole station, in fact—in a state of shock. And in an uproar. Within minutes, the news had spread to every other station in town, flooding the newsroom with calls from curious and concerned colleagues and competitors.

Between the phone calls and frantic visits from many of his staff, Barclay hardly had time to leave his office. Feeling helpless and angry, knowing no more than anyone else, he was forced to simply plead ignorance and defer to Hawke's announcement that afternoon.

Rarely had he been left so far out of the loop, but he quickly discovered he was not alone. The secret had been so well-kept that most of the other management people were as much in the dark as he was.

Shit, he thought. *Leave it to the goddamned paper to learn about it first.*

So he was left biding his time—fending off inquiries and making sure the newsroom was properly prepared to cover Hawke's news conference and employee meeting.

BY NOON, THE PANDEMONIUM had eased and he felt comfortable enough to run across the street to the hotel for a quick lunch. When he returned, he was intercepted by his assistant, Parkett, a hefty former Gopher linebacker who tried to block his way. "You've got to say something, George. The place is wild with rumors."

Barclay tried to push past him. "I don't know any more than you do," he replied for the umpteenth time.

"Nobody's getting any work done," Parkett complained.

"They'd better," Barclay growled, "or I'll have your ass on a stick."

Parkett started to walk away, then turned back. "By the way, there's some woman waiting in your office."

A woman? Who the hell can that be? On a day like this? He'd already cancelled all of his appointments.

Approaching the office warily, he poked his head inside and found a fairly attractive lady about his age sitting on the edge of his frayed guest chair, staring at the TV monitors. "Excuse me," he said from the door. "I'm George Barclay. Can I help you?"

She got up, hand outstretched. "I'm Katie Thorson."

The name meant nothing to him. "Was I expecting you?" he asked, returning the handshake while trying to hide his impatience. "You caught me at kind of a bad time."

"No, you weren't expecting me. But the security people were kind enough to let me in."

She was about five-foot-six, a bit on the heavy side, with blond hair that he guessed wasn't, and a way about her that struck him as somewhere between frightened and determined. Asking her to take a seat, he walked back to his desk and sat down himself, careful not to lean back too far. "So what can I do for you?"

"Rachel Armetage called me. She said you'd talked to her about Jennifer."

Jesus. Word travels fast. "What was your name again?" he asked.

"Katie Thorson. That's my married name. Katie Schmidt when I was single."

They sat for a moment without speaking. Then she continued, "Rachel said you might be interested in looking into Jennifer's murder. And those other women."

He was taken aback. "Hold on," he said quickly. "Please. Rachel may have spoken too soon. I didn't realize Jennifer had died until Saturday night. It came as a shock, although I really didn't know her that well. Naturally, I was interested in how she'd died, but I didn't really indicate anything more."

"So you're not going to look into it?"

He fudged. "I just don't know. I'm not sure what I could do that the police haven't already done."

"You people found out what happened to those three boys a while back, didn't you?"

She was talking about a celebrated investigation into the kidnapping of three young brothers that had happened fifteen years before. Alex Collier, his departed anchor man, had been able to locate the boys, although one was dead and another brainwashed by the time he'd found them.

"Yes, but with a lot of luck."

"And hard work."

"That, too," he admitted.

Her eyes welled. "Everyone's forgotten about Jennifer. Except a few of us who loved her. I know it's been almost twenty years, but, my

God, that doesn't make her any less dead. None of us will rest until whoever did this is caught and punished."

She sniffed, dug a tissue from her purse, then went on, "You knew Jennifer. She loved life. Craved it. Gloried in it. You must have seen that. Surely, you remember that."

"I do," he said. "She was always full of life."

"And detested the idea of death." She was openly weeping now. "She was the best friend I ever had. And then she was gone. Can you imagine her last moments? Feeling the life she so loved squeezed out of her?"

He hated to see a woman cry. "I hear you," he said. "And I sympathize. But . . ." His words evaporated. Then, "Has the case ever been reopened?"

The tears were trickling down her cheeks. "Several years ago, I guess. But it went nowhere. We kept pestering them until they got disgusted with us and stopped taking our calls. We've heard nothing since."

"Them?" he said. "Do you remember the names of any of the detectives?"

"One," she replied, still sniffling. "Jacobs. John Jacobs. But that was years ago."

Her tissue was sodden. Barclay had none in his office, but he offered her his handkerchief. Thank God it was clean.

"Maybe if the police know a station like yours is interested," she said, wiping at the tears, "they'll agree to look into it again."

Maybe, maybe not. He didn't want to tell her that it might not be the same station once this sale was over. Or that he might not be around by then. "Listen, Katie, let me think about this, okay? There are some things happening here that you'll read about and that might have an impact on this. But give me your number and the names and numbers of any of your friends who feel like you do. I'll be in touch. That's all I can promise."

She quickly wrote down several names and numbers and got up. "Thank you so much." Then, looking at the damp hanky. "I'll wash this and send it back to you."

"Don't bother. I have more. And thanks for coming."

As an afterthought, he stopped her. "Are Jennifer's parents still around?"

"Her mother died a few years after Jennifer. Of a broken heart, we think. But her dad's still alive and living here. I'll get his number for you, too."

AFTER SHE LEFT, BARCLAY QUICKLY checked his PDA and picked up the phone.

"St. Paul homicide," said the male voice on the other end of the line.

"John Jacobs, please."

There was a long pause. "Lieutenant Jacobs is no longer here. He retired four years ago."

"Really?"

"Afraid so. May I help you?"

"You can tell me how to reach him."

"Who's calling, please?"

"This is George Barclay at Channel Seven."

"I see. We don't give out personal numbers, even for retirees, but I can check and see if he'll get back to you."

"I'd appreciate that," Barclay said, giving him his work, cell, and home numbers.

Ten minutes later his office phone buzzed.

"George Barclay?"

"Yes."

"This is John Jacobs. They said you called."

"Right," Barclay said. "Thanks for the quick call back."

"I got nothin' better to do." His voice was gruff, impatient. "So what do you need?"

"I'd like to meet with you."

"What about?"

"An old case of yours. Jennifer Bartlow."

There was momentary silence at the other end. "That's history," Jacobs finally said.

"To you, maybe. Not to me. I just learned about her murder."

"So?"

"So I'd like to talk to you about it."

"I'm retired."

"I know, but I'd still like to talk to you."

The silence was longer this time. Barclay strained to hear. Finally, "I can't tell you much."

"More than I know now."

"I don't like reporters. Never have."

"Give me a try," Barclay said.

"When?"

"You tell me."

"Tomorrow night. At O'Gara's in St. Paul. You know it?"

"I can find it," Barclay said.

"Eight o'clock. Ask the bartender. He'll know me."

"Thanks."

By then the phone was dead.

Hawke was standing stiff, almost at attention, in front of the hastily arranged bank of microphones and array of cameras in the studio. Short and dapper, he was clad in a beige Armani suit with a pale-blue shirt, and was—as usual—wearing elevated heels on his shoes. Ill at ease, he shifted from foot to foot, clearly eager to get his little show on the road.

But the assembled photographers paid him no heed, continuing to mill about the studio, setting up their equipment.

Behind Hawke were the three men Barclay had seen earlier in his office. Dressed almost identically in dark-blue suits, white shirts, and striped ties, they stood in descending order of height, like steps in a stairway. However, the tallest one was clearly the leader, conferring frequently, off-mike, with Hawke.

"Please, people," Hawke pleaded. "We have to get going."

Barclay was standing in back of the studio, along with a number of other nervous department heads. "My wife's having a cardiac arrest," the sales manager whispered to him. "She thinks we'll be on welfare and food stamps next week."

"See," Barclay said. "It pays to be single. I get to starve alone."

The guy glanced at him. "Like you'd ever starve," he muttered.

The crowd finally settled down and Hawke cleared his throat. "We did not plan to make this announcement at this time," he began, "but the premature release of some details has forced us to change our plans." He paused to take a sip of water from a glass on the podium.

"As some of you have heard, our board of directors has reluctantly made the decision to sell WCKT-TV to TriCom Communications . . ."

Boos and catcalls rang out from the back of the studio, where a group of technicians and stagehands had slipped into the news conference. "Why sell?" one of them shouted. "You've already got more money than you can spend!" There was scattered laughter.

"Please," Hawke said. "Show a little courtesy. You can ask your questions later."

The room quieted. "TriCom," he continued, "is a major player in the media landscape, owning a number of other television and radio properties, along with many newspapers. They have an impeccable reputation as quality station operators . . ."

"Bullshit!" the same stagehand shouted. "They're scavengers. Bottom-feeders. I checked 'em out. Talk to any of their stations."

Hawke motioned to one of the security guards, then waited as the guard quickly escorted the rebel out of the studio. "The sale has already been approved by the boards of both companies," he went on, "and awaits only shareholder and F.C.C. approval before the transaction is complete."

Turning to the trio by his side, he said, "I have been assured by these representatives of TriCom, whom I shall introduce in a moment, that they've made no plans for immediate changes in station operations or any hasty decisions about employment levels."

He then introduced the men, but so quickly Barclay could catch only the name of the last one, the tall dude, the big honcho, Larry Landeau, who quickly stepped to the microphones, coolly buttoning his double-breasted suit. Thick hair, brushed back, with a straight nose and eyes that roved the room like a sentry on guard. "Thank you, Nicholas, and thanks to all of you for coming on such short notice. I, too, apologize for the unauthorized release of information about this sale . . . but, as you all well know," he chuckled, "we do have a free and aggressive press in this country."

His two comrades chuckled, too. But they were the only ones.

"Until the F.C.C. approves the sale, I am permitted to say little about our plans for the station, or to speak to any of you individually about your future roles. But I can tell you that, contrary to what the fellow in the back of the studio said, we run top-notch operations in all of our stations. Of course we're conscious of costs and dedicated to being profitable for our shareholders, but at TriCom, we believe you can be both good and profitable."

Snake, Barclay thought, *but smooth. Really smooth.*

"One thing I can tell you, however, is that Mr. Hawke has graciously decided to step aside when the sale is finalized and the new management team takes over. He will leave with our gratitude for having governed such a wonderful television station."

There was scattered applause, and a few boos, turning Hawke's already strained smile into a scowl.

"While I would like to answer any questions you might have," Landau said, "it would be inappropriate at this time. However, I'm sure Mr. Hawke will make himself available."

The questions flew like darts from the assembled reporters: How much did TriCom pay? Not ready to reveal that at this time. Was there division on the board of directors? No, there was unanimous agreement. Did you get a golden parachute? That's my business. Will the sale be opposed by community groups? I can't imagine why. What about any layoffs? You heard the man. That will be up to the new owners.

On and on it went, for the better part of an hour. Hawke dodging and ducking, saying little, revealing less. Barclay had to give him credit: it was a premiere performance.

The employee meeting that followed was less rambunctious, apparently because no one wanted to further offend Hawke or the potential new owners. But anger was still in the air, and the questions were still pointed: What about our 401-k's? Will TriCom honor the current union contracts? Will there be severance payments to those laid off? To his credit, Hawke tried to respond to everyone, but it was clear that many of the questions would go unanswered.

Barclay was again in the back of the studio, listening carefully. His assistant, Jeff Parkett was standing next to him. "Can you survive this?" he asked. "Can any of us survive this?"

Barclay shook his head. "Hate to say it, but I'd bet that a lot of us will be gone. They'll bring in their own troops, especially in the top spots. To set a fresh tone, bring in new ideas. But, mostly, they'll want people who think like they do."

"Jesus . . ."

"Hey, try to relax."

"Relax! I've got a wife and three kids."

"Slow down. The changes won't happen that quickly. They'll probably let the situation settle down. But then they'll slowly import their own people, who will bring in their own people. When they hire a new news director, that's the time to worry."

"I'll be toast," Parkett said, wandering away.

As he watched him leave, Barclay had a moment to think about his own future. True, he had only himself to worry about. No wife, no kids. But he hated the thought of leaving. As much as he bitched about the Minnesota weather, he loved the state and its people.

There was little doubt he could find another job. His reputation in the news business was strong enough to assure him of that. But at what kind of a station? In what kind of a city? The idea of rooting for the Yankees or the Indians was too much to bear. Hell, he'd had enough trouble making the few friends he had here, and the idea of starting all over again somewhere else was so scary he didn't want to think about it.

He assumed he'd get some kind of severance package, but money wasn't the issue. He already earned more than he could spend, and had no desire to improve his lifestyle. And no need to leave a financial legacy. In short, he was quite content with the way things were.

But, deep down, he knew all of that could change.

AFTER ANOTHER HOUR OR SO, with the newsroom humming, he felt comfortable enough to leave the office. He needed the break. "I'll be gone for a while," he told Wilson at the assignment desk. "Maybe an hour or so. I have my cell if you need me."

"Want to tell me where you're going," Wilson said.

"No."

The public library was several blocks away, so he stuck to the skyways crisscrossing downtown, escaping the mid-afternoon heat. Once there, he headed for the library's history section and the microfiche newspaper archives. Checking the date on the 1992 article Rachel had given him, he quickly turned to stories on Jennifer's murder in both the *StarTribune* and the *St. Paul Pioneer Press*.

As he expected, both papers had given the rape-murder significant play, emphasizing the possibility of a serial killer at work. He spent more than an hour scanning the papers from the day of the murder to two weeks after, making hard copies of each story he found. He was disappointed that there was not more new information, but he did learn a few additional facts.

•The Ramsey County medical examiner had confirmed that Jennifer had been sexually assaulted, then strangled, apparently by a belt found near the body.

•St. Paul police had been unable to find eyewitnesses to the attack, and had refused to reveal if they had discovered any other clues—beside the belt—at the murder scene. The stories did not say whether any fingerprints were found on the belt, but Barclay doubted it.

•The police also had confirmed that they believed a serial killer was responsible for the deaths of Jennifer and the two other women, but admitted they had no hard evidence to support that belief.

•The chief investigator for the St. Paul police was a Lieutenant John Jacobs of the Homicide division, the retired cop he had talked to earlier, and that he was part of a joint task force that had been formed to investigate the possibility of a link among the three murders.

It was a few days after the murder that the *Pioneer Press* carried a lengthy feature story on Jennifer's life. Giving Barclay—for the first time—a glimpse of what had become of the girl in the years since he had last seen her. It read, in part:

> After graduating from Armstrong High School in the Minneapolis suburb of Plymouth, in 1984, Jennifer went on to college at the University of Wisconsin in Madison, majoring in theater arts. Her lifelong dream, according to her parents, was to become an actress. "She had a marvelous presence on stage," her father said, "and she loved being part of that world."

> In 1989, she went to New York to pursue the dream, taking both voice and acting lessons at the New York University School of Drama. "She did well at NYU," her mother said, "and later got some small roles off-Broadway and in a few television commercials." But, according to her parents, she hated living in New York and yearned to return to the Midwest.
>
> "She also had a boyfriend back here," her mother said, "and he had told her he wasn't about to move out East."
>
> So, in 1990, Jennifer returned to the Twin Cities. But she quickly discovered that acting jobs were more difficult to find here than they had been in New York. "She was very disappointed," said one of her close friends, Katie Schmidt of Minneapolis, "but she was determined to keep trying."
>
> Like a lot of young people, however, Jennifer had to repay student loans and was forced to seek work outside of the theater. She was able to land a clerical position at Ecolab in downtown St. Paul, where she was working at the time of her death. But she never gave up her goals.
>
> "She was an extraordinarily strong woman," her friend, Katie, said. "Smart, independent, and very savvy. It's more than a crime when someone like her is taken from us so cruelly. She had so much to give the world."

Earlier, the article had identified Jennifer's parents as Kevin and Margaret Bartlow of Plymouth. He made a note of that, and of Katie Schmidt, the woman he had met in his office, but could find no mention of the name of the boyfriend for whom she had supposedly returned to the Twin Cities.

Barclay wondered who he was and what had happened to him. He jotted down another note to himself.

Satisfied he had found all of the stories that seemed to exist in that two week period in both newspapers, he gathered up his material and headed back to the station.

He was no sooner back in his office than there was a rap at his door. Parkett stuck his head inside. "Bad news," he said. "Hawke wants to see you in his office. Like right away."

"No shit," Barclay said, heaving himself out of his chair. He knew a summons would come eventually, but he hadn't expected it so quickly.

Maria gave him a wan smile and waved him into Hawke's office.

"Sorry to bring you up here on short notice," he said, "and sorry I was so brusque with you earlier. But I thought we should talk. Have a seat."

Barclay sat, separated from Hawke by his huge desk, which was almost the size of Barclay's office. "Have your visitors left?" he asked.

"They had to catch a plane. Off to another one of their acquisitions, I suspect."

At a loss for what to say, Barclay waited.

"I know we've had our differences over the years," Hawke said.

No shit, Barclay thought. Among other things, Hawke had once tried to block their exposé of a prominent pedophile judge, who happened to be a friend of his. When that failed, and in a fit of anger, he'd fired Barclay for insubordination, but then had reconsidered—leaving their relationship permanently strained.

"Despite that—and I hope you know this, George—I have great regard for your abilities and for the way you have maintained the reputation and ratings of our news department. You've kept us number one despite the increased competition, and I appreciate that more than you know."

Where's all of this leading? Barclay wondered.

"I know," Hawke went on, "that you must be concerned about your future. And I want to quell any fears you might have." He paused, eyeing Barclay across the desk. "As part of our deal with TriCom, we have insisted that you be retained on the staff at your present salary for up to two years after the sale is consummated."

Barclay was truly surprised. "I appreciate that," he said.

But Hawke wasn't finished. "That's the good news. The bad news is that we couldn't get them to guarantee that you'll remain in your present job. So it's possible you may be reassigned to some other position in the department."

The other shoe. Thud. "Like what?" he asked.

Hawke shrugged. "Producer. Reporter. Researcher. I don't know. It'll be up to you and them."

"But you haven't committed me to stay, have you?" Barclay said.

"Of course not. But," and he paused, "if you decide to leave in the first six months after the sale, you'll have to forego your severance package. That's also part of the deal. They want to be assured of some continuity."

Barclay leaned forward, anger in his voice. "So, let me get this straight. I'm assured of a job, but maybe not my job, for two years. But if I choose to leave before six months, I leave with nothing but my memories."

"That's about it," Hawke said. "I did my best, George."

Barclay got up. "What if I leave before they take over?"

"We haven't crossed that bridge, but I hope you won't."

"I'll have to think about all of this," he said. "But thanks for trying to protect me."

Hawke rose as well, smiling. "I'm really not the prick you think I am."

Maybe, maybe not, Barclay thought as he walked out.

7

After the early news, and after trying to further calm the fears in the newsroom, Barclay left the station for the short walk back to his condo. The August heat was unrelenting, but he tried to ignore it and keep his mind on Hawke's proposition: Could he really stay at the station as something other than news director? Living with the humiliation? And do what? Sit around and watch the new owners slowly dismantle everything he had tried to build?

There were larger questions: Did he really want to remain in a business that was changing so dramatically and work for the kind of jerks he had gotten a glimpse of today? He knew it was a new world out there, ruled by conglomerates like TriCom, which talked the talk but didn't walk the walk. He couldn't kid himself; he'd have trouble finding a station that hadn't been infected by the same contagion, an illness he knew had already cost the jobs of many of his old friends in the news business.

But what else could he do? The idea of working for a public relations agency or some government outfit was, at first blush, unacceptable. To be honest, he didn't consider himself capable of anything else. His whole professional life had been dedicated to doing this one job, and the thought of leaving it for something else was beyond his immediate imagination.

Seuss was waiting just inside his condo door, absent his normal scowl, actually looking slightly sympathetic, as if he knew all was not well in Barclay's world. Barclay scooped him up and held him close—

something he rarely did—and, for a moment, he thought he heard the cat actually purr.

The light on his message machine was blinking. Putting the cat down, he hit the button and heard Rachel's voice: "Hi, George. I heard the news, but didn't want to bother you at the station. Do you want to talk? I'm just down the street at the YW, working out. Be here till 7:30 or so. Stop down if you can, and we'll get something to eat. I'll let you buy this time."

He glanced at his watch. Quarter past seven. He had the time, and why not? Maybe talking would help. So he quickly gave Seuss fresh food and water, scooped out his litter box, and exchanged his own soggy shirt for a clean one.

HE FOUND HER JOGGING on the treadmill, hardly breaking a sweat, wearing shorts and a sports bra that clearly displayed what the green silk reunion dress had only hinted at. This was a woman who clearly took care of her body, and, from the look of her nicely tanned skin, spent a fair amount of time in the sun. He stood for a moment, admiring what he saw, before she spotted him. "Hi, George. Glad you could make it. Give me a minute. Another half-mile to go."

He was happy to oblige.

She dabbed at her face with a towel. "Do you work out?" she asked.

"Are you being smart?"

"No," she laughed, "I'm serious."

"I used to," he said. "But not for a while."

She was breathing a little heavier. "Well, I know they have openings here," she said.

He stood back, watching but trying not to stare, until she completed her final half-mile. "I'm just going to jump in the shower," she said as she stepped off. "Want to meet me down at Brit's?"

"Sure." Next best thing to the shower, he thought.

Brit's, as the name suggests, was an English-style bar just down the Nicollet Mall. He made his way there, deciding against the hot sidewalk seating for the cool and dark interior. Finding a small table to one side, he had already finished one beer and was halfway through a second by the time she walked in, squinting to find him in the crowd.

She slipped into a chair next to him. "Have you already eaten?"

"Grape Nuts for breakfast. A piece of cold pizza for lunch."

"George! You have to eat better than that."

"I haven't had much time," he said.

"I can imagine. Tell me about it."

He told her everything—from his early morning encounter with Hawke and the TriCom goons to the employee meeting. "The place is in disarray. Nobody knows what's happening. Everybody thinks they're going to be out of a job."

"What about you?"

"I wish I knew," he said, repeating the deal Hawke had offered him. "I haven't been thinking about much else. For sure, I'll have some decisions to make."

He was again surprised by how much he was telling her. This was a woman who seemed to draw it out of him without much effort.

By then a waiter appeared, took her order for a glass of chardonnay, and—for both of them—an order of buffalo wings and onion rings. Barclay stuck with his second beer.

Rachel asked, "Did Katie Thorson call you?"

"Better than that. She came to see me."

"Really?"

"You work fast, Rachel."

"I'm sorry. I didn't know she'd do that."

Recounting his conversation with Katie, he said, "I wish she wouldn't have cried. That always gets me."

"See. I told you. You've got a soft heart."

"Don't tell people in the newsroom."

"So, what are you going to do?"

"I don't know, but I do have another favor to ask."

"Shoot."

He pulled a small sheet of paper from his pocket. "Katie gave me the names and numbers of some of Jennifer's other friends."

"Okay."

"Would you give her another call? See if you could set up a meeting with these friends in the next week or so. I'd like to meet with them, and have you there as well."

She hesitated. "I'll be happy to make the call, but why do you want me there?"

"For my own comfort level, I guess."

Their wings and rings arrived along with two drinks they hadn't ordered. "A fellow at the bar sent them over," the waiter said.

A tall guy with salt-and-pepper hair gave them a wave. Rachel responded with a smile. "That's Sam Posner," she said. "He used to work with my husband."

"One of your men friends?"

"He's divorced. We dated a couple of times. But he's pretty full of himself. Most successful stockbrokers are, I've found."

"You do have a lot of friends," Barclay observed. "I couldn't believe how many people you seemed to know at that reunion."

"Knowing and *really* knowing are two different things. I have far more acquaintances than friends, I'm afraid."

They sat back, listening to the ebb and flow of conversation around them, not talking, nibbling at their food, sipping at their drinks. Finally, Rachel said, "So tell me more about yourself and Jennifer."

He thought for a moment, then responded with a question of his own. "Who was your first love?"

She gave him a curious look. Then smiled. "Hector Salazar," she said. "In ninth grade. He was a Spanish exchange student. The most handsome boy I'd ever seen." She laughed. "But my parents didn't approve. Almost made me change schools. 'We'll have no foreigners in our family,' they said."

"And how did Hector feel about you?"

"He said he loved me. But remember, this was ninth grade."

"You started younger than I did," he said. "Jennifer was my first love. I mean, real love. But unlike your Hector, she didn't exactly return the favor."

Rachel leaned on the table, her chin resting on her clasped hands.

"She sat in front of me in English," his memory kicking in. "Her hair was so black. Black and shiny, shimmering when the sun hit the window in a certain way. I couldn't take my eyes off of it. She sat up so straight and was so smart. Knew grammar, backwards and forwards. When to use 'lay' and 'lie.' 'Further' and 'farther.' We were all in awe.

"She'd turn around and look back at me now and then. Called me Georgie Porgie from South Dakotie. Thought I was a dork, I'm sure. But, of course, at the time, I thought she was flirting, and was completely smitten."

Rachel smiled. "Go on," she said. "This is great."

"Now, maybe. But at the time, I was miserable. She was all I could think about. I'd wait in the halls to catch a glimpse of her. I'd wait outside school to see her get on the bus, even if it meant missing my own bus. I'd fantasize about asking her to the prom, but, of course, never did. I wouldn't have dared, and it wouldn't have done any good anyway. I was just another drooling kid with the hidden hots for her."

"She never responded?"

"Oh, yeah. I used to get better grades than she did on our theme papers, and I think it drove her crazy. Said I was the teacher's pet. But I didn't care; at least she was noticing me.

"Poor George," Rachel said.

He leaned back in his chair. "I never saw her after graduation. Never knew what had happened to her. But every now and then, even years later, she would pop back into my head. At the oddest times. I've known other women since, of course, but none of them ever measured up to those memories of Jennifer. Maybe that's why I'm still single."

"Seriously?" she said. "She had that kind of impact on you?"

"Sounds silly, I know. But, in a way, she did. I kept waiting for other women to trigger those same kinds of feelings, but it didn't happen. At least not often."

"That's remarkable," she said.

"Strange may be a better word."

"And you never tried to contact her?"

"It would've been hopeless," he said. "Besides, by then I'd moved on. To college. My career. I tried not to look back, but I could never completely shake that childish crush."

"This is very weird, George. Do you realize that?"

"I guess it is," he admitted, wondering if he had told her too much.

Their glasses and plates were empty. The crowd had lessened. "I'd better be going," he said, getting up, leaving a twenty and a ten on the table. "I have to check on things at the station and try to figure out what I'm going to do."

"Thanks for meeting me," she said. "And thanks for telling me about Jennifer."

As they were on their way out, Sam, the man at the bar who'd bought them the drinks, intercepted them. "Hey, Rachel. It's been a while."

"It has, Sam. Nice to see you again." She quickly introduced him to Barclay, who thanked him for the drink and then headed for the door. Waiting a beat for Rachel to join him, then deciding she wasn't going to. "Call me, will you, George?" she called after him. "It's your turn."

He gave a wave, leaving her with Sam, and leaving himself trying to understand the sudden regret he felt.

O'Gara's was a large Irish pub located just off Interstate 94 in St. Paul, a neighborhood bar that managed to attract patrons from all across the Twin Cities. And while Barclay had never been there, he had no trouble finding it.

The first thing he noticed, bolted to a wall just inside O'Gara's, was the battered door from a New York City fire department rescue truck destroyed in the attack on the World Trade Center. He later learned that the bar had helped to raise thousands of dollars in a benefit for the firefighters, that the scarred door of Rescue 4 had been sent from New York as a thank you gift.

On this night, only a few customers sat at the bar and in the booths across the way. One young couple was playing electronic darts, but everyone else seemed to be either staring into their beers or watching the Twins on two TVs hung high on opposite ends of the bar.

Barclay squeezed onto one of the stools and surveyed those around him. No one approached or seemed to take notice of him until the bartender stopped in front of him. "What's your pleasure?" he asked.

"An Amstel Light," Barclay said.

"You got it."

As he reached into the cooler, Barclay said, "I'm supposed to meet John Jacobs here. He said you'd point him out."

"J.J.?" the bartender said. "Haven't seen him yet. But you won't miss him. He's big as a tree with a crew cut." Then, with a laugh, "And watch out when you shake hands. He'll crush you."

Barclay cooled his heels for about ten minutes, sipping his beer and watching the Twins fall behind the Royals, three to two, in the fifth inning. *Not to worry*, he thought, *only one run. They'll come back.*

Intent on the game, he didn't see Jacobs until he was standing next to him, towering above him. "You must be Barclay," he said, his voice as husky in person as it'd been on the phone. "Somebody told me you were carrying a few extra pounds."

Barclay twisted on the stool, startled. "It's mostly muscle," he finally said and grinned.

Jacobs guffawed. "Right," he said. Then he stuck out his hand. "I'm John Jacobs. But most people call me J.J."

Barclay hesitated. "The bartender told me." He took the outstretched hand, grimacing in anticipation. The bartender hadn't been kidding. His knuckles cracked, stuck together like glue.

"But," Jacobs said, finally releasing his grip, "the same guy told me you were okay. Better than most of your buddies in the news business."

"Nice to hear," Barclay replied, wondering who the informant might be. "Can I get you something?"

Jacobs waved to the bartender. "Wild Turkey, straight up."

They took their drinks to one of the booths, which Barclay struggled to fit into. "You oughta' lose some of that weight," Jacobs said. "It's not healthy."

"I'm trying," he said. "Two pounds in the last three days."

"That's a start, but it's probably all water."

In advance of the meeting, Barclay had learned that Jacobs was a tough ex-Marine who'd survived a couple of tours in Vietnam, returning to St. Paul to become a cop in the mid-seventies. That meant he must be over seventy, but—except for his pure white crew cut—you'd never tell it. Six-foot-five or more, with shoulders as broad as his waist was narrow, he appeared to be in top physical condition. His face was ruddy, perhaps from too many Wild Turkeys, but his skin was tight and his eyes a startling blue—which seemed to have a light of their own in the dimness of the bar.

As they talked, Barclay learned more about the man: divorced, the father of two grown children, who now lived by himself in suburban Roseville. "It isn't easy being married to a cop," he said, "and I wasn't the greatest husband to begin with. The wife put up with me until the kids got out of high school, then took off with some friggin' accountant. The prick."

"Sorry to hear," Barclay said. "And your kids?"

"One's in California, the other in Georgia. I hardly ever see them or the grandkids. Maybe at Christmas, but that's about it."

He went on to say he'd been a street cop for the better part of fifteen years before he made sergeant and was assigned to the homicide unit in the eighties. "I was there until I retired," he said. "Twenty-some years."

"That's a lot of murders," Barclay offered.

"You're telling me? I still see 'em in my sleep."

"That include Jennifer Bartlow?"

"Of course. She's near the top of the list."

"Why's that?"

Jacobs eyed him. "Why do you think? Because we never solved it. Because she was a beautiful young woman who didn't deserve to die the way she did. And because the same guy killed two others."

"You believe that?"

"Sure. But we could never prove it. And we never caught him."

Before Barclay could respond, Jacobs said, "I told you on the phone. It's history. I don't like talking about old cases. Especially the ones that got away from us. I've tried to put those behind me."

"I understand," Barclay said. "But you're here, aren't you? Maybe you haven't been able to put this one completely away."

Jacobs grunted and downed the last of his drink. "Maybe not. But what does this woman mean to you?"

Barclay hesitated, then quickly told the story of the reunion. "I didn't know she'd died until then. It piqued my interest. The fact that it's never been solved. Got me curious."

"That's all?"

"I liked her. Let's leave it at that."

"Well, you're a little late." Jacobs said, leaning in. "I can't remember a homicide . . . or series of homicides . . . that got more thoroughly investigated. Dozens of us were involved. A task force looked into every fucking nook and cranny. I bet we interviewed a couple hundred people . . . friends of the women, coworkers, possible suspects. We beat the bushes, but came up empty.

"We even called in the FBI profilers, the pros who've made a career of studying serial rapists and murderers."

"And?"

"They said there are two types of offenders—organized and disorganized. That our guy was probably one of the organized ones. Above average intelligence, a careful planner, who picks and chooses his victims carefully. Likes to taunt the cops, and takes pride in being able to thwart the investigation."

"What else?" Barclay asked.

He glanced across at the bar. "That he could be any one of those dudes sitting over there. An average guy. You'd never pick him out in a crowd as some kind of psycho killer."

Barclay thought for a moment. "Isn't it unusual? Three murders in a few months. Then they stop?"

"Yeah. But that wasn't the only strange thing."

"What else?"

"There was no connection among the three women that we could ever figure out. All from different parts of the cities. Traveled in different circles. Worked at different places. Didn't go to the same bars, or know any of the same people. They didn't even look alike. One was heavy and not very attractive. Another was quite unattractive, as a matter of fact. And then there was Jennifer. Who was beautiful, of course."

"So they were random?"

"Apparently. But even in random killings, the profilers tell us the killer tends to pick out the same kind of women. They like to prey on a certain type."

"So why are you convinced it was the same guy?" Barclay asked.

"Exactly the same M.O. All three raped. All strangled with a belt, their bodies left the same way. The belts were left behind as some kind of symbol, I guess. To taunt us, maybe."

Barclay persisted. "How do you explain the killings suddenly stopping?"

"I can't. Maybe he left town. Maybe got religion. Or his conscience caught up with him. Maybe he got sent up on some other charge, and we never tied him to the murders. It's anybody's guess."

"So you finally just quit looking, huh?" Barclay said.

"What'd you expect?" he replied angrily. "We were getting nowhere."

"So you just put it in the bottom of the pile."

J.J. leaned across the table, his face no more than six inches from Barclay's. "Don't piss me off, okay? I worked my ass off on that case, but at some point you gotta give it up. Move on."

"Okay, okay, relax," Barclay said. When J.J. sat back, Barclay said, "I'm going to get another beer. Want a refill?"

"Make mine a double," Jacobs said.

When he returned to the booth, Barclay said, "Someone told me they reopened the case a few years ago. Why was that?"

Jacobs picked up the glass and took a sip. "I was told that Jennifer's father got some anonymous cards and letters. Stuff that referred to the murder. I don't think the investigation led anywhere, but I was gone by then. Out to pasture. I don't know much more."

"Can you tell me who would?" Barclay asked.

"Maybe. I can check."

"How about the file on Jennifer's case?"

"Not unless I get an okay."

"So you'll talk to somebody?"

"I'll give it a try. See if someone will talk to you."

A little while later, Barclay got up to leave. "Thanks for seeing me," he said. "You've been great." Then he remembered. "One more thing. One of the newspaper stories I read mentioned a boyfriend. You know who he was?"

"I don't remember his name, but it'll be in the file."

"Thanks again," he said, walking away, leaving J.J. to finish his drink. Glancing at the TV on his way out. The Twins were now leading, five to three. He smiled. *Knew it*, he thought.

9

As soon as he walked into the station the next morning, Barclay could tell there was trouble. A crowd had gathered in the newsroom, laughing nervously as they glanced over their shoulders, then scattering when they saw him coming.

It took him only a moment to spot the problem.

Someone had taken a picture of Larry Landeau, the TriCom Communications honcho, blown it up to life size, and hung it from one of the high ceiling's light fixtures, a noose around his neck.

Good God, Barclay thought.

Before he could do or say anything, however, he heard an angry, "What the hell's going on here, George?" Hawke had walked in behind him, but before Barclay could respond, he brushed past him and stood beneath the cardboard cutout, shouting, "Get that thing down. Now!"

Problem was, it was about ten feet off the floor, and the step ladder the guilty party must have used to hang it there was nowhere in sight. And no one seemed to be in the mood to try to find it. In fact, all the bystanders were now back at their desks or fleeing the newsroom, leaving Hawke and Barclay standing alone beneath the dangling Mr. Landreau.

Hawke tried to grab the cardboard feet, to pull it down, but even with his own raised heels, he couldn't come close. Barclay stifled a giggle, but Hawke was fuming. "This is outrageous, George. I want you to get that down and find and fire the responsible party. Now. Today. Hear me?"

Barclay heard him, but knew he had no chance in hell of complying. No one in the newsroom would tattle, even if they knew the culprit, and he suspected the deed had been done in the dead of night, when the place was all but vacant. "I'll try, Nicholas. I'll ask around, and talk to security, but it won't be easy."

"I'm not asking you to *try*," Hawke sputtered. "I'm telling you to *do* it."

Barclay said, "It's a prank, Nicholas. A joke. People are pissed off about the sale. You know that."

Hell, he thought, *you should be happy it's not you hanging up there.*

"This is no way to protest," Hawke grumbled. "Besides, the sale's a done deal."

Maybe so, but Barclay suspected—no, he knew—there would be other copies of the cutout mysteriously showing up in various parts of the station between now and the time the real Mr. Landreau was back.

"We'll get it down," he said, motioning to Parkett to come over. "Get a stepladder, Jeff, and remove our new owner from the gallows."

"Not funny, George," Hawke said as he stomped out. "I want whoever did this."

Barclay walked slowly among the newsroom cubicles, studying each face, searching for hidden smirks or other signs of guilt. Not that he'd probably do anything about it, but he was curious as to who had the balls to pull off this stunt. Despite himself, he couldn't help but feel a touch of admiration.

All he got, however, were guileless expressions from those with enough courage to look up from their desks. And he ignored the smiles and the muffled laughter that followed in his wake.

Once Parkett was down from the ladder, and Landreau was residing in the Dumpster outside, Barclay got up on the elevated assignment desk to address the newsroom. "Listen, people. The fun is over. All you're doing is pissing Hawke off, and he's going to make life more miserable for all of us. Me, especially. Give him a break, give me a break, and cut the bullshit. That's an order."

Fat chance.

The next morning, a new Mr. Landreau had moved to a guest chair in Hawke's outer office, a noose around his neck.

"Do you know what Hawke's doing now?" Barclay grumbled to Parkett after a loud ten minutes in Hawke's office. "He's offering a three-hundred-dollar reward for the head of whoever's doing this."

"Good luck," Parkett replied.

"I'm serious. He's going for blood. He's meeting with the security people. Adding another guy at night."

"It's a big building," Parkett offered. "They can't be everywhere."

Barclay gave him a suspicious look. "You know something I don't know?"

Parkett spread his hands in mock innocence. "No way. I just can't wait to see where Landreau turns up next."

BARCLAY SPENT THE NEXT COUPLE OF DAYS concentrating on the work of the newsroom, meeting with his various assistants, planning the sweep series for the upcoming November rating period. Like it or not, which he did not, the three important rating months, November, February and May, had long been virtually the sole yardstick by which the competing stations—and news departments—were judged. Forget the awards, or the day-in, day-out reporting of breaking events. It was the ratings generated during those three months that determined success or failure. And, to some extent, the futures of the people involved.

What's more, the sweep series had to appeal to the younger audience the advertisers so coveted. The soccer moms and hockey dads out there in TV-land.

Barclay would never forget Hawke once barking at him, "Goddamn it, George. Get your marketing hat on. We need to sell the news!"

Barclay had long felt the time and effort required to research and prepare the sweep series and special reports so depleted newsroom resources that it became increasingly difficult to do an adequate job of reporting the daily events. But his was a voice in the wilderness—and over time he had been forced to accept the inevitable. But so far, at least, the station had been successful—a steady winner in the ratings sweepstakes over the years.

He knew it couldn't last forever, and the pressure to bypass daily news in favor of the more banal reporting would only increase under the new owners.

Maybe, he thought, *it's time to get out of the business.*

THAT EVENING, AS THE NEWS CREW entered the studio to prepare for the late newscast, they found Mr. Landreau propped up in the anchor chair. The noose was gone, but a dunce hat had been placed atop his head.

THE THUNDERSTORM CAME in the middle of the night, crashing around Barclay's condo, rudely shaking him out of what had been another night of restless sleep. He'd known the storm was coming, the evening weather report had told him that, but he was still surprised by its ferocity. Living on the twentieth floor, he felt as if he was in the vortex of the storm, the galvanizing flashes of lightning illuminating his rooms like a thousand Roman Candles, the sheets of rain pelting his windows, cascading down the panes like a mountain waterfall, the cracks of thunder a stereophonic cacophony of kettle drums and cymbals.

He wandered from room to room, frequently flinching at the display of the storm's raw power. Convinced at one moment that he could feel the building sway, but just as certain the next that it was only his imagination. Wishing, briefly, that he might be living a few floors closer to the ground.

The storm went on and on, the winds and rain ebbing then picking up, the thunder and lightning at once more distant, then closer. Sitting at the kitchen table, waiting for it to end, he knew he would never get back to sleep.

With daybreak still a few hours off, he made a pot of coffee, and then retrieved all of the old newspaper clippings and notes he'd made on Jennifer's murder. Sitting at the kitchen table, he reread every story and reviewed every note, looking for answers to the unanswered questions.

Why did a serial killer strike quickly three times, then quit? Why in such different parts of the cities, the victims themselves so different? And why couldn't the combined forces of all those cops—including the cold case investigators—come up with the killer?

He knew that John Jacobs was troubled by some of these same questions, but had long since given up trying to provide the answers.

So who the hell was Barclay to try and figure it out?

HE AWAKENED ABRUPTLY, his head resting on folded arms on the table. The storm had passed, the sun streamed in the windows, the sky a cloudless blue. Sleep had come unexpectedly. And blessedly.

He stretched his arms, arched his back, and rotated his head to get the kinks out of his neck. His mouth was sour, his teeth in need of a brushing, but otherwise he felt amazingly refreshed.

Maybe I should spend more of my nights out here, he thought.

Pouring himself a glass of orange juice, he walked to the balcony and stepped outside, finding the air astonishingly cool and fresh. The storm had not only broken the dry spell but also the heat wave, ushering in refreshing breezes courtesy of a Canadian high pressure system. *God bless the Canadians*, he thought, filling his lungs with the wonder of it.

Sunday morning. What to do? Shower. Get some breakfast somewhere. Then what? He hadn't gone to church for years, although he wasn't sure why—because, deep down, he continued to feel a strong spiritual presence in his life. Perhaps he'd tired of the religious trappings of the churches he'd been raised in, or perhaps it was a simple case of inertia. In any event, church was no longer a part of his Sunday routine.

As he emerged from the shower, the phone rang. He knew immediately it would be his mother, calling from Florida. That was part of the Sunday routine. "Hi, Mom," he said without hearing her voice.

"How did you know it was me?" She always asked that.

"A good guess." He always said that.

"So how are you?" she said.

"I'm fine, Mom. How about you guys?"

"We're fine, although your father's arthritis is kicking up again."

"Sorry to hear that."

"He sends his greetings, by the way."

Barclay was amused. His father rarely spoke to him on the phone, except with a specific question, usually involving some malfunction of his computer. Otherwise, he was content to let Barclay's mother do the talking.

As the conversation wore on, he felt compelled to tell her of the pending changes at the station. "I don't know what it's going to mean, but I may have to find a job somewhere else."

"Oh, no," she said, pausing to whisper an aside to his father.

"It won't happen for a while," he added, "and maybe the new owners will be okay. But I doubt it."

"My goodness, George . . ."

"Don't worry, please," he said, and went on to tell her that he'd been guaranteed a job for at least two years but wasn't sure he'd take the offer.

"Why in the world not?" she asked.

"It's hard to explain, but they may not be the kind of people I'd want to work for."

Another pause, garbled conversation in the background. "Your father says you should be careful. Jobs aren't that easy to find these days."

"I know. Tell him I won't do anything foolish."

This did not mollify her, but he didn't want to say anything more. Until he knew how things really stood.

The conversation ended with her again asking—as she always did—if he had found "anyone special?"

"Not yet, Mom, but I keep looking."

"I hope so," she said, but there wasn't much hope in her voice.

BARCLAY LEFT THE CONDO an hour later, eating a quick breakfast downtown, reading chunks of the Sunday paper as he ate, and then, for a lack of anything better to do, he decided to stop by the station. Knowing that by doing so on a Sunday he would only confirm what everyone there already thought: that he didn't have much of a life outside the newsroom.

And, of course, they were right.

As he walked into the newsroom, he was surprised to find a small group gathered near his office, including Maggie Lawrence, one of the station's co-anchors and the leading news personality in town. It was as if they'd been expecting him.

"What's this about?" he asked.

Maggie said, "We tried to call you."

"I was out, eating breakfast. Left my cell at home."

In addition to Maggie, the group included two weekday news producers, the executive producer, and Jeff Parkett. None of whom would normally have been there on a Sunday morning. "We wanted to meet when there was no chance of Hawke nosing around," Parkett said.

Barclay slid into a chair. "So?" He let the question hang.

They looked from one to another, finally letting Maggie speak for them. "Did you know the bad guys were in town? Monitoring our newscasts?"

"No," he said, but was not entirely surprised.

"Harry Wilson spotted that Landeau guy," Maggie said, "and followed him to the Hyatt. A bellboy friend of his said that he'd been there a couple days. That he'd hauled up a couple of small TV's for him. What else could he be doing?"

"I don't know," Barclay replied.

"Is that legal?" Parkett asked. "I thought they had to keep their hands off until the sale was approved."

Again he said he didn't know.

"I've got some other news," Parkett said. "I talked to a buddy of mine from J-School who works for a competitor of TriCom in Toledo. He put me in touch with a friend of his in Des Moines, who actually works for the TriCom station there. They both say we'd better get our resumes ready.

"And that's not all. They told me TriCom totally revamped the newscasts at the stations they bought within a matter of months. Made 'em rock-and-roll news. If it bleeds, or even hurts, it leads. They could give a shit less about government or politics or anything else that doesn't smack of mayhem or madness."

Barclay wasn't surprised, but he didn't show it.

"What are we going to do?" Maggie asked plaintively. "I'm not going to work for somebody like that."

"You've got a contract, Maggie," he reminded her. "With two years to go, and no out-clause for new ownership."

"They can bite my ass," she said, fire in her eyes. "Let 'em sue me."

"They probably would," he replied.

Parkett stood. "Seriously. We can't let this happen. This place is too special. We can't just stand by and watch it go down the drain. Forget about losing our jobs. We couldn't look at ourselves in the mirror."

"I can't forget about losing my job," one of the producers said. "I just bought a new house."

Barclay said, "First of all, you should all settle down. I hear what you're saying, but I don't know what you can do about it. As Hawke says, it's a done deal."

"Not until the F.C.C. approves it," Maggie said.

"Which brings up a point," he replied. "While I've got to be careful what I say, I do know the F.C.C. has been known to delay—or, in some very rare cases, even deny—a sale if there's enough community opposition."

"What are you saying?" Parkett demanded.

"Figure it out."

"You mean," Parkett said, "that if enough community groups with a little influence find out what kind of outfit TriCom is . . . what kind of stations they run . . . well, they might just try to block the sale."

"You said it, I didn't," Barclay replied, not hiding a small smile.

HE WAITED UNTIL THE GROUP BROKE UP, then asked Maggie if she had a minute to meet with him.

"I guess so," she replied. "Why?"

"It's personal," he said, closing his office door behind them.

Barclay had recruited Maggie from her weekend anchor job in California a few years before. A single mom, she'd left an unhappy past in L.A. to begin a new life in Minnesota. Since then, she'd married one of the producers at the station and had another child. And while she and Barclay had had their occasional disagreements, they'd managed to remain close friends.

"What's going on?" she asked, sitting on the edge of her chair.

"I have a hypothetical question for you. Nothing to do with what we just talked about."

"Okay."

"Say a guy, a not-particularly attractive guy, overweight and kind of a social misfit . . ."

She smiled. "Go on," she said.

". . . suddenly and inexplicably attracts the attention of a quite attractive woman, a widow, who seems intent on cultivating a friendship . . ."

"A friendship?"

"Platonic, she says. But it seems to this guy, despite all of his admitted shortcomings, that it could be more than that . . ."

"Why does he think that?"

"I don't know," he replied. "The attention. A word here. A touch there. But you have to understand—this fellow is quite inexperienced in such things and may be reading it all wrong."

"So?"

"So what would you advise him to do?"

"What does he want to do?" she asked.

"He doesn't know. He's confused. Doesn't want to make a fool of himself."

Maggie looked at him thoughtfully. "Since I don't know the people involved in your hypothetical, it'd be hard to offer advice."

"Try."

"Okay. If you insist." She paused, thinking. "I'd say there are three possibilities. One, that the woman wants exactly what she says she wants, namely, a platonic friendship, and is simply an affectionate person. Or, two, that there is indeed something more that is developing, in which case this fellow—if he's interested—should encourage that development. Without being a jerk about it. Or, third, this lady could simply be a very needy person, who has latched onto our guy as a convenient shoulder to lean on. In which case, he ought to retreat as quickly as possible. To avoid getting hurt."

He leaned forward. "Which do you think it is?"

"I'd have to meet the woman," she answered, getting up.

"Maybe that could be arranged."

"Just let me know," she said. Then, at the door, "This guy isn't trying to lose weight is he? Spiffing up his image?"

"Could be. I'll have to ask."

"Do that," she said with a smile as she closed the door behind her.

Kevin Bartlow's house was in the middle of the block in a tidy neighborhood in one of the older sections of suburban Plymouth. Nondescript, some would have described it, but it reminded Barclay of his own home of so many years before. Small, a one-story rambler, with white aluminum siding, dark-brown shutters and a lighter-brown roof. Nicely maintained with a well-trimmed lawn that had been parched by the August sun and the lack of rain.

Parking in front of the house, he made his way up the driveway, noticing that the houses on either side, and also across the street, looked very much like this one—as if they'd been built by the same contractor decades ago. And he couldn't help but wonder if this was the same house that Jennifer had lived in back then.

He'd soon find out.

It was later Sunday, and he'd phoned Jennifer's father the night before, asking if he might stop by. He'd agreed, although reluctantly, and only—he said—because Jennifer's friend, Katie Thorson, had urged him to.

"I don't like to talk about it," Kevin Bartlow had said on the phone. "It only brings back bad memories. She was our only child, you know."

Barclay didn't know. Until then.

Bartlow came out on the stoop as Barclay approached. Thin and balding, and stooped, he leaned on a gnarled wooden cane for support. In his eighties, or close to it, Barclay guessed, and looking as if he'd suffered through many of those years. Not an easy life, he knew, losing both a daughter and a wife within such a short time.

"Mr. Barclay?" Bartlow held out a wafer-thin hand, the skin barely covering the knuckles and tendons.

"Please call me George," Barclay said, tenderly gripping the hand. "And thanks again for seeing me, Mr. Bartlow."

"If you're George, I'm Kevin," he replied politely, opening the door. The voice sounded as thin as the body appeared. "And please come in. I've got the air-conditioner going."

The interior of the house was as tidy as the exterior. Tiny and simply furnished, but comfortable and welcoming. The only piece of furniture that appeared slightly worn was a La-Z-Boy armchair that sat in front of a large-screen TV.

He must have a housekeeper, Barclay thought. And somebody to keep up the yard. He's too frail to do it all by himself.

"You have a very nice house," he said, following Bartlow inside.

"Thank you. We've lived here more than forty years. Ever since Jennifer was a baby."

Barclay had his answer.

On an end table next to the couch were two pictures, one of Jennifer, the other of a woman who must be her mother. The resemblance was remarkable. He walked over and studied them. The only pictures he'd seen of Jennifer until then were the grainy photos in the old newspapers. This one was in color, a portrait that must have been taken in her college years. Her hair was cut shorter than he remembered, her face fuller, more mature. But, if anything, she was even more beautiful than she'd been in high school.

Bartlow waited patiently, watching Barclay study the photos, but saying nothing. Finally, he said, "I've made some coffee . . . or if it's too warm for that, I also have some iced tea."

"I don't want to put you to any trouble," Barclay said, following him into the kitchen.

"It's no trouble."

"Then I'll take the tea, thanks."

The old man leaned his cane against the kitchen counter as he filled the glasses, pointing Barclay to a chair. "I hope this won't take too long," he said. "If I don't get my nap in, I'm shot for the day."

"I won't keep you long," Barclay promised. Then: "Can I help you with that?"

"No, no. Sit, please."

Unsteadily, hands shaking, he brought one glass at a time to the table, then sank into a chair across from him. "Katie Thorson said you may look into Jennifer's death. Is that right?"

"Maybe. If I think I can do anything the police haven't already done."

"It's been a long time," Bartlow said sadly.

"I know. And that's part of the problem." Barclay went on to explain what he suspected Katie had already told him: how he'd known Jennifer in high school, and how he'd come to learn of her death. "I can't tell you how shocked and saddened I was," he said. "While I didn't know her that well, I knew that she was a very special person."

"You're right," her father said. "She was a wonderful girl. A wonderful daughter. She was an actress, you know. A very good actress."

"I read about that," Barclay replied.

Bartlow leaned back in his chair and recounted Jennifer's time in New York and how frustrated she'd been when she returned to the Twin Cities and found so few acting jobs. "It's better now, I guess. More theaters and all. But back then she had to settle for an office job."

Barclay said, "A newspaper story I read said one of the reasons she came back was because of a boyfriend here. You remember his name? The story didn't say."

"Daniel Kimble. But I haven't seen or heard from him in years."

"So you don't know if he still lives around here?"

"No idea. They broke up shortly after she got back from New York. He was at her funeral, but that's the last I saw of him."

"What was he like?"

"A nice enough fellow, I guess. Maybe a little stranger than some of the others she dated."

"Stranger, how?" he asked.

"Not as outgoing. Quiet. Never said much, at least around me. But polite. And she seemed to be really taken by him."

"You know why they broke up?"

"She never said."

Barclay tucked Kimble's name away, then went on, "I spoke to one of the detectives who originally investigated Jennifer's death, and he said you may have gotten some cards or letters about Jennifer. Anonymous ones."

"A few years ago, yes. But the police took them."

"Can you tell me about them?"

"Not much to tell. Pretty cruel, if you ask me. Birthday cards on her birthday. As if she was still alive. Anniversary cards on the anniversary of her death. I'm just glad her mother wasn't here to see them."

Barclay noticed that he wouldn't refer to Jennifer's death as a murder. But then, of course, neither did he.

"How long did this go on?"

"A couple of years. Then they stopped."

"No writing on them?"

"No. Just the address on the envelope."

Barclay was somewhat surprised by Bartlow's apparent lack of emotion when talking about the case. But, he figured, he's probably lived with the anguish so long that he's learned to speak of it as though it had happened to someone else.

"Do you happen to have Jennifer's old high school yearbook?"

"The police have that, too. They've kept almost everything."

After talking a few minutes longer, mostly about Jennifer's college years and her brief acting career, it became clear to Barclay that the old man was tiring, that his welcome might be wearing thin. "I can't thank you enough," he said, standing up. "For the tea. And for agreeing to speak with me."

"I hope it helps," he replied. "But I doubt it will. Nothing else has in all these years."

Before leaving, Barclay gave him one of his business cards. "Call me anytime," he said. "All of my numbers are on that card."

When he got to his car, Bartlow was still at the front door. Leaning on his cane with one hand, wiping at his eyes with the other.

So much for not showing emotion, Barclay thought.

As he started the car and gave a cursory glance into the rear-view mirror, he found the street deserted—except for a black pickup truck parked half-way down the block. He would have thought no more about it but for its darkened windows, which seemed somewhat odd. He spotted it again two blocks away, and two cars behind him at a stoplight. *Curious*, he thought. The light changed, and he moved across intersection—only to find himself feeling slightly silly as he watched the pickup turn left behind him and speed away.

THE NEXT TIME BARCLAY saw Rachel, it was he on the YW treadmill, walking slowly, passing the one mile mark, his legs already feeling heavy, the calves beginning to tighten. His T-shirt was soaked, stuck to his body like a piece of Cling Wrap.

She did a quick double-take. "George?" she said, walking over to him, head cocked. "Am I seeing things?"

"Not too pleasant a sight, I know," he huffed. "Especially when I keel over and somebody has to pick me up."

She chuckled. "You amaze me. Why didn't you tell me you were joining?"

He put the treadmill into pause, wiping away his sweat with a small towel. "I figured I'd see you here, sooner or later."

"I was hoping you'd call. I thought you might've forgotten about me."

"No chance," he said. "But things have been a bit hectic around the shop."

Truth be told, he had tried to avoid her. After the night at Brit's, when he'd felt that small tug of jealousy, he'd decided it was best to establish some distance. No sense in letting his imagination get the better of him, getting excited over something that was so improbable, if not impossible.

Yet here he was, at her health club. On her treadmill. Facing her. Not too much distance, he had to admit.

"Have you lost some weight?" she asked. "Looks like you have."

He restarted the machine. "A little. I'm working on it."

"Are you eating?"

"Some. Enough."

"I worry about you."

"Don't. I'm fine."

She looked toward the locker room. "Will you be here long? Can you wait until I change?"

He glanced at his watch. "For a while, sure," he said.

By the time she got back, he'd traveled another half-mile. Panting, not sure how much farther he could go. She climbed on to the machine next to his, clad in a different sports bra and shorts, but no less tantalizing than the ones he had seen before.

Keep your eyes in your head, he told himself.

As they both walked, she more quickly than he, Barclay tried to fill her in on what had been happening at the station, and about his visit with the retired cop, John Jacobs, and with Jennifer's father.

She listened attentively, asking a question here and there, then told him, "I talked to Katie Thorson. She's trying to set up that meeting you asked for."

"Good," he replied. Then, as he punched the STOP button, he said, "I've got to get off this thing before I fall off."

"What are you going to do now?" she asked.

"Shower. Then go home, I guess. Feed the cat and drink a beer."

She smiled, coyly. "You have anything for a lady to drink?"

He stopped and thought for a moment. "Wine. Some scotch. Twenty years old when I got it. Two years older now."

"I like scotch," she said.

"Then come on over when you're done," he said, reciting his address. "But let me warn you. As a decorator, you'll be shocked by what you see."

"Maybe I can give you some ideas," she said, not realizing that she already had.

SHE WAS AT HIS DOOR an hour later, looking fresh despite the three block walk, wearing a sleeveless striped yellow sun dress that hung nicely from her shoulders. He, in the meantime, had donned another loose-fitting polo shirt and a pair of clean khakis.

"C'mon in," he said, already ashamed of his sparse and drab surroundings.

But she wasn't looking at any of that. Her eyes immediately fastened on Seuss, now winding his way between her legs. "Oh, what a precious cat," she exclaimed, reaching down for him.

"I'd be careful," he said. "He's not exactly a friendly beast."

But he was already in her arms, clearly savoring the attention. Barclay could hear his purrs from where he stood. "What the hell? He hardly ever purrs for me," he said.

"He must know I love cats. I have two."

Barclay led her into the apartment. "What's his name?" she asked, trailing after him, taking in his condo in a glance.

"Seuss," he replied, quickly explaining how he'd come by his name. "I was kind of forced to adopt him."

"He's gorgeous. I love Siamese. They talk a lot."

"Too much, if you ask me."

She gently put the cat down on the couch and again looked around, wandering from the living room through the dining room and into the kitchen and bedrooms. "I see what you mean," she finally said. "About needing some decorating help."

"It's pretty awful, isn't it?" he said, leading her back to the kitchen. "Water with your scotch?"

"Please. But no ice."

He poured her drink and opened his own beer. "What little decorating that's been done, my mother did. And she doesn't exactly have contemporary tastes."

She took a sip from her drink, then smiled. "You know, I didn't realize what a celebrity you are."

He looked puzzled. "What do you mean?"

"My son, Joe, tells me you're something of a legend in the journalism world. That all of the professors at school know about you, about the kind of newsroom you run. The awards you've won. The people you've sent on to the networks. He was totally impressed when I told him we'd become friends."

Barclay wasn't sure how to respond.

She grinned. "Know what one of the professors said?"

"I can't imagine," he replied.

"Joe thought it was hilarious."

"What?"

"That you have . . ."

He waited.

"I'm embarrassed," she said. Then, "He told Joe that you have," suddenly deepening her voice, "the journalistic balls of an elephant."

Barclay laughed, more at her Barry White rendition than at the description. He'd heard that before.

"I can't believe I said that," she said, blushing slightly.

"What he really means is that I'm a survivor. So far, at least. A lot of my friends are on the beach, through no real fault of their own. Got chewed up in the corporate meat-grinder and the horrible economy."

"What do you mean?"

"They couldn't produce the ratings or the revenues or the cost cutting demanded by their new bosses. It's a tough business these days."

"Joe was shocked," she said, "when I told him the station's been sold."

He laughed. "I hope you told him he wasn't alone."

She put down the drink and asked for a pad and pencil. "Time for a tour," she said, walking slowly back through the condo, making notes.

He followed behind, admiring the way the sun dress clung to her narrow hips, her shapely legs. "Are you ready to spend some money?" she asked.

"I guess so," he replied. "But with what's going on at the station, I'm not sure how long I'll be here."

"It would be a good investment either way." Then, with a look over her shoulder, "But I hope you stay."

She spent the next twenty minutes stopping to study each room, making more notes, before retreating to the kitchen to pick up her drink. "The advice will be free," she said, "but it's going to take more than a few thousand dollars to make the place look decent."

"Money's not the problem, but I don't want to buy a bunch of new stuff and then have to move it."

"I understand. Just let me know when you decide."

Barclay offered her another drink and apologized for not offering her something to eat. "I haven't had the chance to shop, and besides, I'm not much of a cook."

"I should be going anyway," she said, putting her empty glass into the sink. "The kids are coming home in a couple of days, and I have to get the place ready for them."

As she was walking out, she stopped in the middle of the living room—so abruptly he almost ran into her. "I just noticed something," she said, once again looking around. "Beside the picture of your parents and the one of Dan Rather in your office, there's not another picture of another human being anywhere."

He shrugged his shoulders. "Does that surprise you? No kids, no siblings, no wife or ex-wife. It's just me."

"And you never considered marriage?"

He was startled. This lady was direct. "A couple of times, maybe. When I was younger. But I was working a lot back then, mostly nights. Weekends, too. They probably thought I was more interested in the job than I was in them. And I guess they were right."

She persisted. "Not since then?"

"Once. A few years ago. When I lost all of that weight. A lady named Monica. But it never got to the engagement stage."

"What happened?"

"She was quite a bit younger. Wanted babies. I didn't blame her, but I was beyond that. I love kids, but I felt I was a little too old to be a new daddy. Selfish on my part, I know, but that's what happened. We never could resolve the issue."

"And then there was Jennifer," she said. "Lurking in the background."

"Maybe so. Subconsciously, anyway."

She moved toward the door. "You regret that now? That you never married?"

"Sometimes. But I've gotten used to living alone. It's not as lonely as married people like to think it is. It has its advantages."

"Like?"

"You must have discovered some of them by now. Living one life, not two. Responsible for only yourself. Free to be me, as the saying goes."

"I still haven't gotten used to it, but maybe I will."

He opened the door for her. "Thanks for coming," he said. "You made the place seem a little brighter. Even without redecorating it."

She gave him a quick hug. "You're sweet," she said.

The last time he'd heard that, it was his mother talking.

11

Once she was gone, Barclay retreated to his office to search the Minneapolis and St. Paul phone directories for the name of Daniel Kimble—Jennifer's old boyfriend. When that failed, he turned to the Internet, but found no one of that name who appeared to live in the Twin Cities area.

Maybe he's moved, he thought.

Then back to the directories. There were eleven Kimbles in the Minneapolis book, seven in the St. Paul directory. And while none of them identified a Daniel by name or initial, Barclay decided to check them all. Maybe he'd find a relative.

In Minneapolis, his calls got four no answers, three answering machines, and four "I don't know any Daniel" responses. In St. Paul, he struck out on the first two calls, but hit on the third. "Yes, I know a Daniel Kimble," a woman replied. "He's my husband's cousin."

Barclay quickly identified himself, but didn't say precisely why he was looking for the man. "I need to talk to him about an old friend we have in common. Do you know where I can find him?"

The woman, Elizabeth Kimble, was suspicious at first, but apparently was reassured by the fact that Barclay worked for Channel Seven. "I always watch your news," she said. "I just love that Maggie Lawrence."

"I'll pass that on to her," he said. "I'm sure she'll be pleased." Then he paused, waiting.

"He lives in Shoreview, I think," she finally said. "But he doesn't go by Daniel anymore. It's Steven. That's his middle name, but he's made it his first. Steven Kimble."

No wonder I couldn't find him. "Why did he do that?" he asked. "Start using his middle name, I mean."

"He never really explained. Just started calling himself Steven. Surprised all of us, but then again, we were never that close. His father and my husband's father were brothers, but they were kind of . . . what do you call it? Estranged?"

After more conversation, she gave him what she thought were Steven Kimble's address and phone number, but attached a caveat. "Please don't tell him you talked to me. He's kind of a loner, doesn't really like people messing around with him. Like I say, we haven't talked in a long time."

"Is he married?" Barclay asked.

"Used to be. I don't know if he still is."

"Where does he work?"

"Don't know that either. In advertising, maybe."

Once he'd gotten all that he thought he could, he asked one final question. "Did you or your husband ever know a Jennifer Bartlow?"

She repeated the name. "No, I can't say that we did. Why?"

"No reason," he said, then thanked her again and assured her that their conversation would remain confidential.

Before he could punch in Kimble's number, the phone rang. "Barclay?"

"Yes."

"This is J.J. You asked me to call."

"Right. Thanks."

"I talked to the cold case detective. A kid named Bennett. With the Ramsey County sheriff's office. He's willing to talk, but with some pretty strict ground rules."

"Like what?"

"I'll let him tell you. But he also wants me to come along."

"That's great," Barclay said. "When?"

"Tomorrow afternoon, if you can make it. Two o'clock. Rice Park."

Barclay thought for a moment. "I'll be there. One more thing."

"What's that?"

"What can you tell me about Daniel Kimble?"

"Who?"

"Daniel Kimble. Jennifer's old boyfriend."

There was a pause. "Not much. I know we eliminated him as a suspect."

"Why?"

"Can't remember, exactly. Had a good alibi, I think, and we had no way to connect him to the other two women."

"Thanks," Barclay said. "I'll see you tomorrow."

Once he'd hung up, he quickly tried Kimble's number. And let it ring. Ten times. No answer. No voicemail.

He tried twice more during the evening with the same result.

BARCLAY WAS AT WORK BY 8:30 the next morning, but not before having spent an hour on the YW treadmill. Two miles and 200 calories. He was down five pounds so far, thanks to the exercise and some fairly disciplined dieting, but he could hardly notice the change in the mirror. His pants, however, did seem to fit a little looser.

He spent the rest of the morning at his desk, going over the monthly budget figures, signing invoices, and answering an occasional phone call. A number of staff members stopped by his office, asking if there was anything new on the station sale. He could only shrug and advise them to be patient.

Happily, the demeaning cutouts of Mr. Landreau had finally stopped showing up, but—to Hawke's dismay—the mystery culprit remained at large.

Late in the morning, Hawke himself appeared at his door. In good spirits for a change. Their attorneys in Washington, he said, reported that the sale application was moving swiftly at the F.C.C., and that they were expecting approval within a matter of weeks, if not sooner.

"That's good, I guess," Barclay offered.

Hawke pulled up a chair. "Have you thought any more about your own situation?" he asked.

"Not really," Barclay admitted. "I've had other things on my mind."

"I wouldn't dilly-dally. They're going to expect some answers."

Barclay then asked if he knew that Landreau had been in town, apparently monitoring their newscasts. Hawke wouldn't answer directly, but said, "Can't say that I blame him. You can't buy a pig in a poke, you know."

When Hawke left, Barclay walked to the other end of the newsroom, to a small office tucked away in one corner. There he found John Knowles, a longtime newsroom employee who headed the station's I-Team, or Investigative unit. He was hunched over his desk, half-glasses hanging from his nose, which was all but buried in a stack of documents.

Years before, Knowles, a bachelor like Barclay, had worked for the network in Washington, but in the face of some serious drinking problems, had come to the Hazelden Center in Minnesota for treatment. Afterward, he'd decided to stay in the state and had managed to hook on with Channel Seven. He'd been there . . . and sober . . . ever since.

"Hey, John, you got a minute?"

Knowles was startled. "What?" Then, pushing his glasses up, "Oh, hi, George."

In contrast to Barclay, Knowles was slender as a stick, with sunken cheeks, a pale complexion and protruding ears. Not exactly anchor material. Which was okay, since he rarely appeared on camera. But he was the best investigative reporter Barclay had ever known.

Barclay stepped inside the door. "Sorry to interrupt, but I need a favor."

"What's that?"

"I'd like you to find out everything you can about a guy by the name of Daniel Kimble, who now goes by his middle name, Steven." He went on to explain where he lived, and his phone number, but said he knew little else about the man. "You're a hell of a lot better at this kind of thing than I'll ever be."

"What do you want to know?"

"The works. Background. Employment. Personal life. Whatever."

Barclay knew there were myriad sources for that kind of information these days, much of it public and much of it on the Web, but one had to know where to look and have the time to search.

For all his smarts, Barclay was practically illiterate, technically. He didn't Twitter, Tweet or text. He wasn't on My Space or Facebook. He didn't own an I-Phone, and, to this day, still missed his old typewriter. He was not exactly what you'd call a Renaissance man.

Knowles was taking notes. "Care to tell me what this is about?"

"Not at the moment."

Clearly disappointed, he muttered, "Okay. You're the boss."

BARCLAY WAS A FEW MINUTES LATE and found John Jacobs sitting on a bench next to the fountain and pool in Rice Park, across from the Ordway Theater and the St. Paul Hotel in downtown St. Paul. It was another lovely day, and a number of children were wading in the pool, searching for coins.

"'Bout time," Jacobs said, glancing at his watch.

"Sorry. I got held up in traffic," Barclay replied, settling in next to him.

They sat quietly a moment, soaking up the sun, watching the kids splash in the pool. "I don't know this Bennett that well," Jacobs finally said. "He was still in uniform when I retired. But I'm told he's smart."

"On the phone, you called him a 'kid.'"

"He is. To a geezer like me. They usually give these old cases to the new guys. Gives 'em a challenge, I guess. Something to do."

Just then, striding across the park, was a fellow Barclay judged to be in his early-thirties, at best. Trim and well-tanned. "This him?" he asked.

"Yup," Jacobs said.

"I see what you mean."

Bennett had a serious, no-nonsense look about him, but his appearance didn't scream cop. Dressed in khakis and a dress shirt, open at the neck, and a dark blue sport coat, he could have been a teacher, a bank clerk, or a computer whiz.

"Josh Bennett," he said as he shook Barclay's hand. Then to Jacobs, "Nice to see you again, J.J. It's been a long time."

"It has, indeed," Jacobs replied.

To Barclay, "I know and worked with a couple of your reporters. They're okay. Better than most."

"Thanks," Barclay replied. "We try to teach 'em right."

Bennett sat on the edge of the bench. "So J.J. tells me you knew this woman. Jennifer."

"A long time ago. And not that well."

"But well enough to be poking around in her murder now?"

Barclay could only shrug.

Bennett said, "I told J.J. I can't say much. It's still an open case."

"But going nowhere, right?" Barclay said.

"At the moment, no."

"And not likely to."

"Never can tell. We could catch a break."

If Bennett was annoyed by his questions, he didn't show it. So Barclay pressed on. "You the only one working on it?"

"Right now, yeah. And I haven't had it for that long."

"And how much time can you give it?"

"Not much. We're overloaded with current stuff."

Barclay leaned in. "So give me a break. What have you got to lose? I'm not going to screw up your investigation. I might even help. Ask around, I'm an honest guy."

"I don't doubt that," Bennett said. "But there are rules."

"Break a few. Who's going to know?"

Bennett studied him, then looked over at Jacobs. "I checked him out," J.J. said. "He gets high marks."

"So what do you need?" Bennett asked.

"Everything you've got that's not going to jeopardize your investigation. Like the case file. Jennifer's yearbook. And anything that connects her murder to the other two."

Bennett laughed. "Don't want much, do you?"

"That's not all. I need to know what happened to those cards that Jennifer's dad got."

"I can tell you that. Nothing. Dead end. No DNA on the envelopes or stamps. At least not enough to test. And whoever addressed the envelopes used block lettering. No handwriting samples."

"May I see them sometime?"

Bennett again glanced at Jacobs. "Tell you what I'll do. I'll check with my boss. If he says okay, I'll give you what I can, without running the risk of you screwing things up. But with one proviso."

"What's that?" Barclay asked.

"That J.J. here works with you, every step of the way. He knows the case. He's a cop, you're not. He'll know if you're stepping out of bounds."

Barclay turned to Jacobs. "What do you say?"

"I'm retired."

"I could put you on the payroll as a consultant," Barclay countered.

"How much?"

"We'll negotiate."

"Let me think about it. I'll be back in touch with both of you."

That ended the conversation. After Bennett left, Barclay grabbed Jacobs' arm. "Do you have another hour or so? I need to see something."

"Tell me what and where," J.J. said.

GARDEN PARK WAS PRETTY MUCH as Barclay had envisioned it. Tucked away in one of St. Paul's older neighborhoods, it was less than four blocks square—a tiny urban island, lightly wooded with walking paths, a few picnic tables, and a small playground and wading pool at one end.

By day, it was anything but threatening.

Jacobs had ridden with him from downtown, providing directions through a confusing maze of residential streets that eventually led to the park. "Pull over here," he said.

Barclay did as he was told, guiding his old Buick to the curb. "Where the hell are we?" he asked.

"Not that far from the University of St. Thomas," Jacobs replied. "Don't you know St. Paul?"

"Not really," Barclay admitted, hoisting himself out of the car. "I don't get over here much." For all he could tell, he could have been in Milwaukee.

J.J. led him from the street into the park, but only for about fifty feet or so. "This is where the joggers found her," he said, pointing to a cluster of pine trees to their right. "She was lying beneath one of those pines, partially covered by a couple of the low-hanging boughs."

Barclay walked over to the spot, but stood back, feeling as he did whenever he visited a cemetery, fearful of stepping on any of the actual graves. Hallowed ground.

"The trees are bigger now, of course, but they were pretty large even back then," Jacobs said, taking a few steps away. "We figure she was actually raped and murdered over here, then dragged beneath the trees."

"It's so close to those houses," Barclay replied, glancing at the homes across the street. "It's amazing nobody saw or heard anything."

"Yes, but it was fairly late in the evening and dark as hell. No moon that night. People must have been watching TV or getting ready for bed."

Barclay stood back, trying to picture the murder scene. It was such a quiet, tranquil place, impossible to imagine it as a setting for such violence.

"I know about the belt," he said. "But what else did you find?"

"Not much," Jacobs replied. "One of her shoes in the street. Which must have come off when he dragged her into the park. We figured he choked her unconscious, raped her, then finished the job. He must have used a condom, but we did find a few spots of semen on the body."

"No DNA back then," Barclay observed.

"Right."

"Have they tested it since?"

"I expect so, but must not have found a match. Bennett would know for sure."

"Anything else?"

"He must have used some kind of tape on her mouth. There were traces of adhesive, but no tape. Also some bruises on her wrists and stomach. We think he must have sat on her."

"My God."

"Her clothes were found in a trash barrel a couple of blocks away. An old couple found them when they carried out the garbage a couple of days later."

Barclay felt a touch of nausea. He took one final look, then turned and headed back to the car. "Thanks for bringing me here," he said, breathing deeply, fighting off the feeling. "I needed to see it for myself."

"No problem," Jacobs said. "I kinda wanted to see it again, too."

Before heading back downtown, they drove a short distance down the same street, pausing in front of an old three-story, gabled house that could have been built a hundred years before. "This is where she lived," Jacobs said. "The owners converted it into three apartments, and Jennifer lived in one of them, on the second floor."

Barclay leaned back in his seat. "She almost made it home, didn't she?"

"Almost."

12

The next morning, as Barclay sat at the kitchen table, still in his pajamas, thumbing through the newspaper, he spotted the story. While it was only a blurb in one of the columns in the back pages of the business section, it looked huge to him.

> The *StarTribune* has learned that several local minority groups, including the St. Paul chapter of the N.A.A.C.P., may oppose the sale of WCKT-TV, Channel Seven, to TriCom Communications of North Carolina. Officials of the minority organizations would not comment on the record, but it appears they are examining the employment and community service records of TriCom in the various cities where it already operates radio and television stations. One spokesman, who did not wish to be identified, said, "We're talking to our friends in several of those cities, and at first glance, it does not appear that TriCom is the kind of broadcaster we'd like to see in the Twin Cities."
>
> The sale of Channel Seven to TriCom is said to be on the fast track for approval by the F.C.C. in Washington, and it's unclear what impact minority opposition would have on that process.

He was elated. Someone had gotten to the groups. Maybe from the seed he'd planted with his staff. Whatever, the fat was clearly in the fire. And he knew there would be hell to pay when Hawke saw the item.

HE WASN'T DISAPPOINTED. Once at the station, when told there'd be an urgent management meeting in an hour, he had no doubt what the topic would be.

Meantime, in the newsroom, enlarged copies of the *StarTribune* article were posted everywhere. And Barclay could sense a feeling of relief and, perhaps, satisfaction. He found Parkett by the assignment desk. "You have anything to do with this?" he asked, holding up a copy of the story.

"Me?" Parkett replied innocently.

"Yes, you."

"You really want to know?"

Barclay thought for a moment. "Maybe not."

"Good."

The management meeting was held in a large second floor conference room, with all of the station's department heads gathered around an oblong mahogany conference table. Hawke was at the head, in a predictably sour mood.

"Okay, people," he said, taking all of them in with a glance. "You've seen the morning paper and understand the possible implications of this story."

There was general head-nodding around the table. Except for Barclay, who stared impassively at the opposite wall.

"If true, it could delay the sale. Maybe worse. Rumors are that these people have hired their own Washington law firm to investigate the possibilities."

"You've got to be kidding," said the promotion director, the only person of color at the table.

"I wish I were," Hawke replied. "It's late in the process, but maybe not too late. Our attorneys are worried, and TriCom is pissed—hinting they could flush the whole thing if there are too many delays. Or too much bad press."

He went on to say that rival groups like this were not always interested in actually blocking a sale, but in leveraging some kind of financial settlement in return for withdrawing their opposition.

"So what do you want us to do?" asked the sales manager.

"Contact every leader of every minority group you know," he said. "Find out who's behind this. The key players. We need to get to them, to persuade them to back off, if we can. Grease a few palms, if necessary. I want no delays. Once something like this gets going, it can take on a life of its own."

Barclay raised his hand, hesitantly. "But what if they're right? What if TriCom is a horseshit company? That's certainly their reputation. Do you really want to sell to someone like that?"

Hawke shot him a look. "I don't want to hear that kind of talk, George! Not from you or anybody else in this room. I've told you, there's no turning back. TriCom's no worse than any other conglomerate in this country."

Quite an endorsement, Barclay thought.

"Am I making myself quite clear?" Hawke barked, glancing at each of them in turn. "I need information. And I need it yesterday. That's all."

With that, he marched out, leaving those behind staring at one another.

AS MUCH AS HE DETESTED DOING IT, but knowing Hawke would soon be at his door demanding results, Barclay spent the rest of the morning doing Hawke's bidding—calling every leader in the minority community he had come to know in his years at the station.

As it turned out, several of his contacts had already been quizzed by other department heads, who'd been more prompt than Barclay in making the calls. On-the-record, everyone pleaded ignorance. Off-the-record, several hinted that one of St. Paul's black leaders, Nathanial "Nat" Coburn, could be among the ringleaders.

Coburn was a successful attorney, a former prosecutor in the U.S. attorney's office, and prominent in the civil rights field. He was well-respected and well-connected, both in Washington and the Twin Cities.

And while Barclay didn't know Coburn well, he knew that Jeff Parkett did. In fact, they lived only a few blocks apart. Their sons played Babe Ruth baseball together. He found Parkett in one of the videotape editing rooms. "You talked to Nat Coburn recently?" he asked.

"Sure. Last weekend. Our kids play ball together."

"I know that."

"So?"

"So?" Barclay encouraged.

"His kid's a hell of a pitcher. Got a fast ball you wouldn't believe. Left-hander, too."

Barclay smiled. "And you can throw a hell of a curve yourself."

Parkett laughed out loud. "So what do you want to know?"

"I think I already know. And I'm going to have to tell Hawke."

"Why?"

"Because it's my job. But I'll leave you out of it."

Parkett feigned innocence. "Out of what?"

"Keep throwing those curves," Barclay said, walking away.

FORTUNATELY, HE DIDN'T NEED to say anything. Hawke had already zeroed in on Coburn, and had invited him to an afternoon meeting at the station. "I want you there, too," he told Barclay. "You know these people better than I do."

These people?

Barclay protested, claiming truthfully that he didn't know Coburn that well, and, besides, he was needed in the newsroom. Which was also true. An armored car had been robbed and its driver killed that morning in suburban White Bear Lake. And, a batch of severe weather, with possible tornadoes, was moving in from the southwest. But Hawke would have none of it. "This is more important than any goddamned news story," he said. "This is our future we're talking about."

He was right about that.

COBURN WAS ALREADY SEATED in Hawke's office by the time Barclay got there. Along with a woman named Natalie Pearson, who was introduced as his legal assistant. Unlike Coburn, she was quite dark-skinned, and older—dressed in a severe dark business suit that seemed to match her somber mood.

Barclay greeted the pair and apologized for his tardiness, blaming the storm that was raging outside, pelting the cities with drenching rain and marble-sized hail. "We've still got tornado warnings," he explained, "so we've got our crews running all over town."

"Tell me about it," Coburn said. "We nearly drowned just running from the parking ramp across the street."

Coburn was Harry Belafonte-handsome, with close-cropped black hair graying at the temples, an easy smile, and a firm handshake. Casually but expensively clad in a dark-blue linen blazer, a white shirt and a red-and-blue bow tie, he appeared at ease. But his look was unwavering, an intimidating presence that must have served him well in the courtroom.

"I understand you've got a future major leaguer for a son," Barclay said, making conversation.

Coburn chuckled. "Hope so. I'm depending on him for my old age."

He seemed eager to talk about his son's baseball exploits, including a seven-inning no-hitter he had thrown the week before. "Believe it or not," he said, "the scouts are already looking at him. And he's only thirteen years old."

"If he's a leftie," Barclay said, "and can throw the ball over the plate, his career is assured."

"That's what they tell me," Coburn said.

Hawke tried to join in the small talk, but he knew nothing about baseball and was clearly uncomfortable, shifting in his chair, tapping his pen on the desk. Finally, he interrupted. "If you don't mind, perhaps we can get to the matter at hand, Mr. Coburn . . ."

"Nat. Everybody calls me Nat."

"Okay, Nat. We understand . . . and correct me if I'm wrong . . . that you may be involved in an effort to block the sale of Channel. Seven to . . ."

"Where'd you hear that?"

"Ahhh . . . from various sources in the community," Hawke said, less certain now.

"Well, you're wrong," Coburn said. "We're not out to block the sale. We want to buy the place."

Hawke sat back in his chair, stunned, momentarily lost for words. "But," he finally said. "It's already been sold. To TriCom."

"Wrong. You've *agreed* to sell. But there's still the matter of the F.C.C."

"But . . ."

Coburn cut him off. "Let me be blunt. Until the announcement in the paper, we didn't know the station was for sale. Now that we do know, we're interested in making a bid. But first we have to try to delay or deny the sale to TriCom."

"'We' being?"

"A coalition representing a wide cross-section of Twin Cities business leaders, including a substantial number of minority group members."

As Hawke glanced across the desk at Barclay, Natalie Pearson spoke for the first time. "As you know, the F.C.C. is still committed to increasing minority ownership of broadcast properties in this country. Further," she added, "the research I've done suggests that TriCom would not serve our communities of color well. They have an abominable record in the areas of equal opportunity and community service. And while they may be successful broadcasters, they're despicable public servants."

Hawke started to protest, but she waved him off. "And you haven't been that great, either. Our people here deserve better treatment."

Man, she's a tiger, Barclay thought.

"The group I represent," Coburn said, "believes it has the financial resources necessary to match or exceed TriCom's price and complete the acquisition. Of course, we would need your cooperation, if not your endorsement. Which is why we're here today."

Hawke was nonplused. He got up and walked behind his desk. Then sat back down. "I don't know what to say," he finally said. "This obviously comes as a complete shock and surprise. I'll have to speak to our attorneys, of course, and it's probably wise to say nothing further until I've had the opportunity to do that."

"Fair enough," Coburn said, as he and Natalie got up. "I just hope you'll consider what'll be in the eventual best interests of this community." Then, at the door, "I'm sure we'll be in touch."

"I'm sure," Hawke replied.

Once they'd left, he turned to Barclay and issued his two-word assessment of the visitors. "Fucking vultures."

BY THE TIME BARCLAY GOT BACK to the newsroom, the threat of tornadoes had passed, but the wind and rain continued unabated. Trees and power lines were down in many of the western suburbs—causing widespread power outages and snarling traffic.

The situation was further complicated by a tense police standoff with the guy who'd robbed the armored car and killed the driver. He was holed up in a house in north Minneapolis, holding two people hostage and forcing the evacuation of homes within a two-block radius.

It was the first good news day in a month. When it rains, it pours. Literally.

"We've got our live trucks all over the place," Parkett told him. "Two out in the storm area and one with the cops at the standoff. We're waiting for the weather to clear so we can get the chopper up."

"Good," Barclay said, hunkering down at the assignment desk to monitor the coverage. "Need anything else?"

"Yeah. More people. Anybody who's not crippled is out there now."

Barclay watched the array of monitors. They'd already broken into regular programming several times with live updates, and he could see that their competitors were doing the same. "Are we keeping up with the other guys?" he asked.

"Whippin' their asses, so far," Parkett replied proudly.

As Barclay well knew, breaking news was the lifeblood of television news, that TV was at its best on days like this—when pictures, more than words, told the story. When there was no time to be thoughtful or introspective, only to move fast and think fast. Beat the other guys on the air, then pummel them with the best coverage.

It's what made coming to work worthwhile.

He continued to hover in the newsroom the rest of the afternoon, contributing what he could while trying not to interfere with the people he hired to direct the coverage. Aside from writing some of the frequent updates for their website, and overseeing the editing of pictures being fed into the station from the live trucks, he generally tried to stay out of the way and in the background.

That was his style. Hire the best people. Train them. Then let them do their work.

By late afternoon, the crisis had eased. The storm was over. Some of the power had been restored. And the armored car killer had killed himself as the police swat team rushed the house. They rescued the two hostages.

The newsroom began to return to normal.

Barclay found John Knowles hunkered down in his office, totally absorbed, as if he hadn't moved since the last time Barclay had seen him. "I'm back," he said. "Fill me in."

Knowles leaned back, removed his glasses and rubbed his eyes. "Won't take that long," he said. "Your Mr. Kimble appears to be a straight arrow. Squeaky clean. Except for a couple of traffic tickets."

"Married?"

"Was. Divorced ten years ago. After four years of marriage. A woman named Julia. No kids. No abuse. No restraining orders. Nothing like that. He got the house, she got everything else, I guess."

"How do you know all that?"

Knowles put his glasses back on. "Talked to a couple of his neighbors. Said I was doing a security check for the government."

"You lied?"

"Sort of. No harm done."

Barclay swallowed a reprimand. He didn't believe reporters should lie to get at the truth, but decided this wasn't the time for another of his lectures.

Knowles went on. "The neighbors admit they don't know much about him. They rarely see or talk to him, and when they do, he's anything but friendly. Chases kids off his lawn, won't return their greetings, that kind of thing. Keeps to himself, almost never has visitors. Guards his privacy with a vengeance."

"How does he earn a living?"

"Self-employed. Works at home. Graphic design stuff, like packages for cereal companies, I'm told."

Barclay considered what he'd heard.

"You want to tell me now what this is all about?" Knowles asked.

"Okay," Barclay said, then took twenty minutes to lay out the whole story, every detail that he knew or could remember. "Kimble seemed like a logical place to begin," he concluded.

"You just said he has an alibi."

"He does, I guess."

"Think you're pissing into the wind?"

"Maybe."

"And aren't you forgetting something?" Knowles said.

"What?"

"The other two victims. You're spending all your time and attention on this one woman, Jennifer."

He was right. Barclay had hardly given the other two women a second thought. "The cops say they didn't have any connection to Jennifer. Or to each other for that matter."

"Still. It'd be nice to know more about them, wouldn't it?"

"You've got the time to do that?"

Knowles said, "I can give it a couple of days."

"I'll get you their names, along with everything else."

"Good," Knowles said. "I love murder mysteries."

JACOBS WAS WAITING in the same booth at O'Gara's when Barclay walked in that night, sipping on what Barclay presumed to be a shot of Wild Turkey. "Hey, J.J.," he said, squeezing into the booth across from him.

Jacobs gave him a small salute with his glass. "Want something to drink?"

"A beer, but it can wait."

A large bound folder, perhaps three inches thick, was sitting on the table. "Is that it?" Barclay asked.

"You got it. The complete Bartlow file, minus a few things they want to keep to themselves."

Barclay picked up the file and rifled through the pages. "I thought they were going to give us everything."

"You're lucky to get what you got," J.J. said. "Don't push it."

While he continued to examine the file, Jacobs went to the bar to refill his glass and also brought back a bottle of Amstel Light.

"You remembered," Barclay said, looking up.

"I never forget what a guy drinks."

The file contained page after page of typewritten notes, which—at first glance—appeared to be various descriptions of the murder scene, synopses of dozens of interviews, the medical examiner's report, and other material not readily identifiable. It could take hours, maybe days, to digest it all.

"You're not going to find much new in there," J.J. said. "Just more details. Who was interviewed and when, stuff from the scene, lab test results, and so forth. Nothing too revealing, I'm afraid."

As Barclay flipped through the pages, he suddenly stopped. There, shockingly, at the back of the file, was a series of black-and-white photos—shot from different distances and angles.

Of the nude and violated body of Jennifer Bartlow.

He closed his eyes. He could barely breathe.

"Sorry," J.J. said, watching him. "I should have warned you."

Barclay closed the file and took a deep gulp of his beer. He couldn't look again. Not now. Maybe never. One glance had shown him all he would ever want to see.

"Death ain't pretty," J.J. said. "Not this kind of death. To this kind of woman. You should have known that coming in."

Barclay could only nod. "I know," he finally muttered. "I just wasn't expecting pictures."

They sat quietly for several minutes, listening to the muted sounds of the jukebox and the laughter and animated conversations of the people at the bar. People about the same age as Jennifer was when those grotesque pictures were taken. What a waste, Barclay thought. What a horrible, horrible waste.

He could envision her here, now, sitting at the bar, arguing, debating, laughing. Using her brains, her beauty, and her sharp tongue to beguile and befuddle anyone and everyone around her. Just as she had beguiled and befuddled Barclay way back when.

"One other thing," J.J. said, pulling something up from the seat beside him. "Jennifer's yearbook. You said you wanted to see it."

Barclay took the book and quickly flipped through the pages, especially interested in the written inscriptions from her high school friends that filled virtually every empty space in the book. His, however, would not be among them. She'd never asked him to sign it.

"So what are you going to do now?" J.J. asked.

Barclay quickly recited what had happened since they'd last met: his meeting with Jennifer's father, his search for Daniel, or Steven, Kimble, and the fact that John Knowles was looking into the murders of the other two women.

"I've already told you," J.J. said. "The same guy got to all three. Virtually the same M.O. I should know. I worked on the fucking task force."

"I'd just like to know more, I guess."

"And why are you hung up on this Kimble?" J.J. asked, repeating what Knowles had argued. "Read the file. He wasn't a suspect."

"I know he wasn't here at the time," Barclay said, "but that doesn't mean he couldn't have arranged it. You know, figuring that if he couldn't have her, nobody would."

"Forget him," J.J. said. "You're only interested because Jennifer had a thing for him, that's all."

"Maybe. But I'd like to get a look at him."

J.J. could only shake his head.

Before they left, they were able to agree on a small consulting fee for Jacobs' help in the investigation. Barclay also filled him in on what was happening at the station.

"Does that mean you'll be out of a job?" he asked.

"Not for a while, if I don't want to be. But, hell, they could have me mopping the floors, for all I know."

"So what are you going to do?"

"Punt, I think."

BARCLAY SPENT THE REST of the evening at home, beginning the Herculean task of reviewing the file, page by page. He'd never seen a police file like this before, and was amazed at the apparent thoroughness of the investigation. The first twenty or thirty pages were devoted to a series of reports on the crime scene itself, written by a number of different cops—starting with the first to arrive and including the observations of each detective and crime scene investigator who came later.

As he already knew, the body had been discovered partially covered by the pine boughs, but the report and the pictures added more detail: she was resting on her side, legs overlapping, one arm outstretched, as if she was in a deep sleep. The first officers immediately noticed a bluish or blue-gray color to her skin and deep bruises on her neck, the first clues that she'd been strangled. By then, rigor mortis was well-established, and flies were swarming around the body.

He paused, not sure he could read more. Taking a break, he made himself a cup of tea, stood outside on the balcony, breathed in the night air, then forced himself back to the report.

The belt, black, size thirty-eight with a silver buckle, was found a few feet from her head. Lab results would later reveal that it had rarely, if ever, been worn. It was a common brand, which could have been bought almost anywhere, and bore no fingerprints.

Was J.J. right? That the belt was some kind of symbol? It must be. Otherwise, why dump Jennifer's clothes blocks away and leave the belt behind? It couldn't be a careless mistake. Not with all three women.

The report also confirmed what J.J. had told him: that imprints in the grass and marks in the soil indicated that the body had been moved from the spot of the attack to its eventual position beneath the pine tree. And that a sweeping search of the immediate area, and later, of the entire park, would uncover no other physical evidence.

The first examination of the body at the scene, and a later autopsy, revealed evidence of the sexual assault, the other bruises that J.J. had spoken of, on her stomach and wrists, but no other signs of trauma or other wounds.

The next section of the report dealt with the police canvas of the neighborhood. House to house, for several blocks in all directions, questioning every resident that day and over the next several days. Were they out that evening? Had they happened to see Jennifer walking? Did they hear or see anything unusual? Strange cars or trucks in the area? The search was exhaustive but fruitless.

The Metro transit bus driver who had dropped Jennifer off at the corner was located and questioned. He remembered her, and was certain no one else had left the bus at the same time. But he could add little about the other passengers who had remained on board.

Barclay closed the file. It was late. He was tired. His eyes ached. And he still had to monitor the late newscasts.

As he walked to the living room and switched on the four TVs, he again wondered why he'd agreed to become involved in all of this. Especially now that he'd seen the voluminous file and understood how meticulous the cops had been. What, he asked himself, could he possibly do that hadn't already been done?

Probably not much, he decided. But he knew he had to try. If not for his own sake, for Jennifer's.

14

Another Saturday morning, and Barclay was back in his old Buick, heading for suburban Shoreview, the home of the elusive Mr. Kimble. He had tried repeatedly to phone the man but never got so much as his answering machine. Either he was never at home, or on vacation, or communicated with the outside world by some other method. E-mail or cell-phone, probably.

So, finally, he said to hell with it and decided to go knock on his door.

With a map by his side, he finally found Kimble's address on Arbor Lane, located just off Lexington Avenue, a quiet street in an upscale neighborhood that ended in a cul-de-sac. The house was an attractive two-story home with a brick and stucco exterior, its lush front lawn shaded by two large oak trees.

Pulling up to the curb, he spotted a man—in shorts, on his knees, with his back to him—tending a small flower garden that bordered the sidewalk. As Barclay got out of the car, he slammed the door in hopes the man would hear and not be startled by his arrival.

It worked.

He got up and turned, shading his eyes from the morning sun as Barclay approached. Slightly built with spindly legs, a narrow face and sharp features, he first struck Barclay as one of those shore birds that hopped along the Florida beaches. "Do I know you?" he asked, squinting.

"No, but . . ." Barclay started to say.

"Then leave," Kimble said. "I don't know what you want, but I'm not interested."

Barclay kept walking. "Mr. Kimble?"

The man held a small but sharp spade in his hand. "Didn't you hear?"

Barclay stopped a few feet away. The neighbors were right. The man was downright unfriendly. "I'm not selling anything," he said, keeping his eyes on the spade. "My name's George Barclay. From Channel Seven News. I've tried to reach you by phone several . . ."

The man took a step forward. "I don't care if you're George Bush. Fuck off. You're on private property."

Barclay stood fast. He outweighed the guy by at least a hundred pounds. But, then again, he didn't have a spade. "I'd like to talk to you about Jennifer Bartlow," he said. "I understand that you knew her . . ."

That stopped the man momentarily. Almost paralyzed him. His shoulders slumped and—for an instant—his face took on a haunted look. But he recovered quickly. His voice was again filled with menace. "Do I have to call the cops to get you the hell out of here?"

"Actually, I'm working with the cops," Barclay replied calmly. "Looking into Jennifer's death. I thought you might help."

As Kimble turned and headed for the front door, Barclay followed. "Look, I'm not the enemy," he said. "I just want to talk. You must want to know who killed her as much as I do."

Kimble stopped on the top step. "Don't you get it?" he growled. "I did all my talking with the cops years ago. I don't know anything about her murder. I hadn't seen her for months. I wasn't even here . . ."

Barclay persisted. "Then tell me about her life . . . before her murder. I'm told you knew her well. Dated her. Knew who her other friends were . . ."

Kimble came back down the steps, now standing no more than a foot away. His breath smelled of Listerine. "Why do you care about her friends? Or about me? I thought she was killed by a stranger. Some serial killer."

"That's what the cops think."

"And you don't?"

"I have no idea. But they've never been able to find the stranger."

Kimble scoffed. "So here you are, uninvited, invading my privacy, poking around my past. What gives you that right?"

Barclay paused. "Jennifer does, I guess."

That stopped him again. Only for a moment. "Then you must have been talking to her ghost. Just leave me the fuck alone. What's past is past. I'd leave it that way, if I were you."

"That sounds like a threat," Barclay said.

"Take it any way you want," he replied.

With that, he was inside the house. Leaving Barclay on the sidewalk, staring at the closed door. And wondering what Jennifer could have ever seen in a prick like this.

BACK HOME, BARCLAY RETURNED to the thick police file, concentrating now on the interviews the cops had conducted in the days and weeks after the killing.

There was page after page of detailed notes on the conversations police had held with scores of people who had touched Jennifer's life in one way or another. Friends, family members, including distant relatives, coworkers, theater people—the list went on and on. The information from one interview would lead to another, then to another. Links were established, connections made, more interviews held. Relationships were probed, alibis checked. Who was she dating and when? Any problems at work? Any known enemies? The questioning was exhaustive—and seemingly unending. Barclay had to give the cops credit.

He recognized a few of the names, like Jennifer's friends, but most he'd never heard of. And why would he? He didn't even know she had died, let alone whom she had known when she was alive.

The file also confirmed what he did already know: that the investigators had spent considerable time and effort in an unsuccessful attempt to discover a tie between Jennifer and the other two victims.

The questioning of Daniel Kimble also confirmed, in essence, what little Kimble had told him: that he had broken up with Jennifer the winter before her death, and that he was, indeed, out of town at the time of her murder. In San Francisco, at a graphic design conference, an alibi confirmed by several others who were also there.

Kimble did, however, provide police with the names of several of Jennifer's friends whom he had come to know in the months they were together. But, again, none of the names meant anything to Barclay, and apparently had led police nowhere.

Kimble also revealed one new piece of information—that in the months before their break-up, Jennifer had expressed concern over strange calls she was getting at all hours of the day and night. At home and at work. The caller never spoke but would stay on the line until she finally hung up. After a few weeks, she told him the calls had ended as abruptly as they'd begun.

Another dead end.

Kimble had admitted to police that it was Jennifer's idea to end their affair, that it had come suddenly, without explanation. He confessed bitterness and anger at her decision, admitting he had pestered her with unsuccessful attempts to get back together. Until, finally, she would no longer speak to him. But he said he still loved her, and would never have wished her any harm.

Barclay closed the file, went to the refrigerator and opened a beer. He'd read enough, but still had dozens of pages to go—including the medical examiner's report and other documents. But what good was it doing? While he was learning more about Jennifer's life, he was learning precious little new about her death. His hopes that he might—by some miracle—spot something the cops had overlooked were proving to be a pipe dream.

He took his beer and returned to the living room, picking up Jennifer's yearbook—thumbing through the pages, squinting at the scrawled writings of her friends, trying to decipher the notes. It had been years since he'd lost or thrown away his own yearbook, and reading hers brought back memories which had been lost, as well. Faces and names which would have helped him the night of the reunion.

In a way, he decided, reading the yearbook was like reading someone's private diary, although he was not invading Jennifer's thoughts, but those of the people who knew her best.

Yet there were few surprises. Most of the inscriptions were predictable: high school kids saying—in one way or another—good-bye, good luck, been good to know you. The majority were written by other girls, although a couple by boys caught his eye. The longest, signed by someone named Ken, covered most of the inside back cover. Barclay had no memory of a Ken, although he recalled there was one guy Jennifer had spent a lot of time with in their senior year.

Ken's note was gushing, recalling, in sentimental detail, the times they had spent together: the dates, the picnics, senior skip day, the prom. The kind of times Barclay could have only dreamed of.

"I'll never forget you," it said at the end. "Not 'til the day I die. Please don't forget me. You're the most wonderful girl I've ever known. And I'd love to spend the rest of my life with you."

Wow, Barclay thought. *And I thought I was lovesick.*

Another, much shorter note, was signed by a Brian. "You're the sweetest, smartest girl I know. You've got a great future. I hope you make the most of it."

Finally, there was a terse message scribbled in one of the margins. It was hard to make out the name, but Barclay thought it looked like David. "Sorry it didn't work out. Can't say I didn't try. Too bad, too sad. Hope you don't regret it some day."

Beneath that inscription, scrawled by a different hand, Jennifer's? was the single word: "LOSER!"

Rachel's condo was on the third floor of a converted warehouse, one of many that had been transformed on the edge of downtown in the past couple of decades. Surrounded by art galleries, chic restaurants, and an ever-burgeoning population of young and successful business people, along with older retirees who'd left their suburban mini-mansions to be closer to the amenities of downtown living.

Barclay had gotten an unexpected call from her that afternoon, apologizing for the late notice, but asking if he could stop by for dinner that night and meet her son, Joe, who was back from college for a day or two. "He'd love to talk to you about the news business," she'd said. "Is that possible?"

"Sure," he'd said, although he was hesitant, fearful that Joe might be like so many other young, would-be journalists who wanted to be either big-time anchors or network stars without going through all of the necessary hoops.

But the idea of an evening with Rachel had won him over.

Unlike his own modern building, hers remained the same—from the outside—as it had in the days when it actually was a warehouse or factory. Take away the new windows and sand-blasted brick and one would swear that inside would be floor after floor of packing boxes and crates. Or assembly lines busily turning out widgets.

She was waiting at her door when he got off the elevator, wearing a smile and a light-blue short-sleeved dress, buttoned neck to waist and hanging to the ankles. "Thanks so much for coming," she said, squeezing his hand. "Joe's really looking forward to this."

"Glad to do it," he replied, "although I'm not sure I can offer much advice."

As he stepped inside the door, he was immediately struck by what he saw: high, vaulted ceilings, rough-hewn timber beams, brick walls, gleaming hardwood floors, and sweeping views of the downtown skyline. "Wow," he said. "This is gorgeous."

"You like it?"

"Love it," he said, trying to take it all in. So different from his own sterile quarters, it breathed age and Old World craftsmanship, although he knew it must house all of the conveniences demanded in a modern condo.

Walking through the rooms, they were followed by her two cats, one black, one white, like slinking salt-and-pepper shakers. Everything he saw, from the oriental rugs to the furniture to the paintings on the walls, was tastefully, even elegantly, selected, the colors and styles perfectly matching the aura of the rooms themselves.

"You've done a wonderful job," he said. "My place must seem like a dungeon compared to this."

"Maybe we just have different tastes."

"Wrong," he said. "I have no taste."

She laughed. They were in the kitchen now, surrounded by glistening stainless-steel appliances, granite countertops, and tiled floor. "I've opened a bottle of red wine," she said, "but I suspect you'd rather have a beer."

"You've got me pegged."

As they took their drinks back to the living room, her son walked in the front door. "Hi," he said, crossing to them. "You must be Mr. Barclay."

"It's George," he said, taking the outstretched hand. "And it's nice to meet you, Joe."

If Joe, Jr., looked anything like his father, then Joe, Sr., must have been one handsome guy. Tall, over six-two, Barclay guessed, sturdy, well-buffed with his mother's reddish hair. Cut short. Hot, the girls would say, with deep-set eyes and a grin not obscured by a fashionable two-day growth of beard.

They chatted for a moment or two before Joe excused himself, disappearing into the kitchen to get his own beer.

"Nice looking kid," Barclay said, once he was gone. Thinking, here's another would-be anchorman in the making.

"Also a good kid," Rachel replied proudly.

"Older or younger than his sister?"

"Younger. Colleen's a junior at Boston College. He's a sophomore."

Colleen, it turned out, was gone for the evening, at dinner with old high-school friends. But Barclay had seen a picture of her on the fireplace mantle. The genetic gods had been good to this family.

When Joe returned, and they were all seated comfortably, the cats settling in next to them, Barclay said, "So how do you like Missouri?"

"Fine. I was told it had a good reputation for journalism."

"It used to, I know that," Barclay replied.

"I think it's still okay. You can get a lot of practical training. At their television station. Or the student newspaper."

Barclay smiled. "And you're sure you want to get into this crazy business?"

Joe seemed startled. "What do you mean?"

Barclay took a deep breath. "I can't tell you anything you don't already know. That things today aren't like they used to be. Certainly not when I got into the business. Newspapers are disappearing every day, it seems, and television stations across the country are cutting back on their staffs. With no real end in sight. And more competition than ever. With cable and the Web, and who knows what's next. Makes your head spin."

Rachel sat listening, her gaze shifting from one to the other.

"That doesn't mean there won't be opportunities for you," Barclay continued, "but it's a whole new, twenty-four-seven world out there, demanding different things of guys like you. If you stick with television, you know you'll probably be shooting and editing tape as well as writing the stories. A 'backpack journalist,' they call it now. You'll need to be quick on your feet, make quick decisions, and hopefully, have a few ethical bones in your body."

Barclay paused. "Sorry. I must be sounding like one of your professors."

"But they're not in the business like you are," Joe said.

"Lucky for them, probably."

"Any suggestions?" Joe asked.

"Depends on what do you want to do."

"Pretty much what you've done, I guess. Write. Produce. Manage, someday, if that's still possible. I'm not much for the on-camera stuff."

Surprise, surprise, Barclay thought, although the kid certainly had the looks to be in front of the cameras. "That's good to hear," he said. "We need people like that."

"So what should I be doing?"

Barclay thought for a moment. Then the words tumbled out. "If you like to write, keep writing. The business may have changed, but we still need good writers. Maybe more than ever in this on-line world. And read. Every newspaper and news magazine you can get your hands on. The ones that still exist. Know what's happening in the world. And study more than the hands-on stuff they're teaching you in J-School. Economics. Geography. Political science. You'll need every bit of it."

The talk went on for another half-hour, as Rachel went back and forth to the kitchen, preparing dinner. They shared another beer. Then Joe finally excused himself to leave on a date. Barclay promised to give him a tour of the station next time he was in town. "And keep writing," he said as he was on his way out the door.

THEY ATE THEIR SPAGHETTI and Caesar salad sitting on stools at the center island in the kitchen, where they could also watch the Twins on a small TV across the way. Rachel assuring him that the meatless spaghetti sauce was low-calorie, as was the salad dressing.

"It's great," he said. "Best meal I've had in days."

"How are you eating?"

"Enough. Cereal, milk, and dry toast in the morning, Slim Fast for lunch, and whatever I can dredge up for dinner. Leaving room for a beer or two."

"George!"

"I'm also taking vitamins. And walking on that damn treadmill."

"I've told you. You do look thinner."

"Slowly but surely. I can even button my suit coat now."

Their conversation was light and genial. No straining to fill awkward gaps. She laughed easily and often as he recalled some of the strange things he'd seen and experienced as he'd traveled around the country as a news jockey. Especially in the smaller markets.

"At one of the stations," he said, "we had to send a crew out of town for almost a week. With no time to prepare or pack. When they came back and put in their expense reports, they included things like the toothpaste and shaving cream they'd had to buy. The general manager went crazy, said they'd only used a few squeezes of the toothpaste . . . and refused to pay for them."

Rachel leaned back and hooted. "You can't be serious?"

"Oh, yeah. Wouldn't pay for the shaving cream, either."

She took her own turn, reciting some of the highs and lows, the joys and frustrations, of raising two smart and headstrong children. But she spoke little of her late husband, and Barclay didn't ask.

The evening passed so quickly and pleasantly that he'd hardly noticed that the Twins had lost. To Kansas City? *You gotta be kidding*.

Evenings like this made him realize how much he may have missed by spending so many nights alone, or sitting in a television newsroom. Not that the single life didn't have its own rewards, and not that one had to be married to enjoy this kind of conversation, but it was rare for him to feel this comfortable and content.

As she walked him to the door, he could hear the ring of the telephone behind them. "Can you wait a minute?" she said.

"Sure."

She was back in less than a minute. "That was strange," she said.

"What?"

"The phone call. No one was on the other end again. It's about the fourth time it's happened."

"Crank calls?"

"I guess so. Katie Thorson told me she's been getting them, too."

"You have Caller ID?" he asked.

"Yes, but the number's never revealed."

"Nothing's ever said?"

"No, but I can hear breathing. I've started hanging up right away."

"Good. You should also call the phone company."

"Maybe. We'll see. It's probably nothing."

"Probably," he agreed, although he couldn't ignore the queasy feeling in his stomach. And it wasn't from the spaghetti.

16

Knowles was waiting by Barclay's office door when he walked in the next morning. "Jesus," Knowles said. "Where have you been? Your face is beet-red."

"I just got off a goddamned treadmill, if you must know," he growled.

"You're actually exercising?"

"No, I just do it for fun. I like coming to work dragging my ass."

"You do look a little thinner," Knowles observed.

"Two pant sizes," he replied as he opened the office door.

Knowles followed him in. "I've got the information on those two other women," he said.

Barclay fell into his chair. "Good. But it'll have to wait awhile. I need to see what the newsroom's up to."

They arranged to meet an hour later, in Knowles's office.

The morning news meeting was one of three held each day, involving the assignment editor, the executive producer, the assistant news director, the chief photographer, and the producers of the various newscasts. Barclay usually sat in on the morning session, to discuss the day's agenda of hard news stories and feature possibilities.

It was one of his favorite duties. A time to sit back and watch his people at work, to judge their ideas and their enthusiasm for their jobs. He said little, allowing the give and take to swirl around him, only occasionally vetoing an idea or making a suggestion. They also critiqued the late news of the night before, holding it up against their competitors.

The teaching and mentoring, he thought, were as important to him as his job of managing the newsroom. And certainly more rewarding.

As the session ended, the executive producer asked Barclay what he'd heard about the pending sale. "Nothing," he replied. "As far as I know, it's moving ahead." Then he looked at Parkett. "You know anything different?"

He smiled. "No, sir. Haven't a clue."

Still throwing those curves, Barclay thought.

"HERE THEY ARE," KNOWLES SAID, placing two pictures on the desk in front of him. "The one on the right is Sheila Hamsted. She was twenty-two. On the left, April Sullivan, twenty-three."

Barclay picked up the pictures, studying each in turn. J.J. had been right. Neither woman was particularly attractive. One was heavy-set, the other slimmer, but not much. Hamsted, the heavier one, had a square face, with drooping eyelids and dark bangs that covered much of her forehead. Sullivan had more angular features, a thinner nose and lips, and close-cropped blond hair. Neither one, Barclay guessed, would draw many second glances.

"You want to see the crime scene photos?" Knowles asked.

"Not unless I have to," he replied.

Knowles put the pictures aside and turned to his notes. "Hamsted, like Jennifer, was found in a park—Jefferson park, in south Minneapolis, in late October. By a couple of kids. Body was nude, partially hidden beneath a picnic table. Clothes were never found. Like Jennifer, she'd been strangled and raped a few yards away and then dragged to the picnic table."

"Let me guess," Barclay said. "The guy used a condom."

"Right. No traces of semen were found."

"But a belt was?"

"Yup. Black. Size forty. Old. Untraceable."

"No witnesses?"

"Nope. She was killed the night before. Probably around midnight. No one in the neighborhood admits to hearing or seeing anything."

"What did she do?"

"A waitress at a sports bar in Bloomington. Got off work about ten and supposedly headed for home. Never got there."

As Barclay digested the information, a tiny fact suddenly bubbled to the surface. "Wait a minute," he said. "What size belt did you say they found?"

"Forty. Why?"

"Probably nothing. But Jennifer's file says she was strangled with a size thirty-eight. And it was new."

"So?"

"So how about the other woman? Sullivan? What belt size?"

Knowles paged through his notes, pausing several pages in. "Forty. Like the first one."

"Old or new?"

"What?"

"The belt. Old or new?"

"Old, I guess. No mention of new."

Sullivan had been found across the city, in suburban Brooklyn Center, near a pond, her body partially covered by snowdrifts left by a February storm. "Frozen solid," Knowles said. "It was below zero, and she'd probably have been buried in snow 'til spring if a guy out cross-country skiing hadn't spotted her."

He said she'd been a clerk at a nearby Target store, and like the other women, was single with no steady boyfriend. And he confirmed what Barclay already knew: that police had been unable to find anything—work, friends, school, anything—that connected these two women to Jennifer.

Knowles said, "The cops think she was raped and killed somewhere else. Then dumped. It was too damned cold to have happened there."

"But a belt was left," Barclay said.

"Yeah. Only this time it was still wrapped around her neck. Looks like the guy's trademark."

By now, more than an hour had passed and Barclay had to get back to the newsroom. "Make me a copy of your notes," he said. "And keep digging, if you have the time."

He was no sooner back in his office when he found Hawke at his door, looking agitated, as usual. "Got a minute?" Hawke asked.

"Sure. C'mon in."

Before sitting, Hawke quickly surveyed the office. "How do you live in this mess? Looks like a goddamned landfill."

Barclay grinned. "You get used to it."

Hawke dropped into the guest chair, but not before first brushing it off. "We need to talk," he said.

"Okay."

"About our friend, Mr. Coburn."

"What about him?"

Hawke leaned forward. "Our attorneys say Coburn's group has some muscle, that we can't take them lightly. They're talking to the F.C.C. staff, maybe laying the groundwork for a petition to deny the sale. It's just a matter of time."

Barclay could only listen, unsure what to expect next.

"So far," Hawke went on, "we have no firm idea who else is in his group. We have our suspects, but we won't know for sure until the actual petition is filed. And maybe not even then."

"What suspects?"

"Some of the big sports guys in town. Money guys, who'd probably love to own their own VHF station to carry their games. Flush the network. Think about it. The Twins, the Timberwolves, the Wild, all on one station. Combined with their cable networks, they'd own the sports franchise in this market. A sports super station. They'd call all the shots. Control the ad prices."

Unlikely but not impossible. "And Coburn?" he asked.

"We think he's their front man. They need some minority participation to have a chance this late in the game. Coburn and his buddies will probably get a piece of the action, but they'll be a minority minority, if you get my drift."

"So why are you talking to me?" Barclay asked.

"Because I want you and your people to do some digging. Find out who else is in this group. Maybe turn up a little dirt while you're at it. We need to prepare a defense."

Barclay leaned across the desk. "Dirt on whom?"

"Start with Coburn," Hawke said. "There must be some skeletons in his closet. Usually are with those people."

Those people? "You've got to be kidding!" Barclay protested.

"Like hell. We're not playing games here."

Barclay was aghast. Even from Hawke, this was the last thing he would have expected. Poking around somebody's private past for purely self-serving purposes. "Is that even legal?" he asked. "To say nothing of *ethical*."

"Legal, smeegle," Hawke replied. "We need answers. And quick."

"I don't know, Nicholas. I think you've stepped off the deep end. And I don't want any part of it."

"Then you'd better reconsider," Hawke warned. "Like I say, we're not playing games."

"But what if you get caught?"

"We won't."

Barclay thought for a moment. "Tell you what I'll do. We'll try to find out who the others in the group are. But I won't be digging for dirt. You'd better get a private detective for that."

"That's not good enough."

"It'll have to be," he said.

With that, Hawke jumped up and started to stomp out. But he stopped at the door, looking back, angrily. "And clean this pigsty up!"

Yes, sir, Barclay thought. *Right away.*

17

O'Gara's was beginning to feel like a second home to Barclay. Even the bartender recognized him now, putting an Amstel Light in front of him before he could ask for it.

"Waiting for J. J. again?" the bartender asked.

"You got it."

"Might as well set him up, too," he said, pouring a glass of Wild Turkey and leaving it next to Barclay's beer.

Jacobs got there ten minutes later, wearing a pair of shorts and a polo shirt. "Just got off the golf course," he explained. "Sorry to be late."

"No problem," Barclay said. "But I didn't know you played golf."

"I don't, really."

"What'd you shoot?"

"A hundred and six. I suck."

Barclay laughed. He could empathize, but he didn't want to talk about golf right then. He had other things on his mind.

They retreated to their usual booth, and Jacobs asked, "So what's up?"

"Things I can't quite shake," Barclay said as he took out a pad of notes he'd made before coming.

"Like what?"

"Did your task force ever question why a different size belt was used in one of the murders?"

"I don't remember that it was."

"According to the files, it was," Barclay said. "Size thirty-eight for Jennifer, size forty for the other two. Two of the belts were old, hers was new."

"So?"

"So, I'm curious. Who would have known, back then, what size belts were used in the first two murders?"

J.J. paused as he took a sip of his drink. Finally, "Just us. It's not the kind of detail we would ever have made public."

"That's what I figured," Barclay said.

"I still don't know where you're going with this," Jacobs replied.

"I'm not sure, either, and maybe I'm a little loony, but why would the killer use two old, well-worn belts in two of the murders, and a brand new one, of a different size, in the third?"

"Maybe he ran out of old belts."

"Be serious."

"I don't think it's important, okay. And I'm not sure why you do."

"I'll get to that in a minute," Barclay said.

"So, what's next?"

He checked his notes. "Correct me if I'm wrong, but wasn't Jennifer's father the only one to get those bizarre birthday and anniversary notes? Not the parents or relatives of the other women?"

"As far as I know, that's right."

"Does that strike you as strange?"

"A little, maybe. But, remember, the notes came after I'd retired."

"Finally," Barclay said, "there are the women themselves. This guy—this killer—must have known something about these women. Enough to follow them, to know where they'd be when he decided to strike. He wouldn't just randomly wait, hoping that some woman might come along."

Jacobs nodded. "In that sense, no, it probably wasn't random. He might have known who the women were, and what their habits were, but didn't know them personally. Remember, we could never find anyone that all three, or even two, of the women knew."

"I remember," Barclay said, leaning in, "and do you remember telling me about the FBI profilers?"

"Of course."

"That they said that this kind of 'organized' killer tends to pick victims with the similar characteristics—age, appearance, lifestyle. Whatever."

Jacobs nodded.

"So, I ask you again, if he knew who they were, and what they looked like, why would he choose to attack two entirely different types of women?"

"I see where you're going," Jacobs said.

"Tell me."

"You don't think it was one guy."

"Bingo!" Barclay said.

Jacobs leaned back in the booth, finishing the Wild Turkey with one final swig. "You're a piece of work," he said.

Barclay took a deep breath. "I think Jennifer's killer was a copy-cat. He knew about the other murders, about the belts, but he didn't know—couldn't have known, unless he was a cop—the size of the belts and the fact that they were old. He had to be someone who thought he could hide in the shadows of the other murders. And, who, years later, would feel confident enough—and still angry enough—to taunt Jennifer's father with the anonymous cards. I think whoever killed Jennifer knew her. Maybe from a long time ago . . ."

"Someone like you," Jacobs said.

That hit Barclay where it hurt. "Yeah," he finally said, "I've thought about that. Maybe somebody like me. Only with murder in his heart. Someone she'd once rejected . . ."

"I told you," Jacobs said, "we interviewed and eliminated all of her old boyfriends."

"What if it wasn't a boyfriend?" Barclay argued. "I sure as hell wasn't. But I certainly felt rejected, as could others over the years."

Jacobs got up and out of the booth. "I've gotta give you credit," he said. "For your imagination, if nothing else."

Barclay shrugged.

"I'll talk to Bennett," Jacobs continued. "Tell him your theory. And hope he doesn't laugh in my face."

"If he does, he's a fool," Barclay said. "And one more thing. A couple of Jennifer's friends have been getting anonymous telephone calls. Like the ones Jennifer got in the months before she was killed."

"No shit," J.J. replied, frowning. "I'll mention that to Bennett, too."

Then, with a wave to the bartender, J.J. was out the door, leaving Barclay alone with his beer and his theories. And the tab.

SLEEP WOULD COME AND GO, like wisps of fog. Drifting in, then out. Lifting, then falling.

She, too, would be there, then gone. Across the dance floor, her red dress billowing around her, her eyes fixed on his. Beckoning, pleading for him to come to her, to hold her, to float with the music, as soft and gentle as a June breeze.

But he could only stand transfixed, powerless, unable to move, watching sadly as others took her in their arms, whirling across the floor, in and out of the mist. Sweeping past him, her face radiant but flushed, she reached out, her fingers brushing his cheek.

Fingers as cold as the tip of an icicle.

Then, like the fog, she was gone, swallowed up by a sea of darkness.

BARCLAY SAT UP, GASPING FOR AIR. Lost, for a moment, in his own dark depths. Sweating and chilled, at the same time.

Breathing deeply, he reached for the bedside lamp to erase the darkness if not the dream. Foolishly, he touched his cheek, convinced he might still feel the icy imprint of her fingers. Instead, there was only the feverish warmth of his own skin.

Angrily, he threw aside his tangled sheet and heaved himself out of bed. Half the night was gone, and he knew there would be no chance of further rest. Not with Jennifer hanging on to the edge of his consciousness, as she had for so many recent nights, apparently intent on taunting him in death as she had in life.

He could see the signs bobbing in the sun-splashed morning air from a block away. Maybe a dozen people carrying a half dozen posters, walking in a small circle in front of the main entrance to the television station.

Now what's going on? Barclay picked up his pace.

He recognized her before he could read the signs. Natalie Pearson, Nat Coburn's assistant, leading the small parade. Then a couple of the handmade banners became readable: NO SALE TO RACIST MEDIA, and, TV FOR THE PEOPLE. Then, a third, PEOPLE FIRST, PROFITS SECOND.

He paused across the street, in time to see Nicolas Hawke rush out of the building, accompanied by one of the station's security guards. Looking confused, trying—as Barclay had—to read the signs as they passed by him. Then angry. "What the hell is this about?" he shouted loud enough to be heard by Barclay across the way.

He quickly crossed the street, in hopes of preventing a confrontation.

Too late.

"Get the hell off our sidewalk," Hawke shouted as he stepped in front of the protesters, blocking their way. Turning to the security guard, "I want them out of here. Now! If they're not gone in five minutes, get the cops." The guard scurried back into the building.

By then, Barclay was by his side, grabbing his arm. "Hold on, Nicholas. Cool down."

Hawke shook him off. "Not now, George," he snapped. "I'll handle this."

"Not this way," Barclay said, grabbing his arm again and pulling him aside. "Hold your fire, Nicholas. Listen to me. They've got a right to be here. The sidewalk's public property. Keep this up and the cops will arrest *you*, not them."

At that moment, Natalie Pearson stepped out of the line and walked over, her sign by her side. Only then did Hawke recognize her. "It's you," he sputtered. "You were in my office . . ."

"We don't want trouble, Mr. Hawke," she said, speaking easily and with a small smile. "We're here peacefully. To make our point."

"What point?" he snarled.

"That the sale to TriCom is a mistake. That it won't serve the community. Especially our communities of color. If TriCom isn't racist, it's close to it. We know. We've checked. They're bad people, Mr. Hawke."

"I thought you were going to the F.C.C.," he replied, still belligerent but calmer now.

"We have," she replied. "But we want to build public support for our position."

Alerted in advance, the first photographers and reporters arrived on the scene, including those from the newspapers and one from Channel Seven itself. As they began to videotape and snap still pictures, Hawke shrunk back against the building. "Who the hell invited them?" he demanded. "And isn't that one of our people? Get him out of here."

Barclay made no move to obey, knowing that ordering their cameraman away now would cause more of a ruckus than the protest itself. He'd have to fight that fight later.

But if Hawke was surprised by the arrival of the news people, he was aghast at what he saw next. There, joining the parade of protesters, carrying her own sign, was none other than their star anchorwoman, Maggie Lawrence.

Her sign read simply, I AGREE.

Barclay was amazed. Hawke was irate. But Maggie didn't give them a second glance, holding her sign defiantly high in the air.

Hawke was gasping for air. "George!" he finally managed. "Do something!"

The photographers converged on Maggie as Natalie Pearson walked over to shake her hand, and to pose with her before the cameras. And while Maggie refused to say anything on camera, Pearson had no such hesitation. "I believe Maggie Lawrence's presence here demonstrates that some of the people inside this building agree with those of us on the outside—that this pending sale is bad for the station as well as the community. That it threatens the independence of Channel Seven as a locally owned voice of news and public affairs. Maggie and others inside, like us, don't want this station to become part of a giant conglomerate, which couldn't care less about the people who live and work here."

As Pearson spoke, Hawke stood back, simmering.

"You've got to say something, Nicholas," Barclay told him. "You have to respond in some way."

"No way. This is a goddamned circus."

"You have to," he persisted. "Get your head together."

Before he could argue more, Barclay walked over to the crowd of news people, waited for Pearson to finish, then announced that Hawke would have a response momentarily.

By the time he was ready, surrounded by microphones and cameras, most of the protesters—including Maggie Lawrence—had departed. Raising himself on his tiptoes, Hawke began, calmly, "Let me say that I believe these people had every right to be here, to voice their opinions. As much as I may disagree with them."

Right, Barclay thought.

"This is America, after all. But I must tell you that TriCom Communications is a fine, reputable company, which serves its communities—including its minority communities—well. We would never have agreed to sell this station to them if we had believed otherwise."

"Oh, yeah?" Barclay muttered under his breath.

Hawke went on, "What's more, I believe this is an attempt to extort money from us—what we call a 'tribute' in our business—in return for eventually agreeing to drop its opposition."

A shout came from behind the cameras, "That's a racist lie!" It was Natalie Pearson, who had stayed on to hear Hawke. "And you damn well know it."

Hawke ignored her. "Time will tell what their true motives are," he went on. "Where the real truth lies. In the meantime, we'll continue to defend the sale and move forward toward its completion. Thank you very much . . ."

As he began to walk away, questions stopped him. Who's leading the opposition group? How do you know TriCom is so reputable? When do you expect the sale to be finalized? What's the F.C.C. position on all of this? Hawke answered each question calmly and confidently, showing no signs of the panic or anger he had displayed only moments before. Barclay was impressed.

Finally, one of the reporters from a competing station asked, "What about Maggie Lawrence? What was she doing out here . . . and will she face any discipline?"

Hawke paused for a moment. "Of course not. While I'm disappointed that Maggie chose to take part in the demonstration, she has every right to express her opinion, however wrong I believe she might be. That's the American way. And, right or wrong, she's an important part of our Channel Seven family."

Flashing a smile, he made his way through the reporters and cameras and into the front door, with Barclay close behind.

Once inside, however, Hawke's mood changed as fast as the colors of a chameleon. He stopped abruptly in the middle of the hallway and angrily turned on Barclay. "I don't want to see a second of that circus on our air," he snapped. "Not one lousy second."

Barclay's mouth fell open. "What? You can't be serious?"

"Oh, yeah? Try me."

"Nicholas, listen to me." Barclay's voice was plaintive. "We can't *not* run the story. Not when everyone else will. Not when our own self-interest is involved. We'd be the laughing stock of the business. The newspapers will crucify us. To say nothing of the F.C.C., if it hears about it."

Hawke was adamant. "I'll take that chance. Kill the story."

With that, he turned on his heel and began to walk away.

"I won't do it," Barclay said to his back. "Find somebody else."

Hawke spun, his eyes glittering with anger. "You're refusing a direct order?"

"Yes."

Hawke stood for a moment, sizing him up. "I run this candy store, in case you've forgotten. *I* give the orders. You obey the orders. That's how it works."

"Not when the orders are bullshit," Barclay replied, standing his ground.

"Maybe I'll have to find somebody else."

"Not in our newsroom, you won't," Barclay said. "They won't stand for it. You won't have a newscast. You'll have half an hour of black."

Hawke took a step toward him. "You're serious, aren't you?"

"Deadly."

"You actually think everyone in the newsroom would risk their jobs over this? Refuse to work?"

"Absolutely. I know my people."

"And you'd risk the reputation of this station?"

"I'm not risking it. You are."

Hawke stood vibrating with anger. He never had understood news people. Never would. A strange breed. Marched to their own drummers. But it was clear that he was caught between the proverbial rock and hard place. He couldn't put on a goddamned newscast by himself. Or have the time to bring in others who would.

He took a deep breath. "Fine," he said with venom. "You win. This time. Run the fucking story."

Before he could leave, Barclay said, "Thanks, boss. You're doing the right thing."

"Stick it up your ass," Hawke replied, retreating down the hallway.

ALTHOUGH BARCLAY HAD BEEN UNAWARE OF IT, several people had witnessed the confrontation and word quickly spread. So, to his surprise, when he entered the newsroom, he found himself getting a standing ovation, with Parkett leading the applause. "Way to go, George," he said, thumping Barclay on the back as he headed for his office. "We're with you. We're proud of you."

Barclay was touched but wasn't about to admit it. "Then maybe you'll get back to work," he said, with mock anger. "So we don't have to go to black."

"Gotcha," Parkett replied with a salute and a smile.

"And I'll personally handle the protest story," Barclay added over his shoulder. "Let me know when it's ready to edit."

"You're the man," Parkett said.

When he got to his office, Barclay found Maggie Lawrence waiting for him, looking decidedly uncomfortable.

"Where's your sign?" he asked, pausing at the door.

"In the Dumpster."

He walked in and took his seat behind the desk, waiting.

"I'm sorry, George. I had to do it. I know I embarrassed you, and I apologize for that. But I had to do it."

"You didn't *have* to do it," he said. "You *chose* to do it."

"Okay, I chose to do it."

He leaned into her. "And you may have to pay the consequences some day. Hawke doesn't forget things like that. Nor, I suspect, will the new owners. They'll see you as disloyal."

"That's okay. I don't want to work for them, anyway." Then, in frustration, "We can't just sit idly by and let this happen, George."

"It's happening all over the country," he said. "You can't hold back a tidal wave. Not with a flimsy protest sign."

"I had to try. And I'm not alone. Most of the people out there," pointing to the newsroom, "feel the same way."

"But they didn't lug a sign around. I don't want to be a prick about it, Maggie, but you know you can't participate in a public demonstration. It jeopardizes our neutrality . . .our objectivity . . . your objectivity . . ."

"I understand."

"But you did it anyway."

"Yes."

"By all rights, I should suspend you or dock your pay. Or something. But Hawke's already said there'll be no discipline. So I guess we'll have to let it ride. But I want you to take a night off. I don't want you anywhere near that story when it goes on the air."

Maggie got out of her chair. "I'm sorry, George. You're the last person in the world I'd want to disappoint. But I'm still not sorry I did it."

Sadly, he watched her leave, but not without a touch of admiration in his heart.

HE SPENT THE NEXT FEW HOURS in the editing booth, and at his computer, writing different versions of the protest story for the various newscasts, taking his time, knowing that if ever a story had to be fair and balanced—this was it. That it would be studiously viewed by their competitors and the protest group alike—all of whom would be quick to bitch if they found the slightest hint of bias.

By the end of the day, he was exhausted and eager to get home, ready to forego his nightly jaunt on the treadmill, and the off-chance of running into Rachel. But before he could leave, he got two phone calls, the first from John Jacobs.

"Hey, J.J." he said, tiredly. "What do you need?"

"You sound like shit."

"I'm beat. It's been a tough day."

"I'm not going to make it any easier," J.J. said. "Bennett thinks you're full of shit, but he wants to talk with you."

Barclay was amused. "Then why does he want to talk?"

"Got me," he said. "I'm just the messenger."

"I'll tell you why. Because he thinks there may be a grain of truth buried in the shit."

J.J. laughed. "You've got chutzpah, I'll give you that."

They arranged to meet the next day.

The second phone call was a surprise—coming from none other than Nicholas Hawke himself. "This pains me," Hawke said, "but I have to apologize for our little dispute this morning. Several of our directors say you were right to insist that we run the story. That we could have jeopardized our standing with the Commission if we'd withheld it."

Barclay felt a small tug of satisfaction but wisely said nothing.

"However," Hawke went on, "I must make it clear that you cannot, on a whim, defy my orders. That final authority must rest with me. The directors were quite firm about that."

Again, Barclay remained silent.

"George? Are you there?"

"I'm here."

"Did you hear what I said?"

"I don't defy orders on a whim."

"All right, then. We understand each other. Have a good night."

I'm trying, he thought. *God knows, I'm trying.*

BEFORE HEADING HOME, despite his exhaustion, he felt obliged to attack the work that had piled up on his desk. There were time cards and expense reports to be signed, budget analyses to be studied, the latest batch of overnight ratings to be reviewed. Only as he shuffled through the large stack of material did he realize how little time he'd been giving to the normal routine of his job.

Others had begun to notice, though. As he left his office to refill his coffee cup, Jeff Parkett approached and—hesitantly—asked if he'd been out interviewing for another job.

"Of course not," Barclay replied. "Why would you ask that?"

"Because you're not around much," Parkett said. "Some of us are wondering if you're about to abandon ship."

"That's ridiculous. I'm not going anywhere."

"Then what's going on?" Parkett asked.

He hesitated. "I'm just spending some time on a personal project."

"Really? Is that why Knowles has been hanging around?"

"He's giving me a hand, yeah."

Parkett pressed on. "Is there a potential news story in this 'project' of yours?"

"Maybe. It's too soon to know."

"Care to fill me in? In case you get hit by a truck or something."

"Later, if it looks more promising. And I'll keep my eye out for any trucks."

Parkett started to walk away. "Now who's throwing the curves?" he said over his shoulder.

Josh Bennett was waiting on the same bench in Rice Park as Barclay and J.J. made their way along the path past the wading pool. Today, however, they found fewer kids splashing about, thanks to the heavy, overcast skies and the feel of impending rain in the air.

Bennett rose to meet them, and—after a quick handshake and glance at the fast-moving clouds—suggested they retreat to the coffee shop inside the Landmark Center across the park. "Muggy as hell, isn't it?" he said, his words coinciding with ominous rumbles of thunder.

As they hurried inside the stately old building—once the ornate federal court house in St. Paul—the first drops of rain hit the sidewalk. By the time they ordered their coffee, the sprinkles had become a downpour, pooling deep puddles in the street, slowing traffic and chasing remaining pedestrians into the shelter of the nearest buildings.

"Okay," Bennett said, once they'd settled in, "J.J.'s briefed me on some of your ideas."

"I've heard," Barclay replied.

Bennett smiled. "For the record, I don't really think you're full of shit. You've obviously done your homework."

"I've just read the file and talked to people. Tried to think of anything the cops may have missed."

Bennett took a sip of his coffee and pushed back his chair. "Know what the problem is? The case is too damned old. I wasn't even in college when it happened. And J.J.'s task force was abolished years ago. So here I am, looking at Jennifer's murder with no idea if anybody in Minneapolis or Brooklyn Center is doing the same with the other two women."

"Why don't you ask?" Barclay said.

"I have. But, so far, I haven't gotten any answers. And I really haven't had the time to press the issue."

J.J. broke in. "If all three murders had happened in St. Paul, say, or in one of the other cities, they'd probably be getting more attention than they are now. But as it is . . ." His voice trailed off.

"Okay," Barclay said. "Let's forget the other two women for the moment." Seeing no objection, he went on. "You agree it's possible that Jennifer was killed by someone who had nothing to do with the other murders?"

"Possible, but not likely," Bennett replied.

"Why not?"

"Because there's more about the three murders that are similar than dissimilar. The differences you've pointed out are interesting, but not convincing."

Barclay knew he was at a disadvantage because he wasn't privy to all the details of the other murders. Still . . .

"Okay," he finally said, "ignore the differences in the belts, and even the differences in the type of women chosen. Consider the cards Jennifer's dad received, and the fact that Jennifer got anonymous calls in the months before her murder. As far as I know, neither of the other women got such calls, nor did their relatives get such cards. Am I right?"

Barclay wasn't sure, but thought he detected a look of grudging agreement on each of their faces.

"Maybe," Bennett admitted. "But that could be explained in other ways. Maybe this guy became more intrigued with Jennifer after the murder, when he found out more about her in the press. Hence, the cards years later."

"C'mon," Barclay replied. "You don't really believe that . . ."

"And," J.J. chimed in, "a lot of women get anonymous phone calls. Most of which, like Jennifer's, never get officially reported."

"But," Barclay responded, "as far as we know, the other two women didn't get any calls like that."

"That's true," J.J. admitted.

After sitting quietly for several minutes, Bennett spoke up. "I'll give it more thought, okay, and run it by the people I report to."

"Good," Barclay replied.

"And I'll try again to get hold of somebody in Minneapolis and Brooklyn Center who's still around and might know something about the other murders."

"That's all I can ask. Meantime, I'm going to talk to more people. See if I can shake some memories."

"And what about me?" J.J. asked.

"I want you with me," Barclay said.

DRIVING BACK TO THE STATION, Barclay got a call on his cell. "George? It's Rachel."

"Hey, Rachel."

"Sorry to bother you," she said, "but I'm wondering if you have plans for tonight?"

"Not really," he replied.

"Good. I've got tickets for the Twins. Thought you might like to go."

It had been weeks since he'd been to a game. "That'd be great."

"Wait and see. I've got great seats."

SHE WAS RIGHT. MAYBE the best seats in the Metrodome. Two rows up, directly behind the Twins' dugout, a far cry from his usual vantage point in the upper deck.

"How did you get seats like this?" he asked, once they'd settled in.

"From a friend," she'd said.

He didn't press the point.

It was the rubber game of a three-game series with the Seattle Mariners, the Twins last season in the Metrodome before moving to a new stadium. Nick Blackburn was pitching for the Twins, and the place was packed.

"You go to many of these games?" he asked.

"Not now, but I used to. Joe's firm had season tickets."

"He was a big fan?"

"Not really. It was good for business. He'd take clients and I'd tag along. Smile a lot. And flirt if they were especially good clients."

There was a touch of bitterness in her voice, but it was the most she'd said about her late husband since their brunch at the hotel. And Barclay decided to pursue it. "You don't talk much about him, you know. Your husband, I mean."

She seemed surprised. "Should I?"

"Not necessarily, I guess. But it seems a little curious. You know a lot more about me and my past than I know about you."

"Another time, maybe," she replied. Her tone was serious, final.

Okay, have it your way. He sat back, content to savor the game, sip his overpriced cup of beer, and relish the close-up view of the players going to and from the dugout. Rachel seemed to be enjoying herself, too, munching on her popcorn and cheering and booing with the best of them.

Between the second and third innings, he asked her if she'd had any more of the strange phone calls.

"A couple, including one in the middle of the night.

"This is getting weird," he said. "Has Katie gotten more?"

"I don't know. I haven't talked to her."

"You called the phone company?"

"Yeah, but I've decided to just use my cell. I won't answer the home phone unless it's one of the kids."

A moment of panic came after the sixth inning. By then, the Twins had a one-run lead, and the fans were settling in for some traditional between-innings fun. The stadium's Kiss Cams roved the stands, capturing couples on the huge scoreboard screens, the crowd hooting and hollering for an on-camera kiss from each of the couples unlucky enough to be caught in the lens.

Barclay was paying little attention until the people in back of them, and on either side, began to scream in their ears. "Kiss! Kiss! Kiss!" Only then did he glance at the scoreboard . . . mortified to see the giant image of Rachel and himself, looking both shocked and traumatized. The camera crew knew they'd found their patsies.

The crowd was unrelenting. The shouts were deafening. "Kiss! C'mon, kiss her!"

He tried to look away, to ignore the clamor, but there was no place to hide. Then he felt Rachel tug at his arm, laughing. "C'mon, George, let's get it over with. They won't stop until we do."

Before he could respond, she leaned over and kissed him on the cheek. But that was not enough. "More! more!" the crowd shouted.

With no hesitation, Rachel did their bidding. Twisting in her seat, still laughing, she took his face between her hands and kissed him fully on the lips. Lingering for a millisecond more than Barclay thought was necessary. Cheers replaced the jeers.

"I'm so sorry," he said after the camera had moved on. "To put you through that."

"Don't be," she replied. "It wasn't your fault. And it was all in good fun." Then, with a mock coquettish glance at him, she added, "Besides, I kind of enjoyed it."

The game ended with the Twins losing four to two, but Barclay hardly noticed. He was still feeling her moist lips on his. And wondering about that extra millisecond.

Katie Thorson's home was an imposing two-story colonial overlooking the meandering Minnehaha Creek in south Minneapolis—an older, fashionable neighborhood where the homes were surrounded by lush lawns, sheltered and shaded by towering, decades-old oak, ash and the few remaining elms that had survived the scourge of Dutch-Elm disease.

"Not bad digs," J.J. said as he and Barclay pulled up in front of the house.

"Little wonder," Barclay replied. "I think her husband's a big-time lawyer."

Pulsating lawn sprinklers sprayed pistol-like shots of water in every direction, strategically placed to cover the lawn but miss several cars parked in the driveway, all of them—Barclay could tell at a glance—far newer than his aging Buick.

They sat for a moment, letting the engine idle. "Tell me again," J.J. said, flashing a grin, "why are we here?"

"In hopes of learning something new, smartass," Barclay replied. "These women knew Jennifer better than anyone."

"And?"

"Who knows? We'll see." Besides, he wasn't sure where else to go, or what else to do, at the moment.

As they got out of the car, another, with Rachel at the wheel, pulled in behind them. "Is this the lady at the ballpark?" J.J. asked quietly.

The word had spread.

"Don't say a friggin' thing," Barclay warned as Rachel got out and walked toward them, wearing the same yellow sun dress she had worn to his condo.

Jacobs said nothing, but emitted a low wolf whistle.

After introductions, and as they walked up the sidewalk, Barclay thanked her again for coming. "I'm happy to," she replied, "although I'm still not sure why I'm here. I don't know any of these women that well."

"I know," he said. "I'll explain later."

Katie was at the door to greet them, escorting them through a marble-tiled foyer, past an open stairway and into a spacious living room where three other women rose to meet them. Barclay knew in advance who would be there and studied them closely now as Katie made the introductions.

Gloria DeLuca, tall and thin, well-tanned with frosted blond hair, wearing small frameless glasses and a tailored suit that gave her the look of a no-nonsense professional who'd just come from the office. Maybe another lawyer, Barclay thought.

Jackie Shepard, shorter and more matronly, with a fuller face and dimples that punctuated a perpetual smile. A soccer mom, he guessed.

And Annie Russell, clearly the most athletic of the three, still clad in jogging shorts and running shoes, displaying long, muscular legs and a trim, sturdy body. A ponytail hung to the middle of her back. Her face still showed a sheen of sweat, as if she'd just come in from a long run.

Barclay looked again at Gloria DeLuca. "Have we met before?" he asked. "You look familiar."

"We were at the same table at the reunion," she said, "before you suddenly took off."

"Okay," he replied, relieved he could remember something from that night. "I'm sorry about the abrupt departure. Not my finest hour."

"We all understood," she said.

Once they were seated, Katie began, "I can't tell you how grateful we are that you've decided to begin your own investigation."

"It's not exactly 'my own,'" Barclay said, explaining J.J.'s role in the original investigation and in the subsequent serial killer task force. "Although he's retired, he's agreed to help out, but as he'll tell you, he's not very hopeful that this will lead to anything. Nor am I, really."

He went on to report on his own reading of the police files and the old newspaper clippings, along with the fact that he'd spoken to a number of people involved in the case, including Josh Bennett. "In the process," he said, "a couple of things have struck me as strange. I won't go into those now, but they were enough to persuade me to pursue this a little further. But," he added, glancing at each woman in turn, "I don't want to get your hopes up. The case is old and the trail is cold, and the police have done a remarkably thorough job."

The women listened intently and without comment as J.J. briefly took over, recounting details of the original investigation and the possible ties to the other two victims. "George is right about me," he added, "I don't really agree with some of his ideas. But I was in police work long enough to know that the unexpected can happen . . . often when you least expect it. So I'm happy to help in any way I can."

Katie, in turn, told them how each of the women had come to know Jennifer: Gloria in theater arts, participating in several school plays and variety shows; Jackie, the dimpled soccer mom, Jennifer's next-door neighbor, the two inseparable since seventh grade; and, Annie, who ran with Jennifer on the school's cross-country team.

"It's funny," Katie said, glancing at the others. "None of us was that close to one another back then. Jennifer brought us together and kept us together. We all revolved around her."

She paused for a moment, eyes welling slightly. "And, you know, if it weren't for Jennifer we probably would have gone our separate ways, but, even in death, she's managed to keep us together, almost twenty years later."

Each woman then took a turn recounting her own special memories of Jennifer: her intellect and curiosity, her sense of humor, her occasionally acid tongue, and her robust self-image. "She was always a great actress," Jackie said. "As far back as junior high, she'd dress up in some of her mom's old clothes and put on these one-girl performances, which she'd written herself. I was her only audience, of course, but I still remember how awed I was that somebody of our age could do that."

For her part, Annie recalled how Jennifer inevitably finished last or near the back of the cross-country pack but never complained or quit. "I remember waiting at the finish line, sometimes for a long time, for her to hobble in, huffing and puffing, but with a smile as broad as a pumpkin face—wondering if her time had improved at all."

As the stories went on, Barclay found himself wishing more than ever that he'd somehow managed to know this woman—this girl—better, if only a tenth as well as these women had known her.

"But I've also been told," he said, with a quick glance at Rachel, "that there was another side to her. Maybe less noble."

"What do you mean?" Annie asked.

He searched for the right words. "That she put off people, that she didn't have a lot of friends beyond your small group. That she could be particularly tough on guys, lead them on, then drop them like a rock."

If he'd expected an angry reaction, he was disappointed. He found only knowing smiles. "I don't know where you heard that," Katie said, "but it's true. She left behind a long trail of broken hearts."

"I should know," Gloria said. "My husband was one of them."

"Really?" Barclay said.

"Yes, really. I got him on the rebound, a few months after Jennifer dumped him. And I'm not ashamed to admit it. Finishing second to Jennifer was no dishonor."

"What's his name?"

"David. David DeLuca. You met him that night at the reunion, too."

Barclay had no memory of him, but pressed on. "Did she have any steady boyfriends? That lasted, I mean? The police gave me her yearbook, and I read a long note from somebody named Ken . . ."

"Ken Younger," Gloria said. "They went together our whole senior year. To the prom and everything. She never dated anyone else that year, as far as I know. But it never went beyond . . . you know . . . dating. I mean, they were never . . . intimate or anything. We would've known. She couldn't have kept that kind of a secret."

Annie added, "She was deathly afraid of getting pregnant. Not only because she was a good Lutheran, but because she knew what it could do to her future. And she was very fixed on her future."

"So what happened to this Ken?" Barclay asked.

Gloria again spoke up. "He was at the five-year reunion," she said. "I remember because he and Jennifer spent some time together, chatting."

"But they didn't come together?" Barclay said.

"No, no," Gloria replied. "She came with me. Neither of us brought a date."

"And none of you has seen or heard about him since?"

They all shook their heads.

He checked his notes. "There was another name in the yearbook. I could barely make it out. David, I think. He wrote, 'Sorry it didn't work out. Can't say I didn't try. Too bad, too sad. Hope you don't regret it some day.' Does that ring any bells?"

"Not my David, I'm sure," Gloria said quickly, her face reddening. "She would never have asked him to sign it."

Barclay paused for a moment, studying her, then went on. "What about Daniel Kimble?"

"A jerk," Jackie snapped. "None of us could understand what Jennifer saw in him. But she thought he was brilliant. A genius. A great artist. We all thought he was an angry, arrogant bastard, if you'll pardon my French."

"So what happened?"

"When she came back from New York, she finally came to her senses . . . and gave him the boot."

Barclay said, "He told police that she'd been getting anonymous phone calls, which she took as threatening. Did she ever mention those to you?"

"Never," they said, almost in unison.

"Okay," he said. "Before we go any further, let me tell you what I'm thinking. Why I asked Katie to arrange this meeting."

As all of them leaned forward, he briefly explained his copycat theory. "At the time of her murder, the police were mainly looking for someone who might have known Jennifer as well as the other two victims. I'm pushing in a different direction." Then, he leaned forward himself. "I want you to again take yourselves back to those high school days and after—to stretch your memories to the max, to remember anything, anyone who in any way acted strangely around Jennifer. Who may have bugged her in some small, almost incidental way. Someone she may have mentioned, even in passing, as pestering or stalking her."

Annie blurted, "I can't believe this! You actually think someone from high school killed Jennifer? Eight years later? That's unbelievable."

"Maybe so," he replied, unruffled, but to reinforce his point, he reluctantly recalled for them his own long-distance crush on Jennifer, and his adolescent feeling of rejection at the time. "I'm looking for somebody like me, I suppose, only more desperate. A sociopath or psychopath in hiding, who could have been the school geek or the star quarterback, for all we know. Someone the police had no reason to suspect."

As he paused for a breath, Jackie said, quietly, "She spoke of you, you know."

"What?" he said. "Who?"

"Jennifer. I remember now that she talked about you. Georgie Porgie from South Dakotie. How could I forget that?"

Barclay could only stare at her.

"She talked about how cute you were when you tried to flirt with her. In English class, wasn't it? You sat behind her or something."

Was she putting him on? He glanced at Rachel. Had she told them what he'd told her at the bar? Not from what he could see now. "I'm surprised," he finally said. "I didn't think she knew I was alive."

"Well, she did . . ."

Gloria broke in. "Forget that. What you're asking us to do we've all done before. Years ago. I couldn't think of anything else for weeks. None of us could."

"I want you to think again," he said. "Together. Take yourselves back. Talk it through. Maybe one memory will jar another. Talk to others who may have known Jennifer less well who are still around."

Katie stood up. "We'll do that," she said, her eyes roving the circle of women. "Starting tonight. After you leave. It's the least we can do."

"Great," he replied. "But there's one other thing. The reason I've asked Rachel to be here tonight."

She perked up as he unfolded a sheaf of papers. "I've written a letter that I'd like you to send to every one of your classmates, Rachel. Just like your reunion letters. And to those in the class ahead of you and behind you, if you can get lists of those names."

Ignoring their puzzled expressions, he passed out copies of the letter, printed on his personal Channel Seven letterhead.

> Dear Classmates,
>
> My name is George Barclay. I'm the News Director at Channel Seven, and, like you, a graduate of Armstrong High. I have been asked to help in a renewed investigation into the brutal, unsolved 1992 murder of another classmate, Jennifer Bartlow.
>
> I, in turn, am asking for your help.
>
> As you may remember, at the time of her death, police believed Jennifer was the victim of a serial rapist and killer—who had also murdered two other women in different parts of the Twin Cities, using remarkably similar methods. Now, almost twenty years later, all three murders remain unsolved.
>
> For reasons I can't divulge here, and which police do not necessarily share, I believe Jennifer may have died at the hands of a different killer, who may have known her—or of her—for many years, perhaps as far back as high school.
>
> Hence, this letter.
>
> I know the police spoke to some of you at the time of Jennifer's death, especially those who knew her well, asking for your help in finding her killer. Now I'm asking all of you—including those who did not know her well or didn't talk to the police at the time—to search your memories for any information, no matter how trivial, that might lead police to her killer.
>
> What kind of information? Anything you now believe might have a bearing on the case and which you may not have thought of or reported at the time. For instance, strange behavior on the part of anyone toward Jennifer. Something suspicious you may have observed, but felt was too unimportant then to mention. Anything that Jennifer may have said to you which now—with the benefit of hindsight—could potentially be important. In short, anything involving Jennifer Bartlow that struck you then, or now, as unusual.
>
> If you have any information you believe may be helpful, please write or call. Perhaps we can provide justice for Jennifer, and closure for her father and friends. For all of us.
>
> Sincerely,
>
> George Barclay

Once they'd finished reading, he asked, "Any reaction?"

J.J., who hadn't seen the letter before, said, "Just for the record, and with all due respect, George, I think it's a long shot. And our friend, Detective Bennett, may not like it, either. Going public, like this."

"Tough," Barclay replied. Then, to Rachel. "I'll pay for the envelopes and the postage and for any staff help you may need. I'd like to get these out as soon as possible."

"Shouldn't be a problem," she replied. "I've got all of the names and addresses on my computer. I'll try to get the lists from the other classes."

"Good."

"But you should know," she added, "that we never could locate a number of classmates. Thirty or forty, I'd guess."

"I'll need their names," he said.

Katie and the other women sat silent for a moment, Then, Katie asked, "What if Mr. Jacobs is right . . . and this doesn't work?"

Barclay shrugged. "We wait for another brilliant idea. But at the moment, I'm fresh out of them."

She sat up straight in her chair. "Then let's get started," she said. "It's about time we did something."

Once back in the car, Barclay asked, "So what did you think?"

"I think we're chasing our tails," J.J. replied. "Tilting at windmills. Whatever."

Barclay smiled. "You have any other suggestions?"

"Not really."

"What'd you think of the women?"

"What do you mean?"

"Your impressions, that's all."

"If I was thirty years younger, I'd like to take a shot at the one in running shorts. Let her wrap those long, lean legs around me."

Barclay laughed as he pulled away from the curb. "Seriously."

"Shit, I don't know." He thought for a moment. "They'll do what you ask, I suppose. Go through the motions, at least. But, except for Katie, I get the feeling the others think it's as hopeless as I do."

"Maybe so," Barclay said.

J.J. turned in his seat. "Speaking of the women, tell me what's going on with you and Rachel?"

"Nothing. We're friends, that's all."

"Oh, yeah?"

"Yeah."

"Then you didn't see what I saw."

Barclay glanced over at him. "What do you mean?"

"The way she looked at you when you were talking."

"Bullshit," Barclay said.

"I'm serious. I could see it in her eyes. Call it admiration. Pride, maybe. Like she was seeing something in you she hadn't seen before."

"That's crazy. You're the one seeing things."

"Have it your way. But I think you may have something going."

Barclay gripped the steering wheel and stared straight ahead, so intent on what J.J. had just told him that neither he nor J.J. noticed the black pickup truck with darkened windows parked halfway down the block, its lights off, motor idling.

Barclay spent much of the next week once again trying to catch up with the routine station work he'd allowed to pile up. He was late in beginning work on next year's newsroom budget, which was always a painful chore, complicated by the possibility that the new owners—if and when they took over—would probably want him to start all over again, imposing their own bottom-line demands.

What's more, negotiations with AFTRA, the union representing many of the newsroom employees, were scheduled to begin in less than a month—an always stressful and time-consuming process that pitted him against his friends and colleagues in the newsroom.

And then there were the sweep series and special reports, still being developed—which required him to sit in on endless meetings with the producers and reporters.

Meantime, he had given John Knowles Rachel's list of missing classmates, thirty-two in all, and asked him to track down as many as he could. Josh Bennett had also called twice, demanding a meeting to discuss his letter, but Barclay had put him off, blaming his heavy workload.

So far, there'd been no further appearances by the station protesters, but he suspected that wouldn't last forever. He knew they'd called a series of community meetings in those areas with heavy minority populations—to generate more support for their cause.

Hawke had also dropped by a few times, demanding to know whether Barclay's people had uncovered the identities of the still unseen—still unnamed—backers of the Coburn group. Barclay had told him to have patience; they were still working on it.

Although not very hard.

On one of the days, before leaving for home, he took time to make the rounds of the newsroom, stopping to chat, looking over shoulders, hoping to get a feel of things again. He'd been stuck in his office for so much of the time, he'd found himself missing the hum and rhythm of the place.

Quiet as it often was.

In his early years, newsrooms were clamorous caverns—wide open, full of clacking typewriters, blaring police and fire frequencies, squawking two-way radios, and by reporters and producers who could only be heard by out-shouting the next guy.

There were fewer women in the newsrooms back then and far grittier language among the men, few of whom were known for the delicacy of their vocabulary. Guys who spent too much time drinking and too little time with their wives. Hence, a lot of drunks and divorces.

Today, things were far more civilized. Thanks to political correctness, common courtesy, and the kind of people who now populated the place. Family men and women, by and large, with growing kids and homes in the suburbs, who tried—with some exceptions—to treat each other and the language with decorum and decency. Who drank beer or wine instead of martinis, who usually went home after work instead of the nearest watering hole.

The muted clicking of computers had replaced the noisy drumbeat of the typewriters, and the cubicles that housed many of the reporters and producers prevented most noise or conversation from escaping. To an outsider, today's newsroom could be mistaken for an insurance office or an accounting firm.

Barclay missed the old days but knew they'd never return. The world had changed and, with it, television and the television newsroom.

Long gone were the days of "real news," as the old-time journalists would have described it. Thanks to cable and the Internet, the business was infused now with a bewildering mixture of information and entertainment. Hard news replaced, in large measure, by celebrity journalism, where a Britney Spears or a Michael Jackson was better known to television viewers than the vice-president of the United States. Where the latest tryst or divorce of a Hollywood star was likely to get as big a play as the latest suicide bombing in the Middle East.

As one of his news buddies said recently, "There's a lot more icing than cake these days."

Barclay had lived through the transformation, fought against it, but in the end was helpless to do much except to go with the flow. He could only hope that he'd live long enough to see the pendulum swing back, to see the country come to its senses and once again value news that actually affected people's lives.

HALFWAY HOME, HE CHANGED his mind and his direction—heading instead for the YW and the loathsome treadmill. *My mind may be mush*, he'd told himself, *but my legs haven't done shit all day. Might as well give them a workout.*

As he approached the Y, he spotted Rachel leaving, gym bag in her hand and a flush on her face. "Hey," he said, hurrying to catch up.

She waited. "George! I didn't know you were coming."

"I didn't, either. Until a couple of minutes ago."

Although the weather had cooled, she was still wearing shorts, sandals, and a sleeveless blouse that dipped around the neck. All white except for orange striping on the blouse and the sandal straps. Against her tanned skin, the outfit was altogether fetching, he thought.

"You have time for a drink?" she asked.

He glanced at his watch. "Sure." The treadmill could wait.

This time, they picked one of the outdoor tables at Brit's, protected from the sinking sun by an oversized umbrella. Before too long, by early October probably, the outdoor tables would be gone—stored away in the face of another chilly fall and the onset of winter. *Enjoy it while we can*, he thought.

As they waited for his beer and her wine, she asked how much weight he'd lost.

"Going on ten pounds," he replied. "Give or take."

"That's marvelous. Amazing, actually."

"Still a long way to go, but it seems to be coming off in the right places. I'm down almost three belt sizes."

"I can tell," she said, leaning back, appraising him. "But you also look tired."

Admitting he was, he quickly related the long days of dealing with office business. "I may be getting too old," he said. "My brain feels like it's been in a blender."

"Phooey," she said. "You just need a good night's sleep."

If only, he thought.

As the waiter arrived with their drinks, and as they continued to talk, he tried to detect any signs of the affection or admiration in her eyes that J.J. claimed to have seen. If they were there, they eluded him. While she certainly was as friendly as ever, there was no hint of anything more. So much for J.J.'s observations, he decided.

"You should know," she said, "that all your letters have been sent out."

"Already?"

"Yup. I printed the labels and got the letters copied yesterday. Katie and the others came over this afternoon to stuff the envelopes."

"You work fast. That's great."

"It'll take another few days to get the lists of the other classes, but those should be out soon, too."

"You're keeping track of the expenses?" he asked.

"Sure, but don't worry about it."

They sat quietly, enjoying a soft breeze that had come up as the sun was setting, whisking away some of Barclay's stored-up tension and fatigue. *This is the way life is supposed to be*, he thought.

Finally, breaking the silence, he said, "You told me at the ballgame that we'd talk about your late husband some day."

"I did?"

"Uh huh."

"It's not something I like to talk about," she said.

"Why?"

"Because it's painful. What's past is past."

"Okay."

Then, studying him, she asked, "Why is it you're so interested?"

"Because I'm interested in you and your life," he replied, hoping he wasn't sounding too forward. "Because I've already told you more about mine than you probably want to know."

She sighed. "If I'd known this was coming, George, I would have ordered a scotch instead of the wine. Maybe two scotches."

He waited.

"This will sound harsh," she finally said, "but the best thing about my life with Joe was the two wonderful kids he gave me. For that, I'll be forever grateful." She took a sip of her wine. "As I look back, I guess we had what you'd call a sterile marriage. He was obsessed with his career, with making more money than we needed or could reasonably spend, to the exclusion of myself—and, to some extent, the kids. Life with Joe was essentially lifeless. Largely sexless. Most of the time, I felt terribly alone, if not physically, certainly emotionally. He simply wasn't there."

"Yet you stayed with him," Barclay said.

"I know. There were the kids. The security. I admit wanting that. Life was empty but comfortable. Built largely around Joe and Colleen. I kept busy. Tried to stay active. To be the dutiful, attentive wife he expected me to be. But it was all a lie—and worst of all, I knew it was a lie. By the time the kids were older and I realized I had to make something more of my life—he was on his death bed." She paused. "Have you heard enough?"

He shrugged. "Up to you."

She looked off into space. "I admit I was terribly hurt when he died. You can't live with someone that long and not share their pain and suffering. It was such a long, horrible process. Excruciating for him and for me. And, of course, for the kids. But I can't lie now; there was also a sense of relief when it was over. Not only because he was finally free. But . . . so was I."

"Since then?" he said.

"Since then . . . as you know . . . I've tried to throw myself back into life. Renewing my old friendships, making new ones. Like you. Getting involved in everything I can . . . trying to build my little decorating business, doing volunteer stuff, getting my body back in shape, keeping current with the kids. Traveling more, I hope."

"And men?" Barclay asked. Now he knew he was being forward.

If she objected, she didn't show it. "For the first year, nothing," she said. "Except for getting hit on by a couple of married men that Joe knew, who figured that his poor widow must be getting lonely by then."

"You're kidding."

"Believe it. Like I needed some kind of sympathy fuck to ease my sorrow."

Barclay was startled. He'd never heard her utter a four-letter word before.

"Needless to say," she went on, "that turned me off for a while. But since then, I've dated a few times. Nothing serious, nothing special. The ones I've seen, in fact, are a lot like Joe . . . distant, self-absorbed . . . and I decided I'd had enough of that." Then, with a smile, "For the record, I don't include you in that group."

"Thanks."

By now, darkness had settled over the sidewalk table and the cool breeze had picked up. Rachel shivered in her sleeveless blouse. "I'm freezing, and I have to get going," she said, getting up.

He got up with her.

"Can I get the bill?" she asked. "You paid last time, I think."

"I'll take care of it. You'll owe me."

"Okay," she said, starting to walk away. "Oh, I forgot. My daughter Colleen's coming back in town the day after tomorrow. She'd like to meet you."

"Fine," Barclay said, hiding his surprise. "Just let me know when."

She walked back, staring up at him for a moment. "Thanks for not being like the others," she said, raising herself up to kiss him lightly on his bearded cheek. Laughing. "See, I don't even need the Kiss Cam."

Then she was walking down the street, gym bag swinging by her side.

By morning, the weather had changed. A warm front had moved in, leaving the sky overcast and the air dripping with humidity. Barclay and Katie Thorson drove through the gates of Crystal Lake Cemetery in north Minneapolis—Jennifer Bartlow's final resting place.

Why he wanted to be here, to see her grave, he couldn't explain, either to himself or to Katie when he'd called her the night before, asking if she'd mind taking him here. "Of course not," she'd said, never asking for an explanation.

So here they were, slowly winding their way through acres and acres of tree-shaded greenery, part of a sprawling expanse in the heart of the city, past countless markers and monuments of every shape and size, scattered in every direction.

"Why was she buried here?" Barclay asked. "It's a long way from her home."

"Her folks grew up near here and her grandparents are buried here," Katie said. "Her mother now, too. It's where the family plot is."

They drove past a stone chapel with stained-glass windows and a bell tower on top, and by one hillside lined with row-upon-row of small white military headstones, many of them weathered and blackened with age, dating back—Barclay guessed—to World War I, if not before.

As they drove, Barclay said, "Rachel tells me you've been getting some strange phone calls."

"A few, but they've stopped now."

"No idea who?"

"No. He never said anything. All I could hear was kind of a wheeze, like he had a chest cold or something."

"Tell me if you get any more, okay?" Barclay said.

"Sure."

She directed him through the cemetery maze, along a series of intersecting, narrow roads until finally they were there. Section 16, a small sign read. Before they got out of the car, Barclay said, "One more thing. What can you tell me about David DeLuca?"

"Gloria's husband?"

"Yes."

She gave him a strange look. "Why do you ask?"

He shrugged. "Gloria said he was one of the guys who got dumped by Jennifer."

She smiled. "One of several, I'm afraid."

He waited.

"He's a nice guy," she finally said. "I knew him back in high school, of course. I was a bridesmaid in their wedding, but I haven't really seen that much of him since. Socially, I mean. We don't get together that often with our husbands. We tend to keep that part of our lives to ourselves."

"How hard did he take the fall?" Barclay asked. "When Jennifer dropped him."

She hesitated. "Hard, I'd guess, but I don't really remember. What are you thinking, anyway?"

"Nothing. I'm just curious. Except for Kimble, I haven't met any of Jennifer's other rejects."

She looked at him, hard. "You certainly don't think he had anything to do with her . . . death, do you?"

"Of course not. I'd have no reason to think that."

Except, he told himself, *for that strange inscription in the yearbook.*

As they got out of the car, she said, "We have to walk a ways," looking toward a small grouping of trees perhaps a half a block away. "It was a day like this when we buried her," she added. "Just as humid. And even hotter. It seemed like we carried that casket for a mile."

"You were a pallbearer?"

"Sure. All four of us were."

They walked slowly, Barclay pausing now and then to study the names on some of the gravestones.

"You wouldn't believe how many people were at the funeral," she said. "Both at the church, and here. Hundreds. The pastor had to use a microphone for the graveside prayers."

"You think most of them knew her?" he asked.

"Of course. But some, I'm sure, were just curious. Drawn by the publicity, by the fact that she'd been murdered. Hard to understand, but it happens, I was told."

She stopped and pointed to a marker a few feet ahead. "It's right there," she said, but stayed back as Barclay approached and stood by it. Remnants of a wilted bouquet of flowers lay nearby, and untrimmed tufts of grass had begun to invade the edges of the rectangular piece of marble. Not far enough, however, to hide the simple, chiseled inscription:

JENNIFER BARTLOW
1966-1992
MAY SHE FIND PEACE

Next to that marker, separated by a grave width, was another.

MARGARET BARTLOW
1937-1994
WIFE, MOTHER

He knelt down and picked at the clumps of grass, brushing and blowing the dirt from the surface of the marble. Tracing the rough, indented outline of Jennifer's name.

"I try to get here every few months," Katie said, walking up. "To do what you're doing. But it's been a while now."

"Did you leave the flowers?" he asked.

"No," she said, picking them up. "Maybe her dad did, although he doesn't get here often these days. Or maybe another of her friends."

She knelt next to him. "Years ago," she said, "I used to come here by myself and sit in the sun. For hours, sometimes. To talk to her. To myself, really."

Barclay turned to her. "What did you talk about?"

She smiled and looked off into the distance. "Everything, really. Our times together. The silly things we did. The fun we had. Serious stuff, too. About my life. My problems. Our friends. Everything and anything." She paused, wiping at her eyes. "Anybody who saw me must have thought I was crazy. Sitting here, alone, talking and laughing to myself. And crying."

"Can we sit for a minute, too?" he asked.

"If you'd like," she said, as they both settled down on the grass.

"What else?" he asked.

"What else did I talk to her about?"

"Yes."

"Golly, you name it. What was. What could have been. She was a dreamer, you know. She couldn't stop talking about the future. What it might hold for both of us. So I'd sit here and tell her what a great actress she'd be by now . . . on Broadway, in the movies. Married to some Hollywood hunk, with gorgeous kids and a nanny. Living in a mansion in Beverly Hills, with gates and guards and two Jaguars and a Ferrari in the driveway."

Barclay chuckled. "That's quite a picture."

"It probably wouldn't have happened," she went on, "but I'd like to think it might have. She had that kind of talent. And drive."

"Which turned some people off, right?"

"What do you mean?"

"What we talked about the other night at your place," he said, leaning back on his elbows. "Her drive. Ambition. Arrogance, maybe. I keep hearing how she could antagonize people. Her acid tongue and all."

"You're right," Katie laughed. "She wasn't all sweetness and light. She suffered no fools."

"Including me."

She laughed again. "It was the actress in her. She loved that role. Loved verbal combat. To match wits. She hated to lose. And could strike out if she thought someone was getting the better of her."

"I remember," Barclay said, thinking back to English class. "But she pretty much ignored me. I was all but invisible to her."

"I'm sorry you didn't get to know her better. She had a good heart. Trust me on that. There's nothing she wouldn't do for us. She was always there when we needed her. We may have been the same age, but she was more like a big sister to all of us."

They sat a few minutes longer, saying nothing, lost in their own memories. By then, the sky had grown darker, with distant flashes of lightning visible off to the west.

As they got up, Barclay took one of the withered flowers from her hand, fingering it, watching as the remaining petals fell. "How long do you think these flowers have been here?" he asked.

Katie held them up. "A week or more, I'd say. They're in pretty bad shape."

"Do me another favor," Barclay said. "When you talk to your friends, ask if any of them have been here recently and brought the flowers. Maybe check with Jennifer's dad, too."

"Sure," she said, "but why?"

"Just curious. It'd be nice to know who's been here visiting her."

JENNIFER WAS BACK. In the gloom of his bedroom. Standing, in the corner, smiling, her naked body obscured by the shadows. "Georgie, Porgie," she whispered. "Where ever have you been?" She moved closer, floating, leaning over the end of the bed, her pale skin caught now in a sliver of the moon's soft rays passing through the window. Her hand was atop the thin sheet, moving up his leg, slowly, tantalizingly. "Poor Georgie," she breathed, touching him, caressing him. "Oh, how I've missed you."

When he awoke, it was just in time.

23

When he showed up at Rachel's condo, Barclay was surprised to find, not Rachel at the door, but a young woman who must be daughter Colleen. "Hi," he said, quickly looking past her, "I'm George Barclay."

"And I'm Colleen," she replied. "Come in."

He hesitated. "Am I early?"

"No, no," she said, stepping aside. "Mom just realized she was out of beer, and ran out to get some."

He walked past her. "I hope she's not doing that for me," he said.

"For both of us, I think."

He stood awkwardly a moment, unsure of what to do or say next.

"I'm in the kitchen," she said. "Mixing the salad."

As he followed her there, he found it impossible not to admire her slim figure, hips and legs nicely encased in a pair of black Capri pants that also showed off a well-rounded bottom.

Behave yourself, he thought.

"I hope you like chicken breast," she said, "because that's what's on the menu."

"Sounds great," he replied.

If Colleen wasn't a younger mirror-image of her mother, she was close to it. The same slender, well-tanned face, a smattering of freckles, auburn hair that dropped in ringlets to her shoulders, and eyes that seemed to change from green to blue, depending on the light. And a smile that would delight any dentist.

"So," she said, "I'm glad you could make it. Both Joe and Mom have told me a lot about you."

"Like?"

Turning, with a grin, "Like you're quite shy, for one thing."

He returned the grin. "I prefer to think of it as reserved."

She laughed. Her mother's laugh. "She also said you can be a funny man."

He didn't know what to say to that.

"Seriously," she said, as she tossed the salad, "and I don't mean to embarrass you, but I think you've brought a little light into Mom's life. She must enjoy your friendship, or she wouldn't talk about you as much as she does."

Barclay settled onto a kitchen stool. "That's nice to hear," he offered. "I feel the same way."

"And I know she admires what you're trying to do in Jennifer Bartlow's murder. She feels like she's helping a private eye."

He chuckled. "That's more romantic than it is, I'm afraid."

At that moment, they heard the front door open and close. A moment later, Rachel walked into the kitchen lugging a six-pack of Amstel Light. "Hi, there," she said, setting the beer on the counter and giving him a quick, unembarrassed hug. "Sorry I wasn't here to greet you."

"No problem," he said, "but you should have called me. I would have brought the beer."

"It was no trouble," she replied, opening two of the beers for him and Colleen, and a glass of wine for herself. Then she checked the oven. The succulent smell of the roasting chicken filled the kitchen. Barclay breathed it in, savoring the aroma.

"Smells wonderful," he said.

"Hope you're hungry."

"Famished, actually. I've been looking forward to this."

"Be patient. It'll be a little while."

As they retreated to the living room with their drinks, Colleen glanced at him. "Mother tells me you've been losing weight."

"Trying," he replied. "One day at a time."

"I think you look great," she said.

What else could she say? he thought.

Colleen, it turned out, was in her third year at Boston College, hoping to get into med school and become a pediatrician some day. "I love kids, and I'd love to be a doctor, but I'm not sure I'm smart enough," she said, "or have the patience and persistence it'd take. I'll have to wait and see."

Barclay, at her urging, talked about his own time at Northwestern, his various television jobs, and how he'd come to be at Channel Seven. "They were looking for someone who had his roots in the Midwest, who knew the area and some of its history. They just happened to find me."

The conversation was easy, the time passing quickly, and when dinner came, it lived up to its kitchen aromas. Roasted chicken breasts, alongside whipped potatoes, green beans, and Colleen's salad. Barclay hadn't eaten this well since his last dinner here, but again, he was mindful of his portions—refusing second helpings, determined to leave the table slightly hungry.

After dinner, as he helped clear the table and fill the dishwasher, Rachel asked if there was anything new in the investigation. "Not much," he admitted, "but, to be honest, I've been too busy to think much about it."

"Any replies to the letters?"

"A few, but nothing very helpful."

As they spent another half hour talking, sipping after-dinner coffee, Rachel revealed that she had found yet another new decorating client. "It's not much," she said, "just helping out with some color selections and artwork, but it's one more name on the list. And if they like what I do, they might refer some of their empty-nester friends who also plan to move into the city."

"Congratulations," he said. "Maybe you can add me to your list soon."

"Just tell me when."

Later, as he was leaving, Rachel asked if he needed a ride. "No, I got lazy and drove."

"Then I'll walk you to your car."

Colleen, who had left them alone after dinner, reappeared at the door to say good-bye. "I'm glad we could meet," she said, gripping his hand warmly. Then, with a nod toward her mother, added, "And take care of her, okay?"

He laughed. "She takes pretty good care of herself."

WHEN THEY HIT THE STREET, Barclay was surprised to find it already dark. The late summer days were growing shorter. As they walked toward his car parked just down the street, he stopped short. Even in the pale light, he sensed something was wrong.

"Stay here," he told Rachel as he moved slowly toward the old Buick.

"What's wrong?" There was confusion in her voice.

"Don't know. Just stay back, please."

There was a streetlight at either end of the block, but here, in the middle, the shadows were deep, and—at that moment—foreboding. He could see no one else on the street as he walked warily toward the car. Rachel hung back. "George? What's going on?"

He held up his hand, glancing in every direction. Now fifteen feet away, moving closer, he could see what the shadows had hidden. Every window of the Buick was shattered, caved in, leaving tangled webs of splintered glass, the shards littering the battered and dented hood and trunk, and along the street and sidewalk.

He walked closer, his feet crunching on the broken glass.

"George, what is it?"

He looked over his shoulder. "Go back inside, Rachel. Please. Do it now."

She walked closer. "Not until you tell me what's happened."

"Someone took a sledgehammer to my car."

"What?" She hurried ahead, ignoring his orders. "My, God," she said, staring at the battered wreck. "Who could have done this?"

And why had no one heard or seen it? he wondered.

The car seemed to be sitting lower. He bent down, seeing for the first time that every tire had been punctured and flattened.

"Son of a bitch," he muttered.

Rachel grabbed his arm. "We have to call the police," she said.

"We will, but it probably won't do much good." Then he saw that every other car within view, on both sides of the street, appeared to be untouched. "I think somebody got one of my letters."

"What?"

"Nothing. Forget it."

Then she saw the same thing. "Somebody singled you out? Picked you out on purpose?" He could hear the disbelief in her voice.

"Looks that way," he replied, taking his cell phone off his belt.

"But who?"

"Don't know."

"Are you calling the police?"

"Yeah. Then the station. Then my insurance guy. Then a tow truck to get this hulk to the junkyard."

Rachel grabbed his hand. "I can't believe it! Right here on my street. I'm so sorry."

"Hell, it's not your fault. Besides, I needed a new car anyway."

She put her head on his shoulder and he thought he could feel a small shudder.

The cops came and wrote a brief report, commiserating with him as they surveyed the damage, shrugging off the fact that his car was the only one attacked. "Damn shame," one of them said. "Fuckin' kids got no respect for private property." His partner was more philosophical. "You're lucky it's just an old beater."

"That's no beater," Barclay objected. "That's a Buick."

The cop eyed him. "Yeah, right."

"You want us to call the tow?" asked the first.

"I already have," Barclay said. "Triple-A."

"Good enough," one said as they got back into their squad car. "We'll write up the report and get the street guys down here to clean up the mess. And, good luck, fella."

"Thanks," he replied, watching them drive away. *Pricks.*

By now, a small group had gathered on the sidewalk, drawn by the squad car's flashing lights.

"Any of you see or hear anything?" Barclay asked.

One older woman stepped forward, hesitantly. "I heard some banging," she said. "And glass breaking. But I thought they might be collecting the trash."

"At this time of night?"

She shrugged and began to walk away.

"So you didn't see anyone?"

She shook her head. "It was too dark," she replied, disappearing into one of the buildings.

"Anyone else?" he asked.

No one else stepped forward. One by one, they began to depart.

Jeff Parkett was the next to arrive, driving up in one of the station news cars. "The desk called me," he said, getting out, eyeing the wreck. "Goddamn, George, how'd you do that sitting at the curb?"

"It was no accident. Somebody beat the crap out of it."

"No kidding," he said, taking a closer look, walking around the wreckage. "Want a cameraman down here to shoot it?"

"Don't bother. I'll remember what it looks like."

"You know who did it?"

"No idea."

Parkett moved closer, lowering his voice. "This have anything to do with that personal project of yours?"

"Could be," Barclay said.

"Want to tell me about it now?"

"No."

"Have it your way. You need a ride?"

"I need your car. I'll drop you back at the station."

"No sweat," he replied, handing him the keys. "Anything else?"

"Yeah. Tell the desk to forget about this. You, too."

As they waited for the tow truck, Rachel reappeared with Colleen by her side. "This is horrible," Colleen said. "Unbelievable." Looking at her mother, "I thought this was a safe neighborhood."

"It's not the neighborhood," Barclay said. "This was personal."

"Really? But why?"

He looked at Rachel. "I've got a good guess."

Rachel drew back.

"If it was personal," he said, "then whoever followed me might know why I was here. I want you to be careful, Rachel. I don't know who or what we're dealing with, but you've gotta be cautious. Keep your eyes open."

"You're serious, aren't you?" she said.

"Yes."

As they talked, the tow truck finally pulled up, the driver scratching his head as he surveyed the wreck. "What the hell we got here?" he asked.

"A mess," Barclay replied.

"Looks like a goddamned train hit it. What'd you want me to do with it?"

"The scrap heap."

"Not tonight. I'll have to take it to our lot."

"Okay," Barclay said, knowing his insurance man would want to see it, anyway.

As the driver began to load the heap of dented metal and shattered glass onto his truck, Barclay urged Rachel and Colleen to go back inside. "I've got to get home and make some calls," he said. "Try to figure this out."

Rachel squeezed his hand. "Be careful," she said. "And call me."

"You, too," he said, wondering again what the hell he'd gotten them both into.

ONCE HE'D DROPPED PARKETT OFF at the station, and while keeping his eye on the rear-view mirror, Barclay drove back to the condominium, parking the car securely inside the garage.

And inside the condo, after tending to an impatient and disgruntled Seuss, he put in a call to John Jacobs. Getting no answer at his home, he tried O'Gara's. "Yeah, he's here," someone said. "Hang on."

Barclay waited.

"Hello?" The background noise was deafening. "Who's this?"

"Barclay."

"Hey, George. Lemme' get away from the noise."

Barclay waited again.

"You there? What's going on?" The babble was better, but not much.

"There's trouble in River City," Barclay said, his voice raised.

"What do you mean?"

He told him.

"No shit. You okay?"

"I'm fine, but my car's headed for the crusher."

There was a long pause. Finally, "So what do you think?"

"I think we should talk," Barclay said. "Soon."

"Tonight?"

"Tomorrow morning. I'll buy breakfast. The Hilton. 7:30."

J.J. groaned. "I don't get up 'til ten."

"Make an exception."

Another groan. "For you, okay. I'll see you then."

WHEN BARCLAY SHOWED UP AT THE HILTON, he found not only J.J., but Josh Bennett, as well. "He wanted to come," J.J. said simply. "Said you'd been avoiding him."

"Not exactly," Barclay said, settling into a chair.

"What would you call it?" Bennett asked.

"Being up to my ass in alligators," he replied, tiredly.

"You do look like hell," J.J. observed. "Don't you sleep at night?"

"Not a lot," he admitted.

When the waiter arrived to take their orders, Barclay settled for orange juice, unbuttered toast, a bowl of Grape Nuts, and a large glass of skim milk, then watched enviously as the other two ordered bacon and eggs and hash browns.

Bennett paused until the waiter left. "J.J. told me about your car. Totaled, he says."

"Totaled," Barclay agreed.

"The cops made a report?"

"Yeah, but they blew it off. Blamed it on kids."

"So what do you think?"

"That it was a warning," he said, cautiously, "from someone who either got one of my letters or heard about it in some other way. Someone who doesn't like me poking around in the past. Who thinks the whole thing should be forgotten, that Jennifer be allowed to rest in peace, if that's what you can call it."

"Her killer?"

He shrugged. "Maybe. But it could be anybody who doesn't want the whole thing dragged up again. Maybe somebody like that ex-boyfriend of hers, Kimble. Not only is he a mean bastard, but he made it clear to me that he thinks what's past is past. To quote him, 'I'd leave it that way, if I were you.'"

He paused as their breakfasts arrived. "This is not my imagination, guys. Trust me. I don't have enemies that'd go around wrecking my car. I've never been threatened in my life. A few of my reporters have, but not me. And I don't like the feeling. And I don't like Rachel and Katie Thorson getting those anonymous phone calls. That didn't happen before all of this began. And it can't be a coincidence."

Bennett took out a small notebook and pen. "Where's your car? I'd like to take a look at it."

"Why?"

"To see it for myself. Maybe have our crime lab guys go over it."

Barclay gave him the address of the towing company lot.

"And where does this Kimble live?"

"You're going to talk to him?"

"Maybe."

"That'll piss him off, for sure," Barclay said, reciting Kimble's address.

"In the meantime," Bennett went on, repeating the same advice Barclay had given Rachel. "I'd be careful. Watch your back. Whoever did this to your car may want to take a whack at you."

"So you agree," Barclay said, "that there may be something to all of this?"

"Could be. It's worth checking, anyway."

"Good," Barclay said. Then, "Have you heard anything from the cops in Minneapolis and Brooklyn Center?"

"Yeah, finally. They're trying to dig out the files. But who knows how long that'll take."

After Bennett left, J.J. asked Barclay, "Where are you heading now?"

"To look for a new car," he replied.

"I'll tag along, if you don't mind. Watch that back of yours."

To his dismay, when Barclay walked into the station later that morning, he found that word of his crushed car had spread through the newsroom. Several people stopped by to offer their condolences. "You really loved that car, didn't you?" one of them said.

"Yeah, I did," he replied. "We'd been together a long time."

"Know who did it?"

"Not yet," he said. "Probably never will."

Parkett was waiting by his office. "You get a new one?"

"Just now."

"What kind?"

"Guess."

"A Buick."

"Of course," Barclay said as he entered his office, immediately struck by the pile of papers on his desk. "Shit," he muttered, picking through the stack. There was a lot of routine paperwork, but also a number of what appeared to be Armstrong alumni letters.

Parkett was still parked at the office door. "Knowles wants to see you. Said to give him a call."

"Okay," Barclay replied, thumbing through the letters.

"Ready now to tell me what's going on?"

Barclay looked up. "Soon."

"Somebody out to get you?"

Barclay was getting irritated. "Look, Jeff, I don't know. Okay? I'm hip-deep in shit right now and trying to dig my way out. I'll fill you in when the time's right."

"I just want to help."

Barclay threw a paper clip at him. "You can help by getting the hell out of my office."

"Okay, okay," he said, backing out. "Relax."

Barclay settled in behind his desk. There were probably a dozen letters, mostly notes which—like the earlier ones—offered little except encouragement. One, however, was different. The writing was scribbled, but readable.

"I don't know if this will help," the letter read, "but one of the guys in eleventh-grade Chemistry was constantly bugging Jennifer. Flirting, rubbing against her. Trying to get a quick feel. I know because I sat next to them and could see what was going on. He thought it was a big joke, but I could tell she didn't like it. Even complained to the teacher, I think. I don't remember the guy's name, but he was a big dude with a face full of acne. May have played on the football team. The teacher was Mr. Hatcher, but I think he died several years ago."

The letter went on, "The police never talked to me, and I didn't talk to them. Didn't think it was important at the time. But your letter reminded me of it, and I'm glad to get it off my chest. Hope it helps."

Then, there was a P.S. "I'm not giving you my name because I don't want to get more involved. Hope you understand. And Good Luck."

Barclay put in a quick call to Rachel, reciting parts of the letter. "Do you remember a big guy with acne? May have played football."

There was a pause on the other end. "Not really," she said. "There were a lot of big guys with acne."

"He was in Chemistry with Jennifer. Talk to Katie and the others, will you? It might be important."

"Will do. Are you okay?"

"I'm fine. Even got a new car."

"Really? So quick?"

"Yup. I'll give you a ride."

"Good. I'll call you back."

He put the letter aside and was glancing at the others when Hawke suddenly appeared at his door, closing it behind him. "Want to tell me what the hell's going on?"

Damn, Barclay thought. The news had reached the second floor.

"Have you been screwing some married lady?" Hawke demanded.

Barclay couldn't help but laugh. "Why in the world," he finally managed, "would you ask that?"

"Because that's what pissed off, cuckolded husbands do. Take sledge hammers to cars."

This was hilarious. "No," he sputtered. "I don't go around screwing married ladies. Not that I wouldn't like to."

"Then what *is* going on?"

"The cops think kids did it," he replied, stifling his laugh. "All I know is that I had to buy a new car."

"But you're okay?"

"Sure."

Hawke got up and looked around. "Well, good," he said. Then, "I thought I told you to clean this place up."

"It's next on my to-do list," Barclay replied, swallowing hard.

"I hope so," Hawke said. Then he was gone.

KNOWLES WAS WAITING IN HIS OFFICE when Barclay arrived. "Heard about your car," he said. "Too bad."

"Thanks."

"The price of poker may be going up," Knowles added. "I'd watch your ass."

"I've heard that before," Barclay replied.

Knowles then spread out a pile of papers on the desk. "Here's the stuff on the missing classmates," he said. "I've found twenty-one of the thirty-two so far, most of them living out of state, a lot of them in California or out East, which is no surprise. I can't tell you much more about them, except I found no red flags."

"You said 'most.'"

"Glad you caught that. Two of them have actually spent time in prison. One, in fact, is still there."

"No shit," Barclay said. "Who?"

Knowles shuffled through the papers. "Here," he said, picking out two of the sheets. "Tim Eliason and Harvey Pinkston. Eliason got two years for robbery and assault in the mid-nineties, then spent another year for violating probation. He's out now, but still on probation."

"The other guy?"

"More interesting. Pinkston's still behind bars for the rape and attempted murder of an ex-girlfriend. Happened a couple of years ago. He tried to strangle her."

"With a belt?"

"I don't know," Knowles said. "I'm still checking."

Barclay leaned back. "So how did you get all this?"

"From the data bases kept by the Department of Corrections and the Bureau of Criminal Apprehension. You can find almost anything about anybody if you know where to look."

"Sweet," Barclay said.

"Which brings me to the next point."

"Which is?"

"If you'll get me the names of all the men who got your letters, I'll try to find if there are others with a criminal history."

"There are hundreds of names," Barclay said. "It'll take forever."

"Not really. It goes pretty quick with the system I've set up."

"All right. You might start with one name."

"Who's that?"

"A guy named Ken Younger. Jennifer went steady with him through their senior year. But her friends haven't seen or heard about him since their five-year reunion."

"Good. Anything else?"

"Yeah," Barclay said, retrieving the anonymous letter he'd received that morning.

Knowles read it quickly. "Not much of a description of the guy," he said.

"I know."

"I'll see what I can do."

AT HOME THAT NIGHT, BARCLAY took out Jennifer's yearbook again, turning page after page, studying the individual pictures of the senior men. Looking for a big guy with acne. But with a class of over six hundred, about half of them male, and with the pictures touched up—he presumed—to hide any trace of facial imperfections, it proved to be an impossible task.

He also studied the group pictures of the Armstrong football team, but found they were taken from too great a distance, making the details of one face all but indistinguishable from the next.

He snapped the book shut, but not before taking a quick peek at his own class photo. He could hardly recognize himself, with his narrow, beardless face, goofy haircut, and wide-eyed expression. *Talk about a class geek*, he thought.

A few minutes later, Rachel was on the phone—telling him that none of the women could remember any one guy who matched that particular description. "I'm not surprised," Barclay said, relating the results of his own yearbook search. "It looks like a dead end."

The phone went silent for a moment. "You sound discouraged," she said. "Are you?"

"A little, I guess. But I'll get over it."

"Anything I can do?"

"Nothing more I can think of."

"When do I get to ride in that new car of yours?"

"Anytime you'd like."

"On a real date?"

Barclay was stunned, suddenly speechless. Then, collecting himself, "A real date? Or a pity date?"

She laughed. "I think we should have dinner somewhere nice and go dancing. I haven't danced since the reunion. And I love to dance."

Barclay hadn't danced since . . . he couldn't remember when. "I told you once, I'm not much of a dancer."

"That was before you lost twelve pounds," she said.

"Fifteen, actually."

"Even better. You'll spin me around like a top."

"And hope I don't fall on you."

She laughed again. "It's a deal then," she said. "When?"

They agreed on the next Saturday night.

"I'll make all the arrangements," she said. "You just need to bring your dancing shoes."

As if he had any.

Jeff Parkett pushed his way into Barclay's office. "Better come quick. Security's holding some maniac in the outer lobby who's demanding to see you. It's getting ugly."

Barclay pulled himself out of his chair and followed Parkett through the newsroom and down the long hallway. From a distance, he could see two of the security guards struggling to hold the man, one on each arm, pressing him against the wall, avoiding his kicks. And despite the glass security door, he could hear the man's muffled shouts and angry epithets.

Parkett got to the door first, his linebacker body blocking Barclay's way. "Hang tight," he said. "Let me see what's going on."

Still breathing heavily from the run down the hall, Barclay was happy to oblige. Looking over Parkett's broad shoulders, he tried to get a glimpse of the man—but his back was now facing them.

Parkett pushed the door open. "What's going on here?" he demanded.

It was then that the man turned, his face twisted with anger. "Get these goons off me," he bellowed, trying again to break free.

Barclay recognized him immediately. Daniel Steven Kimble.

"Calm down," Parkett warned, nose-to-nose with Kimble.

He stopped struggling momentarily, but remained in the guards' clutches.

"Now what's the problem?" Parkett demanded.

Kimble caught sight of Barclay. "Him!" he shouted. "He's the problem."

Parkett turned as Barclay came through the door. "You know this guy?"

Barclay nodded. "Yeah, I know him. Let him go."

"Not yet," Parkett said. Then, to the guards, "Pat him down."

While one of the guards continued to hold him, the other did as he was told. He found nothing.

"Okay," Parkett said, still standing between Kimble and Barclay. "You ready to settle down?"

Kimble nodded, but his feverish eyes never left Barclay.

"Take him to the conference room," Barclay told the guards. "Stay with him. I'll be there in a minute."

As the guards escorted him down the hallway, Parkett said, "Ready to tell me *now* what the hell's going on?"

"When I'm done with him," Barclay replied. "It's time you know."

HE FOUND KIMBLE SITTING CALMLY at one end of the conference table, his hands folded in front of him. "You can leave us alone," Barclay told the guards. "But stay close to the door, and if you hear anything unusual—like me getting strangled—I want you to take this guy down. Got it?"

The guards gave him a curious look and left. Barclay stood at one end of the table, near the door, with Kimble at the other end. "Okay," he said, "now that you've calmed down, what's going on?"

Kimble spit out the words. "You sicced the cops on me. A goddamned detective shows up at my door, demanding to know where the hell I was Thursday night. He parked his squad car in front of my house, where all the neighbors could see. I told him to fuck off."

Barclay listened impassively. "You should watch that temper of yours. It'll get you in all kinds of trouble."

Kimble leaned forward, his face reddening. "Stuff it."

"Have it your way, but for the record, I didn't sic the cops on you. They did it on their own. My car got all smashed up Thursday night, by somebody who apparently doesn't like me. Your name was one of the first that came to mind."

"Why me?" he shot back.

"Because you were a belligerent bastard when I was at your house and tried to ask a few simple questions about Jennifer Bartlow. Because you basically threatened me for nosing around you and the past."

"I've got a right to my privacy," he declared.

"And I've got a right not to have my car broken to bits."

"But that has nothing to do with me."

"Maybe not, but the cops wanted to make sure."

Kimble settled back in his chair. "It's none of your goddamned business, but I was at Orchestra Hall Thursday night. I've still got the ticket stub to prove it." With that, he pulled out the stub and pushed it down the table. Then, "And I still don't get what all of this has to do with Jennifer."

Barclay hesitated, but then decided to tell him about his investigation and his letter to Armstrong alumni. "I may be way off base," he said, when he'd finished, "but I think I rattled somebody's cage. I don't have that many enemies."

What little remained of Kimble's anger seemed to evaporate. "Look," he said, "I loved Jennifer, okay? More than you or anybody else will ever know. There's no way I could ever have hurt her."

Barclay watched him carefully. He was near tears. Hard not to believe him. "So tell me," he asked. "Why did she break things off?"

Kimble shrugged. "I wish I knew." He paused. "New York changed her. When she got back, she said she wanted more room, more freedom. Said I was too possessive, too serious. And I suppose I was. But only because I wanted to make a life with her."

Then, "And her friends never liked me. I don't know why, but they kept pushing Jennifer to dump me. Finally, she did. End of story."

Barclay got up and balanced himself on the edge of the conference table. "Now that you know what I think . . . what do you think? Could Jennifer have been killed by someone she might have known?"

"I just don't know . . ."

"Except for her girlfriends," Barclay pressed, "you were closer to her than anyone back then. Think back. Besides the phone calls, did she ever talk about being harassed in any way? Even in the distant past?"

Kimble shook his head slowly. "Not that I can remember," he said. "She never had any enemies I knew about. The calls bothered her, of course, but she never mentioned anything else that I can recall."

"Give it some more thought, will you?" Barclay said. "And call me if you come up with anything."

"I will," Kimble replied, getting up. "And I'm sorry for causing the ruckus. I was pissed off."

"I understand. But, like I told you at the house, I'm not your enemy."

AS PROMISED, ONCE KIMBLE LEFT, Barclay took Parkett aside and briefed him on the details of his investigation.

"That's a hell of a story," Parkett said. "Maybe the biggest of your life if you can help nab this guy."

"That's a big maybe."

"Anything I can do to help?"

"Just keep things going here. And keep quiet about all of this. I don't want Hawke or anybody else to know what's going on."

"Not a problem. Just take care of yourself."

THE CALL FROM JOSH BENNETT CAME a few minutes later. "You didn't touch your car, did you? When you found it?"

"I don't think so," Barclay replied, trying to recall. "Why?"

"We found blood on some of the splintered glass. Your buddy may have cut himself while doing the dirty work."

"Good. I hope he bled to death."

"Sorry. There wasn't that much blood. We're analyzing it now, but it probably won't tell us much, except the type."

"Anything else?" Barclay asked.

"Not really. We've got the car in our garage, going over it more carefully. I'll keep you informed."

LATE THAT AFTERNOON, as he was about to leave, Harry Wilson, on the assignment desk, stopped him. "Thought you should know that some guy's called three or four times, asking for your home address and phone number."

"What guy?"

"He wouldn't leave his name," Wilson said. "Said he's an old friend."

An old friend? Strange, Barclay thought. "I hope you didn't tell him anything."

"Of course not. He said he'd find out some other way."

"Okay. Let me know if he calls again."

In ordinary times, he wouldn't have thought much more about it. But these weren't ordinary times. Not with his investigation partially in the open, and his battered car in the police garage.

It was time for caution.

Now, whenever leaving the station or the condo, he'd pause for a moment to survey his surroundings—glancing in each direction, feeling somewhat foolish in the process.

Fear had never been part of his life. Aside from a near head-on collision with a semi years before, he'd never really felt fear for himself. For a couple of his reporters, yes, when they'd put themselves in perilous situations. And almost every day for the pilot of the station helicopter, and whoever happened to be riding along, knowing that many news helicopters had gone down over the years.

And while he didn't exactly feel fear now, he was apprehensive. He couldn't easily forget the sight of his old Buick, and what one angry man with a purpose and a sledge hammer could do to a ton and a half of metal and glass.

All he could do, he told himself, was to stay on guard, and hope for the best.

AS IF LIFE WASN'T COMPLICATED ENOUGH, when he got home he was surprised—shocked—to find a message from Stanley Hoffer, the general manager of Channel Ten, their major television rival. "Sorry to bother you at home," the message said, "but I want you to know that if things get rough for you over there, I'd be happy to discuss opportunities here at Channel Ten. I've always admired you as a competitor and would be delighted to work with you as a colleague." Then, "This is in confidence, of course. Let me know if you're interested."

The message ended with Hoffer providing his home and cell phone numbers.

Damn, Barclay thought. *That's all I need.*

Despite the turmoil at his own station, the idea of working for a competitor had never entered his mind. Could he actually do it? Legally, there'd be no problem; he had no non-compete clause and no legal obligation to provide Hawke with anything more than a two-week notice.

But that was not the issue.

The idea of crossing the street, of working for the other guys, was—at first blush—unthinkable. To say good-bye to everything and everyone he had held dear for so long, to walk into a strange newsroom and suddenly work for the very people he had been trying to whip for all these years . . . well, he just couldn't imagine it.

Yet Hawke and the others at Channel Seven had made decisions that could dramatically affect his life without his knowledge or consent. If they succeeded, life under the new owners would likely be as different—maybe worse—than it would be working for Hoffer at Channel Ten.

Others had made the jump in the past. Not often, and not many, but switching stations was not unheard of, especially as the news business changed and old loyalties faded. And, the more he thought about it, there could be worse places to work: Channel Ten, like his own station, was still locally owned, and apparently still committed to providing a strong local news product.

What's more, he thought, it would provide a new challenge. Force him to meet new people, hear new ideas. Develop a new newsroom. Feed his competitive juices. Especially if he would be facing new owners at Channel Seven.

And—it would allow him to remain in the Twin Cities.

A few weeks ago, he would have laughed the call off. But, now, surprising even himself, he tucked away Hoffer's numbers. Who knew what the future might hold?

27

Seuss lay sprawled on the edge of the bed, watching intently as Barclay stood in front of the mirror, struggling to tie his goddamned necktie. Each attempt had ended with one end of the tie longer than the other, until finally, after the sixth try, he figured they were about as close as they were ever going to get.

He stood back from the mirror, examining himself. The new suit was two sizes smaller than the one he'd worn to the reunion. Dark gray, close to the tint of his graying beard, and lightweight enough—he hoped—to keep him from sweating too much. His white shirt, too, was aimed at minimizing any sign of perspiration should the jacket have to come off some time during the evening.

"What do you think, Seuss? Pretty spiffy, huh?"

The cat yawned.

He took one more glance in the mirror. He was looking better. Not great, but better. The exercise program had not only helped shed the pounds, but lifting weights—which he'd also begun to do—had started to firm up his body. Still a long way to go, he thought, but not bad. Presentable, at least.

He'd spent the past two hours showering, trimming his beard, even giving himself a manicure. He couldn't remember the last time he'd done that. Nor, for that matter, could he remember his last real date. With Monica, maybe, although there had been a few go-nowhere blind dates since. But certainly no outing that had prompted this much effort.

His preparations were interrupted once by a phone call from his mother, who was more excited than he to learn that he was actually going out. "Who is this girl?" she'd asked. "Do I know her?"

"She's not a girl, Mom. She's a woman. My age. And, no, you don't know her."

"Is she nice?"

"Very nice, yes."

"A single woman?"

"A widow, Mom. With two kids. Both in college."

That had stopped her for a moment. "Really? And she's your age?"

His mother had never stopped thinking of him as a twenty-something. "Yes, Mom. She married quite young."

She would have pressed on with more questions, but he'd begged off, saying he had to get ready.

"I'll call you in the morning," she'd said. "To see how it went."

"I might not be here in the morning," he'd replied.

"What? George, you behave!"

"Bye, Mom."

He could picture her—rushing to repeat the conversation to his father. Who'd probably be thinking: Good, he may finally get laid.

RACHEL WAS WAITING AT THE DOOR of her building when he pulled up. He was out of the car and holding the passenger door open by the time she got down the steps, treading carefully on semi-high heels. She stopped a few feet away. "Wow," she said, admiring the new Buick. "Look at that."

But Barclay was looking at her. Wearing the same green silk dress she'd worn the night of the reunion, clinging to her, accentuating but not flaunting the soft curves of her body. Over her bare shoulders, a slightly-darker green sweater, loosely-knotted in front, as a hedge against the cool evening air.

"Forget the car," he said. "Look at you. You're gorgeous."

She laughed. "Aren't you sweet," she said. "Is that a new suit?"

"Just off the rack. Haven't even spilled on it yet."

She laughed again, walking the length of the car, trailing her hand along the polished blue finish. "I love blue," she said. Then she ducked her head inside. "And leather seats, too. My goodness."

"Heated, I'll have you know," he replied proudly.

"I'm doubly impressed," she said, slipping in.

He closed the door after her, then took a quick look around. He'd been cautious driving here, but traffic was light on this Saturday night and he'd spotted nothing suspicious.

"So where are we going?" he asked, pulling away from the curb.

"To Angelo's," she replied. "The seafood's great, and they've got a small combo and a nice dance floor."

Barclay had never been there, but he'd heard about it. Located in suburban Bloomington, it had a reputation as a quiet, classy, pricey restaurant.

"So you've been there before?" he asked.

"Several times. You haven't?"

"Afraid not."

"Then it's about time," she said, moving a little closer to him, allowing him a whiff of whatever delicious scent she was wearing. He could happily breathe that in all night long.

As they drove, she asked about the investigation and what, if anything, new was happening at the station. He told her about the confrontation with Steven Kimble and the later phone message from the GM at Channel Ten.

"Would you actually consider that?" she asked.

"Probably not. But it's nice to know there may be something to fall back on, if worse comes to worse."

"I just can't see you doing it," she said. "Not after all of the wonderful things you've said about the station and the people there."

"I know," he admitted. "But all of that could change."

ANGELO'S WAS EVEN MORE ELEGANT than Barclay had imagined: small and intimate, with subdued lighting—the atmosphere sweetened by the lilting music of a small combo. Piano, clarinet, drums, and bass. Something from Sondheim, Barclay thought.

While the place was crowded, it seemed not to be; there was enough distance between tables to provide a sense of space and privacy, almost as if they'd be dining alone. The maître-d' led them to a table off to one side, augustly seating Rachel before spreading linen napkins in both of their laps. "Edward will be with you in a moment," he said, leaving book-like menus the size of a small tabloid in front of each of them. "Enjoy your evening, and don't hesitate to beckon if there's any problem."

Beckon?

"So what do you think?" Rachel asked, settling back into her chair, looking around.

"Seems wonderful," he replied, "although a bit off my beaten track."

"It's one of my favorite places," she said.

He resisted asking who she'd been there with before, and simply said, "Thanks for letting me tag along."

She grinned. "You are cute, you know that?"

Like a ghost, Edward suddenly and silently appeared, offering the evening's specials, none of which appealed to Barclay, and asking what they'd like to drink. They'd already decided on a bottle of Australian white, and he promptly slipped away to fulfill their wishes.

While waiting for the wine and studying the menus, Rachel told him how much Colleen had enjoyed meeting him. "She liked that you listen. That you seemed genuinely interested in her, and what she's doing."

"I was," he said.

"And that she had to persuade you to talk about yourself. Most of her friends, it seems, are more interested in talking about their own lives than hers."

"I know what she means," he said.

By the time Edward returned with their wine, they had decided on their orders: grilled salmon for her, poached trout for him, with a Caesar salad to start.

As always, their conversation before and during dinner was light and relaxed, touching on subjects of interest to each or both of them. Everything from politics to sports to art to world affairs. And once again, he felt utterly captivated by the ease of the conversation, and by the gentle, carefree way about her.

Until now.

"It's time," she said, after their plates had been cleared and after they'd finished their first cup of coffee. "Are you ready?"

The combo had begun playing again, a slow tune that he recognized but could not name. "Are you sure you want to do this?" he asked.

"Positive," she said, reaching across the table to take his hand.

He said a little prayer, then found himself on the dance floor, moving slowly, holding her loosely, mindful of her toes. Fortunately, they were not alone; others had joined them, crowding the small floor, pushing them closer together. With his hand on her back, he could feel the warmth of her skin beneath the silk dress, and in front, the slight pressure of her breasts against his chest.

My God, he thought. *If this isn't heaven, it's close to it.*

"What were you worried about?" she asked, looking up at him. "You're a nice dancer."

She wasn't putting him on. He was doing okay, surprising even himself. It had been years, but he moved easily, even light-footed. The lost weight was making a difference, he thought; he felt far less awkward, or conspicuous, than he would have all of those pounds ago.

Of course, he was helped by her skill, staying with him, never leading, but guiding, nonetheless. He was immersed in the fresh scent of her hair, and when he looked down on her, he found her eyes closed, a small smile on her lips. She was somewhere else, he thought. But that was okay; she was in his arms now.

By the third dance, "Misty," her arm tightened around him, her breasts heavy against him. Their hips together for an instant, then apart. Then together again. Feeling the heat. He fought to control himself. But failed.

"Oh, my," she whispered.

As the song ended, they stood for a moment, swaying slightly. Holding on. Her cheek pressed against his chest, hot. His own face flushed. He didn't know what to say, couldn't have spoken anyway. He could barely breathe. Something important had just happened, he knew that. Some threshold had been crossed that he had never expected to cross. Lost for words, he could only relish the moment.

Finally, they parted. She took his hand, gripping tightly, and led him back to the table. They sat quietly a moment—until a wayward thought hit him. Despite himself, he grinned. And it caught her eye.

"What are you thinking?" she asked.

"Nothing," he said.

"Yes, you are. You're smiling."

"It's nothing."

"What?"

He couldn't erase the grin. "You'll get angry."

"Try me."

It was too late to retreat. "I was thinking about Sam Malone in *Cheers*."

She looked at him curiously. "What about him?"

"The time when he found himself in," he glanced over his shoulder, "a . . . similar situation. With Diane, I think. Or maybe Rebecca."

"And?"

"And . . . remember? Him yelling, 'Fire down below!'"

For a moment, she seemed confused, but then threw her head back and hooted, loud enough to draw stares from the nearby tables.

"You are something else," she said, ignoring the stares.

"I'm sorry. It was just such a great moment . . ."

"Don't apologize," she replied, trying to stifle her giggling. "Trust me. You weren't the only one feeling the fire."

It was then, as they settled back, still smiling, enjoying their final sips of wine, that he felt the vibration of his cell phone against his hip. *Son of a bitch! Ignore it*, he told himself. But he knew he couldn't. Too many years in the news business had taught him that.

"Sorry," he said, pulling the phone out.

Rachel was disbelieving. "You've got a call? Now? Here?"

He could only shrug. And turn away. "Barclay," he answered.

He listened for a moment. Then his head drooped. "Okay, I'll meet you there. It'll probably be an hour."

He put the phone away. "That was J.J.," he said. "There's been another attempted rape and murder. Same park where they found Jennifer. The guy left a belt."

Once in the car, Barclay was back on the cell phone, punching in the number of the assignment desk. He waited three rings for an answer. "This is Barclay. Who's this?"

"Stenerson."

Nathan Stenerson. A new kid on the desk.

"Hey, Nate. Anything on the police radios about an attempted rape and murder in St. Paul? In Garden Park?"

"Yeah," Stenerson said, "Our photog's already there."

"Good. Tell him I'll meet him."

"You will? Why?"

He ignored the question. "And call Parkett at home. Tell him to meet me there, too."

"Okay," he said, clearly confused by the attention this relatively routine police call was getting. "Want to tell me what's going on?"

"Just make the call," Barclay said.

Putting the phone down, he glanced apologetically at Rachel. "I'm sorry the evening's ending this way," he said. "But I have to . . ."

"It doesn't have to end. I'd like to go with you."

He hesitated. "I'm not sure that's a good idea."

"Why?"

Struggling for a reason, he said, "You'll freeze to death, for one thing. You've just got that sweater."

"I'll be okay. And I'll stay out of the way. Besides, you'll just waste time by dropping me off at home first."

She had a point.

The last few minutes at Angelo's had been a blur. Hurriedly paying the bill, rushing out, Rachel trailing behind, shaken, asking questions he could not answer. Another attack. Another belt. How could this be?

Despite the rush, he drove cautiously—staying well within the interstate speed limits, not wanting to risk a traffic stop with a few glasses of wine in his system. But as he swung off I-35W and onto I-94, heading east into St. Paul, he suddenly realized that he had no idea of how to get to Garden Park . . . that he'd been absolutely lost when J.J. had led him there.

He switched on the overhead light and reached for his Twin Cities map, regretting now that he'd declined a GPS in the new car. He handed the map to Rachel, asking her to try and locate the park. "It's near St. Thomas," he said. "That's all I remember."

She spread the map out on her lap, bending over, using her finger to trace their path. She worked quickly. "Take the Cretin Avenue exit," she said, "then a left on Marshall. It's a couple of blocks from there."

"Thanks."

She smiled. "See. I can be a help."

He followed her directions, and in another ten minutes, they arrived. Three squad cars were parked along the street, their flashing lights off, in deference, he guessed, to the late hour and the peace of the neighborhood. But he could still make out the fluttering police tape, flashlights bobbing in the park, and the shadowy figures of the cops moving about.

They parked a few car lengths down the street. "Maybe you should stay here," he told Rachel. "Until I see what's happening."

"No, thanks. I'll stick with you, if that's okay."

"All right. I've got a jacket in the trunk. Should keep you warm."

They walked slowly down the darkened sidewalk, looking for J.J. Clearly, whatever excitement there had been was long since over. Now close to midnight, few lights were showing in any of the houses along the street.

As a bus passed down the block, behind them, Barclay suddenly realized he was following the same path that Jennifer had taken so many years before. In the same direction. On the same sidewalk. Past the same darkened houses. Not as warm as that night, but probably just as spooky.

Rachel must have felt it, too. She gripped his hand, pressing against him. "He did it here to send a message, didn't he?"

"Probably." *What else could explain it?*

They found J.J. standing next to his parked car, arms wrapped around himself against the chill. He did a double-take when he spotted Rachel but quickly recovered. After a quick hello, he told Barclay, "I hated to call you on a Saturday night, but I thought you'd want to be here."

"I'm glad you did," Barclay said, then introduced Rachel to Bennett, who was standing nearby.

"So what happened here?" he asked.

"You won't believe it," J.J. said.

Barclay looked at Bennett. "A carbon copy of Jennifer," Bennett said. "Only with a happier outcome. The woman got attacked right over there," pointing to a spot a few feet down the sidewalk, "and got dragged into the park. By a big guy. With gloves and stocking mask. Ripped her skirt off and tried to strangle her, but she managed to get a scream off . . . and some fellow walking his dog in the park ran over, yelling. The guy took off. But left the belt."

"And the woman?" Barclay asked.

"Some bruises. Badly shaken up. But she should be okay. Ambulance took her to Region's hospital. She was lucky."

Barclay could only shake his head.

"It gets even stranger," J.J. said.

"How's that?"

Bennett looked across the street at the park. "Our guys found a college class ring in the grass."

"The woman's?"

"No," Bennett said, watching Barclay closely. "Jennifer's."

"What?"

"From Wisconsin. Her initials are on it."

"I didn't know she had a class ring . . . or that it was missing," he said.

"It wasn't in the file," Bennett replied. "It's one of the things we kept to ourselves."

He held up a small plastic bag, the gold ring inside.

Barclay slumped against the car. "You're telling me this guy held on to this ring all these years. Then decides to drop it here?"

"Looks that way," Bennett said. "To taunt us, I'd guess."

"Not us, me," Barclay said.

Rachel had stayed in the background, listening closely, but suddenly, unexpectedly, she broke in, facing Bennett. "Sorry," she said, "but does this finally convince you that George has been right all along?"

Barclay was taken aback, but Bennett grinned. "Yes, ma'am. I'm afraid it does."

"Good," she said, stepping away.

At that moment, Parkett and the station cameraman, Zach Anthony, walked up the sidewalk, emerging from the darkness. "Hey, boss," Parkett said.

Barclay quickly made introductions. Then, to Anthony, "When did you get here?"

"Before anyone else," he replied, "But after they took the woman away. Too dark to get much on tape, except a few cops milling around."

Parkett spoke up. "Is this what I think it is?"

"Yeah," Barclay replied. "Looks like our guy struck again."

"You're sure?"

"I'm sure."

Bennett stepped forward. "But you can't report this, you know."

"Report what?" Parkett asked.

"The connection. To Jennifer."

"What do you mean, we can't report it?" Parkett demanded. "If we know it's the same guy, we have to report it. What the hell? A rapist strikes again? After damn near twenty years? That's a hell of a story."

Bennett looked at Barclay. "Tell him."

"He's right, Jeff. We can report tonight's attack, like everyone else. But nothing more. Nothing about Jennifer."

"You've gotta' be kidding me," Parkett said, heat in his voice. "I don't believe this."

"Calm down," Barclay said. "And listen to me. The only reason we know what we know is because Bennett here leveled with me. On the promise I won't screw up his investigation."

"Wrong," Parkett persisted. "What we know is because of *your* investigation, not his. With all due respect to Detective Bennett, you're the one who made the connection, not him. It's your story. *Our* story."

"Our story will be when they finally catch the guy," Barclay said, irritably. "Until then . . ."

"And what if one of our competitors gets it first?" Parkett argued. "What if somebody else remembers that another woman was raped and killed years ago in this very same park? And gets it on the air before us?"

"That's a chance we'll have to take," Barclay said.

Parkett, turning to walk away, said disgustedly, "And here I thought we were in the friggin' news business."

BACK IN THE CAR, RACHEL ASKED, "Do you and Parkett often argue like that?"

"Not often, but he says what he thinks. That's okay. And he's right, you know. About reporting this story."

"But you still won't?"

"I can't. I gave my word. But, when I did, I never expected something like this to happen."

She was sitting close to him, both of them warmed by the soft purr of the Buick's heater. And by the soothing strains of Tchaikovsky's "Serenade for Strings" from the car's CD player.

Several minutes passed before she said, "There's something else."

"What's that?"

"The woman who was attacked. She could have been killed."

"I know." Then, after a long pause, "Because of me."

"I didn't mean that."

"I know, but I haven't been thinking about much else."

True. Ever since getting the call at the restaurant, it had been weighing on him. An innocent woman assaulted because of his zealous—some would say obsessive—pursuit of a decades-old killer. A woman who'd be forced to live with the horror of this night because he'd insisted on stirring up an old pot of hate and revenge. Him, George Barclay. Who'd never intentionally hurt anybody in his entire life.

"You couldn't have known this would happen," she said.

"Maybe not. But after my car got whacked, I should have expected something else. I did expect something else. Just not this."

"Thank God she's going to be okay."

"I know. I just wish I knew what to do."

Should he give this all up? To keep someone else from getting hurt or killed? Leave it to Bennett and the cops? Maybe so, but then again, where would they be without him? Maybe nowhere.

But at least the woman wouldn't be lying in a hospital.

WHEN THEY PULLED UP TO RACHEL'S CONDO, Barclay let the motor idle, keeping the warmth inside. Sitting quietly, her hand in his, still surrounded by Tchaikovsky's sweet-sounding strings, he wanted to speak—to tell her how wondrous, how unforgettable the night of dinner and dancing had been, but he was afraid to, knowing he would never find the right words. That anything he could say would fall far short of what he felt.

So he simply sat, holding her hand, inhaling her nearness, hoping she could sense what he could not express.

She must have. Leaning over, snuggling against him, her head on his shoulder, she whispered, "Would you like to come up?"

He closed his eyes and drew a deep breath. Ever since they'd left the dance floor, he been hoping for—yet dreading—these words. Struggling with what he'd do or say if that invitation was ever offered.

"Well?"

Her other hand was on his thigh. The tips of her fingers featherlike, dancing. Spreading heat. Then her lips were on his. Moist. Warm. Slightly open. Tentative. The tip of her tongue, exploring. His own, responding.

My God, he thought. Feeling himself harden with her touch.

Her breast was in his hand, cupping it, filling it. Softer than the silk that covered it. He could hear her breath quicken, matching his own. Mixing with it. Sweet, still with the hint of wine.

"Come," she whispered, taking his hand, reaching for the door.

"No," he heard himself say, not believing he'd said it.

She looked around, surprised. "What?"

"I can't."

"Why?"

He didn't answer. He didn't know the answer. Maybe it was being at the park. The stark reminder of Jennifer. Knowing it had happened again. Or maybe it was none of that. Perhaps he was simply scared.

Again, she seemed to know. "Are you afraid?"

"Maybe."

"Of what?"

"I don't know. Of disappointing you. Of risking that. It's been a long time."

She took his face in her hands, brushing his lips with hers. "For me, too," she said. "But trust me. You won't disappoint me."

She kissed the tip of his nose. His forehead. Back to his lips.

"Come," she said again.

This time, he went. And never looked back.

Barclay was fresh out of the shower, still in his robe, thumbing through the Sunday paper in search of some mention of the attempted rape, when the phone rang. His mother. Must be. "Hi, Mom."

Laughter at the other end.

Rachel.

Damn!

"Sorry," he said. "I thought it'd be my mother . . ."

"I heard."

". . . she always calls on Sunday morning."

"Always?"

"Most of the time. Especially if she knows I've been out the night before. To make sure I behaved myself."

"You didn't."

"I know."

"And I'm glad. That's all I wanted to tell you. And to wish you a good morning."

God, he loved the sound of her voice.

"You're wonderful," he said. "Did I tell you that?"

"Yes," she said. "Several times."

"May I tell you again?"

"Yes."

"You're wonderful."

It had been awkward at first. She, it turned out, was as shy as he. But, in the darkness of her bedroom, the silk dress was soon gone, his new suit a crumpled heap on the floor. Then, the slow, tantalizing process of discovery. Of exploration. And now, each moment was so deeply etched in his memory that he could vividly recall every touch, every whisper.

"No regrets?" he said.

"None. And you?"

"Of course not."

"You're sure?" she said. "I felt like I was—"

"I'm sure. You were wonderful. Have I told you that?"

She laughed again. "Yes."

After more banter, they agreed to meet later at the YW, then to move on to the Hilton for a drink and an early dinner.

"Say hi to your Mom, when she calls."

"I will. I'll also tell her what a winsome wench you are."

"Please do."

NOT A HALF HOUR LATER, he had his chance.

"So how did it go?" his mother asked.

"Just fine. I had a good time."

There was a pause. "Tell me about this lady. Is she special?"

Knowing she would not rest until he responded, he told her—as briefly as he could—how they'd met, her family, and where they'd gone the night before.

"You actually went dancing?"

"Yes," he said. "And I did okay."

"That's nice. Your father never would dance, you know."

"I know."

"Are you okay?" she asked. "You sound a little cranky."

"I'm okay. I just have a lot on my mind right now."

He was surprised. She took the hint. "Then I'll let you go. Your father sends his love."

"Love you both," he replied. "I'll call you later in the week."

TWO HOURS LATER, HE FOUND HIMSELF in the nearly-deserted lobby of Regions hospital in St. Paul, summoned there by J.J., who was sitting by himself, thumbing through a dog-eared copy of *Today's Health*. Sunday, apparently, was not a busy day at the hospital.

"Bennett's upstairs," J.J. told him, "talking to the woman."

"How's she doing?"

"Satisfactory condition. But bruises and a broken wrist, where the guy grabbed and pulled her. They're going to keep her for another night, for observation. That's all I know."

Barclay settled into a chair next to J.J., repeating what he and Rachel had discussed the night before. "It's my fault, you know. For flushing this guy out of the bushes."

J.J. didn't argue, but simply looked at him. "Shit happens," he said. "Be grateful she's not in worse shape."

"Trust me, I am," Barclay said.

"And look on the bright side. We may be a step closer to finding this shithead. Now that he's come out from behind those bushes."

"How's that?"

"He's acting stupid. Taking chances. If he keeps this up, he's bound to make a mistake. Maybe he already has."

"Then why's he doing it?"

J.J. shrugged. "I'm no psychologist," he said, "and who knows why killers do what they do? But I'd bet the guy feels challenged. Leaving that ring behind was like throwing down the gauntlet. His way of saying find me if you can, kind of thing."

When they looked up, Bennett was crossing the lobby, a large plastic bag in his hand. "Hey," he said, sitting down next to them.

"Tell us," Barclay said.

"Considering what she went through, she's in remarkably good spirits. Still hurting, but on pain meds. Knows she's lucky to be alive. Her mother's up there with her now."

"Who is she?" J.J. asked.

"A waitress at one of those restaurants near the Xcel Center. Nineteen years old. Amazingly, she shares an apartment in a house one door down from where Jennifer lived. Got off the same damn bus.

Never knew what hit her. Guy appeared out of nowhere, got her from behind. Never said anything. Just dragged her into the park. That's all she knows, except . . ."

"Except what?" Barclay asked.

"She took a big bite out of his arm. Tasted blood. Turns out it was his scream, not hers, that got the attention of the guy walking the dog."

"Gutsy girl," J.J. said.

"For sure," Bennett replied.

"What's in the bag?" Barclay asked.

Bennett held the bag up. "Her clothes. Going to the lab. Her blouse may have some of his blood on it."

"Anything else?" Barclay wanted to know.

"If you're talking about semen or something, no. He never got that far."

"How about the belt?"

"Black. Size 38. Same as, same as."

As they got up to leave, Barclay said, "I don't suppose there's any chance of my talking to her."

"No way," Bennett replied. "You'll never even know her name."

"Then will you let me know what the lab says?"

"Sure. As long as you keep your part of the bargain."

WHEN BARCLAY WALKED INTO HIS CONDO, the phone was ringing and the message light on the phone was blinking. He picked up the phone.

"Mr. Barclay?" The voice was soft, frail.

"Yes."

"This is Kevin Bartlow." Pause. "Jennifer's father."

"Of course. How are you?"

"About the same," he said. "You left your card with your number. I've tried several times."

"I'm sorry. I just got back."

"More of those cards came." The voice was halting. "Addressed to Jennifer."

Barclay pressed the phone to his ear. "When? How many?"

"Yesterday. Two of them. I was going to call the police, but I don't know who to call anymore."

"Do you still have the cards?"

"Yes. Right in front of me."

"Did you open them?"

"Yes. I had to."

"If it's okay, I'll come pick them up. And get them to the police."

"I'd appreciate that. I don't get out much anymore."

"I'll be there this afternoon."

"Good. I'll look for you."

Seuss was winding around his legs, tail up, whining. He picked him up and cradled him in his arms as he sat down on the sofa. Things were moving too fast. He felt momentarily overwhelmed.

Then he remembered the messages. Still holding Seuss, he retrieved the first. From Jeff Parkett, apologizing for their confrontation of the night before, "I was out of line. I'm sure I embarrassed you in front of your friends. You're the boss, and I should trust your judgment. It won't happen again."

The second was from John Knowles. "I've got some of the information you asked for. Let me know when you want to talk. You still work here, don't you?"

HE HAD NO TROUBLE FINDING HIS WAY back to Kevin Bartlow's house, taking his time in the new Buick, enjoying what had turned out to be a crisp, late summer day. Some trees already had begun to turn, but he knew it would still be a few weeks before they'd all be in their full and glorious color.

He'd lived a lot of places, but still believed Indian summer in Minnesota was as lovely as you could find anywhere. Only New England might rival it.

As always, he'd been vigilant about the traffic around him, even taking a couple of extra turns when he thought one particular vehicle had been following him for too long. But it had turned out to be nothing.

Bartlow was at the door as soon as he pulled into the driveway, looking even more fragile than before. Thinner, more bent over, leaning more heavily on his wooden cane.

He held open the door. "Come in. I'll heat up some coffee."

"I won't stay long," Barclay promised.

"I've had my nap. And I don't have many visitors these days."

The house was as cozy and as immaculate as before, although smelling slightly stale—as though it had been a while since the windows were last open. As they walked into the kitchen, Barclay saw at a glance the cards lying on the kitchen table.

"I was careful opening them," the old man said. "Just touched the corners and used a letter opener. The police told me to do that if I ever got more cards."

Barclay guessed the police had told him not to open them at all, but he wasn't about to say anything.

"Was there writing inside?" he asked.

"Yes. Look for yourself."

Barclay carefully pulled the cards from the envelopes. One was a sympathy card, inscribed with a scribbled "You still miss her? Too bad, old man."

The second was a birthday card, with the same scribbling. "Your daughter was a whore. She deserved to die!"

Talk about cruel.

Bartlow set the cups of coffee on the table and sat down himself. "Cream or sugar? I don't remember."

"Neither, but thanks."

Barclay pointed to the envelopes. "I'm so sorry you have to go through this."

The old man blew on his coffee before taking a tentative sip. "You know, it's strange, but the cards didn't bother me as much this time. I know that whoever's writing them is an evil person. That he never really knew Jennifer. He couldn't have."

"When was her birthday?" Barclay asked.

"Friday. The day before the cards arrived. She would have been forty-four."

Barclay said, "I know you've thought about it a thousand times, but can you think of anyone who'd be capable of sending cards like this?"

"No, of course not. Why do you ask that?"

He paused. "Because I think whoever sent these cards, whoever killed Jennifer, may have known her and, perhaps, you, as well."

"What?"

As briefly as he could, Barclay explained his theory and what had happened since they'd last met. "Just last night, someone attacked another woman in the same park where Jennifer was found. He even left Jennifer's old class ring behind."

Bartlow fell back in his chair. "You can't be serious."

"It's true, I'm afraid."

"Is the woman okay?"

"I think so, yes."

"Thank goodness."

Bartlow got up to refill their cups, a tremor in his hand and in his voice. "I'm too old for this, you know. First, Jennifer. Then her mother. Now, this. I thought it was all in the past. It's too much."

Barclay could feel his pain. "It must be horrible for you."

Bartlow seemed to pull himself together. "So what can I do?"

"The same thing I've asked others to do. Think back. Think hard. It may have been somebody Jennifer knew, however long ago, and felt uncomfortable about. Somone who may have bothered her or harassed her in some way."

Bartlow could only shake his head. "I'll try again," he finally said. "But it's been so long . . . and my memory's not as good . . ."

"I understand. I can only ask you to try," Barclay replied.

Before he could leave, Bartlow asked if he'd like to see some of the family's old photo albums.

"Of course," Barclay said.

They retreated to the living room and sat together on the sofa as Bartlow opened the first of a stack of albums sitting on the coffee table—apparently put there in anticipation of his visit.

The first two albums were devoted to Jennifer's early years: predictable photos of family activities—at the playground, the beach, around the Christmas tree. There was Jennifer's baptism, her first day of school, her birthday parties, her confirmation. Page after page of aging black-and-white pictures, some barely clinging to the albums' pages, the pages themselves frayed at the edges from years of turning.

For Barclay, it was fascinating to see this fast-forward record of Jennifer growing up, from her first pictures as a baby in her mother's arms through her clumsy adolescent years—to her transformation from the awkward, spindly-legged kid to a self-assured young woman.

"This is how I remember her," he said. "As a beautiful young woman."

"They didn't get much prettier," Bartlow agreed, smiling.

The final five albums were devoted to those later years, in high school and beyond, including her time in various theater productions. He bent over the albums, studying each picture carefully, recognizing in some of the photos the women he'd met at Katie's home. But there were many other faces he did not—could not—know.

Three pages of one album held at least a dozen pictures of Jennifer and the boy Ken Younger, her steady boyfriend, including some that were obviously taken at the prom: Jennifer in a formal gown, smiling, looking radiant, standing arm-in-arm with Younger under a flower-filled arch.

Barclay asked, "How well did you know this fellow?"

"Ken? We knew him well. He was around all the time."

"Do you know why they broke up?"

"No. Or if I did, I've forgotten."

The last pages included shots of Jennifer and Daniel Kimble in their happier times, and a number of photos taken on the streets of New York—and from a couple of the off-Broadway plays she'd been in.

Finally, after the last album was put aside, Barclay asked, "Did the police ever see these?"

"I suppose so, but my wife wouldn't part with them."

"May I borrow the last few? I promise to get them back to you."

Bartlow hesitated. "I guess so. But, please, don't keep them long. They're all I have left."

"And one more thing," Barclay said.

"What's that?"

"The guest register from Jennifer's funeral. Do you still have it?"

"I think so. I'll have to look."

"Would you? It might be important."

Bartlow disappeared into an adjacent bedroom, reappearing a few minutes later, carrying a thick, bound book. "It was in a closet," he said. "I haven't looked at it in years."

Barclay took it and put it with the albums. "I'll bring all of these back soon. They may help."

"I hope they do. I don't want to die without knowing who took my Jennifer."

AS BARCLAY NEARED DOWNTOWN, he first tried calling Josh Bennett, and when that failed, he punched in J.J's number, quickly telling him where he'd been and what he had.

"Did you open them?" J.J. asked.

"They were already open."

"And you read them?"

"Yeah," Barclay replied, reciting what each had said.

"Bennett's going to be pissed."

Barclay grunted. "The old guy didn't know who else to call."

"Okay. I'll try to reach Bennett," J.J. said. "Where will you be?"

"Home for a while. Then out."

"Another date, Romeo?"

"Buzz off."

"She have an older sister?"

"No, and even if she did . . ."

"A mother?"

"You're a sick bastard, you know that."

"Not sick, just jealous," he said, and hung up.

Three times during the night, the phone rang, shattering the darkened quiet of the condo, sending Seuss flying off the end of the bed, scurrying to who knew where.

Each time, there was only silence on the other end of the line.

The calls were spaced an hour or so apart, giving Barclay just enough time to drift off to sleep before being wrenched awake again. Finally, he simply gave up, made a pot of tea, and sat by the phone—waiting.

After the second call, he had no doubt who the caller was. And when the phone rang for the third time, he was prepared. "Hey, buddy," he said in his friendliest voice. "Nice to hear from you. I don't often get the chance to talk to a monster like you. Are you proud of what you did to that poor woman in the park? Someone you didn't even know, who'd never done anything to you. Big, tough guy, aren't you?"

He thought he could hear the soft intake of breath.

"You're dead meat, you know that? Sooner rather than later, I'd guess. A week or two, give or take."

Whoever it was, was still listening. A captive audience of one, and Barclay decided to make the most of it. "And what did Jennifer do to you? Called you the pathetic creep you are? Told you to get lost in that weird, psychotic world of yours? Must have hurt, huh? What'd you think? That she could actually fall for somebody like you? You gotta be kidding."

Still there, his breathing more audible now.

"You were clever, doing what you did. I'll give you that. Fooled a lot of people for a long time. But you made a couple of mistakes. And the cops are only a step or two behind you now. The charade is over."

Seuss had returned, slinking into the room, glancing warily in all directions before leaping into Barclay's lap, snuggling against him.

"You still there? Enjoying this as much as I am?" He expected no answer and got none. "Well, sorry to say, I gotta go. Call again any-time. And have a nice day, okay? But watch your behind."

There were no more calls.

KNOWING SLEEP WOULD NEVER RETURN, Barclay spent the rest of the early morning hours poring over the photo albums, using a magnifying glass to study each individual picture. Not knowing exactly what he was looking for, but hoping at some point to show the albums to Katie and her friends—on the off-chance the pictures might jar their memories.

To be truthful, however, he also coveted another, closer glimpse of Jennifer—to see her in ways and in places he'd never had the chance to see her in person. To share her life, in a way, through these photos, to discover things about her that he'd never been privileged to know.

Small things. A wide-eyed look of surprise. A flip of her hair. The wiping away of a tear. Sitting, cross-legged, in her bed, in pajamas. In a bikini, at the beach. On a swing, flying high. In costume, on a stage.

Again, as he moved from photo to photo, he could only marvel at her beauty, whether dripping with sweat from a cross-country run or perfectly made up for the prom. If beauty was in the eyes of the beholder, then everyone she touched was beholden.

He, of course, had never seen or known her beyond the boundaries of the school. What he would have given to have been in even one of these pictures. To have been that close, even for a click of the shutter.

AS HE WALKED INTO THE NEWSROOM the next morning, he got a call from Josh Bennett, demanding to know where the Bartlow cards were, and what the hell he was doing with them.

"In my hand," Barclay said. "In a sealed envelope. Waiting for you to pick them up."

"You should have called me," Bennett insisted.

"I tried. Later."

"Not later. Before. Those cards are evidence, for Christ's sake. They've got to be protected."

"They were," Barclay said, patiently explaining that Kevin Barlow hadn't known who to call. "We've become friends," he added. "He trusts me."

"Still, you should have called me first," Bennett said. "I'm on my way to pick them up."

"I'll be here," Barclay replied.

JOHN KNOWLES WAS WAITING FOR HIM outside his office door. "You have time to talk now?" he asked, "or should I come back later?"

Barclay glanced into the newsroom. Everything seemed to be operating normally. "No, c'mon in. We've got some catching-up to do."

Knowles settled into a chair. "Parkett told me about the woman at the park. Looks like things are heating up."

"In more ways than one," Barclay said, and went on to tell him about the nocturnal phone calls that had kept him up most of the night, and the new cards that Jennifer's father had received.

"About those phone calls," Knowles said. "You think it's wise to taunt this guy?"

"Probably not, but he's pissing me off."

"The guy's a killer. It might pay to be a little cautious."

"Duly noted," Barclay said.

"You're not afraid?"

"For myself?"

"Yes," Knowles said.

He thought for a moment. "Yeah, I suppose so. Who wouldn't be? I know what he did to Jennifer and the other woman in the park. What he did to my car. And what he'd probably do to me, given the chance."

"So?"

"So what do you want me to do? Quit? No, thanks. I can only try not to give him that chance."

Sounded brave, but Barclay knew he'd never done anything remotely heroic in his life. Never had his courage tested. Never fought in a war, or fired a gun, for that matter.

Knowles studied him for a moment, as though seeing something in him that he hadn't seen before. Then he opened a thick folder that he'd brought with him. "Here's a rundown on the names you gave me. Almost a thousand men in all, if you remember."

Barclay had forgotten how many there were. "How long did it take?"

"Longer than I thought it would. Hours to cull out the duplicate names, double-check addresses, and all the rest. Kind of tedious work, you want to know the truth."

"And?"

"I had a few more hits. A dozen or so. Of guys who've actually spent time in the prison system. Or were in and out of the courts. Fewer than I expected, actually, considering the number of guys. But I can't pretend I got everybody.

"And you can forget that Tim Eliason," he added. "He's back in jail. Has been for a couple of months. Another probation violation."

"Okay," Barclay said. "Let's go with the new ones you have." He went down the list of names, quickly noting what offenses had landed the men in prison. Only two were for sexual assault. Again, the names meant nothing to him. "How about Ken Younger? Could you find him?"

"Yup. Lives in Des Moines. Married. Three kids. Mr. Clean. Forget about him, too."

"You have his phone number?"

"Yeah. Right here."

"Good. I may need it sometime."

He leaned back in his chair, a headache forming behind his eyes, probably from too little sleep. "So what'd we do now?" he asked, more of himself than of Knowles. "We can check these guys out further, I suppose. Or have Bennett do it. See if Katie or her friends recognize any of the names. But, you know . . . we may be sniffing the wrong tree."

"What do you mean?"

"Think about it. We're looking at guys with criminal records. Convicted rapists. Thugs. Whatever. I don't think our boy is like that.

Violent, yeah. A psycho, maybe. But not a serial rapist. He went after Jennifer specifically. And attacked this other woman to thumb his nose at us. He may never have spent a day in prison. At least not for rape."

Knowles studied him. "I'm not sure I agree, but say you're right, where do we go from here?"

"Back to the beginning." He got up, staring out into the newsroom. "We know it has to be someone who knew Jennifer, even obliquely, who must have had some connection to Armstrong, who's big and strong, even now, who may be a psychopath, but may not have a criminal record. He could be living a fairly normal life. Hiding in plain sight, if you will."

"So we are back where we started."

"Not entirely. For one thing, we know he's still around. Not dead, not in prison. Walking the streets. We've got samples of his blood, and the few specks of semen he left on Jennifer. And . . . we've eliminated a few people. Not many, I admit, but some. Things could be worse."

If Knowles was convinced, he didn't show it. "Are they doing DNA tests on the blood and semen?" he asked.

"I'll ask Bennett. But that can take weeks, maybe months. And then you gotta find a match. I wouldn't count on DNA in the short run."

Knowles got up. "Anything more I can do?"

"Keep working on the names. Maybe something will turn up."

"Okay."

"One more thing."

"What's that?"

"Tell your computer to sort out the Davids from all of those names."

"The Davids? Why?"

"Just curious."

BY LUNCHTIME, AN ANGRY JOSH BENNETT arrived to retrieve the Bartlow cards. "I'm dead serious about this," he said. "You should have called me."

"I know," Barclay said. "I apologize. It won't happen again."

"I hope not."

For fear of further irritating him, Barclay decided against reporting his one-sided late night phone conversation, or about the photo albums and funeral guest book that he'd borrowed from Bartlow. But he did tell him about the list of names that Knowles had developed. "Turns out that at least a dozen guys who were at Armstrong about the time Jennifer was there have since spent time in prison. Including a couple for sexual assault."

Bennett was clearly impressed. "You've got those names?"

"Here," Barclay replied, handing him a copy of the list.

"How'd he get these?" Bennett asked.

"He ran them through the Corrections Department and BCA data bases. He says there could be others that he missed."

"Impressive."

"I noticed that four or five are still in prison," Barclay said, "so you can forget them. But the others might be worth a look."

"Of course," Bennnett said, getting up to leave. "And before I forget," he added, "the cops in Minneapolis and Brooklyn Center finally got back to me. They've got nothing new in either case, but confirmed what you suspected—that as far as they know there have been no cards or other communication with either of the women's families since the murders. And no one remembers the women getting harassing phone calls."

"Good. But one more thing."

"What's that?"

"Are you doing a DNA check on the blood and semen?"

"When I can," Bennett said. "But the labs are so backed up it's going to be a while."

"I figured."

At the office door, Bennett turned back. "Believe me, I do appreciate your help in this, and I don't mean to be a prick, but I don't want to lose this guy because somebody screwed up the evidence along the way."

"I hear you," Barclay said.

31

Six hours later, he would hear from Bennett again.

Barclay was on the treadmill, pushing himself at four miles an hour, dripping sweat, breathing hard, but determined to keep going as long as Rachel did, running on the machine next to his.

She slowed for a moment. "Is that your cell phone?"

The phone was in his duffel bag next to the treadmill.

"What?" he gasped.

"Your phone. I think I hear it."

He stopped the machine and stepped off.

It was Bennett. "You've got a problem. We've got a problem."

"What's that?" he asked.

"I just got off the phone with some reporter at the *Pioneer Press*. He mentioned Jennifer's murder . . ."

"Son of a bitch," Barclay muttered.

". . . and wants to know if there's some connection to Saturday's assault."

Barclay waited.

"A neighbor across from the park who lived there when Jennifer was attacked called the paper and reminded them of her murder."

Parkett's fears of that night had just been realized. The cat was scratching its way out of the bag.

Barclay walked across the gym and slumped into a chair. Rachel watched him curiously from her treadmill. "What did you tell him?" Barclay asked.

"I lied," Bennett replied. "Played ignorant. Said I didn't know of any connection. But that I'd check into it. I left it at that."

"Good," Barclay said.

There was a pause on the other end. "I don't like to lie. Not even to reporters."

"I understand."

"I'll have to get back to him at some point. I can't fog it out forever."

"What's he going to do in the meantime?"

"Nothing, as far I know. He didn't seem all that excited, like some editor had told him to make the call. Couldn't tell, but he may not be the brightest bulb."

"Okay," Barclay said. "Maybe we've got some breathing room."

"Maybe. But don't count on too much."

Barclay returned to the treadmill and quickly repeated the conversation for Rachel. "What do you do now?" she asked.

"I don't know," he said. "Try to speed things up, if that's possible."

"Anything I can do?"

"As a matter of fact, yes. Call Katie Thorson and see if she can arrange another meeting with her friends. Tomorrow night, maybe."

"To do what?"

"To look at some old pictures," he said. "A little show and tell."

ONCE THEY'D EACH SHOWERED and shared a quick drink at Brit's, they split up—Rachel to meet some potential decorating clients, Barclay to keep an appointment he now wished he'd never made. But it was too late to cancel it.

Days before, as a courtesy, he had returned the call from Stanley Hoffer, the general manager of Channel Ten, intending to thank him politely for his interest and to say that he was committed to stay where he was—at least until the ownership issue was decided.

Hoffer had said he understood, but persuaded him to meet anyway, if only to get acquainted. So here they were—sitting in a dimly lighted corner of Morton's steak house, further obscured from view by a divider that separated them from most others in the restaurant. Clearly, Hoffer was as interested as Barclay in keeping this meeting private. To be seen together would cause rumors and gossip to fly faster than the Concorde once did.

While Barclay had seen Hoffer at a couple of local broadcast functions, he had never actually met the man. In his fifties, he guessed, Hoffer was tall and erect with wavy black hair that seemed too dark to be natural, with straight, well-tanned features and an air about him of quiet self-confidence.

In a crowd, one glance would peg him as some kind of haughty executive. But, in person, he proved to be affable and gregarious, greeting Barclay warmly, and quickly ordering a beer for both of them. "Amstel Light, right?" he asked.

"You've got it," Barclay replied, impressed.

Turned out, he knew a lot more about Barclay than his preference in beer. He could recite his whole history, from where he'd grown up and gone to school to every station he'd worked at. "I do my homework," he said in answer to Barclay's look of amazement. "I like to know whom I'm dealing with."

As impressed as he was, Barclay couldn't escape an uneasy feeling that his life had just been strip-searched by a stranger. A competitor, at that.

For his part, Hoffer told a fairly familiar story of a young sales executive who had traveled from station to station, much like Barclay, rising steadily in the sales ranks to various management positions—eventually landing the top job at Channel Ten five years before.

"I've watched you from a distance," he said, "admired what you've done over there. The kind of shop you run. The people you hire. Your investigations, your kick-ass journalism. You're a hell of a competitor."

"I appreciate that," Barclay replied, at a loss for what else to say.

"I know you're going through some tough times. Word on the street is that Hawke may be history and that TriCom may be ready to pull the plug. What'll happen then is anybody's guess. You could be working for a sports super-station."

"I doubt that," Barclay said. "The public wouldn't stand for it. A VHF network affiliate going all-sports? Won't happen."

"Don't be so sure. If TriCom drops out, it'll probably go to the highest bidder. And that could be Coburn's group."

Barclay didn't want to argue. He was there to listen, not debate. And he had to be careful what he said. He didn't really know this man or what his actual agenda might be. In competitive terms, he was still the enemy, and someone to be wary of.

"As I told you on the phone," Barclay said, "I want to see this thing through. I've got too much at stake in the station, too much of my life invested there to make any rash moves."

"I understand. But we live in an uncertain world."

By then their dinners had arrived. A massive T-bone for Hoffer, a dinner salad for Barclay.

"I heard you're on a diet," Hoffer said.

"Painful, but true," he replied, eyeing the steak enviously.

"How much have you lost?"

"Going on twenty pounds, give or take."

As they ate, the conversation—to Barclay's relief—stayed on neutral ground: mutual friends in the business, their experiences at some of the smaller stations where each had worked, and the historic distrust between news and sales staffs.

Listening to him, Barclay couldn't help but contrast this man to Hawke. While Hawke was a gruff, rough-and-tumble, take-no-prisoners kind of guy who spoke his mind, often in expletives, Hoffer was as smooth as a dollop of syrup. He might never have uttered a four-letter word in his life.

Which left Barclay feeling slightly uncomfortable. And suspicious. There had to be more to the man than he was seeing across the table. Appearances, he knew, do sometimes lie.

"Can we talk about a 'what if?'" Hoffer asked between bites of his steak.

"I'm not sure what you mean."

"What if you were to change your mind? Decide to come over to our place?"

"I've already said . . ."

"I know, but what if?" He paused. "Just so you know. You'd have total control of the newsroom and its budget. Hire and fire whomever you'd like. Have the final word on which anchors stay or go. A secretary. Company car. Profit-sharing. And fifty thousand dollars more than whatever you're making now."

Barclay sat back in his chair, stunned. A deal like that in these uncertain economic and competitive times? When many stations were cutting salaries and people?

But Hoffer wasn't done yet. "A three-year contract, guaranteed. And no interference from me or the sales department."

Hoffer waited for a reaction, but when he saw none, he added, "Of course, all of that is negotiable."

"And in return . . . ?" Barclay let the question dangle.

"Simple. You give me the same kind of balls-to-the-walls news department you run now. I want to be number one in this market, and I think you can take us there."

Barclay took a final sip of his beer, trying to absorb what he'd been told.

"Think about it," Hoffer told him. "No rush."

As they prepared to leave, Hoffer asked, "Just for the record, do you have a non-compete clause in your contract?"

"I don't have a contract."

"Really?"

"Really."

"That'll make things easier, if the time ever comes."

Who knows? Barclay thought. *Like the man said, it's an uncertain world.*

LATER THAT NIGHT, AT HOME, he sifted through a couple dozen letters and notes from Armstrong alumni that had arrived in the past day or so. In all, he suspected, he had received more than a hundred replies—none of which, sadly, had shed any new light on the investigation.

Most of this batch, like the others, simply expressed appreciation for his efforts and the hope that they might prove successful. A few of the writers had known Jennifer well, but many others had not. Almost all expressed doubt that her killer might actually be a classmate from Armstrong. And a couple even chastised him for suggesting it.

He read each of the new notes twice, then skimmed the others that he'd already read in the past. Searching for anything he might have missed, however trivial.

Several mentioned the name of Ken Younger, and two others provided the names of three boys they thought she'd also dated. But Barclay had already cross-checked those names against Knowles's list and found that all three were living out of state.

There seemed to be no end to the dead ends.

Before heading for bed, he got two phone calls. The first was from Rachel, telling him the meeting with Katie's friends was on for the next night. The second from John Knowles, who said he'd found thirty-two Davids among his list of male Armstrong alumni.

"Tell me now," Knowles said, "why the interest in a David?"

Barclay hesitated. Finally, "My gut, that's all. Someone named David, at least I think that's the name, left an inscription in Jennifer's yearbook which sounded a little ominous to me. And none of Jennifer's friends could recall a David who might have written it. Or who knew her well enough to have even signed her yearbook."

"What exactly did it say?" Knowles asked.

"Let me get my notes." There was a pause as he shuffled papers. "Here it is: 'Sorry it didn't work out. Can't say I didn't try. Too bad, too sad. Hope you don't regret it some day.'"

"That's it?" Knowles asked, skeptically.

"I know it isn't much," Barclay said, "but we don't have much. Except for a big guy with a dose of acne."

"So what can I do now?" Knowles asked.

"Humor me a bit longer," Barclay replied tiredly. "Check those thirty-two Davids. Where they live, what they do, what you can find."

Knowles sigh was audible. "Okay. It'll take awhile, but I'll do my best."

BARCLAY CAME AWAKE SUDDENLY, emerging from the deepest sleep he'd had in many nights. The bedroom was pitch black, save for the glow of the luminous numbers on the clock radio. 2:33. Sitting up, holding the sheet tight around him, he listened but heard nothing save the soft wheezing of a sleeping Seuss at the end of the bed.

He slipped out of bed and into his slippers, treading softly out of the bedroom and into the darkened hallway. Pausing, listening again. Then into the kitchen, flipping on the lights, moving on, warily exploring the rest of the condo, room by room.

Finding nothing but silence.

I should have known, he thought sheepishly. *No one's going to get through the building's elaborate security system and into a tightly-locked condo.*

But what had brought him out of his sleep?

Then he knew. The conversation with Knowles. His gut feeling.

He walked into his office and pulled out Jennifer's police file, flipping through it quickly, searching for the police interviews. Page 43, the first of twelve pages. He ran his finger down the typewritten lines, one page after another. He knew it was there, buried in the file as it had been in his sub-conscious.

Then he found it. Page 49. David Casperson. Twenty-six at the time of the interview. Unmarried, living at an address on Ewing Avenue in south Minneapolis. Interviewed by police because he and several others had appeared in a high school play with Jennifer in their senior year. The interview was brief and non-productive, one of perhaps fifty that the cops had conducted with Jennifer's classmates. But—as Barclay studied every page of the interview section—while there was a Derek, a Davis, a Darrell, and David DeLuca, Gloria's husband, Casperson was the only other David listed. The only other David actually interviewed by the police.

You're going off the deep end, he told himself. Get a grip.

Still.

He reached for the phone and called Knowles's home number. Three rings, then a groggy, "Yeah?"

"You awake?"

"Now I am."

"Awake enough to remember something?"

"I guess."

"When you're checking those Davids, put David Casperson at the top of the list."

"Jesus Christ, George. It's three o'clock in the morning."

"I know."

"You gotta get a grip."

"I just told myself that."

"Then listen to yourself. You're obsessing. And costing me sleep."

"Sorry."

"What was the name again?"

"Casperson. David Casperson."

"Okay. Now take your teddy bear and go back to bed."

32

The photo albums of Jennifer's high school years were spread out on Katie Thorson's dining room table, surrounded by Katie and her three friends—Gloria, Jackie and Annie—with Rachel and Barclay standing off to one side, observing.

For the women, it was almost a festive occasion. Katie had provided wine and hors d'oeuvres, which they nibbled as they stood by the table, bent over the albums. "These are wonderful," Gloria said, flipping the pages. "I've never seen most of these pictures before."

They were lost in the past, oohing and aahing at some of the photos, laughing at others. Barclay could only stand aside and wait, patiently, pacing the floor, sipping his wine, chatting with Rachel. Finally, he decided, it was time to get to work.

The chatter and laughter stopped.

"Here's what I'd like to do," he explained. "Each of you take an album. Study the pictures, make notes, then pass the album on until each of you has had a chance to see all of the pictures. Look for anyone who doesn't belong, who you don't know. Or that Jennifer might not have known that well. An interloper, if you will. Someone you may have forgotten about. Then we'll collect the notes and see if anything turns up."

The women looked at one another. Then at the stack of albums. The fun and games were over.

Barclay bided his time. Waiting and watching. Not knowing what to expect, but pleased that the women were now taking the exercise seriously, intently studying picture after picture, page after page, occasionally making a note on the pads he'd provided, sometimes consulting one another, pointing to a particular photo, whispering.

More than an hour went by; albums were passed along. More of the wine and the munchies were consumed. Katie got up once to make coffee, then returned to the table.

After another hour, the task was over. The albums were stacked at one end of the table, along with the empty coffee cups and wine glasses. The women appeared exhausted, rubbing their eyes and working to get the kinks out of their necks and shoulders, "I don't care if I never look at another picture," Jackie said. "Ever. And I mean that."

"Amen," Annie added.

Barclay grinned. "You've done a hell of a job," he said. "Now let's see if you've found anything."

He collected their notes and quickly went through them. Knowing that not all of the women would know everyone in all of the pictures. But hoping to find one or more that none of them knew.

There were four. Identified by album and page.

He reached for the first album, flipped to the page. Found the picture. "What is it?" he asked.

"Senior skip day," Gloria said. "At the St. Croix State Park. We had a big picnic."

The photo showed a group of kids, maybe a dozen in all, gathered around a picnic table, the St. Croix River in the background. Gloria pointed to a boy on the far left, almost out of the picture. "We don't know him," she said, glancing at the other women. "I don't know where he came from."

Barclay studied the photo. The boy seemed taller than the others, with broad shoulders, long, reddish hair, and a smirk on his face.

He showed the picture to Rachel. "You know him?"

She shook her head.

Gloria said, "He's in another picture, too."

"Which?" he asked.

She reached for a second album. "Here," she said, pointing to a shot of Jennifer and about seven other kids, including three boys. In costume, on stage. "That's him, on the right."

It was. Same build. Same red hair. Same smirk.

"They did *Skin of Our Teeth* as a senior class play," Annie said. "I saw the play, but I don't remember him."

None of the others did, either.

Barclay turned to Gloria. "I thought you were in theater with her?"

"I was, but not in this play. I hate Thornton Wilder."

Barclay asked, "Does the name David Casperson mean anything?"

He found only blank looks. "Why?" Jackie asked.

"He was one of the students the cops interviewed. He'd been in a play with Jennifer."

Again, no response.

They moved on to the other suspect pictures. One of Jennifer at a beach, with a boy—blondish, well-tanned and in sunglasses—kneeling next to her. "That may have been when they were on vacation in Florida," Gloria said. "I don't recognize the beach . . . or the guy."

Another showed Jennifer dancing, in the arms of someone in a blue tux, with short, dark hair, his face in profile. "That was at the senior prom," Annie said. "I recognize her dress. But we have no clue who she's dancing with."

"I thought she went to the prom with Ken Younger," Barclay said.

"She did," Annie replied, shrugging.

The final photo was one of Jennifer and Steven Daniel Kimble with another man, who stood a head taller than Kimble and was twice as broad. With the look of someone who spent a lot of time in a weight room. "We know that's Kimble, of course," Katie said. "But we have no idea who the other fellow is. You'd have to ask Kimble."

"I'll do that," he said. Then, "Just so I'm clear. There are no other pictures of Jennifer with someone that none of you recognize. Right?"

Katie looked at the others. "Except for some with her family, with cousins and uncles and all. All of us knew who all our friends were. We didn't keep any secrets."

"And among those you did recognize, there's no one that Jennifer had a problem with?"

"No," Gloria said. "We've talked about that."

"Good," he said. "I appreciate what you've done. I don't know if it will do any good, but at least we've gone through the motions."

As they were about to leave, Katie pulled him aside. "I need to apologize."

"For what?" he asked.

"Remember our visit to the cemetery . . ."

"Of course."

". . . and you wondered about the flowers. Who might have left them?"

"Right."

"I'd forgotten to call you back," she said. "And I didn't think about it again until I made another visit to the grave a couple of days ago."

"And?"

"There was another bouquet. Fresh, this time. And I checked. None of us put them there. Neither did her dad. He said he hasn't been to the cemetery in months."

"Interesting," he said.

"Important?"

"Probably not, but I've read that killers sometimes like to pay their victims a visit."

She shrunk back. "That's creepy."

"I know," he said.

ONCE IN THE CAR, Barclay repeated for Rachel what Katie had told him.

"You actually went to the cemetery?" she said. "You never told me."

"I forgot, I guess."

She turned in her seat, staring across at him. "I don't understand. Why did you do that?"

"What? Go to the cemetery?"

"Yes."

He didn't answer for a moment. Finally, "I don't know. I couldn't explain it to myself, actually. I just knew I wanted to go. To see the grave for myself."

She drew back, her face in shadow, then in and out of the lights of the passing cars. "That's a little strange, George. Do you know that?"

"Maybe."

"Are you still obsessing?"

"I don't think so. But I'm not sure."

She waited.

"I know it doesn't make much sense," he finally said. "But this whole investigation has brought me closer to her. The pictures. What her friends and her dad have told me about her. It's like I'm finally getting to know her. Like I never did when she was alive. She's become a real person now."

"But she's dead, George."

"Of course. Maybe that's why I had to see her grave. To convince myself of that. It had nothing to do with you . . . or us."

"Wrong. It has everything to do with me . . . and us," she said.

Nothing more was said for several minutes. Her face was turned, staring out the side window, leaving him feeling very much alone. The silence went unbroken until they pulled up in front of her condo building, and she finally turned back to him, saying quietly, "You know, George . . . that I can't, I won't, compete with a corpse."

She could have shouted the words. They had the same impact. His head swiveled, but any words were lost in his throat.

"Think about it," she said, getting out of the car, walking swiftly to the door.

This time, there was no invitation to follow her in.

Maybe it was his confusion. His brain focused on everything but what he was doing. Or the exhaustion brought on by his almost perpetual insomnia. Whatever it was, he was in a fog-like state when he drove into the condo garage and pulled into his reserved parking spot.

He sat for a moment behind the wheel, letting the motor idle, listening to the final notes of Copland's *Fanfare for the Common Man*. Closing his eyes, willing himself to forget the sight of Rachel closing the door behind her, without a glance back.

Her words, etched as in stone: "I can't, I won't, compete with a corpse."

What the hell have I done?

Wearily, he shut off the engine and opened the door, pulling himself out of the car. Standing. Seeing only the flicker of a shadow from behind.

Then, the pain. Excruciating. Numbing.

The first blow was to his back, near his kidney, the next to the back of his head, behind and below the ear. One, two, in quick succession. Like pistons firing. He heard himself scream, felt his face hit the concrete, sliding, gouging his cheek.

He tried to curl up in a ball, covering his head to ward off more blows. Leaving his stomach and back open to the kicks that came next. One, two, three. More. Then he lost count. And consciousness.

But only for a moment.

He heard the footsteps pounding across the garage floor, heading for the door. He raised his head, hoping to see, only to hear the door slam. He could taste the blood, his blood, see it pooling on the concrete beneath his head.

He tried to raise himself up but fell back. The pain was everywhere. Persistent, penetrating. He gasped for breath. For the first time since looking into the headlights of that oncoming semi years before, he thought he might die.

Too young, too young! was all he could think.

Then, another set of headlights, burning into his eyes. And, finally, screams, not his, "Call Security! Call Nine-One-One!"

THE VOICES WERE ALL AROUND HIM. Their moving faces a blur. He was on his back. Something cool was on his cheek. Something soft beneath his head. "Lay still, sir," said one of the voices. "Help is on the way."

In the background, a woman's frantic cry, "What happened? What happened?"

His stomach was a knot of pain. His head, throbbing. A fireball. He tried to move his arms, to flex his fingers. Then his legs.

Sheer, undiluted agony.

He could hear the sirens. Far away, then closer.

"Move aside, move aside, please."

Paramedics hovering above him, their hands moving over his body, exploring, testing. His body flinching at virtually every torturous touch.

Checking his pulse, his blood pressure, holding his head steady.

He tried to speak, but his throat was a closed trap.

Something was over his nose and mouth. Oxygen. Filling his lungs.

"Anybody know his name?" One of the paramedics.

"Barclay. George Barclay." The same woman's voice. "He lives on the twentieth floor."

"Are you taking anything, George?" The paramedic, leaning close to his ear. "Any medications?"

Barclay managed to move his head, no.

"Okay. You're going to be all right. We're going to put a collar on you, okay? A neck brace. Then we're going to lift you on to a backboard. Like a stretcher. Take you to the hospital. Okay? Grit your teeth."

Arms beneath his shoulders. His back. Under his legs. Lifting. A scream.

Was it his?

Then he passed out.

THE AMBULANCE. THE EMERGENCY ROOM. All but lost to him. Whatever they'd given him for the pain had dulled every other sense. Groggy, he was aware only of darkness and light, bright light, of rushed movement and hushed words. Stripped of his clothes, poked and probed. But gently.

Until finally, focus.

A woman in green scrubs leaned over him. "Mr. Barclay. You're in the emergency room at the Hennepin County Medical Center. You understand me?"

He stared at her, not fully comprehending. Then, turning his head, he saw the white curtain enshrouding them. An IV bag hanging over him. Eyes back on the woman. Older, graying hair, pulled back. Brown eyes. Concerned, sympathetic.

"Mr. Barclay?"

He swallowed, his throat parched. "Yes."

"Do you know where you are?"

"Yes. I heard."

"Good. You've been badly beaten, but we think you'll be just fine. Apparently no broken bones. Cuts and bruises, but your vital signs are good, and there's no indication that any internal organs have been damaged. Do you understand?"

"Yes."

She put a hand on his arm. "We're going to transfer you to a hospital room, where you'll be more comfortable. There'll be more x-rays, more tests, but they'll take good care of you upstairs, and a doctor will stop by to tell you more afterwards."

"Good." Then he pointed to his mouth, licking his lips.

She picked up a glass of water and put a straw into his mouth. "Only a sip," she said. Then, "I need to know who to call. Your wife? One of your children?"

"I have no one," he managed. "Jeff Parkett at Channel Seven. Tell them who you are and they'll give you his home number."

"No relatives?"

"Not here. I live alone."

As she was about to leave, she said, "The police were here. They'll be back when you're settled into your room."

"Okay. Thank you."

HE WASN'T SURE HOW LONG HE'D SLEPT, but when he awoke, the hospital room was filled with light. And Jeff Parkett was sitting by the bed.

"Hey, boss."

"Hi, Jeff."

"Did you hear about this old man on a bench in the mall . . . ?"

"What are you talking about?"

"A young kid with multi-colored spiked hair—yellow, green, blue, purple, red, you get the picture—walks up and sits down next to him. The old man looks at him. 'What are you staring at?' the kid asks. 'Haven't you ever done anything wild in your life?' The old man thinks for a moment and says, 'Yeah, years ago, I got drunk and fucked a parrot. I thought you might be my son.'"

Parkett doubled over, barely able to contain himself.

Barclay could only smile. It hurt too much to laugh. "You're a piece of work," he mumbled.

Parkett pulled his chair closer. "Then there's this woman whose hip replacement goes bad. The screws come loose. After the doctor finishes examining her, he looks up and asks, "So what's a joint like this doing in a girl like you?"

This time, Barclay had to laugh, despite the pain. "You're going to kill me, asshole."

"Looks like somebody else got to you first," he replied, suddenly serious.

"I guess," Barclay said, grimacing as he shifted his weight in the bed.

"So what the hell happened?"

"I don't know. Got out of my car in the garage and got whacked. Don't remember much more."

"You didn't see him?"

"His shadow, that's all. But he packed a hell of a wallop."

"Your face is a mess."

Barclay felt the bandage on his cheek. "That's what kissing concrete will do for you."

"I talked to the nurse at the desk," Parkett said. "She says you'll probably be here for a couple of days."

"We'll see. If I can walk, I'm out of here."

Parkett smiled and sat back in the chair, shaking his head.

"You haven't told anybody about this, have you?" Barclay said.

"Only Hawke and the newsroom."

"What?"

"C'mon. They deserved to know. Besides, you can't keep something like this a secret. Police reports and all. I suspect it'll be in the papers by tomorrow. And on our news tonight. Shit, you could have been killed."

"But I wasn't."

"I also called your friend, Jacobs. He should be here soon."

Barclay said, "You know what people will think, don't you?"

"What?"

"An old, single guy gets the shit beat out of him in a parking garage. Gay-bashing, right?"

"Not anybody who knows you."

There was a light knock on the door, and J.J. poked his head in. "I'll be damned," he said, gawking.

"Don't stare," Barclay said. "It's impolite."

Jacobs walked to the bed. "You are a sickening sight. I thought I told you to watch your back."

"I forgot."

"You think it was our friend?"

"Who else?"

"How'd he get into the garage?"

"Probably followed my car in," Barclay said. "It wouldn't be that hard. I should have kept my eyes open."

"Well, lemme tell you," J.J. said, "he's starting to piss me off, too."

Barclay managed a small chuckle.

"I called Bennett. He's talking to Minneapolis P.D. Sends his best."

They sat and talked for several more minutes, but then Barclay's eyes began to close. "You guys better get out of here," he said. "Before I start to snore. I'll let you know when I'm set to leave."

"I'll be back tonight," Parkett said. "After the early news."

"And I'm not going anywhere," Jacobs said. "And I'll handle the cops when they show up."

Barclay didn't hear. By then, he was dead asleep.

He was in an out of sleep all day, waking only to tell the nurses to hold all calls and allow no visitors. Except for Parkett and J.J., who refused to leave the room or the floor.

"You must have better things to do," Barclay told J.J. during one of his waking moments.

"Name one," Jacobs said.

The cops had come and gone, not waking Barclay, allowing J.J. to tell them what little there was to tell. For their part, the officers said they'd been unable to find witnesses to the attack or anything at the garage that might help identity the attacker.

The doctors were in and out, too, telling Barclay that the deep contusions on his face would heal with time, but might leave some scars. "You may want to keep that beard of yours," one said. The severe bruises on his back, stomach, and legs would also mend, they said, but more slowly. There was no kidney damage, and while they'd once feared he might have a concussion, they now felt it would be okay. "But you'll probably have headaches for a while."

When the early news came on, he watched with apprehension—knowing there'd probably be some mention of the attack. It came after the first commercial, with Maggie Lawrence on the screen, Barclay's picture super-imposed behind her.

"We regret to report tonight that our boss here at Channel Seven News, George Barclay, was attacked and beaten last night in the garage of his Minneapolis condominium. He survived the attack and is hospitalized at the Hennepin County Medical Center in fair condition. Police do not know if the assault was an attempted robbery or car-jacking, or a simple mugging. The investigation is continuing." Then, she added, "If you're watching, George, our very best wishes go out to you tonight, for a speedy, complete recovery. We already miss you here."

Barclay flicked off the TV. "Now why'd they have to do that?" he muttered.

"Because they love you," J.J. said, grinning from his chair.

"Bullshit."

Two large bouquets of flowers sat on the window ledge. One from the staff of the newsroom, the other—hard to believe—from Nicholas Hawke.

He'd also received a frantic call from his mother—who'd heard about the attack from a former Minneapolis neighbor, who'd heard a report on the radio.

"Why didn't you call us," she'd demanded. "We're worried sick."

"I'm okay, Mom. The doctors say I'm going to be fine. Just some bumps and bruises."

"Who did this to you?"

"I don't know. Some mugger, they think."

"Well, I'm coming up there," she'd said. "Your father's trying to arrange for the plane tickets now."

"Please don't," he'd pleaded. "You know how you hate to fly. And I'll be out of the hospital by the time you'd get here."

After more argument, and more reassurances from him, she'd reluctantly agreed to wait. "I'll call you, if I need you," he'd said.

He could hear her talking to his dad in the background.

"You promise?"

"I promise."

Twenty minutes later, Parkett was at the door. "You see the show?"

"Newscast, not a show, but, yeah, I saw it," Barclay said. "I wish you wouldn't have done it."

He walked in, nodded to J.J. "Too bad. Everybody sends their best."

"Thanks. I got the flowers."

"Are you better?"

"A little," Barclay said. "The pain pills are working. But I can barely keep my eyes open."

"Your lady friend's in the lobby."

"Rachel?"

"They won't let her up. Your orders, they say. She's refusing to leave."

"Sweet Jesus. J.J., will you go get her?"

"Sure," he said.

"So what's happening at the station?" Barclay asked.

"Same old, same old," Parkett replied. "Whoever said 'no news is good news' was full of shit. We're having trouble filling the half hours. But everybody's breaking their ass."

"No other problems?"

"No."

"How's Hawke."

"Haven't seen him," Parkett replied. "It's like he's in hiding."

"He must be around. He sent me flowers."

Despite himself, he dozed off, for how long he wasn't sure. But when he awoke, Rachel was next to the bed, holding his hand—a solitary tear making its way slowly down her cheek.

J.J. and Parkett were nowhere to be seen.

"Hey," he said, in a whisper.

She wiped the tear away. "You big oaf. Why didn't you call me?" An echo of his mother.

"I'm sorry you got stuck downstairs. I didn't know you were here."

She leaned down and kissed him, on the side of his lips not covered by the swath of bandage. Then on his good cheek. On his forehead. He breathed in the familiar, wonderful scent of her hair. The night before, he wasn't sure he'd ever smell it again.

"I didn't know until I saw the news," she said. "I couldn't believe it. I still can't."

He tried to raise himself up, but a stab of pain in his lower back kept him down. She saw the grimace, held his head up and pulled the pillow beneath it. "J.J. told me what happened. He says you're going to be okay."

"Easy for him to say," Barclay managed, with a smile.

"Listen to me now. When you're out of here, I want you to stay with me. I'm no nurse, but I'd like to take care of you. Get you back on your feet."

He thought for a moment. "That's a great offer. There's nothing I'd like more. But I can't. In fact, once I get out of here, I don't think we ought to see one another until this thing's over . . . until this guy is—"

"What?"

"I'm serious. He smashed my car right outside your condo. He has to know about you, Rachel. And Kate and the other women, too. Getting roughed up myself is one thing, but the thought of him doing this to you or the others . . . well, it's unthinkable. He's a madman. I want to keep a distance from all of you until the cops get him."

The tears reappeared. "That's not acceptable," she said. "Who knows how long that might take?"

"Not long, I hope," he said. "We must be getting close. He's getting more desperate."

She sat quietly, not bothering to wipe the tears away this time.

"Hey," he said. "You know I can't stand to see a woman cry."

"Tough," she replied.

J.J. and Parkett reappeared at the door. "Is this little love fest over?" Parkett asked.

"Oh, oh," J.J. said, spotting the tears. "We'll come back."

"No, that's okay," Rachel said, getting up. "I have to go. I'll call you tonight, George."

Then, leaning over, whispering, "Forget what I said last night. I'll compete with anybody. Dead or alive. Bring 'em on."

Parkett and Jacobs stood aside, watching her leave. "Wow," Parkett said, once she was gone, "you're the man."

Barclay smiled. But even that still hurt.

J.J. had reluctantly agreed to go home for the night, but told Barclay that he'd alerted the nurses' station and hospital security to keep a close eye on his room. "We don't want that prick taking a second shot at you. You look bad enough already."

"Do me a favor," Barclay said. "Go check my car in the garage. There's some photo albums and a big, bound book in the backseat. Bring them to me tomorrow, will you?"

"Will do."

Barclay gave him the garage security code. "One more thing. Take my cat to my neighbor in twenty-oh-four. Mrs. Ashburn. She loves him. And he must be going crazy by now. Hungry as hell. And angry, probably. You might want to be careful."

Jacobs got up to go.

"I'm going, too," Parkett said. "Gotta keep that ship afloat while the captain recovers from his wounds."

"Tell everybody thanks," Barclay said. "I'll see 'em soon."

HE SPENT TWO MORE DAYS in the hospital. Walking the halls, at first with help, later by himself with a walker. There were more tests and x-rays and more visits from the doctors—but by the third day, the pain in various parts of his body had begun to subside. The bruising and swelling had not gone away, but the bandage was off his face, and he'd begun to eat again—albeit not much.

The pounding headaches, however, did not stop.

Except for nights, J.J. was always there—or not far away. Rachel came at least twice a day, and—despite his protests—so, too, did a parade of other visitors, mostly from the newsroom. Everybody, it seems, wanted to get a peek at him.

Even Hawke stopped by, trying to be cheerful, but looking as morose as Barclay had ever seen him. "Things are going to hell in a hand basket, George," he said. "The whole goddamned deal could fall through."

Barclay said, "I'd heard things weren't going well."

Hawke drew himself up, "Coburn and his buddies—those pricks—are now claiming that TriCom may have ties to organized crime. That one of its corporate directors is a convicted felon, a fact they've hidden from the F.C.C. for years."

"What?"

"TriCom denies it, of course, but our lawyers say the Commission may have little choice but to investigate and perhaps even hold a hearing. Which could take months, if not years."

"My God," Barclay said. "So what happens next?"

"TriCom could pull the plug. The drop-dead provision in the purchase agreement is just a week away, which allows either side to cancel the deal. They could choose to get out of this mess. Meaning the whole deal is down the drain.

"What's more, our board is blaming me—claiming I've mishandled the whole thing. Making me their scapegoat. I may not even have a goddamned job."

"What about Coburn's group?"

"They're waiting in the bushes, I suspect. Ready to pounce."

Watching his distress, Barclay actually felt a pang of sympathy for the man. He wanted to offer words of encouragement, but couldn't find it in him. Besides, he guessed Hawke probably had more money in a sock than everybody else in the station, combined. "So what are you going to do?" he finally asked.

Hawke pulled himself up straight. "The only thing I can do," he replied. "Bury the bastards before they bury us."

BARCLAY SPENT HIS EVENINGS reviewing work from the station that Parkett brought him, and going over page after page of entries in Jennifer's funeral guest book. He knew from the FBI profilers that it was not uncommon for killers not only to visit the graves of their victims, but to attend their funerals, as well. It was a long shot, he knew, but the same could be said for everything else he was doing.

Katie had been right; the funeral had been attended by at least a couple hundred people. As usual, most of the names meant nothing to him, but he jotted down those that did.

David Casperson's name was not among them.

BY THE FOURTH DAY, HE WAS ready to leave. But not alone. J.J. brought a suitcase to the hospital, insisting that he move in with Barclay—for the time being, anyway. "I'll sleep on the couch," he said. "Or anywhere else you want to put me. But I don't want you out of my sight until we put this guy away. You're a wimp to begin with, and now a wounded wimp."

Barclay argued vehemently against it, to no avail.

"I've got a conceal-and-carry permit, you know," J.J. said.

"That's scary," Barclay countered.

J.J. patted his upper chest, beneath his sport coat. "I haven't carried in years, not since I retired, but I am now."

Barclay said, "Just make sure you shoot the right guy, okay?"

For the next three days, Barclay closeted himself inside the condo, using his phone, fax, and computer to communicate with his world. He avoided the outdoors, walking the hallways for exercise, and sleeping—for hours on end. Letting his wounds heal further.

Gradually his strength returned and the pain eased, except for the headaches. He'd quit the pain pills before leaving the hospital, for fear of becoming addicted, and allowed nature and Tylenol to do their jobs. And, so far, they seemed to be working.

Seuss was back from the neighbor's, as grouchy as ever. Some things never change.

Meantime, J.J. became something of his man-servant, doing the shopping, fixing meals, answering the phone, and running any necessary errands. He'd made a little nest for himself on the couch, not far from the TVs, and seemed quite content with the arrangement. "Hey," he said, "as long as there's Wild Turkey in the cupboard, I'm fine."

The only visitor was Jeff Parkett, who shuttled between the newsroom and the condo with paperwork that needed Barclay's attention. In return, he would send Parkett back with written critiques of each major newscast—to share with the producers and others at the station. "I want 'em to know I'm still alive and watching," he said. "I may be lame, but I'm not deaf and dumb."

More flowers arrived at the condo, including one bouquet from his parents, another from Rachel, and still another from Katie Thorson and her friends. "We feel so bad," their note read. "We feel responsible and can only hope that you make a quick and complete recovery. And don't worry, we're being careful."

He spoke by phone to Rachel at least once a day, and despite her protests, continued to insist that she keep her distance. "I don't want you anywhere near me," he told her. "In fact, I wish you'd leave town for a while. Take a quick vacation."

"Like where?" she asked.

"Boston, maybe. Go see Colleen. It's a great city."

"I know. I've been there."

"Go again."

"Forget it. You're not getting rid of me, George. Okay?"

"Okay. But are you watching your backside?"

"Yes."

"I wish I could."

She laughed. "You are getting better. I can tell."

"Do me a favor," he said. "I'm going to e-mail you that picture of the red-headed kid from Jennifer's album. Also the guy she was dancing with. Will you pass them around to some of your other classmates? See if anyone recognizes either one?"

"Sure. I'll copy them to some of those on the reunion list."

"Terrific," he said.

Once off the phone, he called J.J. into the office. Pulling out Jennifer's police file, he turned to page 49, and pointed to the interview with David Casperson. "Back then. Did you talk to this guy?" he asked.

J.J. took the file. "If I did it, my initials would be on the bottom of the page."

He held the file up to the light. "Nope. McIntyre did. See the initials. Mc."

"Who's McIntyre?"

"Eugene McIntyre. Another homicide cop. He died six or seven years ago. Heart attack."

"Shit."

"Even if he were still alive, he couldn't tell you much. Hell, it's been too damn long, and we did dozens of those interviews."

Barclay closed the file and put it away.

"So who's this Casperson?" J.J. asked.

Barclay explained the yearbook entry.

"Pretty thin straw, I'd say."

"Tell me something I don't know," he replied.

THE NEXT MORNING, AS J.J drove him to the station, Barclay was amazed to see, hanging over the front door, a big banner, black on white:

WELCOME BACK, GEORGE!

"Goddamn," he muttered.

"I told you they loved you," J.J. said.

Jacobs was behind the wheel of the Buick, about to pull into the station's underground ramp. Barclay sat next to him, defying J.J.'s demands that he sit in the back seat, out of sight. "You can stick that idea right up your ass," he'd said.

He'd been dreading this first day back at the station because he knew he'd spend half of it explaining to everyone what had happened and accepting their good wishes. He just wanted to get to work, to catch up, but he knew there was little hope of doing so.

Aside from a slight limp and a slow gait, he showed few visible signs of the attack. His face wounds were mostly healed, and even his headaches had finally subsided. But, still, if he got up too quickly from a chair, or out of bed, he'd feel momentary dizziness. The doctors had warned him about that.

J.J. dropped him off inside the ramp. They had agreed that Barclay wouldn't leave the building without alerting Jacobs on his cell phone. He was to go nowhere without J.J. alongside.

Instead of using the elevator, he hobbled up the back steps—hoping to avoid as many people as possible. At the top of the steps, he found himself surprisingly short of breath, knowing then that it might be awhile before he could get back on the treadmill.

Not that he'd miss it much.

He walked slowly down the long hallway, pausing long enough to thank well-wishers before moving on as quickly as he could manage. When he reached the newsroom, there was a shrill whistle from across the room—and, when all heads turned, immediate and spontaneous applause. He grinned and waved, hoping to make it to his office before being inundated.

No such luck.

Finally, after about ten minutes, he freed himself and walked to the raised assignment platform. There was another piercing whistle and people gathered below him. "First of all," he said, hoping his voice would carry, "thank you all very much for the flowers and your support. I was very touched. But, as you can see, I'm getting along fine and am ready to get back to work. If you'll let me. We have a lot to do, and the sooner we all forget about this little incident of mine, the more we'll get done. Thanks, again."

As he hoisted himself off the platform, someone from the back of the room shouted, "Have they got the guy yet?"

Barclay paused. "Not that I know of." Then, with a grin, "But you know our motto: If it's news, it's news to us."

Laughter followed as he made his way through the crowd, Parkett out front, clearing the way. "Are you really okay?" he asked. "You still look a little pale."

"I'm not ready to run a marathon," Barclay replied. "But, then again, I never was. So, yeah, I'm okay."

When they reached his office, he stopped short. There, standing between a brand new desk and credenza, was a smiling Maggie Lawrence. "Welcome home, George," she said. The office had been totally made over, including the new desk and guest chairs, and new carpeting.

"What the hell?" he mumbled, stepping inside the door.

Not only were the all new furnishings, but the mess he'd left behind, the clutter that had so irritated Nicholas Hawke, had been cleaned up. His books and tapes were arranged neatly on shelves, and the old newspapers and scripts that once littered the office either had been filed away or thrown away. Even the windows overlooking the newsroom were sparkling clean.

"Hawke gave us the okay to buy the stuff," Parkett said, from behind him. "And Maggie did the rest."

"I can't believe it," Barclay said, standing back.

"I hope you like it," Maggie said, giving him a quick hug.

He walked behind the desk and sat, swiveling in the new chair. "It's beautiful."

Everything that needed his attention was stacked in several neat piles on the desk. There was even a cup full of newly sharpened pencils. And off to one side, a stack of what appeared to be greeting cards. He picked them up and flipped through them. Get-well cards, he guessed.

"They've been coming in every day," Maggie said, as she prepared to leave. "You have a lot of fans out there." Then, at the door, she stopped. "Are you really okay? We were so worried about you."

"Trust me. I'll be fine."

Once she was gone and he was alone, he quickly opened the cards. Word of the attack must have spread on the Internet, for some of the cards came from old news buddies in various parts of the country. Another was from Stanley Hoffer, the GM of Channel Ten.

At the bottom of the pile was a card with a typed address on the envelope. And no return address. Inside, a blank card with a menacing message: Hope you're feeling better, asshole. Back off.

Barclay felt a slight shiver, momentarily reliving the nightmare in the garage. Whoever he was, the bastard was not going to go quietly.

Except for an occasional interruption or phone call, he spent most of the day behind his office door, sifting through the stacks of material that needed either his review or his signature. He did take time to attend the morning news meeting, and to make a courtesy stop at Hawke's office—to thank him for the flowers and the new office furniture—only to find him gone for the day.

Late in the afternoon, he got two phone calls. The first was from J.J., who said Josh Bennett wanted to have dinner with them, and the second from Katie Thorson. "Rachel told me you were back at work," she said. "I hope I'm not interrupting something important."

"No, that's fine, Katie. And thanks to you and the others for the flowers."

"That's why I'm calling," she said.

That took him back. "About the flowers you sent?"

"No, no. The other flowers."

He was still puzzled. "What do you mean?"

"I can't get it out of my mind. What you told me. That it might have been Jen's killer who left those flowers at her grave."

He gripped the phone more tightly. "That's not exactly what I said, Katie. I said the FBI profilers say killers sometimes do that, visit the graves of their victims."

"I understand."

"Okay."

"So I have a plan," she said. "Gloria, Jackie, Annie, and I, and others, if we can recruit them, are going to take turns sitting out at the cemetery, watching Jennifer's grave."

"Wait a minute . . ."

"No, listen." She was breathless. "We'll do it from a distance. With binoculars, if need be. And only when we have the time. If someone does come, we'll try to get a look at him, and maybe at his car license plate. That's all. We'd never approach him or anything like that."

"Katie, you listen to me. Please. That could be dangerous. And a big waste of time. The chance of seeing anyone, let alone her killer, is about the same as seeing me walk on the moon."

She was not dissuaded. "You knew what you were doing could be dangerous," she said.

"And look what it got me," he replied tersely. "It's not worth the risk, Katie."

"We'll have to decide that, I guess. We'll let you know if we see anything."

"Katie, please . . ."

By then, she had hung up.

BENNETT WAS WAITING in the restaurant, his face hidden behind a menu, when J.J. and Barclay walked up and sat down. "We're here," J.J. said.

The face reappeared. “Hey. Good to see you.”

“And you,” Barclay replied.

Bennett put the menu aside and studied him. “You don’t look that bad. Considering.”

“Thanks. You should’ve seen the other guy.”

Bennett chuckled. “I understand you didn’t.”

Barclay smiled. “You got that right. He ran scared when he thought I might get up off the concrete. Chicken-shit bastard.”

“In your dreams,” J.J. said.

“By the way,” Barclay said, showing them the anonymous greeting card, “I heard from him again.”

“Son of a bitch,” J.J. said as he studied the card and passed it on to Bennett. Who added, “This is one determined dude. Can I keep this?”

“Be my guest.”

A waiter appeared to take their drink orders and to announce the specials of the evening. Then he disappeared.

“We’ve got a lot to catch up on,” Bennett said. “Want me to go first?”

“Go ahead.”

“First of all, the blood we found on the woman’s blouse in the park and on the broken glass from your car is a match. Doesn’t tell us much, since it’s type A-positive, which is about as common as you can get. But it’s something. And, we’ve submitted those blood samples and the old semen samples found on Jennifer’s body for DNA testing. But as you know, it could take weeks or longer to get the results. Old, cold cases like this don’t have the highest priority. But at least the process has begun.”

“But,” Barclay interrupted, “even if there is a match, you still have to find out whose DNA it is. Right? It has to be in the system somewhere.”

“That’s right. And if your theory is correct, if this isn’t some kind of sexual predator we’re dealing with, then it may not be.”

“What else?”

“The names you gave me. The ones Knowles found who had spent time in prison, or were still there.”

"Yeah."

"They led nowhere. We checked them all out."

"Figures."

Their drinks came, and they put in their orders: fish for Barclay, red meat for the other two.

"So, what have you got?" Bennett asked.

He quickly filled him in on everything he could think of: the pictures from the photo albums, the funeral guest book, the flowers at the grave, and Katie Thorson's latest plan.

"Is she serious?" Bennett said.

"I tried to talk her out of it. But she thinks they have to do something."

"They're living in a fantasy world," J.J. offered.

"I agree," Barclay replied, sinking back in his chair, once again overcome by a deep sense of disappointment and frustration. "But we've gotta keep going," he finally said. "We're getting close to the guy. I can feel it. And he knows it. He's shitting his pants out there somewhere."

"It's a big somewhere," J.J. said.

"I know, I know," Barclay said. "But we've narrowed it down. We know a lot about him. Except who he is. And he must be feeling the heat. Or he wouldn't be doing what he's doing."

"Maybe," Bennett said, "but look at it another way. He could be playing games with us. With you. Getting his kicks. Flexing his muscles. And his brains. Staying one step ahead. Having fun."

"Why do you say that?" Barclay asked.

"Because if he was truly scared, he'd simply hunker down, lay low like he has. Play it safe. I've told you before. I think he sees this as a challenge. A game of one-upmanship. Cat and mouse. With no fear that he's ever going to get caught."

Barclay asked, "Do you really believe that?"

Bennett thought for a moment. "I don't know. I just think this guy's too smart to be scared."

That's a hell of a note to end on, Barclay thought.

When he and J.J. got back to the condo, Barclay dug through his notes, finally finding a telephone number Knowles had given him days before. He quickly punched in the Des Moines area code and number. A woman answered.

"Ken Younger, please."

There was a pause. "Who's this?"

"My name's George Barclay, with Channel Seven in the Twin Cities."

"Really?"

"Yes. Is Mr. Younger there?"

"I'll get him."

As Barclay waited, J.J. said, "You don't give up, do you?"

"Not easily," he replied.

After another minute or two, Younger was on the phone. "Yes?"

Before Barclay could explain who he was, Younger interrupted. "I know who you are. I got your letter. I guess everybody did."

"Good. Then you know why I'm calling."

"Not really. I told the police everything I knew back then."

"I know," Barclay said, "but I have a couple of questions of my own, if you don't mind."

"Okay."

"You went with Jennifer for a long time. Knew her well."

"That's true."

Barclay went on, "I found a picture taken of Jennifer at the prom. The prom I'm told you took her to. Dancing with someone else. A guy in a blue tux, with short, dark hair. Who none of her friends seem to remember or recognize. Do you happen to know who that might have been?"

There was a long pause. "I'd have to think," he said. "She danced with a lot of other guys. They wouldn't leave her alone."

"Even though she was there with you?"

"That made no difference to them. Or to her. She just wanted to have fun."

"There's another picture," Barclay said. "Of a red-headed kid at the senior skip day picnic. At the St. Croix state park. Does that ring any bells?"

There was another pause. "Not really," he said.

"Do you have an e-mail address?"

Younger gave it to him.

"I'll send you the pictures I'm talking about. Get back to me if you know who they are. Okay?"

"Sure. I'll do anything I can do to help." Then, in a whisper, "I would have married her, you know. If she would have let me."

"From what I'm gathering," Barclay said, "you weren't alone."

WHETHER IT WAS HIS BODY'S WAY of healing or something else at play he couldn't say, but since leaving the hospital, he'd never slept better. Going to bed early, sleeping late, rarely waking in between. And so it was on this morning.

Ignoring the alarm, he was roused only by the whiff of coffee and the muted sounds of the radio coming from the kitchen. He found J.J. at the kitchen table with his coffee, engrossed in the morning paper. "You'd better read this," he said, pointing to a headline in the business section of the *StarTribune*.

> TriCom "Turns off"
> Channel Seven
> GM Hawke Assails Opponents
>
> TriCom Communications, the North Carolina media giant, has ended its attempt to purchase WCKT-TV, Channel Seven in the Twin Cities,

deciding to exercise a "drop dead" provision of the purchase agreement—which allowed either party to pull out of the deal as of yesterday.

The sale of Channel Seven to TriCom was announced several weeks ago, but immediately faced stiff opposition from local minority groups, citing what they said was TriCom's "dismal record" in equal opportunity employment and public service in a number of cities where they own broadcast and newspaper properties. TriCom denied those and other charges, but the Federal Communications Commission (FCC) has delayed approval of the transaction pending an investigation.

Larry Landeau, TriCom's vice-president for acquisitions, said, "We foresaw a protracted legal battle over this purchase and finally decided that it would be in everyone's best interests to simply end our efforts as quickly as possible."

Nathaniel Coburn, a local attorney and one of the leaders of the opposition group, hailed the decision by TriCom, calling it "a great day" for television viewers in the Twin Cities, especially those in our minority communities."

But Nicholas Hawke, vice president and general manager of Channel Seven, said the station and TriCom have been the victims of "a vicious, unwarranted attack" by Coburn's group, adding "this is racial blackmail, plain and simple."

"Holy shit," Barclay muttered as he continued to read. "Beaten again on our own goddamned story."

No wonder he couldn't find Hawke when he'd stopped by his office.

"Can Hawke really say that?" J.J. asked.

"What?"

"That it's racial blackmail? Pretty serious charge, if you ask me."

He was right. And there was more toward the end of the story.

Hawke said the opponents had conducted "a scurrilous campaign" of lies and deceit to impugn the reputation of TriCom and to "sabotage" the deal in their own self-interest. "Talk about playing the race card," Hawke said. "They did it in spades."

Coburn reacted angrily to the charge, saying Hawke's words amounted to "racism of the worst kind." He said his group acted in the community's best interests, not their own, and took special exception of Hawke's use of the word "spade." "If that isn't a stereotypical racial slur, I've never heard one."

Barclay looked up from the paper, disbelieving. Remembering Hawke's words, "I'm going to bury the bastards before they bury us."

He looked at J.J. "I think Hawke just fucked himself." Then he picked up the phone and hit the speed dial. Parkett answered.

"You see the paper?" Barclay asked.

"In spades," Parkett replied.

"Smart ass. Where's Hawke?"

"In a spider hole, I'd guess. Nobody's seen him."

"Try to find him. Tell him we're going to need some kind of statement for our own story. And track down Coburn. I'll be in as soon as I can. The shit's gonna fly, and I want us to be on top of it."

"Gotcha."

WHEN HE GOT TO THE NEWSROOM, he found an air of jubilation. Larry Landeau's cutout was again hanging in effigy, the noose tied tighter than ever, with people damn near dancing in the aisles. "This is a great day," Parkett said, escorting him toward his office. "The troops are happier than hell."

"I can see," Barclay said.

"I've left messages for Hawke," Parkett said, "but, so far, no response. And we just got word that Coburn and others from his group are holding a news conference this afternoon. Word is that they're going to demand Hawke's resignation."

"Surprise, surprise," Barclay said. "I'll see if I can dig him out of his hole."

MARIA FALLON WAS SITTING PRIMLY at her desk when he arrived at Hawke's office. "He's not here, George," she said immediately. "And I don't know where he is. That's the truth."

"I've got to find him," Barclay said. "A storm's brewing out there and he's in the middle of it."

Her carefully controlled façade began to crumble. Her eyes welled, and she turned away. "The poor man," she whispered, wiping at the tears with the back of her hand. "He's been under such pressure. You wouldn't believe it, George. The protesters. The board.

Those awful people from TriCom. They've all been after him. It was finally too much, I think."

He walked over to her and touched her shoulder, hoping to console her. "Maybe it's time, Maria. A blessing in disguise. No one should live with that kind of stress. It'll kill him."

She looked up, still sniffling. "But what happens to me?"

"Depends on what the board decides to do. If they sell to somebody else, we may all be out of a job. But I'm sure you'll be well taken care of."

That seemed to mollify her. She grasped his hand. "Thanks, George. If I hear from him, I'll call you."

"You think he's meeting with the board?"

"That's my guess, but I don't know where. The chairman called this morning, quite angry."

He's dead meat, Barclay thought, walking out.

LESS THAN AN HOUR LATER, he got his own call from Harold "H.T." Thomberg, the chairman of the board of WCKT-TV. Someone he'd met no more than a dozen times in ten years. "George? I understand you've been trying to reach Nicholas."

"That's right, sir. We need his comments regarding the sale and the statements quoted in this morning's paper. Yours, too, for that matter."

"That's why I called," Thomberg said. "Nicholas will be holding a news conference in an hour, at the station. To apologize for his statements and to announce his retirement, effective immediately."

"That's too bad . . ." Barclay started to say.

"The promotion department is alerting the other media, and I've spoken personally to Mr. Coburn, expressing the board's apologies for the inappropriate remarks made by Nicholas."

"Will you be at the news conference?"

"No. But I'm issuing a written statement on behalf of the board."

"So what happens next?" Barclay asked.

"I may want to talk to you about that, George. We're going to need someone to run the station until we can find a new general manager."

"Are you talking about me?"

"Yes."

"Sorry, sir. My plate's full, as it is."

"Don't be hasty. You seem to be the only one around there with any sense."

"Sir—"

"It's H.T."

"Okay, H.T. I really think you should—"

"We'll talk. Once things settle down."

Then next thing he heard was a dial tone.

TO BARCLAY'S SURPRISE, Hawke appeared fit and relaxed, even sprightly, when he walked into the studio. Dressed in a dark-blue suit, white shirt, and polka dot bow tie, he strode about, smiling, shaking hands with everyone in sight.

Turning to the podium, he waited patiently as the cameras and microphones were set up. "Are we ready?" he finally asked, a smile still on his lips.

Given thumbs up by one of the photographers, he began. "I have two items to discuss with you today, but please, no questions afterwards." He paused, his eyes traversing the crowd. "First, I'd like to extend my heartfelt apologies to Nat Coburn and the group he represents for my unfortunate comments quoted in the newspaper. The words were uttered in anger and frustration at our inability to consummate the sale of Channel Seven to TriCom Communications, which I still believe would have been in the public's best interests. And while I continue to believe that racial politics played a role in the outcome of this endeavor, I am not now, nor have I ever have been, a racist—and will happily stand by my record in that regard.

"Second, at the request of our board of directors, I am announcing my retirement, effective at the end of this news conference."

Maria Fallon, standing next to Barclay, uttered a small cry.

"I leave with a heavy heart," he continued, "but with great pride in what we have accomplished in my more than twenty years in this position. This is a great television station, and with the help of all these people gathered here, it will continue to be. My wife and I leave tomorrow for a Caribbean vacation, which I believe I have more than earned. Thank you, very much."

With that, he left the podium to a smattering of applause and plunged once again into the crowd of onlookers, shaking hands, patting backs, whispering in ears. For all the world, he looked like a man who had just walked out of prison and into the bright sunshine of a new day.

When he came to Barclay, he wrapped his arms around him and squeezed. "George," he said. "I'm going to miss you more than anybody. You've been a giant thorn in my side, a pain in my ass, but I admire and respect you—and hope that you have a speck of respect left for me."

"I do," Barclay mumbled.

"I'll keep in touch," he said, then moved on.

As Barclay watched him go, he had to admit he might actually miss the little bastard.

WHEN BARCLAY GOT BACK TO HIS OFFICE, Parkett said he had a phone call waiting. "You may not want to take it. He wouldn't give his name."

He picked up the phone anyway. "Yes?"

"So, do you want to be a baseball announcer?"

"What?"

It was Stanley Hoffer, the GM of Channel Ten. "What'd I tell you? The sale's off and Hawke's gone."

"You were right," Barclay admitted.

"And all of the big sports guys in town are waiting in the wings. Hiding behind Coburn, ready to turn your place into the sports super-station."

"I still can't believe that," Barclay replied.

"Well, when it happens, remember our conversation. I'm still interested."

"I appreciate that."

"You feeling better?"

"A lot."

"Good. Take care."

BARCLAY SPENT THE REST OF THE AFTERNOON working with the producers, fashioning the story of the botched station sale and Hawke's "retirement." The piece featured not only a portion of Hawke's goodbye statement, but also a segment from Nat Coburn's news conference.

Coburn accepted the station's—and Hawke's—apologies with good grace, and went on to say, "Now that TriCom has bowed out of the picture, our group plans to approach the Channel Seven board with our own bid for the station."

To which one reporter asked, "When are you going to reveal who's in your group?"

"In good time," Coburn replied.

Another: "Where's the money coming from?"

Coburn: "Sources that will remain nameless."

The same reporter: "Any truth to the rumors that you want to create a sports super-station?"

"I don't comment on rumors."

As Barclay watched the tape, witnessing Coburn's evasiveness, he was suddenly convinced that Hoffer might be right. And Hawke, too. That the whole protest may have been a cleverly-orchestrated charade.

Poor Hawke. He lost both the battle and the war.

But, Barclay thought, *that's show business*.

37

As they stood outside the door of the condo, fiddling with the keys, J.J. said, "Don't be shocked, but there's a surprise waiting inside."

"What?" Barclay said.

"You'll see."

He opened the door, and there—standing in the middle of the living room—was Rachel, with Seuss in her arms. "Hi, guys," she said. "Dinner's in the oven. And the beer's in the refrigerator."

"I'll be damned," was all he could say.

She put the cat down and walked over to give him a hug. "Is this okay? Coming here? J.J. suggested it. Said it would be safe. That you needed a lift and that he was tired of cooking."

"Of course it's okay," he said, momentarily dazed. "It's great."

She was wearing a light-blue scooped-neck sweater and white slacks that tapered to her ankles. A thin gold pendant hung from her neck, with matching ear rings and bracelet. It was the first time he'd seen her since the hospital, and he couldn't help but stare.

"What's the matter?" she said.

"You're gorgeous, that's all."

She laughed. "And you're full of it."

They retreated to the kitchen, and while she stood by with her glass of wine, J.J. reached for the Wild Turkey and Barclay for a beer. "There's roast beef in the oven," she said, "but it's going to need another half hour or so."

"Just so you know," J.J. said, "after dinner I'm taking off for a while. Let the two of you get reacquainted."

"You don't have to do that," Rachel said.

"No problem. I'm told profits are down at O'Gara's since I've been away."

Back in the living room, with their drinks, and with Seuss cuddled between them on the couch, Rachel said, "You've had quite a day, haven't you? I saw it all on the news."

Barclay nodded. "I actually felt a little sorry for Hawke. He truly believed the TriCom deal was a good one. And, who knows? He may have been right, if we end up as some kind of sports station."

He also told them about his phone conversation with H.T. Thomberg, the chairman of the board.

"That's wonderful," Rachel said. "Are you going to do it?"

"Probably not."

"Why in the world not?"

Good question, he thought. He knew that over the past thirty years or so, large numbers of news directors had gone on to become successful general managers at stations across the country. But . . .

"I don't know," he finally said. "I just don't think I'm cut out for it. Not now, anyway. I love news, but I get freaked out if I'm around too many suits. Besides, who knows how long this investigation's going to go on?"

"Speaking of that," Rachel said, "I have some news of my own."

"What's that?"

"I don't know if it's important, but—like you asked—I forwarded that picture of the red-headed kid to a number of my friends."

"And?"

"A couple of them knew who he was. Or is. His name's Davis Stratford. He was in our class, but kind of a loner, I'm told. I certainly never knew him."

"Did you say Davis?"

"Yes. Davis Stratford. I checked my records. He's only been at two of the reunions. The tenth. And this last one."

"Really? He was there this time?"

"I guess so. He signed up, anyway."

Barclay got up and hurriedly went to his office, returning with Jennifer's police file—flipping through it to the interview section.

"What are you looking for?" J.J. asked.

"The guys you interviewed back then. When I was looking for more Davids . . . and found David Casperson . . . I remember other names. And I think Davis was one of them."

J.J. stood by him, looking over his shoulder.

"Here it is," Barclay said, pointing. "Davis Stratford. Interviewed on the same day as Casperson. By the same cop, McIntyre. He was in the same school play. David. Davis. The similarity in names never occurred to me."

He put the file down and went back to his office, returning with both Jennifer's yearbook and the funeral guest book. He gave the funeral book to Rachel. "Can you see if his name's in there?"

Then to the yearbook. Finding the inscription that had bothered him so much for so long. *Sorry it didn't work out. Can't say I didn't try. Too bad, too sad. Hope you don't regret it some day*. "Look closely," he told J.J., holding the book up. "The scribbled signature. I thought it said David, but I never was sure. It could be Davis."

"I guess," J.J. conceded, but showing far less excitement than Barclay.

"I found it," Rachel said, sliding closer to him. "He did come to the funeral."

Barclay got up and paced the floor, rubbing his hands. "What'd you just tell me, Rachel?"

"About the funeral?"

"No. The reunion. You said this Davis was at the tenth reunion, right?"

"That's what the records show."

"And wasn't that the reunion where you honored Jennifer's memory?"

She caught on. "That's right."

He looked at J.J. "I think we may be on to something."

J.J. stifled a yawn. "And I think I've heard that before."

Barclay walked to the kitchen to get another beer, and to refill their glasses. Returning, he asked Rachel, "Do I have time to make a call before dinner?"

"Sure."

He went to the phone and called John Knowles, who answered on the second ring.

"John, this is Barclay."

"Hey, George."

Barclay quickly related what they'd just discovered. "I need to find out everything I can about this Davis Stratford."

"I'll get at it first thing in the morning," Knowles said. Then, "This sounds more promising than most."

"I hope so."

THE BEDROOM WAS HALF IN LIGHT, half in dark, the light spilling in from the hallway. Dinner was over, J.J. was off to O'Gara's, and they were alone. "For a couple of hours, at least," he'd told them. "Have fun."

Seuss lay on the bed, watching with interest.

Rachel was unbuttoning his shirt, slowly. "I want to see that bruised and battered body of yours," she whispered. "Up close, and personal."

Halfway down the shirt, she stopped, spreading it open, kissing his chest, his neck. Lingering there. Then up to his lips, her tongue exploring, as it had that first time in the car.

He stood straight, helpless to do anything but feel. And wonder.

The buttons were free, the shirt off. The belt went and the pants fell.

"Come," she said. "Into the light."

She knelt next to him, running her fingers over the welts and bruises that remained on his legs and back. "You poor thing," she said, her hands as smooth as the silk she once wore. "You're still black and blue all over."

Then she was in his arms, holding on. Slowly, he did to her what she had done to him, feeling the warmth of her breasts against his chest. Hearing her breath quicken. Small moans, barely audible, even against his ear.

"You're wonderful," she whispered. "Have I ever told you that?"

"This is a dream, isn't it?"

"No, it's real."

They were on the bed, pushing Seuss aside, their bodies, intertwined, in and out of the light, glistening. The frantic, pulsating urges of their first time together had quieted, allowing them to explore hidden, unexplored places that provided Barclay, at least, with pleasures he had never known before.

When it was over, they lay quietly. Absorbing, cooling. She leaned over him, running her hands down the length of him. "You've gotten so much thinner," she said. "It's hard to believe it's the same you."

It was true, although he deserved little of the credit. The time in the hospital and since seemed to have cut more of his weight than the weeks on the treadmill.

She snuggled back against him. "We're a perfect fit, you know."

"I know. And I still can't believe it."

She chuckled. "Who would have ever thought?"

"Not me. God, not me."

BY THE TIME J.J. GOT BACK TO THE CONDO, they were settled in on the couch, watching a late Twins game, from Seattle. The Twins were trailing, but it was only the middle of the fifth.

"So how'd it go?" J.J. asked.

"Great," Rachel replied. "We've just been sitting here, reading and watching the game."

"Uh huh. And I just got back from outer space."

Barclay laughed. "Are you sober?"

"As a judge."

"Good," Rachel said, "because I've got to get home."

Barclay walked her to the door. To J.J. "Take good care of her. Walk her all the way inside her place."

"Who do you think you're talking to? I'm a cop, remember."

As Barclay opened the door, Rachel turned and kissed him fully on the lips, oblivious to J.J. standing to the side. "When can we do this again?" she asked.

"You mean read and watch TV?"
She grinned. "Yes."
"Soon, I hope."
"So do I." And she kissed him again.

The reverberations from Hawke's sudden departure were still echoing in the newsroom when Barclay walked in the next morning. Small clusters of people gathered in every corner until they saw him. Then they began to scatter.

"What's going on?" he demanded.

"That's what everyone else is wondering," Parkett replied. "What is going on? Who's running the place?"

"Not the inmates, I'll tell you that. Get 'em back to work."

"Seriously," Parkett said, trailing him toward his office.

Barclay stopped at his door. "I don't know. Somebody else is going to have to figure that out. But as far as I know, I'm still running the news department."

"Yes, sir," he said, clicking his heels.

"And stop that clicking shit," Barclay said. "It makes me crazy."

"Yes, sir." *Click. Click.*

"Asshole," Barclay muttered.

Both the *StarTribune* and *Pioneer Press* were replete with stories of the Hawke and Coburn news conferences, and with speculation as to who Coburn's backers might be. Coburn wasn't saying anything more, nor was anyone else connected with his group.

For his part, H.T. Thomberg had refused comment, except to say, "As of his moment, the station is no longer for sale." Adding that an interim general manager would be named as soon as possible.

Two hours later, John Knowles was in Barclay's office, looking even gaunter than usual. He slumped into the guest chair, his glasses again hanging from his nose. He took out a small notepad. "Here's some preliminary stuff on Stratford. I'll get more later, but thought you should see what I have so far."

"Good."

"He's forty-four years old. Married for the third time, and lives in Richfield. Works construction, a carpenter, I guess. No significant problems with the law, although he does have two DUIs and one disorderly conduct conviction. Served thirty days in the county workhouse. He's also has been in and out of debt, with a couple of bankruptcies to his credit."

"Kids?"

"Two. Both living away from home."

"Anything else?"

"Maybe. The disorderly conduct charge came in a plea bargain. He was originally charged with assault. Apparently he beat the hell out of some guy in a bar fight."

Sounds familiar, Barclay thought.

"You've got his address?"

"Yup."

"And where he works?"

"Right now he's on a job in south Minneapolis. Building an apartment house or something. I've got that address, too."

"Great work, John."

"One more thing. I'm going out to the construction site this afternoon to see if I can get some pictures of the guy. From a distance, of course."

"Tell me when you're leaving," Barclay said. "J.J. and I would like to tag along."

Knowles had no sooner left than Bennett was on the phone. "J.J. told me about your new theory," he said.

"Another long shot, I know," Barclay replied tiredly.

"Maybe not," Bennett said. "After J.J. called, I did some of my own checking. One of my buddies in the Minneapolis PD dug out the file on his assault charge. The beating Stratford gave the guy in the bar was remarkably similar to yours. Blind-sided him, kicked the crap out of him."

"He's got big feet, I can testify to that," Barclay said, then related what Knowles had just told him.

"That would seem to fit the profile of the kind of guy we're looking for," Bennett said. "Bad marriages, bad credit, bad temper. In short, a loser. You may be on to something."

"But you once said you thought he was smart."

"Maybe I was wrong. Maybe he's just clever, not smart."

"So, what are you going to do?" Barclay asked.

"For the moment, nothing. I don't have the time. I'm up to my shoulders in new shit."

Barclay heaved a sign. "Okay. We'll keep in touch."

THE CONSTRUCTION SITE WAS NOT FAR from Cedar Lake, near the city's chain of lakes, a three-story brick building that looked about half-way done. Scaffolding rose on two sides of the structure, with at least a dozen men and women moving around the building, some on the scaffolding, laying the bricks.

Knowles, Barclay, and J.J. were crowded inside the white I-Team van, with darkened windows on each side, and the lettering D.H. Plumbing inscribed in black on the outside. The van had seen better days, dirty and rusting-out, part of the non-descript look they needed.

Parked down the street, they were squeezed between a car and another van. Outside, the day was bright and warm; inside, it was dark and cool, thanks to the van's air-conditioner. Knowles was at one of the windows, sighting through the viewfinder of the digital long-lens camera.

"The only thing we know about him," Barclay said, "is that he has red hair. Or used to."

"They're all wearing those damned hard hats," Knowles said, adjusting the focus.

Barclay and J.J. waited patiently, sitting on big camera cases stored in the back of the van. Ten, then fifteen, minutes passed.

"Wait a second," Knowles finally said. "I think I may have him. He just came out."

They heard the camera shutter click. Several times, in quick succession.

Barclay picked up a pair of binoculars. "Where?"

"On the right side of the building. He just took his hard hat off."

Barclay found him. Leaning against the bricks. Draining a water bottle. Then lighting a cigarette. His red hair tied in a ponytail. Big, maybe six-foot-three, with broad shoulders and a slim waist. Wearing a red muscle shirt that revealed biceps that could only have come from a lot of time in the weight room.

"Son of a bitch," Barclay muttered. "I know that guy."

"What? Lemme see," J.J. said, snatching the binoculars from Barclay. "Holy shit. He looks like a friggin' wrestler."

"He was at the reunion," Barclay said, a tremor in his voice. "Drunk on his ass. Tried to pick a fight with me."

"Why?" J.J. asked.

"Got me. I'd never seen him before. He didn't like the way I looked, I guess."

"You're shitting me."

"His hair's longer. And it wasn't tied in a ponytail. But that's him, I swear."

Knowles continued to shoot until Stratford flicked the cigarette butt and went back into the building.

Barclay couldn't curb his excitement. "What now?" he asked.

"I'll take you back to the station," Knowles said. "Make some prints for you. But I want to come back to see where he goes and what he does."

"Great," Barclay replied, "but don't let him catch sight of you."

Knowles gave him a look. "And end up looking like you?"

BACK IN THE OFFICE, BARCLAY found a message waiting from H.T. Thomberg. "Call me, ASAP," it said, leaving his number.

Barclay picked up the phone. "Barclay here, returning your call."

"Good. Have you thought any more about our talk?"

"Yes, sir, I have. I think I'll have to decline. For now, anyway."

"You're sure?"

"I'm sure."

"That's what I was afraid of," Thomberg said. "So I'm planning to ask Hal Hughes to steer the ship for a while."

Hughes was the station comptroller. A bean counter. A surprising choice, and someone Barclay knew only—and perhaps unfairly—as a meek little twerp. "Okay," he said, hoping to keep the doubt out of his voice. "I'll do what I can to help."

"I knew you would. But just remember, this is an interim appointment. I hope we can talk again in the future."

"I'd be happy to. The timing now is just not right."

"I understand. You're a good man, George. First rate."

BY LATE AFTERNOON, KNOWLES was back in the newsroom, spreading the prints on Barclay's desk, all remarkably clear. Including not only the shots Barclay had seen him take at the construction site, but others after work: Stratford climbing into a black pickup truck, a Ford F-150, going in and out of a bar, Tandy's Pub, and—from a greater distance—getting out of the truck in the driveway of a small, white rambler.

"These are great, John. I hope he didn't spot you."

"No way. I never got that close."

"So what do you think?"

Knowles shrugged. "Hard to know. From what we saw today, he's just a working stiff. Certainly did nothing strange. But I'd like to keep an eye on him for another day or so."

"You've got the time?"

"I'll make the time."

ONCE KNOWLES WAS GONE, BARCLAY was on the phone to Katie Thorson. "Hey, Katie," he said, "I'm glad I caught you. You've been at the cemetery?"

"I was earlier," she said. "Gloria's there now. We're taking four-hour shifts."

"How's it going?"

"Boring. But we're getting lots of reading and knitting in. And we feel like we're doing something that might help."

"You're keeping a distance?"

"Yes," she said. "We're not taking any chances."

"Good. But I have another favor to ask."

"Sure."

Barclay picked up one of the pictures Knowles had left, a close-up of Stratford standing outside the new apartment building. "I'm going to e-mail you a picture of a guy that we took today, the adult version of the red-headed kid we spotted in Jennifer's album. The one none of you knew."

"Okay."

"Rachel found out that his name's Davis Stratford. Ever heard of him?"

"No, not that I remember."

"Here's the deal. While you're at the cemetery, I'd like you to drop by some of the nearby florist shops with the picture. Ask if they remember selling a bouquet to him recently. He's pretty distinctive looking—big, with his red hair in a ponytail. They might remember."

"Okay," she said, hesitation in her voice. "But what should I tell them?"

He thought for a moment. "Say he's your long-lost brother. That you're trying to find him, that he might have left a bouquet at your mother's grave. Something like that."

"You think he may be the one?"

"Possible. But it could also be another dead end."

There was a long pause at the other end of the line.

"Katie?"

"Sorry," she said. "I was just saying a little prayer."

Hal Hughes was an officious little man, hardly taller than Hawke, who clearly enjoyed his new-found power as interim general manager. Sitting at the head of the big conference table, twirling his glasses, he looked smugly at the people around him—once his co-workers, suddenly his subordinates.

"Okay, people," he said, echoing one of Hawke's favorite phrases. "Listen up. It's time to get to work."

Barclay glanced around. He wasn't the only one trying to hide a smirk.

"I have been entrusted with an awesome responsibility," Hughes went on, puffing up. "By Chairman Thomberg himself. And I take that responsibility very seriously."

Spare me, Barclay thought.

"We are facing many unfinished tasks. Budgets to finalize, labor negotiations to prepare for, promotional plans to develop." Then, shooting a hard look at Barclay, "It'll take all our undivided attentions."

Barclay returned the look. "What are you trying to say, Hal?"

"Just that, George. I know you've had your troubles recently, with the attack and all. That you've been gone a lot. But from now on, I want us all here, working twenty-four hours a day, if necessary."

"I don't think that's possible, Hal. I need my beddy-bye."

There were muffled chuckles around the table, not including Hughes. "I'm not amused, George. And I think I deserve some respect."

Barclay leaned across the table. "You'll have to earn that, Hal. Don't take yourself so goddamned seriously. You're not king, and we're not your serfs. We're all in this together, right? And we'll do our jobs. Trust me."

Hughes rose up, the glasses now clenched in his fist. "I may not be king," he said, spitting out the words. "But I'm the one sitting at the head of this table, not you."

Barclay couldn't resist. The smarmy little prick. "Only because I declined," he said.

There was a collective gasp, everyone caught by surprise, including Hughes. "I don't believe that," he sputtered.

"Then ask H.T," Barclay said. "I only mention it because I think we should get off on the right foot, Hal. You're our boss, okay, but lighten up. And give us the same respect that you're demanding."

Hughes sat back in his chair, studying Barclay. "I think you and I should spend some time together, George," he finally said. "Get some things straight."

"That's a good idea," Barclay replied. "Just give me a call."

With that, the meeting was quickly adjourned.

BARCLAY WAS NO SOONER BACK in the newsroom than he was hailed by Parkett, holding up a phone. "You've got a call. Lady sounds excited."

"Mr. Barclay?"

It was Katie Thorson, a tremor in her voice as her words tumbled out. "You were right! A florist just three blocks from the cemetery recognized the picture. Said he remembered the ponytail . . . that the man was in a week or so ago."

Barclay could feel his chest tighten.

She rushed on. "I even went back and got the bouquet from the grave. Showed it to him. He said it was one of his, that it could have been the one that this Stratford bought."

"Great work, Katie. Did he fall for your story?"

"Absolutely. Asked me to leave my name and number in case my brother came in again."

"You didn't, did you?"

"Of course not. I thanked him but told him he may have already left town."

Bright woman, Barclay thought. And, for once, a long shot might actually be paying off. "Katie, listen to me. From now on, you and the others should stay away from the cemetery. We may know who the guy is now—"

"No, we'll stick it out. We still haven't seen him at the grave itself."

"And you probably won't," Barclay said. "Go home, please. This could get hairy."

"Like I told you before," she said, "we'll have to decide that."

DESPITE HIS OBJECTION TO BARCLAY being out in public, J.J. had finally agreed that they could meet with Bennett after work at O'Gara's. "Hell," Barclay had argued, "if I'm not safe with two cops, when will I be? Besides, I need to get out of the newsroom and smell a little stale bar air."

Bennett was waiting in a booth, nursing a Mountain Dew. Barclay joined him while J.J. stood at the bar, ordering their drinks.

"You feeling better?" Bennett asked.

"Yeah. Almost back to normal."

"Good," Bennett said. "So why the urgent meeting?"

Barclay showed him the picture of Stafford, and quickly and excitedly told him what Katie had learned from the florist.

Bennett said, "He's sure it's the same guy?"

"That's what he says."

"Is that it?"

J.J. returned to the booth, a drink in each hand.

"What do you mean, 'Is that it'?" Barclay said, taking his beer. "It's another piece of the puzzle. It fits. This is our guy."

"Maybe," Bennett said.

Barclay stared at him

"I've seen too many eyewitnesses who were dead wrong," Bennett said. "Especially looking at a photo lineup. I'm not saying this flower guy is wrong, but it would pay to be a little skeptical."

"But Katie said he was positive."

"Trust me, they all do. And, hell, even if it was your guy, he could've brought the bouquet to some other grave. You never know."

Barclay couldn't disguise his disappointment. He'd already decided that if this proved to be another false lead, another dead end, he'd give up the chase. No one could blame him for that, not Katie or her friends, or Jennifer's father, or even Jennifer herself.

But what else was there? He'd followed every lead, however thin, and obeyed every instinct, however silly. He'd read every police report, talked to everyone and anyone who'd had any kind of contact or relationship with Jennifer, in the process coming to know her far better than he ever could have imagined.

She was no longer a ghost out of the past.

But what had he gotten for all of his trouble? Himself roughed up, another woman attacked, to say nothing of the neglect he'd given his job and the people who depended on him in the newsroom.

It was, he'd decided, time to end it, one way or another.

"Okay," he finally said. "So what do you suggest?"

"Keep watching him," Bennett replied. "But play it safe. Keep your distance. Maybe he'll do something foolish."

"That could take forever."

He shrugged. "What do you want me to do? Get a search warrant, or arrest the guy, on what we know now? Give me a break."

J.J. broke in. "Getting some of his DNA might help."

"How the hell do we do that?" Barclay asked.

"You'd need a court order," Bennett said. "And you won't get it."

Barclay sank back in the booth. "Shit," he muttered. "This is a story without an ending. And I'm running out of gas."

J.J. put his arm around him. "Perk up and drink up, Georgie. We'll think of something."

AS IT TURNED OUT, JOHN KNOWLES already had. In fact, he was way ahead of them.

As they sat in O'Gara's, stewing, Knowles was slouched on a stool in Tandy's Pub, which, for a recovering alcoholic, was the last place in the world he wanted to be. A stool apart from him sat Davis Stratford, wearing another of his muscle shirts, grimy and stained from his day on the job. He was hunched over a bourbon and water, dragging on a cigarette.

Knowles was amazed. Smoking in public places, including bars, had been prohibited in Minnesota for several years, but Stratford and others were obviously paying no heed to the law. And no one seemed to be complaining. Not in this joint. They'd probably be out on their asses if they did.

Knowles had followed his F-150 from the construction site, deciding at the last moment to trail him into the bar. "What the hell," he told Barclay later, "the guy had never seen me, didn't know me."

And he was right. Stratford had paid him no heed, barely glancing his way as he'd climbed onto the stool.

Tandy's was a typical neighborhood tavern, the likes of which Knowles had seen hundreds of times in his drinking days. Old, somewhat run down, but comfortable—with a pool table and dart boards, and Twins, Vikings and Wild banners hanging on the walls.

He didn't see the bartender until he was suddenly standing in front of him. "What'll it be, friend?"

"Ginger ale," he said, "with a shot of Canadian Club on the side. And a pack of Marlboro Lights, if you've got 'em."

"You know there's no smoking in here, don't you?" the bartender said. Then he winked.

Knowles hadn't smoked in fifteen years.

The place began to fill up. A blue-collar crowd, mostly men, mostly, like Stratford, in work clothes. And mostly, like Stratford, ignoring him.

The bartender put the drinks and cigarettes in front of him. "Wanna run a tab?" he asked.

"No, thanks," Knowles said, putting a ten spot on the bar. "I'll pay as I go. But I'll need some matches."

He took a sip of the ginger ale and opened the pack of cigarettes, lighting one up, trying not to inhale, fearing he might choke. He looked toward Stratford, who was just snuffing out his own cigarette. "Mind if I share your ash tray?" he asked.

Stratford said nothing, but pushed the ash tray down the bar toward him.

At that moment, someone slid on to the stool between them, apparently a friend of Stratford's. The noise in the bar prevented Knowles from hearing what was said, but the distraction allowed him enough time to quickly pluck Stratford's two cigarette butts out of the ashtray as he was snuffing out his own.

So far, so good. He looked around. No one had seemed to notice his sleight of hand. Little wonder. The bar was getting jammed, filled with shouts and laughter and the noise from two large TVs hanging from the ceiling.

He wasn't finished, but there was a problem: What to do with the shot of C.C.?

He lifted the shot glass to his lips, momentarily overcome by the smell of it, and pretended to take a sip. Then, after a quick glance around him, slipped the shot between his legs, spilling it on the floor.

Moments later, the bartender returned. "Want another one?"

Knowles thought for a moment. "I think I'll just stick with this for now," he said, pointing to the ginger ale. "Slow as you go, you know."

A half hour passed. Then an hour. He was forced to order two more shots, dumping both, and two more ginger ales, all the while keeping an eye on Stratford and his buddy, who continued to talk and drink. Their voices grew louder and louder, rising with the bar noise and the effects of the booze.

Finally, as he was about to leave in frustration, Stratford and his friend got up and walked toward the door. Staggering slightly. He waited until they were gone, and after a quick glance toward the bartender at the other end of the bar, slid onto the next stool and moved Stratford's glass in front of him, as if it were his own.

He waited ten minutes. Then, with another look around, he carefully wrapped a napkin around the glass and stuffed it into his pocket.

He was out the door, Stratford's DNA burning a hole in his pockets.

"YOU DID WHAT?" BARCLAY shouted into the phone.

He and J.J. were back at the condo, eating the last slices of a low-cal pizza.

"Jesus, John, what were you thinking?"

He listened, then covered the receiver and turned to J.J., repeating what Knowles had told him. "Says that between the cigarette butts and the glass there may be enough to get a DNA sample."

J.J. hooted. "Hot damn! Gutsy little bastard, isn't he?"

Barclay went back to the phone. "Where are you now?" Pause. "Okay. Hang tight until we call Bennett."

Barclay cradled the phone. "Can you believe that? While we're sitting at O'Gara's talking about Stratford's DNA, he's out getting it. He's at the station, waiting to hear from us."

J.J. wiped the remnants of the pizza from his hands and face. "I'll call Bennett," he said, "but don't expect him to jump for joy."

"Why not?"

"Because even if there's enough DNA there, it may have been spoiled by Knowles handling it. And then there's the question of how he got it. Hardly a legal search and seizure."

"But," Barclay argued, "it may tell us if we've got the right guy. Legal or not."

"True. But you heard what Bennett said about how long it'll take to get it analyzed."

"Maybe he can put it on a fast track."

"Doubtful," J.J. said as he picked up the phone.

AN HOUR LATER, THEY WERE ALL crowded behind the closed door of Knowles's office. J.J. was right: Bennett was less than excited to be there, or with what Knowles had done. "I admire your bravado," he said, "but what you did was risky, especially if this is the guy you think he is."

"Didn't seem risky at the time," Knowles answered. "Scary part was having that booze an inch from my nose. I can still smell it."

He'd spent the past twenty minutes reciting what had happened at Tandy's, step by step, moment by moment. "I felt like I was all but invisible," he said. "Just another nobody sitting at the bar, guzzling."

"Maybe so," Bennett said, "but in a neighborhood joint like that, they tend to notice strangers hanging around."

By now, the two cigarette butts were sealed in plastic bags, as was the drinking glass. "I kept my fingers away from the rim," Knowles said, "and wrapped the napkin loosely. And I picked up the butts by the snubbed ends. So maybe there's something still there."

Bennett took the bags. "I'll see what I can do," he said. "But I make no promises. The BCA's in a new laboratory, so maybe—if my bosses agree—they'll be able to speed up the process."

Barclay said, "Is there anything I can do? Put pressure on somebody? Use the station's leverage? Shit, we could be close to solving a twenty-year-old murder. That should excite somebody. Somewhere."

Bennett stood up, bags in hand. "You'd think so, wouldn't you?"

40

Knowles was not about to rest on his laurels. For the next two days, he was back at the construction site—arriving each day at a different time, parking in a different location, using a different car, moving a couple of times a day, but always staying within sight of the apartment building.

Hunkered down in the car, he would raise himself up whenever he caught sight of Stratford—who, he found, maintained a remarkably predictable routine. Out of the building twice each morning and afternoon for a cigarette and a water, or coffee, break. Sometimes he was alone, at other times with someone else, including the guy he'd been with at Tandy's.

Never once did he cast a glance in Knowles's direction.

"Nothing's happening," he told Barclay. "Zero. But I'm going to give it one more day."

On the third morning, as he sat slumped in the car, engine off, idly listening to the beat from one of the rock stations, the car itself began to rock. Up and down, side to side, violently, like he'd been caught in a small tornado. His head spun around, glimpsing for the first time at least five burly guys behind and on one side of the car, bent over, lifting the car, then dropping it. Again and again.

Where had they come from? Had he dozed off?

He felt sudden fear, but also wonder. *How can they do that?*

As he tried frantically tried to reach the key, the rocking stopped, replaced by a pounding on his side window. Not with a fist, but a hammer. The glass cracked, Stratford's face pressed against it. "Who the fuck are you?" he shouted. "Why the fuck are you watching us?"

He hit the window again. It splintered. Knowles twisted away, shielding his face. Trying to think. "Building inspector!" he shouted. "Building inspector! Are you crazy?"

Finally, he found the key. The car came to life. The engine raced. Knowles threw it into gear. One of the men, not Stratford, was sprawled across the hood. The rocking began again, even more violently.

"Bullshit," Stratford shouted, trying to push his gloved fist through the crumpled window. "You were in the bar. Who the hell are you?"

Hitting the accelerator, Knowles nearly flipped the man off the hood. He could hear the rear wheels spin, stones fly. Someone else was on the roof, pounding.

He threw the car into reverse, then forward, then back, trying to shake the men free. Doing some rocking of his own.

The window on the passenger side splintered. Then the back window.

He spun the wheel, gunned the engine. The tires screeched and fishtailed into the street, hearing flung rocks bouncing off the back of the car.

He was free.

He was also scared to death.

BARCLAY WAS FURIOUS, STANDING OVER a still-shaken Knowles in his office. "Bennett warned us," he bellowed. "Warned *you*. You could have been killed, for Chrissake."

"I doubt that," Knowles said, although he could still feel the fear.

"I should never have let you go back again," Barclay said, more mildly. "It's my fault."

Knowles stood up. "It's nobody's fault. I had no idea they'd spotted me. There or at the bar. I still don't know how they did it. I took every precaution."

"Whose car was it?" Barclay asked.

"Mine. I used Parkett's yesterday, and Wilson's the day before."

"So they've probably got your license plate."

"I suppose."

"So they'll know who you are. Where you live."

"Maybe, although the state's not supposed to give out that information."

Barclay settled behind his desk. "They'll find a way."

They sat quietly for a moment, studying one another. Finally, Knowles asked, "What do you want me to do?"

Barclay leaned forward, chin out. "I want you out of town. Today. On assignment somewhere. You pick the place. J.J. can take you home to get packed, and then to the airport. I don't want you back here until this thing's over."

"That's a little extreme," Knowles said.

"Is it? This guy doesn't play games. I've got the bruises to prove it."

Knowles stood by the door. "Okay. Call J.J. I'll figure something out. But you'd better tell Parkett. He's expecting something from me for the November sweeps."

"He may have more than he bargained for," Barclay said. "Thanks, in part, to you. Now get your ass out of here."

IF ANYTHING, JOSH BENNETT WAS even angrier than Barclay when he heard what had happened to Knowles. All Barclay could do was hold the phone away from his ear as Bennett delivered the expected tongue-lashing.

When there was a brief pause, Barclay asked, "Are you through?"

"Not yet."

"Tell me when."

"I'm tired of you guys playing cop. Seriously. I warned you something like this could happen. You're going to mess this case up yet."

Barclay waited. "Now?"

There was a deep sigh. "I guess."

"Good. Then let's talk about what happens next. What about the DNA?"

Bennett said, "My boss is on it. He's in tight with the BCA people and hopes he can work something out."

"Hopes?"

"He'll get it done. Maybe in a week or so."

"Terrific," Barclay said. "Until then?"

Another deep sigh. "I think it's time I paid our mysterious Mr. Stratford a visit."

He wasted no time.

TWO HOURS LATER, BENNETT PULLED UP to the construction site in his unmarked Crown Victoria, accompanied by Erik Winslow, a Minneapolis homicide detective with whom he'd been conferring about the old Sheila Hamsted rape and murder.

Bennett had spent the drive time updating Winslow on the whole bizarre situation, including Barclay's and Knowles's role in the investigation.

"Sounds like they're doing your work for you," Winslow said with a sly smile.

"Pisses me off."

"Still, it's a stretch, wouldn't you say? Trying to tie this guy to a twenty-year-old murder because he may have left flowers on the woman's grave?"

"There's a little more than that," Bennett said, "but not much."

They got out of the car and walked toward the building, quickly drawing the attention of those working outside. Bennett had with him a picture of Stratford and Knowles's vague description of the others involved in the car rampage.

Approaching the first worker, they stopped and flashed their badges. "Your foreman here?" Bennett asked.

The man looked skittish. Glancing around, shuffling his feet. "Yeah, I'll get him," he finally said.

A couple of minutes later, a tall, muscular young guy walked toward them, bare-chested, with a heavy tool belt hanging around his waist. Sweat clung to his chest hair and dripped down his cheeks. Butch something. He mumbled his last name.

Bennett and Winslow identified themselves, aware they were

being watched from several parts of the building. "Understand you had a little ruckus here this morning," Bennett said.

"Don't know nothin' about that," he said.

"Really? When five or six of your guys were involved? Beat the hell out of a car down the street and scared the shit out of the guy inside? You didn't know about that?"

"No way. I've been working inside."

Bennett smiled at him. "Butch, buddy. C'mon. It doesn't pay to lie to a cop."

"I ain't lying."

Bennett showed him the picture of Stratford. "This guy work for you?"

Butch glanced at the picture, then away. "Yeah. That's Davis Stratford."

"Get him."

"He ain't here. Went home sick an hour or so ago."

"That's convenient."

"He came down with somethin'."

"Okay. Then get your other guys out here," Bennett said.

"What? We got a job to do."

Winslow stepped forward. "It's either here or at the precinct."

"Son of a bitch," he muttered, but turned and gave a sharp whistle.

Slowly, about a dozen to fifteen men and women, mostly men, filed out and gathered around their foreman.

"Okay, ladies and gentlemen," Bennett said, "here's the deal. We know some of you were involved in an assault this morning. We have descriptions, and we have the guy who was in the car ready and willing to identify you."

Winslow broke in. "So you've got some choices. We can call for a bus to haul all of you down to the precinct and put you in a lineup. Which could take hours, of course. Or, we can take names and numbers and wait for you to call us. You know who you are. We're not necessarily interested in making any arrests, but we are interested in who put you up to it. That guy may get arrested. Understand? So, it's all of you or him. Take your choice."

He stepped back. "Oh, yeah," he said. "We'd like those of you who were involved to ante up about five hundred bucks apiece. To pay for the damage you did to the car. Give the money to Butch here, and we'll tell him where to send it. If we don't see the money in like three days from now, we'll be back to see you."

"Any questions?" Bennett said.

"This is bullshit," one of the guys muttered.

"What you did to the car was bullshit," Winslow replied. "Know what the penalty is for assaulting a federal agent?"

That got their attention, and a double-take from Bennett, who smiled as he walked back to the squad car to get a pad and pen.

"Hang in here," Winslow told the men, "until we get your names, numbers and addresses. Then you can get back to work. And have a nice day."

BEFORE HE DROPPED WINSLOW OFF and returned to St. Paul, Bennett drove into suburban Richfield, winding up in front of the address Knowles had given him—Davis Stratford's home. His Ford F-150 was not in the driveway. No car was.

"Looks like nobody's home," Winslow said.

Bennett climbed out of the car. "We'll see."

He tried ringing and rapping at both the front and back doors, to no avail.

Back in the squad, he said, "I suspect he got the word."

"Probably. Or he's so sick he's in the hospital."

"Yeah, right."

"Want to try that bar?" Winslow asked. "Tandy's?"

"I doubt that he's there. It'd be pretty stupid if he was."

"Then take me home," Winslow said. "I don't wanna' miss supper."

41

When Katie Thorson pulled out of the driveway, heading for her shift at the cemetery, she looked in both directions, as she always did, but saw only the black top of the F-150 pickup truck parked down the street, around a curve, all but hidden by her neighbor's high hedges. She gave it only the briefest of glances as she turned into the street.

Nor did she see it pull out behind her, once she'd made it around another curve, keeping its distance, waiting until she'd moved into heavier traffic, then mixing in with the cars behind her.

Katie had traveled this same route a half-dozen times in the past week, knew it almost by heart, and allowed her mind to drift, paying little heed to anything but the road ahead. Forgetting, for those crucial minutes, the words of caution she had repeatedly received.

She was due to relieve Gloria DeLuca at the cemetery, although she doubted Gloria'd still be there. She had called earlier, saying she had to schedule an emergency dental appointment and would probably leave early.

Katie hoped the excuse was true, although she knew Gloria and the others had tired of the graveside watch and were finding more and thinner reasons either to miss their shifts, leave early or arrive late. Their patience and endurance were waning, and she wasn't sure how much longer they would hang with it. Even Katie's husband was losing what little enthusiasm he'd had for the project, hinting more strongly now that she should consider giving it up.

And she had considered it—until each time she walked to Jennifer's grave, and stood over it. Then it was back for another day.

It took about half an hour to get from her home to the cemetery and never once did she spot the pickup truck that always managed to stay several car lengths behind her, and which pulled to the curb as she drove through the gates of the cemetery.

As she'd suspected, Gloria had already left their usual spot, almost a block away from Jennifer's grave and behind a couple of taller monuments which partially obscured a view of her car, but which gave her a clear view of the gravesite itself.

The cemetery seemed busier than usual, especially for a weekday. Driving in, Katie had passed by one graveside service, in progress, and now, off to her left, she could see a backhoe at work, digging yet another grave. Several cemetery trucks weaved in and out of the intersecting roads, loaded with shovels, hoes, and other equipment—including lawn mowers and trimmers.

With all of the activity, it was not surprising that she paid little attention to yet another pickup truck, the black F-150, which had slowed to a stop and parked a block or so behind her, itself partially hidden by yet another cluster of monuments.

Settling back, Katie felt at ease, the car window open to a gentle breeze in the protective shade of an aged and towering oak, whose birth must have preceded the deaths of many of the mortals buried here. Whose sprawling branches had seen as many seasons as lives come and go.

Truth was, Katie was comfortable with the idea of death, perhaps because—with Jennifer's murder—she'd been forced to come to grips with it at so young an age. Since then, there'd been a still-born child, and both of her parents, dead at an early age.

Her husband thought it strange, but the first thing she often turned to in the morning paper was the obituaries, not out of morbid curiosity or because she expected to find anyone she knew there, but because it gave her a unique glimpse into the lives of people she would otherwise never have known. For many grieving families, she realized, it was their first and only chance to tell the world about their loved one—what they had accomplished in life and who they had left behind.

Many of the stories were poignant and heart-rending, almost all filled with love. And she read virtually every one.

Today, there'd been no time to read at home, so the paper was now spread over the steering wheel, open to the obituaries. Engrossed as she was, she didn't see or hear him. Not even the rustle of a fallen leaf or the snap of a twig. Until his face was behind her, pushing through the open window, his mouth close to her ear. "What are you waiting for? To see her rise again?"

Frantically, she twisted in her seat, wrenching her neck. A scream stuck in her throat, throttled there, never reaching her lips. His gloved hand was clamped over her mouth, smelling of sweat and oil, his breath of beer, hot and acrid on her cheek. The other hand held a clump of her hair, pulling her head back, stretching her neck until she thought the bones might snap.

The newspaper scattered as she grabbed for his arm with both hands, trying to wrestle the glove away from her mouth, but his grip grew only tighter. Twisting from side to side, she fought to pull away, to lunge for the other side of the car.

For a second, as he tried to pull open the door, his hand came free of her mouth. She saw a flash of bare, hairy skin above the glove and bit into it. Hard, gnawing at the flesh, refusing to let go.

He yowled, "You bitch!" and slapped her across the head with the hand that had been pulling at the door. Her head stung, her teeth lost their hold, but with one hand free, she reached forward and twisted the key in the ignition, hearing the engine roar.

She screamed and hit the horn, pressing against it, the blast echoing across the expanse of the cemetery. One of his hands snatched hers away from the horn, the other grabbed her throat, squeezing, the glove like sandpaper against her skin.

My, God, she thought, *this is what he did to Jennifer!*

"Wouldn't let it go, would ya?" he snarled, his breath sprinkled with spittle. "Stuck him on me, didn't you?"

Blindly, as she fought for breath, her fingers found the window switch on the armrest and pressed, holding it down, hearing the window slowly rise, about to trap his arms in the ever-narrowing gap. One of his arms came free, and as she gasped, her fingers found the door lock. She heard the click. Then his other arm was gone—barely escaping the glass vice.

Her head swiveled and she saw him. Standing, staring wide-eyed, mouth agape, as if amazed by what had just happened. No red hair, no ponytail. Blond now, cut short. But it was him, of that she had no doubt.

Hands shaking, she threw the car into gear and hit the accelerator. As she sped off, she saw him in the rear-view mirror, turning and running.

THE CALL CAME NOT FROM KATIE but from her husband, Greg Thorson, who was irate, almost incoherent, raging as Barclay picked up the phone, "You almost got my wife killed, you know that?"

Barclay held the receiver away from his ear "Who the hell is this?" he demanded.

Thorson told him.

Despite his two visits to Katie's home, Barclay had never met the man, and was relieved that he wasn't facing him now. "Hold on," he said. "Slow down. What are you talking about?"

Thorson was not about to be calmed. "That psycho attacked her," he screamed. "At the cemetery. Tried to strangle her, for Chrissake."

Barclay's ear was ringing. "Easy as you go. Are we going to talk, or are you going to keep on shouting?"

There was a pause and a deep sigh at the other end. "We can talk."

"Okay. Was it Stratford?"

The voice mellowed. "Who'd you think? He must have followed her there."

"Is she okay?"

"Besides some bruises on her neck, yeah. But scared shitless."

"I'm very sorry," Barclay said. "Where is she now?"

"With my mother, heading for our lake cabin."

"Did Katie tell you to call?"

"No. She was going to call herself, from the cabin."

Now Barclay's own anger was beginning to show. "Did she tell you I'd warned her and the others to stay away from the cemetery?"

"Yeah, but . . ."

"Did she tell you I'd warned her time and again that we were dealing with a dangerous nut here . . . that he almost certainly knew that she and the others were involved in this thing with me?"

Thorson was now on the defensive. "Yes, I know."

"Your wife's a brave lady, Mr. Thorson. And I can't tell you how much I admire her courage. And the help she's given me. I would have done anything to see her not get hurt. But you can't lay this one on me. I think Katie would tell you the same thing."

"She already did."

"Then why are you on my friggin' back?" Barclay demanded. "I'm not the bad guy here. Stratford is. And we've got to get his ass off the street before he does any more damage."

"Okay, okay," Thorson said. "Sorry I jumped on you. What can I do?"

"Tell me exactly what she told you so I can tell the cops. Then give me the cabin number because they're going to want to talk to her themselves."

Thorson repeated what his wife had told him.

"So he's a blonde now? No ponytail?"

"That's what she said. Short hair."

"And she's certain it was him?"

"Positive."

"Did she call Rachel and the other women?"

"She tried. Got hold of all of them, except Rachel."

Barclay caught his breath. "What do you mean . . . except Rachel?"

"Katie talked to her daughter," Thorson said. "She said Rachel went to the Mall of America."

"Alone?"

"She didn't say."

"Son of a bitch," Barclay muttered. "I've told her to stay close to home."

"I'm sure she's okay," Thorson said.

"I hope so. I'll try her cell."

"Katie already did, but got no answer."

Barclay leaned back in his chair, hoping to relax.

"Is there anything else?" Thorson asked.

"Yeah. Get up to that cabin yourself. Don't let Katie out of your sight until this thing is finally over."

BEFORE HE COULD TRY RACHEL'S CELL, or to reach J.J. or Bennett, Gloria DeLuca was on the phone, frantic with worry about Katie's well-being and her own safety. "My, God, I was there, at the cemetery, just before Katie! He could have done that to me."

He tried to reassure her while urging her and the others to take even-greater precautions. "After what happened with Katie," he said, "I doubt that he'll try anything else soon . . ."

"What are you talking about!" she screamed. "He's a raving psychopath. Don't you get it?"

"I get it, trust me. But please, calm down. Stay at home, Gloria. Stay inside." Then, taking a deep breath, he asked, "Have you talked to Rachel in the last hour or so?"

"No," she said, more subdued. "I thought you would have."

"I haven't had the chance, and now I'm told she might be at the Mall of America."

"I don't know anything about that."

"Okay. But if you do happen to hear from her, have her call me right away."

"I will, but we don't talk that often."

HE LEFT SEVERAL MESSAGES FOR BENNETT, but it was another hour before he finally reached him and described what had happened. "Holy shit," Bennett said. "Is she all right?"

"Bruised, but okay, I guess. Does that sound familiar?"

"Did she report it to the Minneapolis cops?"

"I don't think so. Just told her husband and the other women and headed for their lake cabin."

"But she was sure it was him?"

"That's what she says."

"I'll need to talk to her."

"She's expecting you to," Barclay said, giving him the cabin number. "One more thing. Katie couldn't get hold of Rachel, and now I can't reach her, either. She went to the Mall of America."

"So what's the problem?"

"It makes me uneasy, that's all. She doesn't know about the attack on Katie."

"I wouldn't sweat it," Bennett replied. "But I'm going to call my buddy Winslow and alert the Richfield PD. It's time we finally reel our Mr. Stratford in."

Barclay knew that Bennett had stopped at Stratford's home and job site several times in the days since the attack on Knowles, but had never found him. His wife claimed not to know where he was or when he might return, telling Bennett that he often took off without explanation—to Canada fishing or to Vegas to gamble. Bennett said he knew she was lying, but he had no authority then to search the house. With the attack on Katie, however, the situation had changed.

"I'm coming along," Barclay said.

"No, you're not."

"Yes, I am. I'll stay out of the way, but you owe me that."

There was a long pause. "I'll let you know when I'll be by."

BARCLAY TRIED TO REACH RACHEL twice more on her cell—to no avail—then tried her condo. Daughter Colleen answered. "Colleen? This is George Barclay."

"I thought it might be you," she said.

"You're back from school?"

"For a few days."

"I've been trying to reach your mother," Barclay said.

"So have I. After Katie called and told me what happened to her. It's horrible."

"I know. But I'm told she's going to be okay."

"Good." Then a pause at the other end. "Are you worried about Mom?"

"Not worried," Barclay said. "Just concerned."

"She left me a note, saying she was driving to the Mall to meet a couple of friends for dinner and a movie."

"I know, and I still can't believe it," Barclay said, disbelief—and anger—in his voice. "She knows this guy's a maniac."

"I'm sure she thought she'd be okay," Colleen replied. "What's safer than the Mall of America?"

Barclay paused, not ready to argue. "You're probably right," he finally said. Then, "Did she take her cell?"

"I assume so, but she may not have turned it on. She sometimes forgets."

"Do you know the friends she's with?"

"Only one of them. Suzanne Otis."

"Try to reach her," Barclay said. "Tell her to have Rachel give me a call. I'm sure everything's okay, but I'll feel better once I talk to her."

"So will I," Colleen said. "This feels kind of creepy."

When they arrived at a rendezvous point, a Walgreens's parking lot about a half mile from Stratford's home, Barclay was in the back seat of Bennett's Crown Victoria, with J.J. in front. On either side of them, an unmarked Minneapolis squad car, with Eric Winslow inside, and two Richfield black-and-whites, manned by four uniformed officers.

They'd already driven past the house once, seeing no sign of either the F-150 or any other vehicle outside. The garage doors were closed and the window blinds drawn tight, at least in the front. The lawn was overgrown, and—at a passing glance—the place looked deserted.

"I doubt he's there, but we've got to make sure," Bennett said. "Here's how it's going to go. The Richfield guys will cover the sides and the back of the house, and Winslow and I will take the front. If there's a problem, Richfield will have more backup at the end of the block."

"And if he's not there?" Barclay asked from the backseat.

"Then we'll keep looking," Bennett replied. "Every cop in the state is watching out for his pickup."

"Good," Barclay said.

The drive took less than five minutes, and from Barclay's perch in the back seat, it looked like a scene from a low-budget movie. As all four cars pulled up in front of the house, the Richfield cops—wearing flak jackets, shotguns at the ready—rushed to take positions against the side and back walls, away from any windows. Bennett and Winslow moved just as quickly to the front stoop, standing on either side of the door, guns by their sides.

It wasn't exactly a swat team operation, but close to it.

As Barclay hunkered down in the back seat, J.J. in the front, Bennett pressed the doorbell and waited. Then, Winslow opened the screen door and rapped hard on the inside door.

One of the window blinds pushed aside, then back.

Finally, after about three minutes, the door opened, but only a few inches. Bennett stood back, holding his badge in front of the opening. "Police," he said. "Come on out, hands in front of you."

The inside door opened wider, then the screen door, and a large woman in a drooping housedress emerged with her arms outstretched, as if feeling her way. Her face was full of fear, eyes wide, seeing the guns.

Bennett knew her from his previous visits. He took her arm and pulled her away from the door. "Mrs. Stratford, is your husband inside? I need to know the truth, right now."

She shook her head. "No. Honestly. I haven't seen him since you were here last. I don't know where he is, and that's the truth."

"Have you heard from him?"

She hesitated. Looking around, seeing if the neighbors were watching. "A few hours ago. He called, but he didn't say where he was. Said he might not see me for a while. That he was in more trouble."

"He's right about that," Bennett said.

"Bad trouble?" she asked.

"Could be," Bennett replied. Then, as Winslow showed her the search warrant he had gotten an hour before, he said, "We're going to look inside. You should wait out here."

"Go ahead," she said, slumping down on the front stoop.

Quickly, they moved inside, first one, then the other. Again, just like the movies, Barclay thought, watching from the car.

Ten minutes passed. The Richfield cops were back in their squad cars. The garage doors came open, revealing an old Ford Escort but no pickup. Mrs. Stratford sat, head in hands, weeping. A few of the neighbors had come out of their homes, watching from a distance, one talking into her cell phone.

"Now what?" Barclay wondered aloud.

J.J. turned in his seat. "Buck up. They'll find him. Only problem is, there's a lot of black F-150s out there, and he could easily have switched license plates. So it may take a while."

"What the hell's he going to do in the meantime?"

"Good question. But I'd say he's running out of options."

Another quarter hour passed before Bennett and Winslow walked out of the house, stopping briefly to speak to Mrs. Stratford. Then they were back at the car, Bennett carrying a small plastic bag, and relaying what the woman had told them. "She's scared, but promised to call me if she hears from him again. And the Richfield guys are going to keep an eye on the place."

"What's in the bag?" Barclay asked.

"His toothbrush and comb. For DNA testing, in case the stuff Knowles got doesn't work. We couldn't find anything else."

"That's it?" Barclay said.

"Not exactly. His wife says he's got a gun."

Barclay slumped back in his seat. "Mother of God," he mumbled.

ONCE HE WAS BACK IN HIS OFFICE, Barclay made a quick call to Katie, at her cabin. She still seemed in shock, a quiver in her voice as she re-told her frightening story. "I've never been so scared," she said. "For an instant, when his gloves were around my throat, I felt the horrible fear that Jennifer must have felt. The panic. The helplessness."

"Yet you survived," Barclay said.

"By the grace of God. And automatic windows."

"I can't tell you how sorry I am."

"Nonsense," she shot back. "I have no one to blame but myself. I should have listened to you. Should have been watching. It was stupid."

He started to reply, but she was quick to interrupt again. "And where would we be without you? Nowhere, that's where."

That left him momentarily speechless. "The cops are sure they'll get him," he said, finally. "It's just a matter of time."

"Let's hope so," she replied. "But I don't want to hear another apology from you. Ever. Okay?"

"Okay."

"Are you all right?" she asked.

"Yup. J.J.'s my constant companion. He doesn't trust our security and is sitting outside my office as we speak. He won't leave."

"Good."

IT WAS NO MORE THAN TWENTY MINUTES later that he got a call from Colleen, a tremor in her voice. "I reached Suzanne Otis, one of the women Mom was supposed to meet at the Mall. She hasn't seen her. She didn't show up . . . and left no message."

"Sweet, Jesus," Barclay muttered, concern quickly escalating to worry.

"She must have gotten delayed somewhere, right?"

"Let's hope so," he said. "Keep trying to reach her. So will I."

"I'm getting scared," she said.

"Try to relax. Keep the faith. We'll alert the cops at the Mall. We'll find her."

As Barclay clicked off the cell, he wondered if his words sounded as hollow to her as they did to him.

43

The Mall of America parking ramp was jammed, as it usually was, even in the midst of the recession. As one of the most popular tourist and shopping destinations in the country, it attracted people by the thousands, day in and day out, becoming—in effect—a city within a city, with its own amusement park, hundreds of stores, and a security force the size of many major police departments.

Rachel spent about fifteen minutes trying to find a parking space. She came to the Mall fairly often, but usually by light rail from downtown Minneapolis, and was not that familiar with the ramp itself. Today, she had decided to drive—because her plans for shopping, dinner and a movie would have made a late-night return home by train too spooky for comfort.

That was her first mistake. Driving.

Her second? Paying too little heed to her surroundings.

Once parked, and already late for her meeting with her two friends, she took a quick glance in the mirror to check her hair and make-up, then grabbed her purse and slipped out of the car into the shadows of the ramp. She locked the door, but had taken no more than three steps when she felt an iron grip on her arm. And a guttural whisper in her ear. "If you want to live, do not speak. Do not scream. There is a gun in your back."

Taking no chance, his hand moved from her arm to her mouth, covering it, muffling any sound that might escape. Not to worry. Rachel was so stunned, so shocked by the sudden attack that she was momentarily immobilized. And voiceless.

Holding her tight against him, his head swiveled, searching in every direction for anyone passing nearby.

They were alone.

Rachel suddenly came alive, her momentary paralysis over. Struggling to free herself, she frantically twisted and turned, kicking at his legs behind her, digging her fingernails into the hand that gripped her mouth.

Until she felt the cold steel of the gun against her neck.

"Stop!" he said, pulling her backwards, the steel hard against her skin. "I don't want to hurt you, but if you fuck with me, I will. I have no bitch with you. You're not like those other women."

Hearing those words, she felt herself relax slightly, almost by force of will, knowing that unless someone came by it was fruitless to struggle, that it would be insanity to risk running from a gun, even if she could free herself.

His hand came off her mouth, but held her arm tightly. "You scream, you die," he said. "I have nothing to lose."

By now he had pulled and dragged her several yards to his black pick-up, parked behind and slightly to the left of her own car.

He must have followed me from home! How could I have not been watching? How could I be so stupid? So careless?

Barclay's endless warnings echoed in her ears.

"You're Stratford, aren't you?" she said, finally turning to face him, recognizing him now—despite his altered appearance—as the drunk who had confronted Barclay at the reunion.

He opened the pick-up door. "Get in."

"No," she whispered, pulling back.

"Do it! Now." The gun came within view, pointing at her head.

She studied his face, seeing only blank, blue eyes staring back at her. His expression lifeless, devoid of feeling. Like those of a dead man.

Be careful what you say or do, she told herself, hoping to calm the tremors that racked her body like a high-grade fever. *He's a mental case, walking a thin line, quick to anger, and capable of the most horrendous things. Tread lightly.*

"Where are you taking me?" she finally said, quietly.

"For a ride."

"Where?" she asked plaintively. "And why me?"

"You can't figure that out?"

"No."

"Then you're not as smart as I think you are," he said, pushing her through the door and onto the passenger seat, the gun still in his hand.

"I don't understand . . ."

"Because only you can bring him to me."

"Him? Who?"

"Your boyfriend. Barclay. We need to talk. Face to face."

"You're crazy," she said, forgetting her own caution. "Out of your mind! He'd never come to face you. Not alone. Not after what you did to him in that garage. After what you did to those women."

He walked around the front of the truck, the gun leveled at her through the windshield, and climbed into the driver's seat. "You sell yourself short," he said. "He'll come, and I don't care if he comes alone or not. He needs to know the truth about Jennifer Bartlow. The world needs to know. Why I did what I did."

"Give yourself up" she pleaded. "Turn yourself in. Talk to him then. He'll listen. I know George. He can get you help."

He laughed and started the truck. "Help with what? I got no job, thanks to him, no money, a pig for a wife, and looking at the rest of my life behind bars or in some looney bin. No thanks, been there, done that."

With that, he put the truck in gear, and drove out of the ramp.

"Buckle up," he told her. "Wouldn't want to see you get hurt."

44

By now, it was common knowledge in the newsroom that something was up with Barclay. The circumstantial evidence was strong: the unsolved attack on him, his frequent absences from the newsroom, the sudden and unexplained departure of John Knowles, whom everyone knew had been working closely with him, and, finally, the presence of J.J., the ex-cop who was making no secret of the fact that he was there to protect their boss.

No one but his assistant, Parkett, knew exactly what was happening, except that it involved some kind of high-powered investigation, the details of which were closely guarded. Speculation was rampant, but even the most experienced reporters on the staff were unable to glean any significant information.

And it was no longer just inside speculation.

With marriages and other relationships spanning the various stations, even their competitors were aware that Channel Seven was on the edge of a potentially big story, the theories ranging from a major statehouse scandal, involving the governor himself, to the discovery of a huge Internet-based child pornography ring based in the Twin Cities. Along with other, even more intriguing, theories.

Barclay parried every thrust, including calls from the TV columnists responding to the rumors. For someone who hated to hear the phrase "No comment" from others, he found himself using it time and again.

That is—until Hal Hughes, Barclay's new boss, appeared at his door, shutting it behind him and settling into one of the chairs. "Okay, George, what the hell's going on?"

Aside from a couple of budget meetings, and one session with their ad agency on the fall promotion plans, Barclay had seen little of Hughes. In fact, this was the first time he'd stepped inside Barclay's office.

"Hey, Hal."

Hughes smiled. "I don't want to tussle with you, George. I just want to know what the rumors are all about. I think I deserve that."

"You're right," Barclay said. "You do. We got off to a bad start. And I apologize for that."

"As do I," Hughes replied, moving his chair to the edge of the desk, elbows on top, hands clasped beneath his chin, waiting.

Barclay began at the beginning, from the night at the reunion, cutting no corners, reporting on everything he and the others had done, including every frustrating wrong turn and dead end. "We think we've got the right guy," he said, "and if we can get him—without anybody else getting hurt or killed—it could be the biggest story this station has had in years."

Hughes listened intently, never moving, never interrupting. When Barclay finally finished, Hughes leaned back in the chair. "Did Hawke know about this?"

"No. Only Parkett and Knowles."

"This is the same guy who attacked you?"

"I think so, yes. And the others, too."

"Sounds like a bad dude."

"He is."

Hughes got out of his chair, pausing as he reached the door. "You need anything else? Money? More people?"

"No. Just a promise to keep all of this to yourself."

"You've got it," he said. "And good luck."

THERE WAS STILL NO WORD from, or about, Rachel. Colleen called twice more, confirming again that her mother had failed to meet her friends at the Mall, that she had not called or answered her cell phone. By now, there was panic in her voice. "I've called my brother at school," she said, "and he's trying to decide whether to come home or not."

"Tell him to hang on," Barclay said. "Until we know more." Then, "I'm going to need a description of your mother's car and the license number, if you can find it."

"It's a green, two-thousand-seven Honda," she replied. "I don't know the model or license number, but I can look in her desk."

"Do it."

Barclay hung on the phone for several minutes, fighting the ever-growing queasiness in his stomach, until Colleen came back on. "It's a Honda Accord. License number MTP-715."

"Good. I'll have my cop friend Bennett call Mall security. See if they'll search the ramps and check their security cameras. That's about all I can do for now."

"Please call me with anything," she pleaded. "Anything. I feel so helpless, and . . . God . . . so scared."

"You'll be the first to know," Barclay said. "That's a promise."

NO SOONER HAD HE HUNG UP than Parkett was at his office door.

"Whatever it is, I don't have time," Barclay said, barely glancing up.

"You've got to talk to the newsroom," Parkett said. "The rumors are flying, and people aren't getting shit done."

"It's your job to see that the shit gets done."

"I'm trying."

"Try harder."

"There's a goddamned sheriff's deputy at the back door, checking everyone coming in. And we've got security guards all over the place. To say nothing of J.J. here, camped outside your door. The people are freaking out. They think we're going to be invaded or something."

All of this was news to Barclay. "Bennett must have put the deputy there," he said, "and Hughes now knows what's going on . . . so he must have added the security."

"Won't you say something to the staff?" Parkett pleaded.

"Whatever I say will be all over town in ten minutes," Barclay replied. "We can't afford that. Not now. Do your best. Calm things down. This may be over sooner than we think."

45

Rachel had no real idea of where they were, or where they were going. And Stratford wasn't talking. In fact, he'd said virtually nothing since they'd left the Mall, refusing to answer any of her questions, once angrily telling her to "Shut the fuck up."

She was restrained not only by the truck's seat belts, but bound by a pair of plastic handcuffs, the kind she'd seen in TV movies. Blessedly, they did not fit tightly, allowing her to retain some freedom of movement. But any thought of escape was folly. The pistol remained in his lap, and they'd stopped only once—to let her pee by the side of the road.

She did know they had avoided the freeways, sticking to the back roads, avoiding towns whenever possible. And even those towns they did pass, she did not recognize.

Not that it would have done much good to know.

Darkness had begun to settle in, and the nausea that had kept her stomach churning was now replaced by hunger. It had been hours since she'd last eaten, but when she complained, he simply mumbled, "You'll eat soon enough."

While she no longer felt the extreme panic that had paralyzed her at the Mall, and while her tremors had finally subsided miles before, she could not shake the deep-seated fear that seemed to permeate every bone in her body. These kinds of "rides" never ended well.

Stay strong, she kept telling herself. *Stay calm. Don't let him sense your fear. Pray. Think of the kids, of home, of George. Think of anything but the here and now.*

But that was impossible.

She had no doubt that he could—and would—do to her what he had done to the other women when she no longer served his purposes. Like if she could not bring Barclay to him, face to face, for whatever crazed confrontation he craved. Or after she did.

But when and where that would happen, and what he would do to her afterwards, she had no clue.

Only the fear.

BARCLAY'S OFFICE HAD BECOME a command post of sorts. Bennett was there, J.J. was there, along with Parkett and a detective from Bloomington, where the Mall of America was located. An hour before, Mall security had discovered Rachel's locked car in the ramp. But none of the Mall's network of security cameras had shown Rachel either entering or leaving the many entrances or exits of the Mall itself.

"We have to assume," Bennett said, "that Stratford somehow got to Rachel. He must have followed her after attacking Katie at the cemetery."

"There may be some other explanation," Barclay offered, although his words lacked any conviction.

"Maybe, but not likely," Bennett replied.

"So what do we do?" Barclay asked.

"Wait. We've got every cop in the state and the neighboring states on the look-out for his truck."

"That's a needle in a haystack," Barclay complained. "Like J.J. said before, there are hundreds, probably thousands, of trucks like that out there. And who knows? He could have switched vehicles, or changed license plates, at the least."

"You have any better ideas?" Bennett said, challenging him.

"No," Barclay admitted, sinking back into his chair.

Barclay had never felt so depressed. Or helpless. No matter how he cut it, there was only one conclusion: It was all his fault. If he'd left well enough alone, if he'd let this vicious sleeping dog lie, none of this nightmare would have happened. Rachel would be safe, Katie would be unhurt, and that innocent woman in the park would not be living with her own personal nightmare.

True, Jennifer's murder would remain unsolved, and her murderer would still be living an undiscovered life. But what the hell? As it is, he's still free, still on the loose, only now he might hold Rachel's life in his bloody hands.

HARD AS SHE HAD TRIED TO STAY ALERT and awake, Rachel had finally dozed off—lulled, perhaps, by the rhythm of the road, or by the darkened warmth in the cab of the truck. Or perhaps by something he had slipped into the water he had given her with a sandwich an hour before.

When she awoke, it was totally dark, and the truck was parked, its motor off, in an open space, surrounded by trees, but with not a sound to be heard—aside from the heavy breathing and occasional mumbling of the man sitting next to her. Now and then he lit a cigarette, but he thoughtfully opened a window when he did.

She had no idea of where they were or what would happen next.

It was like a bad dream from which there was no escape.

"Where are we?" she finally asked.

"In a park," he answered simply.

"A park?"

"No more questions," he said, reaching into her purse to retrieve her cell phone. "It's time to make the call."

He handed her the phone. "Call him. Say nothing except you're safe. Tell him you'll call again in the morning with instructions."

She held the phone in her hand, unmoving, staring at him in the darkness.

Without warning, he grabbed her wrist and twisted. Pain shot up her arm.

"Do it," he growled.

BARCLAY WAS DOZING, TOO, when he was brought wide awake by the sound of his cell. He snapped it to his ear. "Barclay."

"George, it's Rachel."

"Thank, God," he said. "Where are you?"

"With him, but I don't know where."

"Are you okay?"

"Yes."

"He hasn't hurt you?"

"No. I'm okay," she said, ignoring the throbbing in her arm.

"Let me talk to him," Barclay said.

"He won't talk to you, not now. He told me to tell you we'd call again in the morning. With instructions."

"Rachel, wait!"

The phone went dead.

Park ranger Tom Nesbitt was making his routine, early-morning rounds of the St. Croix State Park, checking to see which campsites were open and available—to report back to headquarters in St. Paul for posting on the Internet. Sleep still filled his eyes, his body yearning for the warm bed and the warm body of his wife which he had reluctantly left only an hour before.

Wake up, he told himself, *you've got a long day ahead*. A double-shift that would keep him in the park until after dark.

With summer over and school back in session, there were fewer campsites occupied now than normal. Yet he knew that would change again soon—as people returned in greater numbers to savor the autumn air and witness the brilliant changing colors of the oaks and maples.

For Tom Nesbitt, the forest rainbow of Indian summer was his favorite season of the year.

The sun had not yet cleared the trees, and he had just poured the second cup of coffee from his thermos, when he passed the Ford F-150 pick-up parked beneath a canopy of oaks at one of the more secluded campsites. Curious, he thought, since there was no sign of a tent, or fire, or any movement behind the darkened truck windows. Still, it was early, and not that unusual for people to sleep in their vehicles.

After slowing, and jotting down the truck's plate number, he moved on. He'd check later, he decided, when they were up and about, to see if they had the required park sticker.

It would have ended there had not Minnesota state trooper Forrest Zahn stopped by park headquarters to chat with Nesbitt and bum a cup of coffee from his thermos. They'd been friends for years, and it was part of Zahn's daily routine. To drop by at the end of his shift and the beginning of Nesbitt's.

Before he left, Nesbitt handed him a slip of paper with the pick-up plate number on it. "Do me a favor. Check this out on your squad computer. It'll save me calling it in."

"What is it?" Zahn asked.

Nesbitt told him.

"What kind of pick-up?"

"Ford F-150. Couldn't see anybody around it."

Zahn glanced at the slip of paper. He took a deep breath. "I don't need to run a check," he said. "Every cop in the state knows this plate by now." Then, "Are you here alone?"

"Except for a maintenance guy, yeah."

"Okay. Get him to use every available vehicle you've got to block the entrance to the park. Trucks. Bulldozers. Whatever."

"What the hell . . ."

"Now. I mean now."

Zahn glanced around the room. "You've got firearms here, don't you?"

"A shotgun. And a Glock."

"Take 'em. Stand by the entrance—until I can get some backup here. If the pick-up tries to leave, stop him. Shoot the tires out, if you have to. Whatever."

"Holy shit," Nesbitt said. "What are we dealing with?"

Zahn told him. "He's armed and has a woman hostage with him. He's already killed another woman and hurt a couple of others. He's nobody to fuck with."

Nesbitt was shaken. He'd never faced anything like this in his life. He was a park ranger, after all, not a big-city cop.

"Now," Zahn said, "tell me exactly where this pick-up is."

BARCLAY'S NEWSROOM COMMAND POST had become something of a dormitory. A couple of them had slept on cots that had been brought in for the night while others had simply stretched out on the floor, trying to sleep. But now, shortly before seven, all of them were wide awake and upright, drinking coffee and eating doughnuts that one of the young dispatchers had brought to them.

To Barclay's dismay, his cell and office phones had remained mute throughout the night.

Finally, at about eight, Bennett's phone broke the silence.

He listened, then, covering the mouthpiece, "They found the truck."

"Where?" Barclay almost shouted.

Bennett kept listening. "At the St. Croix State Park," he finally said. "At a campsite. A park ranger spotted it and told a state trooper. They've sealed off the park, but haven't approached the truck. No sign yet of Stratford or Rachel, but they may be inside the truck."

"Son of a bitch," Barclay muttered. "I should have guessed. He's back where it all began. Where that goddamned picture was taken."

"The state patrol is there in force," Bennett said. "Along with the sheriff's people. They're awaiting instructions."

IT WAS LIGHT WHEN RACHEL'S EYES OPENED. Dark, then light. Where had the hours gone? She remembered little, except another trip outside the truck to relieve herself, held in check by a leash tied around her neck. Then, another sandwich. More water. "What did you give me to make me sleep?" she demanded, thinking of the water.

"Nothing to worry about," he replied.

The handcuffs that once shackled her wrists now bound her legs, allowing her to move her arms and hands and upper body. He had even provided a pillow that was now stuffed into a corner of the truck cab.

"What time is it?" she asked, looking out the truck windows, seeing nothing but the same trees she had seen in the gloom of night.

"Early," he said.

She rolled her neck and stretched her arms, trying to relieve the kinks of the cramped night's sleep. "I need to brush my teeth. Wash my face," she said.

"Are you kidding? No way."

It suddenly struck her. "You said we're in a park, didn't you?"

"So?"

"It's the St. Croix State Park, isn't it?"

Surprise showed on his face. "How do you figure that?"

She eyed him, a small smile on her lips. "The picture," she said.

"What picture?" He seemed genuinely puzzled.

"On senior skip day. I saw it. In Jennifer's photo album. You, with Jennifer and the others."

"*With* her?" he laughed. "You gotta be kidding. It was the last time she blew me off. Called me a creep and told me to get away from her and her friends. It was right over there," he said, pointing to the right of the truck. "They were all having a great time, fucking around, playing games. Taking pictures. I remember, now, what you must be talking about. I ducked in on one of the shots, which really pissed her off. She had no goddamned time for me. And I never forgot it. Not for all those years. Never spoke to her again . . . not until . . ."

"Until when?"

"That night."

"The night you raped and murdered her."

He shrugged. "I don't wanna talk about it. Not to you."

"So here we are," she said. "Back at the park."

"Good place to end it, don't you think? Seems right, somehow."

The words were no sooner out of his mouth that she felt him stiffen, staring out the rear window. "Looks like we've got company," he said.

She looked where he had looked. There, behind a stand of white pine, stood a state patrol car, its lights flashing. And behind that, another.

"Time to make that call," he said, hunkering down, handing her the cell phone with one hand, tightly gripping the pistol with the other.

47

The state patrol helicopter hovered above a deserted edge of the Grand Casino parking lot near Hinckley, seventy-some miles north of the Twin Cities and about fifteen miles west of the state park. Below, two state patrol cars waited as the chopper slowly made its descent.

Inside, strapped in, were Barclay, Bennett, J.J., and the assistant chief of the state patrol, Steve Ramsey, who, along with the local sheriff, would be officially in charge of the operation facing them.

Jeff Parkett had pleaded that a photographer be allowed to ride with them, but Bennett was adamant: No room in the helicopter, and no time for a video circus.

They'd moved fast after receiving that first call on the location of the truck. In fact, they were already at the helipad when Rachel's call came through—with Stratford demanding the face-to-face meeting with Barclay. "He says I won't get hurt if you come," Rachel had said, a tremor in her voice, "and if the police don't try to interfere."

Barclay had tried to respond, to keep her on the phone, but that was the beginning and end of the call.

To his surprise, Bennett had not tried to hold him back. "You may be our only chance to get her out alive," he'd said. "But I want to make myself clear: you're no cop, you're no hero. You will not expose yourself to this mad man. You will follow our instructions explicitly. Got it?"

Barclay nodded.

Now, as the rotors slowed and they emerged from the chopper, Bennett repeated his warning, shouting over the dying whine of the helicopter engine. "Remember, if you try to play hero, if you do anything foolish, I will knock you flat on your ass. That's a promise. You're a negotiator, that's all. Period. Exclamation point."

"I heard you the first time," Barclay said as they walked toward the waiting patrol cars. "I just want to make sure Rachel's safe."

"Then do what we tell you. And put that fucking flack jacket on."

RACHEL WAS AMAZED AT HOW STRATFORD could remain so calm. He'd crack the window from time to time to smoke a cigarette, but that was the only sign he was feeling any tension. He occasionally glanced out the windows, but seemed to have no fear that the waiting cops would do anything rash or stupid.

For her part, Rachel could only concentrate on controlling her own nerves. Her own emotions. She fought an impulse to lash out at him, but knew it would do no good and might well trigger the anger she could sense was simmering below the surface.

She tried to make conversation, but got grunts for a response. So she could only sit back, trying to think of anything that could divert her mind from the present. She thought of Jennifer—of here, where her eventual death sentence was born, of Barclay and whether there would be a future for them, and of Joe and Colleen—whom she knew must be beside themselves with worry. She had pleaded with Stratford to let her call them, but he'd refused. "If things go my way," he'd said, "you'll see them soon enough."

JOE AND COLLEEN WERE ALSO on Barclay's mind as he sat in the back of the patrol car racing down Highway 48 from Hinckley to the park. Colleen had begged to come along, but Bennett had refused. "We've got enough civilians as it is," he'd said. "Tell her to stay home and stay calm. We'll do everything we can to keep her mother safe."

As they pulled into the park, Barclay was amazed to see the array of patrol and sheriff's cars that had been assembled at the entrance and inside the park. He had been told enroute that all the nearby campers in the park had been safely evacuated, and that a swat team perimeter now surrounded Stratford's pick-up.

As they got out of the cars, they were met by Trooper Zahn. "Still no sign of them," he said, "but we know someone's inside. We can't see through the tinted glass, but we did see a little smoke coming out of the driver-side window."

"Cigarette smoke?" Barclay asked.

"Must be."

"No sign of Rachel?"

"No, but we have to assume she's in there."

Bennett took Zahn, the deputy patrol chief and the sheriff aside, conferring for several minutes before returning to face Barclay and J.J. "Here's the plan," he said. "We'll move you up near the truck, keeping you behind one of those swat team shields, until we make contact with Stratford. And you'll wear this helmet," he added, handing him one.

"Are you serious?" Barclay said, grimacing.

"Put it on," Bennett snapped. "Who knows what this guy will do?"

They drove into the park, stopping behind the cordon of patrol cars and trees on one side of the truck, perhaps twenty yards away. With the shield in front of him, Barclay could barely get a glimpse of it.

"Ready?" Bennett asked, once they were in place.

"Yes."

"Call her."

Barclay punched in her cell phone number. And waited.

INSIDE THE TRUCK, STRATFORD WATCHED with interest as the drama unfolded outside. "The party's about to begin," he said.

When Rachel's cell sounded, he waited . . . for what seemed to Rachel like several minutes. "Aren't you going to answer it?" she asked.

"In a minute. There's no hurry."

She scrunched down in her seat and closed her eyes until she finally heard him say, "Barclay?"

BEHIND THE SHIELD. "Let me talk to Rachel."

"Sorry."

"I don't talk to you until I talk to her," Barclay said.

There was a pause at the other end of the line.

"George?" Rachel's voice

Barclay took a deep breath. "Are you okay? Has he hurt you?"

"No. I'm okay. Talk to him, please. Get this over with."

Stratford was back on the line. "See. Nothing to worry about."

"Look, Davis, this is ridiculous. Let Rachel go, get rid of your gun, and come talk to me, face to face. Nobody's going to hurt you."

"No way. Besides, I can see you from here, hiding behind that goddamned shield. With that silly-looking helmet. This is close enough."

Ignoring Bennett, Barclay stepped out from behind the shield. "Okay. So what do you want to say?"

"That you're a persistent bastard, for one thing. Don't give up easily, do you?"

Barclay said nothing, resisting as Bennett tried to pull him back.

"Brave sucker, too. I should have killed you in the garage."

Again Barclay waited.

"So how did you do it?" Stratford asked.

"Do what?"

"Find me."

"DNA. You left a few drops of semen on Jennifer. And the belts. You used a different size belt than the other guy."

"Not that."

"What do you mean?"

"You, asshole. How'd you settle on me?"

Barclay debated. This was bizarre. But what could he do? If he wanted to talk, he'd talk. "Long story, Stratford. Process of elimination. The yearbook, mainly."

"What?"

"What you wrote in Jennifer's yearbook. 'Too bad, too sad.' Remember that? That she might 'live to regret it?' Struck me as strange, maybe a little threatening. I didn't have much else."

"You're crazy, man. I never signed her yearbook. You think she'd let me sign her yearbook after what she did to me?"

My God, Barclay thought, *can this be? That I've been following the wrong scent, but ended up cornering the right skunk? Unbelievable.*

"Did you know her?" Stratford asked.

"Jennifer? Yes, but not well."

"Did you know she was a prick-teaser?"

"I've heard some stories."

"You don't know shit. She led me on like a dog on a fucking leash." His voice went to falsetto. "'Davis, you're so funny. You make me laugh so hard I wanna wet my pants.'" Back to normal. "We went out twice, even when she was goin' steady with that Younger kid. Nobody knew. Not Younger. Not her stuck-up girlfriends. Snuck out after the play, made out like rabbits in the back seat of my old Dodge. First time, she sucked my tongue like a lollipop. Second time, held my pecker in her hand, then laughed. Let me grab a feel, but that was it. Left me sitting there with nothing but hot rocks."

Inside the truck, Rachel listened to the one-sided conversation, terrified, mesmerized.

Barclay was disbelieving. This was a truly crazy man. "You can't tell me that you killed this woman years later because she wouldn't have sex with you in high school?"

"That wasn't the half of it. She ignored me after that. Would barely speak to me, except when she'd run into me in the hall, and call me 'itsy-bitsy, teensy-weensy,' then laugh."

"Meaning?"

"What'd you think? Even called me Spider. You know, 'itsy-bitsy spider.' It was goddamned humiliating. I'm sure she told all her cunt friends. I could tell by the way other kids looked at me. It had to be all over the goddamned school."

"No, it wasn't," Barclay said. "She didn't tell her friends. They didn't even know who you were."

That seemed to take him back. He remained quiet for a long moment.

Barclay had little doubt that he was telling the truth, but it made little difference now. "She was probably just joking," he finally said. "She liked to taunt people. I've heard that."

"Oh, yeah? That's the other thing. That's why I wanted to have this talk. So somebody finally knows the truth. Everybody thought she was such a sweet babe, a goody-two-shoes. I knew different—that she was a prick-teasing, tongue-sucking whore. And I knew that someday

I'd make it right. That she'd pay. That I'd finally get inside her pants. And, what do you know? I got my chance."

Okay," Barclay said. "Now I know. You've had your say. Give it up."

"No, thanks. Like I told your lady friend here, I got no future. I did jail time once. No more."

With that, the phone connection was broken, and Barclay's tension soared.

STRATFORD TURNED to Rachel and leaned back, staring, his eyes never leaving hers. As if debating.

What?" she demanded, defiantly returning his gaze.

He smiled and touched the barrel of the pistol to her chin, moving it like a steel caress from one cheek to the other.

She didn't move. Didn't flinch. Determined not to show her fear.

The stare lingered until he finally lowered the gun. "You're quite a lady," he said. "Gutsy. I like that."

She huddled against the door, arms tight across her chest. "What are you going to do?"

"I don't think you wanna' know," he said, glancing one last time out the truck window. "But we made a deal. You held up your end." He leaned over and removed the shackles from her legs. "Best unbuckle yourself and take off. I suggest you run like hell and don't look back."

"Don't do it," she pleaded, unsnapping her seat belt. "Give it up. Get some help."

His smile faded. Swallowing a sob, he reached across her and threw open the door.

"Go!" were the last words she heard.

As she ran, she glimpsed Barclay sprinting after her. The next thing was a volley of gunfire, shattering the silence of the woods, sending dozens of birds fleeing for the sky.

When she finally looked back, Rachel saw Stratford sprawled on his back beside the truck. Unmoving. Within sight of the picnic table where he'd once stood, uninvited, for the picture.

The gun was still in his hand. Unloaded. Unfired.

Barclay stood in the back of the massive news control room, flanked by Knowles—who had quickly returned from his exile—Rachel, J.J., and Bennett, all watching as the two clocks above the bank of monitors moved slowly, second-by-second, toward news time. Sitting ahead of them, on two tiers, were the director, the producer, the technical director, and other members of the news and engineering staffs.

"Five minutes to air," the director said into his headset mouthpiece. "Let's run a fax check, quick-like." In rapid succession, the microphones, the TelePrompTer, the graphics, the robotic cameras, and other facilities were tested.

A dazzling array of more than a hundred color monitors stared back at them from the control room walls, each dedicated to a specific purpose. Rachel, holding Barclay's hand, leaned over, whispering, "How can they possibly keep track of all this?"

Barclay chuckled. "I don't know and I don't ask. That's why I run the place."

"One minute and counting," the director said.

In the studio, the anchors were in place, giving their scripts a last-minute review. In the back of the studio, behind the cameras, sitting on folding chairs, were Katie, Gloria, Annie, Jackie and their husbands, and Kevin Bartlow—all of whom Barclay had insisted should be there in person to see the story unfold.

Also there watching—reporters from the *StarTribune* and the *Pioneer Press*, who'd been alerted to the story and were promised a later briefing by Barclay and Bennett.

"Okay, folks," the director said, "fifteen seconds to air. Let's make it a good one." Ten seconds . . . five . . . two . . . the countdown ended, and Maggie Lawrence was on camera.

Barclay followed along on his script:

Live on Maggie	Good evening everyone. Leading the news tonight, in an exclusive Channel Seven report, the apparent solution to the nearly twenty-year-old unsolved rape and murder of a former Armstrong High School student, who was found dead in a St. Paul park in July of 1992.
Take Sil VT: (pic of jennifer)	The nude body of Jennifer Bartlow, who was twenty-sx years old at the time, was found in St. Paul's Garden Park, the apparent third victim of a rapist-killer who had months earlier murdered a woman in south Minneapolis and another in Brooklyn Center.
Live on Maggie Back to VT: (pic of stratford) (pic of rachel) (pic of barclay/knowles)	But investigators now say that Bartlow's death was not connected with the others, that she was the victim of a former Armstrong high school classmate, forty-four-year-old Davis Stratford. He was shot and killed this morning by police in Minnesota's St. Croix State Park, after a stand-off involving a hostage, forty-three-year-old Rachel Armetage, who was released unharmed. Police termed the killing of Stratford as a "suicide-by-cop" death.
  (pic of bennett) (pic of jacobs)	Channel Seven news director George Barclay and I-Team reporter John Knowles have been investigating the cold case for the past several weeks, working with Ramsey County sheriff's detective Josh Bennett and retired St. Paul homicide detective John Jacobs—who was one of the original detectives assigned to Bartlow's rape and murder.
Live on Maggie: Take SOT:	Barclay, who was himself a classmate of Bartlow's at Armstrong, was encouraged to become involved in the investigation by several of Bartlow's friends—who were determined to see her murder solved. One of them was Katie Thorson:
(Title: Katie Thorson)	*We never gave up hope. Jennifer was a wonderful girl, beautiful and smart, who wanted to become an actress, and whose life was cut short by her brutal murder. None of us was going to rest until her killer was caught. I just wish he were still alive so we could all face him in court.*

Back to Sil VT:	Stratford admitted to the killing in a telephone conversation with Barclay shortly before his death. Police are now
(pic of stratford) vinced	analyzing DNA and other evidence, which they are con- will confirm that he was the killer who, as they say, has been "hiding in plain sight" for almost twenty years.
Live on Maggie: on	Police also believe Stratford was responsible for attacks both Barclay and Knowles, in an attempt to discourage their investigation, and for the recent attempted rape of another young woman in the same park where Jennifer Bartlow's body was found.
Take SOT:	Detective Bennett said it's unlikely the case would have been solved without Barclay's efforts:
(Title: Josh Bennett)	*He should have been a cop. He followed every lead and every hunch to narrow the search and finally find the guy. Long after most people would have given up, Barclay kept at it. He and Channel Seven deserve all of the credit.*

As Barclay and the others continued to watch, the story went on to reveal more details of the investigation and to report on the personal and criminal background of Stratford himself. There were also more interviews, including one with Jennifer's father—who haltingly expressed his thanks that his daughter could finally rest in peace—and another with J.J., who said closing the old case had finally given him closure and peace of mind.

In all, the story ran close to six minutes, a lifetime in a thirty-five-minute television newscast. When it was over, and after they'd switched to a commercial break, the control room crew turned as one to look back at Barclay—breaking into spontaneous applause, a first in his vagabond news career.

And in the studio monitor, he could see Maggie and the others at the anchor desk giving him a big thumb's up.

In response, all Barclay could do was step back, smile, and give Rachel's hand a squeeze.

After the broadcast, Hal Hughes insisted on hosting a small celebration in the station's party room, complete with an open bar and a tableful of hors d'oeuvres. All of Barclay's guests were there, along with Parkett and the entire night TV crew, and, surprisingly, even Nicholas Hawke—back from the Caribbean, invited by Hughes to share in the festivities.

Which showed a little class, Barclay thought, remembering, too, Hughes's earlier offer of support. This guy might be all right, after all.

There were toasts and short speeches, all expressing their thanks, congratulations, and admiration.

For his part, Barclay stood back, accepting—albeit reluctantly—the fact that he was the center of attention.

He and Rachel had decided early on that they would never repeat all of what Stratford had said about Jennifer. While believing that much of it was true, and while knowing he could never again think of her in the same way, Barclay saw no value in tarnishing other people's memory of her.

The angel still had wings. They just weren't as lily white.

Among the last to leave the party was Kevin Bartlow, who had come with Katie and her husband. His eyes were glistening with tears as he took Barclay's hand in his. "How can I ever thank you," he said. "I never thought it would happen, but now I'm finally going to be able to die in peace."

"Not soon, I hope," Barclay said, with a small smile.

"I'd like you to have something," the old man said, reaching into his pocket. "The police gave this back to me." His gnarled fingers held out Jennifer's gold class ring.

Barclay glanced at Rachel. "That's very kind, Kevin, but I couldn't. It wouldn't be right. Katie deserves it far more. And she would appreciate it even more than I would."

"You're sure?"

"I'm sure."

Barclay felt a soft squeeze from Rachel's hand.

"But you'll come to visit me sometime?" Bartlow said.

"Of course. Tomorrow, if it's okay. To bring back your photo albums and all."

"Good," he said, hobbling away, leaning on Katie for support.

WHEN ALMOST EVERYONE ELSE WAS GONE, and as Barclay and Rachel prepared to leave, J.J. and Knowles came up to them. "So what's next?" J.J. asked.

Barclay thought for a moment. "First, I'd like Knowles here to try and find out who the hell actually signed that yearbook. Start with David Casperson, but go even further if you have to. I'd like to know who I was really chasing all that time."

Knowles objected. "Does it make any difference now?"

"Maybe not," he said, "but I'd like to know. For the record."

Knowles smiled. "You're the boss."

"Then," Barclay said, with a glance at Rachel, "we're going to take a quick trip to Florida, to visit my folks . . ."

"You'll knock 'em dead," J.J. said to Rachel.

"Then," Barclay said, "I'll be back here for the AFTRA negotiations and other unfinished business."

"Like what?" J.J. asked.

"I thought you would have guessed," he said.

J.J. looked puzzled.

Barclay smiled. "Remember Sheila Hamsted and April Sullivan? We've still got two more murders to solve."

"You're kidding."

"Am I?" with a smile.

"Oh, shit," J.J. said.

Acknowledgments

This novel has been a long time in the writing, and I want to thank those people who have provided support, suggestions and encouragement during that process. Among them, of course, my wife, Carol, and my children and grandchildren, who have always been there in times of frustration and self-doubt. A special thanks to my son, Greg, who provided needed direction at a crucial time, and to my brother, Gordy, and his wife, Liz. and to retired detective Ron Allard. But there were many others who were also by my side, sometimes from long distances, including friends Dave Nimmer, Sharon Nesbitt, Nancy Mate, Don and Petie Kladstrup, Quent and Bee Neufeld, Dana Benson, Dan and Kathy Wackman, Jack Caravela, Bonnie Jedlund, Anne and Arnie Weimerskirch, and the late Al Gullickson.

Finally, to my publishers at North Star Press of St. Cloud, Corinne and Seal Dwyer, who believed in this book when others did not.

To them, and to all, my heartfelt appreciation.

Ron Handberg is an award-winning journalist. He has been news director as well as vice president and general manager of Emmy and Peabody winning station WCCO television, a CBS affiliate in Minneapolis/ St. Paul. He lives in Minnesota.

Learn more about Ron and his books at:
ronhandbergbooks.blogspot.com
Or follow Ron on Facebook
Or, contact Ron directly at: Ronbooks.2010@gmail.com